Julia [illegible] attended school in Yo[illegible]terests include history, [illegible] w discoveries), Persian cats, mythology and astrology. Miss Fitzgerald also writes under the pen-names of Julia Watson and Julia Hamilton, and now lives in Chester.

JULIA FITZGERALD

Salamander

BART
NEW YORK

Reprinted by arrangement with the author.

ISBN: 1-55785-103-4

First Bart Books edition: May 1989

Bart Books
155 E. 34th Street
New York, New York 10016

Manufactured in the United States of America

I hate and love. You may ask why I do so. I do not know, but I feel it and am in torment.

Catullus

For stony limits cannot hold love out.

(*Romeo and Juliet,* II.ii.67)
William Shakespeare

For Marjory Chapman with thanks

PART I

THE MARRIAGE OF CONVENIENCE

CHAPTER ONE

Marningham Hall, set amongst the rolling Cheshire hills, had never seen so much bustle and activity since the twelfth century when it was built. The four daughters of the Duke of Chester, their mother, the Duchess, and their Irish nurse, Hannah, were putting the last touches to packing for their visit to London.

Amrica, the youngest, was pirouetting before a mirror in the beautiful oaken hallway with its linenfold panelling and scent of beeswax. She was admiring herself in her new furred cloak and hat, made especially for the coming journey. Amrica was sixteen, delicately beautiful, with large turquoise eyes and long golden hair which curled at the ends. She had a petite, retroussé nose, full, gently rounded lips, and a trim healthy figure. Pampered and cossetted all her life by her close-knit, loving family, Amrica was on the verge of a great and tremendous adventure. She was to be presented to King Henry the Eighth, her father's cousin, and Henry's Queen, Katherine of Aragon, at their Palace of Greenwich; for Amrica had been chosen to be maid-of-honour to the little Princess Mary, the King's only daughter and heir.

Ever since the news had arrived she had been overwhelmed with excitement but, all the same, slightly apprehensive about the post. As maid-of-honour and companion to the King's only child, Amrica's position would be one of much importance, her influence on the little Princess possibly one of immense value – that was, if she lived up to everyone's expectations of her.

Amrica's mother and sisters had reassured her over and over again that she would soon settle in at Court and that the Princess Mary would love her in no time at all, just as they did. Being such a close, loving family, they could not envisage any which was not the same and all the rumours which reached them of King Henry, his wife and his daughter told of a devoted family dedicated to one another. The poor Queen had had many miscarriages, one of her sons had died after only a few days of life. Amrica must always treat her with the greatest compassion and tenderness, so her mother had instructed her, for Queen Katherine had a great cross to bear.

Although Amrica was the youngest, she was remarkably unspoiled, her nature being sweet and loving, her heart generous. But she also had a strong will and a spirit to match. She had been told by her mother than she would, of necessity, have to quell the latter whilst at Court, for Queen Katherine was a lady of great dignity and composure, which was the result of her stern Spanish upbringing by her own mother, the saintly Isabella the Great. Amrica had known some misgivings on being told this. How could she quench her spirit? She definitely had a mind of her own, and strong opinions; would it not be a great pity to repress them?

'Nonetheless you must,' her mother had said, 'for you are not going to Court to air your opinions, my sweeting. The King and Queen have plenty of those of their own and excellent ministers to provide what they feel they might lack. The Queen will tell you how she wishes her daughter to be raised; she will not expect you to tell her. The Princess Mary, so I have heard, is skilled on the virginals despite the fact that she is only four years old. When certain foreign ambassadors visited her a year ago while her parents were absent, she entertained them regally, playing for them on the virginals and quite dazzling them with her grace and composure. So you will see, Amrica, that the King and Queen have managed to rear their child rather successfully without your aid hitherto.' The Duchess's eyes had twinkled and she had tapped Amrica under the chin lovingly.

'Then I shall be found wanting,' Amrica had wailed, 'for I cannot play on the virginals at all.'

'You can learn, my sweeting. Perhaps the Princess Mary will teach you.' Her mother had smiled again.

'But she is supposed to be learning from me, not I from her.'

'It is rarely that all the teaching is on one side only. There is always much to be learned on both sides, by the pupil and the teacher.'

'What if the Princess Mary does not like me? What if she thinks I am a Philistine because I cannot play on the virginals?'

'Now you are making problems out of nothing,' the Duchess said firmly. 'The Princess, like yourself, will be guided by what the King says. He and the Queen have decided that you are the most suitable companion and maid-of-honour for their precious daughter and naturally the Princess Mary will accept their decision. She is, above all, obedient to her parents' wishes, just as Queen Katherine always was to her parents' wishes.'

'Have you decided upon the gifts you will be giving the Royal Family?' Amrica asked.

'Yes. A ruby crucifix for the Queen, a pearl and diamond ring for the Princess, and a jewel-studded saddle for the King, for his favourite horse.'

'I have heard that he tires out eight horses each morning before Mass. Is that so, Mother? He must be a very vigorous man.'

'That is correct. He is a great sportsman and a great hunter, too. You will find him very tall when you first meet him, but remember not to look surprised, for that is the height of bad manners. The Queen is quite small and tending to be on the plump side.'

'And how tall is the King, Mother?'

'Six feet, two inches.'

'But he is a giant!'

'That is what he is called: a giant among men, a giant

among kings. But do remember what I said, you must not look surprised at his height. He is the King and he can do no wrong.'

'I will remember, Mother.' Amrica vowed to suppress any unsuitable words which might spring to her lips at her first sight of the Royal Family. She thought of the chests of clothes she would be taking to Court with her: the satin slippers and many pairs of woollen stockings, smoothly knitted; the garters which criss-crossed over the knee and which were embroidered with love-knots and rosettes; the lace chemises; the shimmering satin and brocade underskirts over which her gowns would be worn. Queen Katherine adored splendour, and so Amrica's gowns were splendid. There was cherry silk fretted with goldwork, turquoise-blue satin embroidered with lilies, russet velvet spangled and beaded, rose-pink cloth-of-tissue interlaced with needlework in silver and deeper pink, ivory silk serge, silver tissue decorated with brilliants and, for very special occasions such as Royal birthdays, a gown of cloth-of-gold decorated with silver raised-work. The heavier gowns were lined with fur speckled lynx, black-spotted weasel or sable, for the colder days. Then there was her new fur cloak and hat with a ruby *broche d'or* stuck in the brim in the fashionable manner.

And now the cedarwood trunks containing all these gorgeous new clothes were being loaded onto the roof of the Chester coach which stood outside Marningham Hall awaiting its occupants. On the doors of the coach the family crest was splendidly displayed: the white owl carrying a rose in its beak.

Chatter, laughter and men's shouts filled the courtyard as the coach was laden with boxes and chests belonging to Amrica's sisters and mother. The horses were pacing impatiently, eager to be off, and the servants had gathered to watch their mistress and her daughters leaving for London.

It was some time, nonetheless, before everyone was

packed into the coach, including old Hannah, who would not have missed this visit to London for anything, despite her rheumatics.

Amrica sat in the coach, gazing out of the window to take her last look at her beautiful, beloved home. There were tears in her eyes as she waved goodbye to the servants who had cared for her and loved her all her life. They waved in answer, calling out their good wishes and blessing her. She was leaving so much behind, all that was dear and familiar, to take up a completely new life, one which she could, as yet, only imagine. To live with a King and Queen and a Princess, to be the focus of all eyes, of Royal attention – yes, it was a daunting thought, but she was sure that she would be able to cope with it. If only she did not have to leave her beautiful home . . .

As the coach trundled off down the drive Amrica fought back tears, telling herself that a new life and great adventure lay ahead of her. She was going to be the Princess Mary's maid-of-honour. She, out of all the eligible young girls in England, had been chosen. She must remind herself how very, very fortunate she was.

Amrica's sisters seemed somewhat quiet, too. They would soon be losing the youngest member of the family, one with whom they had shared much laughter, pleasure and merriment over the years. The sisters, Arabella, Violette and Marjorie, looked at their sister, who was surreptitiously wiping her wet cheeks, and then at each other. None of them could deny that they were going to miss Amrica sorely, but she was going to a splendid future and they all envied her, particularly Arabella, who would have liked to be the recipient of all the beautiful new clothes and to be taking up a position at Court, where one dressed up every day.

Thinking of the finery worn at Court made Arabella's thoughts turn to her father and her brother, who were in France, Paul for the last six years having been resident with a distant cousin of the Duke's whose home was near

Paris. It had been a hard separation for the family, but it was customary for the sons of nobles to be raised away from their homes for it was believed to be character building.

The Duke had been in France as King Henry's ambassador to the King of France, Francis the First, and he was about to return to London where he would meet his family before leaving for the Court of King Charles of Spain. Why he was going to Spain his family did not yet know. Possibly his journey there would be concerned with Royal secrets, in which case he would not disclose them to his wife and daughters. It was enough for them to know that he was vastly important to King Henry as one of his favourite and most successful ambassadors.

Arabella had asked her father to bring her one of the new-style French hoods as her gift from Paris; Violette wanted a riding habit cut in the French mode, and Marjorie wanted a copy of *The Goodman of Paris*, a famous household and cookery book. Amrica was longing for a length of Genoese velvet in deep rose-pink so that she could make an outfit for the masques which the King and Queen loved to hold at Court. The Duchess had asked for sables, for she adored furs of every kind but most particularly luxuriant sable.

As the miles progressed, the carriage taking them farther and farther away from their home, everyone except Hannah, the Irish nurse, became more and more excited and exhilarated at the thought that they would soon be seeing the Duke in London, that most thrilling city. They might be parting with Amrica very soon, but she would be able to visit them at Marningham Hall and they would be able to visit her at Court, so it was not a final parting by any means, and the prestige of having a relative at Court was incalculable.

They took the journey at a comfortable speed, stopping for

long lunches and settling themselves into their coaching inns reasonably early in the evening. If they stopped at a suitable venue then they went sightseeing, but usually they were so tired and aching from the jolting and heaving of the carriage that they were glad just to rest. They stayed overnight at Lichfield, Coventry, Daventry, Stony Stratford and St Albans, and they arrived at the Fleece Inn, London, on a fine, warm Thursday afternoon. Rooms had been booked for them there while they awaited the berthing of the Duke's ship.

The relief at the cessation of the journey was immense. No more rolling and lurching, no more clutching at one another as the carriage wheels delved into pits or jerked over stones, no more begging the help of passers-by when their coach jammed itself in a muddy ditch.

Amrica had thrilled at her first sight of the City of London. Never had she seen so many spires twisting their way up towards Heaven, nor so many buildings crammed together one upon the other. The streets were narrow and the houses built so closely together that people could shake hands out of their bedroom windows. After the wholesome air of Cheshire there was no doubt that London was malodorous. People felt free to throw all their rubbish and refuse, including the contents of their chamberpots, out into the streets, where the resulting stinking mounds attracted blowflies by the score. Half-starved cats and dogs roamed the alleys, nosing amongst the refuse heaps. In the midst of all this, people were selling their wares on wooden stalls. As their coach rolled past, Amrica took note of what was being sold. Was there anything new and exciting which she had never seen before?

Manchets of bread, some nearly black, some pale brown and some almost white, fashioned in many different shapes. Fresh cooked pies with thick golden crusts – coffyns, as they were called. Marchpane sweetmeats, coloured in blue and red and green, and decorated with sugared fruit and nuts. All manner and shape of fish, including eels (Londoners were very partial to eels, the Duchess commented). One stall displayed nothing but hand-fashioned leather shoes; another capes, cloaks and hoods in the French style; yet another, hose, laces, garters and ribbons.

As they rounded the corner and came face to face with the Fleece Inn, Amrica was conscious that she had had her appetite whetted to see more of London, so it was with a feeling of immense disappointment that she heard her mother saying firmly:

'Now remember what I have said, my treasures; London is a dangerous and sinful city, and we shall not be venturing forth to explore it until your father has arrived.'

'We cannot go out until then?' Amrica wailed. 'But there is so much I want to see, Mother. I have been saving up for so long so that I can shop in London.'

'And what if something befell you?' demanded the Duchess. 'What if you were set upon by cut-purses and had all that hard-saved money stolen from you? What would your father say to me then, if I let such a thing happen? No, he has besought me to take extra special care of you all now that we are in the city. We have but a day or two to wait the arrival of his ship and then we can explore all that we please.'

'Oh Mother, may we not?' Amrica said again, crestfallen, thinking of the money in her purse and all the things she wanted to see.

As they alighted from the coach, her eyes fell on a large and colourful poster.

> *'Hoffman and his Dancing Dogs. Zita and her Troupe of Dancing Gypsies. Marja and her Giant Dancing Bear. Lord Valzi and his Tumbling Men.'*

Then beneath, in gigantic scarlet letters:

> *'Come and see them all at Polski's Fair. Four nights only, 28th, 29th, 30th, and 31st of May.'*

And where was Polski's Fair? In black lettering underneath the scarlet Amrica read: '*Bunting Square*'. She wondered where that was, but she could ask someone in the Inn. With all her heart she wanted to see Polski's Fair and the marvellous acts which comprised it. She had never seen dancing dogs before and she tried to imagine what they would be like. Would they dance in time to music, or would they rise on their hind legs to cavort? She had once seen a small performing bear which had visited Marningham Hall with a troupe of travelling players, but she had never seen a 'giant dancing bear'. And the gypsies sounded marvellous; they would be dressed in scarlets and bright emerald green and gold and purple, with flaring skirts and tambourines flashing as they whirled round and round. Their hair would be long and loose and very dark and their eyes would flash as brightly as the spangles on their scarves.

The hubbub of the Fleece Inn did nothing to dispel Amrica's ambition to see Polski's Fair. When she and her sisters and mother had settled in their rooms she mentioned the poster to the Duchess, who threw up her hands in horror.

'A fair, a travelling fair? Just the place for cut-purses, mountebanks and vagabonds! No, Amrica, I cannot think why you should even want to go. Why, they would divest you of your money and all your clothes, and every piece of jewellery you wore before you knew what had happened to you. There would be vermin amongst the crowds, and disease; you would catch a fever. Remember you have lived in the fresh country air all your life and are not used to the miasmas of city life.'

'Oh but Mother – what is the use of coming to London if we are not going to see it? I am strong and healthy; you *know* that I shall not catch any disease! Besides, it would be far more unhealthy to stay cooped up in these stuffy rooms.'

The Duchess partially relented. 'When your father

arrives you have my permission to ask him if you might view the fair, but only if we can get suitable seats. I will not have you pushed in amongst a crowd of verminous beggars, covered in dirt and sores.'

'But Mother, by the time Father arrives the fair will have gone! It is here for only two more days.'

'Well, if it is gone then it is gone, my sweeting, and there is nothing that we can do about it. There will be other fairs and far more exciting things than that for you to see, I promise you.' The Duchess patted Amrica's cheek, but her daughter was by now feeling highly rebellious. She wanted to see the gypsies, the giant bear and the dancing dogs, and she did not intend to be kept shut up in the room at the Fleece Inn like any wayward child. She had done no wrong, and she knew that she could take care of herself.

Her resolve to see the fair increased as the hours passed. She unpacked her hand-case and tried on some of her new gowns. They had brought with them a family heirloom, the Rosetta Jewel. The Rosetta Jewel was a beautiful rose-pink diamond, Amrica's favourite colour, and she had begged her father by letter to let her wear it for her Court visit; he had agreed. Amrica was not at all superstitious, so she ignored the story that the jewel was cursed, for her grandmother had fallen off a balcony while wearing it and had been killed. Since then, the Jewel had been shut away in the family vault until now, when it was to grace Amrica's neck at Greenwich. The diamond seemed to spring to life against her flesh, there seemed to be a sparkling eye deep within it. How could anyone say such a perfect and beautiful gem was cursed? She longed to be able to dress up now and go out into the city wearing one of her splendid new gowns and with the jewel hanging from a fine gold chain around her neck. If they all went out together surely they would be all right?

But the Duchess greeted Amrica's proposal with horror, as did Hannah.

'Bless us and save us!' exclaimed the old nurse. 'Are ye

wanting us all to be murdered before the Duke arrives? And what would he say to that, indeed, when he finds his family slaughtered? What would he say to ye all then?'

'I do not know, for he would not be able to talk to us, would he, Hannah?' said Amrica pertly, at which the Duchess rebuked her sternly.

'Amrica, you are being most unlike yourself. What has come over you, child?'

'I only want to see the sights of London, Mother. Anyone would think that I had suggested we rob the Queen.'

'*Amrica!*' the Duchess gasped.

Amrica apologized, but only half heartedly. This whole thing was too foolish for words. But an idea was boiling in her mind. The next day she decided that if her mother would not give her permission to go sightseeing, then she would go without permission. Now there was only one day left to see the fair and she was determined not to miss it.

That evening Amrica was so deliberately intractable that she was despatched to bed early. She knew that she had over an hour before her sister Violette, with whom she shared a room, came to bed – an hour in which to see Polski's Fair and blow the consequences! If she were quick about it, she could be back in bed before Violette arrived and no one would even know that she had been out.

Forgetting that she had the Rosetta Jewel round her neck, Amrica pulled on a cloak over her gown, pulling the hood well forward so that her face was concealed. Cautiously she peered round the door of her room. There was no one in the corridor outside. From way below in the depths of the inn she heard the noise of revelry, of people vigorously intent on eating and drinking and having a good time. Even though there was no one about, Amrica stepped out carefully, slipping silently along the corridor. She was nearly at the head of the stairs when she heard a crashing noise and shrank into herself, stepping back into the shadows. It was a drunken man stumbling into his bedroom. The sound of a wife's angry scolding reached Amrica's ears as the door closed behind the man and then there were muffled curses as he fell over something in the dark. Smiling to herself, Amrica found her way downstairs to a side door and began to struggle with its huge, heavy bolt, praying that no one would come out of the room which resounded with the noise of carousing and laughter.

After a great deal of heaving she managed to unlock the door and swing it open just wide enough for her to slip through. It was then that she saw the boy curled up on the straw by the door, and she stopped in alarm. Would he raise a hue and cry and bring the revellers out into the hall? But no, why should he? He was just another guest at the inn. He looked up at her sleepily, and she whispered to him to be sure and open the door for her when she returned. To persuade him she handed him a coin, a golden angel; it was generous enough to make his jaw drop open. Overcome with gratitude, he grinned and agreed to do what she said. Then, yawning, he dropped back to sleep amongst the straw, the angel securely hidden in his doublet.

Outside, the night air was heavy with odours, but they were not the fragrant scents of the country and Amrica wrinkled her nose in distaste, remembering the pomander which was in the pocket of her cloak for just such an occasion as this. Now she took it out of her pocket, sniffing at its orangey perfume spiked with cloves to stifle the noxious smells. Looking round her, she saw to her disappointment that the streets surrounding the Fleece were empty. All those who were not inside the inn enjoying the noisy revelry must be at home sitting in front of their fires. She had been hoping to see somebody so that she could ask the way to Polski's Fair: now she wished that she had asked the boy.

Walking on, Amrica at last saw some people standing

by a pump, laughing and quaffing wine from leathern bottles. They did not look up as she passed by in her dark cloak. A woman stepped out of the shadows. It was a painted whore, wearing the characteristic scarlet hood, who had thought she was a customer. Snarling, the woman stepped back into the shadows.

Amrica walked on, her skin tingling, her senses alert. She saw two lovers kissing in the shadows and a flush rose to her cheeks. They turned their faces as she passed, and to her surprise she saw that they were both young men. She was too nervous to ask them the way to Polski's Fair. She had never seen such a thing before and it brought fresh colour to her cheeks.

The smarter area surrounding the Fleece Inn was now giving way to a more rundown part of the city, and gradually hovels and decrepit homes were coming into view. Wonderment at all she saw led Amrica ever onwards, oblivious to the fact that she had wandered into one of London's most disreputable quarters.

Sudden shouts and a flying body made her clutch her cloak around her. A street fight had erupted. Two men were beating at one another with their fists and roaring obscene words. The sudden violence so close to her made the hairs on her neck stand on end. She wanted to stay and watch how the fight progressed, and yet she dared not. Turning hurriedly, she almost fell over a beggar. On looking down she saw that both his legs were missing. Suppressing a shriek of horror, she stumbled on, falling over more beggars who were arranged in a line, all with similar shocking deformities. They were preparing for their usual evening work: horrifying and shaming passers-by into parting with their money. Amrica threw them all the money she had, thirty groats, and hurried on, hoping that the hovels around her would soon make way for more fashionable buildings. If not, she must return soon the way she had come; that was, if she could not find someone suitable to ask the way. So far she had not seen anyone whom she dared approach.

The alleys were now becoming narrow and dark. She knew that she would have to turn back. Regretfully, she did so, and it was then that the gang of louts appeared. Seeing Amrica in her fine clothes they headed for her as one man, filling the alleyway along which she had come so that she could not escape that way and instead must run towards the narrow dark streets.

Unknown to her, she was now entering London's notorious brothel area, where no self-respecting young woman would ever dream of going by day or by night. She thought of little except the feet pounding behind her, the coarse shouts of the youths who were in pursuit. She knew nothing of the horrors of this shadowy world where more than a thousand beggars plied their trade, many of them having been maimed at birth by their own parents so that they could earn a living by begging. Even the poorest passer-by could be set upon in this seamy, squalid district, and no sooner had Amrica slipped down a side alley, thinking that she had given the youths the slip, than she found herself being surveyed by scavenging, hostile eyes. A gaggle of aged crones were standing in a doorway, staring at her, their greedy eyes fixed on her cloak. Elbowing one another out of the way, they stumbled towards her. It was then that the youths caught up with Amrica.

'Keep off, keep off! She is ours!' screamed the hags, baring toothless gums.

For a moment the men hung back and in that moment one of the women lunged at Amrica with a club, hitting her a crashing blow on the head from behind. Amrica immediately lost consciousness, slumping to the cobbles.

She felt nothing of the hands stripping off her clothes until only her chemise was left and that tattered and torn by the clawing greedy fingers – which paused only momentarily when the marvellous Rosetta Jewel came into view.

Could such a jewel be real? Whether it was real or no, soon it had been torn from Amrica's neck and the men and hags were fighting over it savagely.

Those men who were deprived of the jewel and who had not been successful in grabbing any of the girl's luxurious clothes, now eyed one another before advancing on the inert body on the cobbles. If they could not have jewels or clothes there were other things that they could obtain, things which would not last but which could be even more pleasurable than material items.

One of them had his hands on Amrica's breasts, another was running his fingers through the streaming silver-gilt flow of her hair on the cobbles, a glistening moonlit river.

It was then that the coach trundled past on its way to the docks. The coach's door opened and a middle-aged man jumped out, shouting angrily to the men, telling them to clear off. Deciding they were no match for the furious stranger, his coachman and servants, the louts slunk off into the shadows where they belonged.

The middle-aged man, Lucien, Comte de Deverelle, who had been about to return to his home near Paris after a stay in London, approached the body of the girl on the cobbles with his heart thudding in his breast in the most painful fashion. He hardly noticed the fact that there were only tatters to cover the body. What had caught his eye as he rode past was the long, flowing, silver-gilt hair spread out on the cobbles.

'Athena, Athena, you have come back!' he whispered, and in his bemused mind the girl lying before him was his daughter, Athena, who had been the light of his life and to whom he had been devoted until she had died of a fever when she was aged sixteen. He had never got over her death, and now here she was again, golden hair and all, and, by the looks of it, in desperate need of his care and attention.

'My daughter,' he whispered, his mind erasing the years since Athena's death, seeing only Athena's face as he bent over the unconscious Amrica. And, while part of him believed that Athena had returned, the other, smaller, part realized that this child, so like Athena, was not in truth his daughter but someone very like her. On closer inspection he saw that not only the long golden hair was like Athena's, but the face also: the delicate, exquisite planes, the tilting curves, the rosebud lips, the arched, golden brows. God was good, He was giving him a second chance. This poor little waif, whoever she was, would be brought up as he would have brought up Athena had she lived. But surely this *was* Athena? His confusion increased, many thoughts passing through his lonely, strange mind as he gestured to his coachman to lift the girl into his coach.

Soon Amrica was wrapped in warm sables, nothing but her face and the long golden hair showing, and as the Comte instructed his coachman to ride on, he sat gazing at the girl, at the still, quiet face and the closed eyes, wondering what colour those eyes would be. Then he remembered that he had ordered only one cabin on the *Marie Claire* for his journey to France. What if they did not have room, an extra cabin, for the girl? But it did not matter, she could have his bunk if needs be; he would tend her himself. His poor Athena, his poor, precious Athena, so ill of a fever. He would care for her gently and devotedly, and perhaps this time he would save her life . . .

Who was going to question a rich Comte, one famous for his eccentricities? The Captain of the *Marie Claire* did not quibble about providing an extra cabin for the young girl introduced by the Comte as his daughter Athena, and soon Amrica was tucked up in a bunk, still unconscious from the blow to her head.

The Comte sent for water and linen and soon he himself had bathed and soothed Amrica's wound and washed the mud of the cobbles from her body. Her head he bound up carefully in fresh linen, but she remained dead to the world.

*

The Comte did not sleep that night. He sat by the bunk watching over Amrica, all the time thinking of her as Athena, his daughter, and how he had been given a second chance. He did not care if the girl spoke roughly when she awoke, if she was just a common vagabond, as well she might be although her skin was soft and velvet and her hair silky and luxuriant. No well-bred young lady would have been found alone in that notorious slum section by the London docks.

Many thoughts came into his mind as he kept watch, but his overriding notion was to care for this girl, to protect her and not let her out of his sight. He must not lose his Athena again, that must not be allowed. His daughter had been returned to him: God was good, indeed He was.

Morning saw the *Marie Clarie* setting sail for France, at which the Comte heaved a sigh of relief. Very soon they would be out into the waters of the Channel, and then his beautiful Athena would truly be his, no one could take her away from him then. He had not thought of what he would say to the girl when she regained consciousness.

The Comte de Deverelle was fifty years old, an eccentric who loved practical jokes, who lived on a shoestring despite the appearance of great wealth. He gambled when he was especially desperate for money, but he needed no one to tell him how empty his life had been since Athena's death. He had loved Athena's mother dearly, but she had died giving birth to Athena, endowing the child with her long golden hair and pale blue eyes. To lose one beautiful and adored woman had been a tragedy, to lose two had been too much for the Comte's mind. He had never been himself again since, not truly himself. He had long periods of lucidity when he appeared quite normal but then, in the midst of being very logical and quite sane, he would say or do something quite astounding or improbable so that those around him would know that things were not quite right with his mental state. He had never done anything violent or behaved in any way approaching such a frightening lack of control, but once he had sat next to a golden-haired lady at a dinner and quite terrified her by insisting on calling her Athena and behaving as if he knew her intimately. He had further alarmed her by anticipating that she would be returning home with him to his house that night. Finally, two of his servants had taken the woman's husband aside and carefully explained to him about the Comte, after which the servants had distracted their master while the woman's husband had quickly led her away.

Now it appeared that the Comte's patience had been rewarded for his golden-haired Athena had returned, as young and beautiful as before, and infinitely as lovable.

The Comte stood up, approaching the bedside of the invalid. Rivulets of silver-gilt hair had spread themselves around the pillow, her face was as white as the bandages around her head, and there was a blue light to the skin around her mouth. She looked pinched and ill, which indeed she was, but nothing could eradicate the beauty of her finely sculpted bone structure, the dark lashes shadowing her cheeks, the full, undulating curve of her mouth. The Comte stood gazing down at her, his knobbly fingers reaching out to coil themselves in the skeins of luxuriant hair which felt like silk against his skin, silk spun by some enchanted faerie . . . When he had been divesting her of her tattered chemise the night before and bathing the mud and dirt from her body, he had thought nothing more of her naked form than would any loving father, noticing only the dark stains left by the cobbles, the contusions on her back and hips where she had fallen, and the deep wound on her head. Over and over as he had worked he had thought, 'Athena, Athena, my beloved daughter, please get well, please be all right. Oh, what would your mother say if she knew that you were so ill? Pray God, let the fever not be too serious!' For, in his mind, he was nursing his daughter through the fever which had killed her at sixteen, only now he had forgotten that Athena had ever died. Was she not here again, and alive? The time between was reduced to nothing.

It was midday when Amrica recovered consciousness. The first thing she saw was the Comte leaning over her, then she felt the gentle lurching of the ship and realized that she was not on land. Looking round, she saw the panelled confines of the cabin, then her eyes came to rest again upon the face of the middle-aged man who was looking at her with such anxiety and such devotion in his gaze.

'What – what has happened?' she whispered. 'Why am I here?'

'Athena, *ma trésor*,' said the Comte in his excellent English, 'I was fetching you from the convent in England when an accident befell you and you received a blow to the head. I am nursing you now, *ma trésor*. Soon you will be at home in my château.'

'We – we are on a ship?'

'Yes, we are on a ship, Athena.'

'Where are we going, sir?'

'To France, to my château.'

Amrica searched her mind for some memory of who she was, of what she was doing here, but there was nothing, just a great dark emptiness. She could not remember anything at all; not her name, who she was, where she had come from, where she had been, where she was going. There was nothing in her head except a terrifying blank.

'Who am I?' she said in a little voice, feeling small and insignificant and greatly at risk.

'Why, *ma trésor*, you are my daughter, my cherished daughter, Athena de Deverelle.'

'Your daughter? So that is who I am . . .' Amrica gave a tremulous smile, then a pain shot through her head from the wound in her scalp and she raised a hand to feel the bandages gently 'How was I injured?'

'You fell and struck your head,' replied the Comte. 'I fear that it was a nasty bang and you will take some time to recover, but do not fear, for when we reach Calais my coach and servants will be waiting to take us to the Château Deverelle.'

'So – I banged my head. Is that why I cannot remember anything – Father?'

A brilliant light shone in the Comte's eyes at her words. He had half expected protestations when the girl awoke, although an inner voice kept telling him that she was his daughter and that of course there would be no difficulties. He had not anticipated the girl regaining consciousness to proclaim that she had lost her memory. That seemed an all too benevolent stroke of fortune for him and he prayed that it would last. He prayed that before she regained her memory they would be safely at the Château Deverelle and that by then she would have come round to loving him, to realizing that he meant her no harm but only wished to cherish her.

'Yes, *ma trésor*, that must be why you can remember nothing. Is that really so? Have you forgotten – everything?' His heart hardly daring to beat, the Comte awaited her reply.

'When – when I try to think to remember, there is nothing: just a great blank in my head. It is most strange, Father – frightening.'

'It is not unknown for head wounds to cause such a reaction, my love. I have heard of it before.'

'Will I remember again?'

'I am sure that you will, in time. But for now we must concentrate on getting you strong again, must we not? Are you thirsty, my love? Can I get you something to eat?'

'Oh yes, terribly thirsty,' Amrica whispered, suddenly conscious off how parched was her throat. 'My head aches so.'

'I will get you a pain-killing draught, my love, and of course a drink. We must revive the body's humours, must we not, after such a terrible shock as a blow to the head?'

Amrica watched the man going out of the room, feeling

a sense of loss as the door closed behind him. He had such a kind face, so sincere and honest. She felt that she could trust him. But, of course, that would be natural if he were her father. She only wished that she could remember, but there was nothing . . . nothing except the big dark void. The effort of trying to recall was making her headache worse. She lay back, trying to relax, trying to clear her thoughts so that the headache would lessen, and she succeeded a little. But she could not lose the sensation of strangeness, as if she were in an unknown place with unknown people, a place she had not expected to be. On board a ship . . . For some reason which, of course, she could not remember, she had not expected to be on board a ship. She should have been at – and there she could remember nothing: it was just impossible. And the pain returned the moment she tried to strain her thoughts.

The door opened and there stood the Comte, smiling, holding a tray laden with drinks and medicaments. His light brown eyes were round and twinkling, and the dimples in his creased face were showing. Amrica had no difficulty in believing that she loved her father dearly.

Placing the tray on the bed, the Comte pointed out the things lying upon it.

'Now, what would you like to drink *ma petite*? We have fresh orange juice, or a posset, freshly made by my valet, or goat's milk, which is famous for its strength-restoring properties.'

'The orange juice please, Father. That is just what I want, my throat is so dry, so tight.' Amrica took the orange juice and began to drink in great, marvellously quenching gulps, at which the Comte put out a restraining hand.

'Slowly, slowly, my love. Remember that you have been ill.'

When the orange juice had disappeared, the Comte handed Amrica the pain-killing draught.

'Sip this very slowly,' he told her, 'and then you must try and sleep.'

'How far do we have to go now? What if the ship reaches land while I am still asleep, Father?'

'Do not let such things trouble you, *ma petite*. My servants will carry you to the coach if you are still asleep. Have I not told you to leave all such problems to your father, who is quite capable of attending to everything on his own?' The Comte beamed.

Something occurred to Amrica and she spoke out without thinking.

'Father, where is my mother?'

The question caught the Comte by surprise, but nonetheless he found himself replying steadily: 'Your sweet mother, may the Blessed Virgin protect and guard her soul, died when you were born, Athena.'

'What was I doing in England?'

'Your mother and I were living in England at the time of your birth, my dove. I left you in the Convent of the Virgin of Dolours to be raised by the nuns, as your mother would have wished. I visited you regularly. Do not think that I left you there and forgot you. Far from it.'

'I am sure that you would not forget me, Father.' Amrica gave a little smile. But sleepiness was stealing over her and she yawned.

Immediately the Comte stood up, picking up the tray. 'I will leave you now to rest.'

Amrica knew no more, until, wrapped in sables, she woke as she was being gently placed in the Deverelle coach at Calais. But she roused only momentarily, and soon curled up comfortably asleep again. Next time she woke it was to find herself in a massive and comfortable tester-bed in the Château Deverelle just outside Paris. She was desperately thirsty, calling immediately for a drink, which a maid-servant brought her, the Comte arriving on her heels.

'So, you are awake! Ah, it is good to see you looking so well, there is some colour in your cheeks.' He sat on the edge of Amrica's bed and took one of her hands in his, squeezing it tenderly. 'Have your fruit juice, my little one, and then we shall talk if you are up to it. I expect that you are very hungry by now.'

'My head does not hurt nearly as much,' said Amrica thankfully.

'That is good to hear. We shall soon have you well again, do not worry.'

Amrica noticed the maid-servant then. She was standing at the side of the bed, staring at her curiously. Servants should not stare. She wanted to tell the girl so, but the task seemed too great for her in her weakened state. The Comte did not seem to notice anything amiss, and shortly the girl bobbed a curtsy and left the room.

Downstairs, the rest of the staff were waiting eagerly for the maid's report.

'What is she like?' demanded Elise, the youngest of the servants. 'Tell us, what is she like, Marie? Does she look like the Comte? Is it really his daughter?'

'Well, she has the long golden hair and her eyes are nearly the same blue as those of the girl in the portrait in the Long Gallery' (this was a painting of Athena, executed when she was eleven years old).

'What else, tell us what else, Marie?'

'How do you think she just appeared out of the blue like this when we all thought that she was dead?' This from Pierre, the Comte's under-valet.

'Well, we knew that when he was living in England a few years ago a child of his died of a fever. At least, we think we know that; we have had to piece it together from snippets and rumour and gossip we have heard.'

'It does not help with us all having been taken on so recently,' added Pierre. 'I have always wondered why the Comte got rid of all his old servants. Have you not wondered, too? I mean, we all came to this house and it was empty, there was not one servant here. We are all new, and we know nothing of the Comte's past except what we have managed to fit together bit by bit.'

Marie put her head on one side. 'The girl is very pretty, she looks high-bred, every bit as ladylike as the portrait of Athena in the Long Gallery.'

'Why should she not look high-bred, Marie?' asked Claude, another of the servants. 'What have you been thinking?'

Marie half closed her eyes. 'Truth to tell, it had occurred to me that the Comte might have picked up some drab from the streets to bring home as a mistress. He has always been a strange one, as we know, and I thought that this might be his way of introducing a mistress into the household.'

'A *mistress*? But if he wants a mistress all he has to do is take one. There must be dozens of women who would be eager to meet with his favours.'

'He has never been one for doing things in a straightforward manner, Pierre,' Marie said, unconvinced.

'Perhaps he has another daughter,' put in Claude, 'one which we have never known about. Perhaps she really has grown up in a convent as he said.'

'She must be a bastard,' Marie breathed.

Then Lazare, the coachman, spoke up. 'But he said – that is, he told me – that this was Athena, his daughter, and the daughter of his wife who died giving birth to her sixteen years ago. And she does look about sixteen.' Lazare had been paid handsomely by the Comte to make everyone believe that Athena really was his real daughter. 'She has the long golden hair, more or less the same colour eyes – and who can trust a portrait anyway? And why should the Comte lie to us? He has no reason to do that; he is the lord and master here, he can do as he wishes. I say that she is his daughter.' Lazare nodded his head firmly.

'Lazare is right,' put in Pierre. 'What possible reason could our master have for lying to us? No reason at all that I can see –'

'I looked long and closely at the girl,' Marie interrupted, 'and all the time I was looking at her I was remembering that portrait of Athena. I know that there is some difference in their ages and that girls can change very much between the ages of eleven and sixteen, but I say that the girl is truly Athena, his daughter, as he claims. The rumours we have heard in the past must have been wrong, or else it was another daughter who died. We would be wrong and foolish to mistrust our master's word; besides, who would dare? We would be dismissed for insolence.'

'I had no intention of disbelieving our master,' said Claude.

'Nor I,' added Pierre.

'Nor I,' said Lazare firmly.

And so the matter was closed.

CHAPTER TWO

The Comte was skilled in the use of herbs, and he treated Amrica accordingly. Twice a day she was made to drink the juice of the leaves of adder's tongue mixed with the distilled water of horsetail; this was to speed the healing of the wound on her head. A green balsam of olive oil and adder's tongue was applied directly to the wound, and to protect her from the wound becoming inflamed she was given the juice of comfrey to drink. No sooner had the balsam been applied to her wound, along with clean bandages, than it was time to drink one of the concoctions which the Comte had mixed for her, and then it would be time to drink another, and then time to have the wound treated again.

'I do not know what I would do without you, Father,' Amrica said on the fourth day, as the Comte stood back from the bed after applying a clean bandage to her head.

'I only do what I do for the one I love most in all the world,' the Comte said expressively, his brown eyes moist with emotion.

Amrica's turquoise eyes responded in kind. She reached up to take the Comte's hand and squeezed it affectionately.

'You are a dear, and I can never thank you enough for what you have done for me.'

'But I would never forgive myself if I did not care for you to the utmost of my capabilities, *ma petite*,' the Comte beamed. 'You are my one and only daughter, truly my treasure. If anything happened to you I would never recover. I think you know that, Athena.'

'Yes, Father,' murmured Amrica.

'I want you to get well and strong again; that is all I dream of, all that I pray for. I want to see you walking in the gardens of the Château Deverelle and riding my horses across the meadows; I want to see you listening to the birdsong and picking flowers and choosing new gowns. Nothing would please me more. And when you are truly better, we are going to have a grand ball in your honour. All my neighbours will want to meet you and there will be many young gentlemen from Court, I vow, who will be eager to attend upon such a lovely young heiress.'

'I am an heiress, Father?'

'But, of course, *mon trésor*. Had I not told you, do you not remember? In two years' time you will inherit your *grandmère*'s fortune. Oh yes, there will be many young men eager to pay suit to you.'

In the Comte's muddled, disturbed mind he had devised the greatest practical joke of his life, without considering the consequences for the girl who lay in the bed before him. He was going to tell everyone that Athena, his daughter, would one day inherit an immense fortune. He would encourage suitors to woo Athena and then, when they had made fools of themselves, he would tell them that she was not an heiress. It would be the most successful practical joke he had ever played, and he would have reason to congratulate himself. There were many smirking, pompous youths and gentlemen at Court who could do with being taken down a peg or two and he would delight in doing just that.

'Now, my love,' he continued, 'you will also be able to learn how to speak French, and I will teach you to play the lute and you will learn French songs. And of course you must learn the Court etiquette that we have here in Paris, for as my daughter you must be fully informed on all matters.'

Court etiquette. The phrase whirled round in Amrica's head. It reminded her of something, but she could not think what. Then, just as suddenly as it had come, the vague feeling of familiarity left her.

In the following weeks, Amrica rapidly regained her energy and vigour. If any of the servants had had misgivings about her, they put these feelings aside in the face of her sweetness, grace and charm. Here was no arrogant aristocrat but a lively, pleasant-natured young girl with sparkling eyes and high spirits – as befitted her age – and it was plain that their master doted on her. He had never looked happier or more contented. Soon Amrica was able to be carried downstairs in the strong arms of Lazare or Pierre, who would place her in a comfortable chair on the terrace in the June sunshine, or by the window in the music-room or the library.

When she was in the music-room the Comte would come and join her and show her how to play the lute. He was also teaching her how to speak French, and she found that learning French songs was the perfect way of becoming familiar with French pronunciation. She was an adept pupil, taking to the strange language as if she had known it all along – a fact which delighted the Comte. Obviously her French blood facilitated her learning the language, he told himself, and despite her upbringing in an English convent she was still truly French.

The Comte started to tell Amrica something of the French Royal Family and the Court in Paris. He told her about the King's mother, Louise of Savoy, and the King's sister, Marguerite. He said that Louise, Marguerite and King Francis were known as the Trinity because they were so close and devoted to one another. Poets wrote songs and verses in their honour. Nothing could divide or separate them.

'These are qualities well worth nurturing in your own life, *mon trésor*,' the Comte said to Amrica, lightly touching her cheek with one of his gnarled fingers. 'Both the Queen Mother and the Duchess Marguerite write verses proclaiming their love for one another and for the King. Let me read you one written by the Duchess and then, if you feel inclined, you may set the lines to music and sing them for me.' And standing by her side he began to read:

'Tis but one heart, and so will ever be.
I promise it a heart that's yours or mine;
Whatever may befall all you or me,
Neither our blood or reason would agree.
And so to this myself I do resign,
I give my will to yours, between your hands,
Both words and deeds I place,
Since by this means you shall myself displace.
'Tis but one heart!

While so complete I thus commit, you see,
Myself to you and so shall henceforth be
Better than formerly, yet please yourself remind
Of our accord that we shall thereby find
It everlasting since only in you am I free.
'Tis but one heart!'

Amrica, who in our story is now to become Athena, delighted in the verses. They moved her romantic heart and she thoroughly approved of such singular devotion, whether it was between relatives or lovers. She told the Comte so, at which he patted her hand and, with a twinkling smile, said:

'You are at the age to think of lovers, *ma petite*, and soon you shall have more suitors than you can count on both hands. All of Paris is longing to see you.'

'How do they know of me, Father?'

'I have told them, of course,' he said, smiling at her fondly. 'I have let it be known that my fair daughter Athena is now resident at the Château Deverelle.'

'Oh how I wish that I could remember! I know nothing, only what you choose to tell me. No, no, I did not mean it to sound like that, I did not mean to suggest that you are hiding anything from me, Father. It is just that there is so much I cannot remember, so much I may never know.'

'I have explained to you how it can be so after a severe blow to the head, but you must not fret. All my friends and neighbours, the courtiers who will be coming to see you, they all know the truth, that you are Athena, my beloved daughter – not only beautiful, but a great heiress.'

'Oh, but is it wise to tell them that I am an heiress? Will it not attract the wrong type?'

'I shall be superintending everything,' the Comte reassured her. 'I shall not let you fall into the wrong hands. Any man who wishes to marry you must meet with my whole-hearted approbation. He must be a man of integrity and honour, a man of sincerity, and he must treat you with perfect gentleness and kindness.'

'And with love too, I hope, Father,' Athena said, raising her golden brows. 'He must love me; I could not dream of marrying a man who did not love me.'

'It is customary for parents to arrange marriages for their children,' the Comte said, somewhat stiffly.

'So I am to be forced into an arranged marriage?' asked Athena, her heart sinking. Not to be able to remember her past, to have no memory whatsoever, was bad enough, but to know that she would be obliged to marry some man who might not meet with her approval was highly disturbing, to say the least.

'Trust your father,' he said firmly. 'Now, you know me well, do you not? Can you see me forcing you to do anything against your will? Do you think I would see you marry a monster, a wedding of a Beauty and a Beast? Not while I live!'

'He would not need to be a monster, Father. Not physically, that is. I would find him unacceptable if he were cold, graceless or unloving. Any one of those things would not find favour with me. To be tied to a cold man – oh, I cannot think of anything more horrible!'

'How could any man be cold married to you, *mon trésor*?'

'I would rather be married for love and not for my gold, all the same.'

'A pretty sentiment, little one.'

Tears came into Athena's eyes. 'You will distress me if you persist in talking of my being married, Father. You only brought me home a few weeks ago; we have barely had time to get to know one another thoroughly, and that is something I dearly wish to do before I am asked to leave you.'

The Comte was moved. He took Athena's hands in his. 'Now now, my child, do not upset yourself. Be assured that I shall not part with you that easily.'

'But, the suitors, Father, these men of whom you talk, the men who will want to marry me – what of them?'

'Men can be kept at arm's length for a great deal of time, my dove, especially when one is as fair and as wealthy as you are to be. They will be waiting on your every word with tongues hanging out. They will be obedient, attentive, generous, and most amiable.'

'Acts put on to impress me,' Athena said, sounding almost bitter. 'They will be actors. I shall not see the true men behind the façades. How shall I know which one to choose? How shall I know which one is sincere and which one loves me if they all profess to love me because they think only of my fortune?'

'Believe me, we shall weed them out. Between us we shall find the one who is worthy of you.'

She sighed, but held her tongue. Clearly, there was nothing to be gained by arguing with him now.

In the ensuing weeks, Athena recovered her full vigour, learning how to speak French tolerably well, to play the lute and to sing in French. The slightly outmoded dresses that she had been wearing, hurriedly acquired for her by the Comte while she was still languishing in bed, were soon to be put aside, for now the Comte had told her that she was to be able to choose new gowns and slippers. He promised her hoods in the fashionable style, shaped like a crescent moon edged with jewels and goldwork with a fall of black velvet dropping gracefully behind the head. She would have a *vasquine* of fine silk and camlet, and a farthingale of stiffened taffeta and linen. She was to choose *cottes* of silver taffeta embroidered with gold thread, which would be placed over the farthingale and beneath the gowns. The height of July was approaching, so she should have some gowns in the Moorish style, fashioned like bernouses, loose and flowing in fine, light silks, and of course clusters of pretty feathers of many different colours, all garnished with gold spangles, to be placed in the hat or the hood or pinned to the bodice or the cloak.

And there would be jewels to choose; the Comte had instructed merchants to call with their wares so that Athena could select what she wished. He did not, of course, tell her that he could ill afford to furnish her with new robes and jewels. He explained away the old-fashioned clothes in the wardrobes by saying that those had been the garments which the nuns had made her wear in their ignorance, and she accepted what he said, as she accepted everything which came from his lips – even the talk of marriage.

Athena had only to see his kind, wrinkled, brown face, the twinkling light brown eyes, the tightly curled mop of brown hair striped with grey, to feel a warm and loving response within her. She did not doubt for one moment that she was his daughter, that she loved him and that he loved her. Indeed, what reason had she to doubt this?

Lazare, the coachman, had served his master faithfully for many years. He was the only servant whom the Comte had not dismissed when he was broken-hearted at the real Athena's death. And Lazare would not speak out. Nothing would make him reveal how his master had found the strange girl lying on the cobbles by the docks in London. If this strange girl made his master happy – and it was obvious that she did – then Lazare was happy too. So ran the thoughts of a devoted servant. He had never spoken to anyone of the real Athena's death, for after she had died the Comte had taken him on one side and told him that all must go on as before but that he must never speak of anything he had seen or heard in the Château Deverelle or in England.

How conveniently everything had worked out now, as if it had all been carefully planned beforehand by the Comte. The real Athena had died in England, which made things even easier. No one but the Comte had seen her die. Should any of his friends or colleagues remark on the sudden appearance of his daughter, he had but to say that they had been mistaken, that Athena had not died in England but had gone into a convent, or some such tale. He knew that when the time came he would manage a suitably convincing story; practical jokers were excellent at telling lies.

So would run his thoughts when he was undergoing one of those periods when he knew that the beautiful young girl in his care was not his true daughter.

Athena revelled in the visits from the many merchants instructed by the Comte to show her their wares. Goldsmiths from the Rue d'Antoine brought her rings and beautifully chased carcanets for her neck, jazerines – exquisitely wrought gold chains – to hang on the bodice of her gowns, and jewelled *ferronières* to wear in the centre of her forehead when her hair was loose. One of these she particularly loved: it had a drop pink pearl, fat and glossy, and there was a matching carcanet from which was suspended a pink pearl, the twin of the one hanging from the *ferronière*. When she looked at the pink pearl she experienced the strangest sensation. She could not explain it. It was both eerie and somehow pleasing. She felt as if she stood at a border and across the border was some great and marvellous secret which she was about to learn. And then, just as she thought her mind was grasping the secret, it would flit away, disappear completely, leaving her with a feeling of poignant sadness. The pink pearls reminded her of something, but she could not remember what, however hard she tried.

The visits from the cloth-merchants were some of the

most invigorating. They brought her rolls of material: glowing, embossed silks; rich heavy brocades in cerise and dark gold, in emerald green and coolest ivory; sumptuous velvets in dense gold, rich blues, amethyst, lemon yellow, pale beige, rose-pink; cloth-of-tissue, of silver and gold; and, for the most important occasions, black cloth-of-gold, which she considered quite dazzling but too mature for her age. There were rolls of lace, too, so delicate and fragile; stars and roses, daisies, all brought to life in the most delicate stitchery imaginable.

Furriers brought sables and marten, spotted lynx, miniver, and rich furs from Tartary.

There were scented and embroidered gloves; fur-lined cloaks with jewelled hoods; pantofles – slippers – for her feet in every hue and design; hoods in the French style, the Italian style, the German style, encrusted or embroidered, edged with filigree-work, embossed with gold, adazzle with jewels of every variety, or stiff with pearls. Even the garters, heavily embroidered, were encrusted with jewels, and the hose were of the finest cloth in as many and varied colours as the materials.

Athena sat like a queen, surrounded by merchants all trying to outdo one another to gain her attentions. She wore an outmoded gown which was too tight under the bust and the arms, and shoes which pinched when she walked too far, and her hair was coiled up in a blue silk snood. She looked more like a merchant's daughter than a nobleman's, and yet here were all these merchants virtually on their knees before her, desperate for her approbation – desperate also for the Comte's money.

By nightfall Athena was pleasantly tired. The Comte had told her to feel free to choose as many of the items as she desired, but all the same she had been very selective. She found the colour rose-pink particularly pleasing, and so she had selected different materials in this colour; she had decided that the gown she would wear for the ball in her honour would be in rose-pink, and with it she would wear the *ferronière* and carcanet with the rose-pink pearls.

During the next few weeks the Comte was like a gleeful child as he organized the coming ball and feast. He was a past master at living on a shoestring, and it did not matter to him that he was spending money he did not have. All that mattered was that he had a daughter again, and that she was going to be presented to all the important people that he knew. Sometimes, when he was alone, he giggled to himself as he thought of the suitors who would plead for Athena's hand: men who would believe that she was one day to become immensely wealthy. He could not wait for the farce to begin. He knew that he was going to enjoy himself more than he had ever done before. It was going to be a grand lark.

For a moment – but only for a moment – he thought enviously of Francis, the King of France, and the extravagances of the French Court. Francis never seemed short of money, nor in difficulties with his economic situation. It was reputed that he spent three hundred thousand crowns each year on presents for ladies of the Court, some of them little better than *filles de joie*. On the first day of January each year, Francis gave these *filles de joie* gifts, and generous gifts at that. And, according to ancient custom, the ladies reciprocated by giving the King a bouquet of flowers each May Day. What the Comte would have given to have possessed just part of the King's enormous income, to be able to spend money as liberally as did he . . . He half closed his eyes, imagining his pockets bulging with gold crowns, thinking of his empty coffers and imagining them similarly filled. But he would not lose heart. If necessary, he would take to gambling again, for fortunes could be won on the toss of a dice, as he knew from past experience. That they could also be lost he knew too, but he preferred not to dwell on that aspect. If ever the thought of his penury tempted him into a fit of depression, he had only to think of his beautiful daughter, with her trusting face. He would not dream of disappointing her, nor would he shock her by telling her the truth. She was young; nothing must stop her being happy, nothing must stop her blossoming freely, without anxieties.

He could not wait for the night of the ball, to see her in her finery, to hear the lilt of music, and have the French windows thrown open onto the lawns and gardens as they had been in previous years when his fortunes had been in a better condition. In his mind's eye, he saw the swirl of coloured gowns, the glitter of jewels, heard laughter and the deep, male voices of his guests. And the suitors . . . He chuckled to himself. They would be like foxes after a chicken, a young, plump, and succulent bird; their fangs would be sharp, their claws unsheathed. They would be groomed and pluméd, splendidly garbed, richly begemmed. But, he vowed, not one of them would have her.

He loved his daughter, he wanted her company, he had no wish to lose her. If the thought occurred to him that he might rescue himself from an intolerable financial situation by marrying his adored Athena to one of the wealthier men in France, he did not linger over the idea. She was *his*: and he intended to keep it that way.

Dress-fittings took up hours of Athena's time. The *couturière* who had come especially from Paris to robe her, Madame le Brun, was a garrulous creature, with opinions on everything. Athena was to learn quite a few snippets of information about the French Court from the lips of Madame le Brun.

As the woman pinned and shaped, snipped and fitted, she told Athena of the poor, unhappy Queen of France, Claude.

'*Madame la Reine, hélas*, is not comely and well-made, nor does she have the raven hair which the King so admires in his –' Madame le Brun paused, her eyes sparkling – 'mistresses.'

'The King has mistresses?' Athena gasped.

'Oh yes, my dear. Not like the King of England, who is devoted to his Queen.'

'Why should a man want mistresses when he has a wife?' asked Athena in all innocence.

'That is not for me to say, not where the King is concerned.' Madame le Brun shrugged her shoulders. 'Who can say what makes a man turn to other arms? It is boredom, or curiosity, or perhaps he is seeking what he does not find in his wife?'

'Would a man become an adulterer merely because he likes women with black hair and his wife does not possess it?'

'That I cannot say, Mam'selle. I only know that it is so, that King Francis is a man of generous and splendid appetites.' Madame le Brun lowered her voice. 'Has M'sieur le Comte told you of the ladies who accompany the Court wherever it goes, from Royal palace to Royal palace?'

'Yes, he did mention something along those lines, about the King giving these ladies gifts.'

'Ah yes, it is the custom. They make a great show of it.'

'Are these – are they . . . common women, strumpets?' Athena asked hesitantly.

'If they were not attached to the French Court, yes, they would be common, low women. Certainly strumpets. But these are *belles jolies filles* and although few of them are of high breeding, they are picked for their beauty and grace, their charm, and various other talents.' Madame le Brun's small green eyes glittered even more brightly.

'Then the Court of France is a scandalous place,' Athena said, feeling extremely daring at criticizing the King's Court.

'To say the least, Mam'selle, to say the least. But it is all done with such grace, such dignity that words like low and common do not spring to mind. Be assured, Mam'selle, that if you should visit Court with your esteemed father, or even if you should have to reside there for some time, there will be nothing that you will find openly offensive; rather you will be impressed, filled with awe. Ah, the jewels, the silks and satins, the brocade, the cloth-of-gold, the pearls and rubies and diamonds that blaze there, the dancing and the masques! Many times have I wished that I were half my age and nobly born, for if that were so I would be frolicking at Court most happily. Oh, the handsome gentlemen you will see there! They take your breath away with their beauty.'

'Is the King handsome, Madame? Tell me of him.'

'His Majesty is twenty-four years old. He is tall and well-made, but slim, you understand. He has glossy chestnut hair which he wears quite long, cut just below the ears, in a bob. He has a very fair complexion, and the colour of his eyes matches his hair. He has a shapely mouth, with the lower lip fuller than the upper, and his nose dominates his face. His eyebrows are thin and dark, and arched high. It is said, and frequently, that he is the most handsome King France has ever had.'

'He is very tall?'

'Six feet, so they say.'

'That is tall, indeed.' For a moment a vague thought flittered through Athena's mind: a King who was extremely tall, six feet or over. That sounded familiar to her; where had she heard it before? Perhaps it had been her father when he had been speaking of Francis. Yes, that must be it.

'Oh, things have changed since he became King, Mam'selle. It is all feasting and merrymaking now; every courtier dressing as if he were the richest man in Paris, every courtesan determined to outdo the other. Which is, of course, good for my business. In the last few years since King Francis came to the throne, I have trebled my income. It began immediately Francis became King in

1515 – his triumphant entry into Paris dazzled all those who saw it. There were, they say, twelve hundred Princes and Dukes, Counts and noblemen taking part. The King wore white and cloth-of-silver with a white velvet bonnet, and he rode on a white Arab stallion with a white canopy. *Largesse* was thrown freely to the crowds. A salamander was much in evidence on all the livery.'

'A salamander? What is that, Madame?'

'It is the King's own personal emblem, chosen by his mother, Madame Louise. The salamander is a fabulous lizard which flourishes amongst flames. It has been the King's emblem since he was ten years old, and of course for many years before he became King he did indeed flourish among flames, for he was the old King's heir only if the old King did not have any sons. By the old King I mean Louis the Twelfth, the son of Charles, Duke of Orléans. Louis had two wives, Anne of Brittany and Mary, the sister of Henry the Eighth. By Anne he had two daughters, Claude, the present Queen, and Renée. But all those years that he was married to Anne, when he was a younger man, Francis and his mother lived in dread of Louis producing a son and thus ousting Francis from his position as Dauphin – heir to the Throne. Fortunately for Francis, all Anne of Brittany's sons died in infancy.'

'So King Francis is not the son of Louis the Twelfth?'

'Indeed not, Mam'selle. Charles, Duke of Orléans, had a brother, Jean, Count of Angouleme, who married Marguerite de Rohan. Their son was Charles, Count of Angouleme, and he married Louise of Savoy, and it was their son who became the present King.'

'That must have been a tortuous time for King Francis and his mother,' mused Athena.

'Madame Louise never lost hope. At all times she believed that one day her son would be King; she was an example to us all. A woman of grat strength and courage, Madame Louise. Married at twelve and widowed at nineteen . . .'

'How sad for her!' Athena exclaimed.

'Her husband was not one to be mourned, Mam'selle. He was unfaithful many times, he cared only for himself, a great womanizer. She was well rid of him,' declared Madame le Brun.

'But he gave her two handsome children you say, and it is clear she dotes on them both.'

'That is *all* he gave her.' The seamstress rolled her eyes heavenwards. 'Ah, men –! They are all the same. Take, take, take . . . So few of them ever care to give.'

Madame le Brun had finished pinning the hem of Athena's new gown, and she stood back to survey the length to see that it was exactly even. As it appeared to be so, she gestured to Athena to stand before the long mirror. Athena did so, and was pleasantly astonished by the reflection that she saw there: a young girl with shimmering silver-gilt hair stood looking back at her, dressed in an equally shimmering blue gown. Then something strange happened. Athena put her hand to her throat as if in search of some jewel. She looked in the mirror; there was nothing there hanging at her throat, and yet for a single flash of time she had had the strongest sensation that there should be something hanging there, something beautiful and splendid which she would love. Then she remembered – the carcanet with the pink pearl, that must be what she was thinking of, but she would be wearing that with her pink gowns of course, not with her blue.

'Who will be coming to the ball in your honour, Mam'selle?' Madame le Brun asked as she took out a pin and rethreaded it more carefully.

'Many courtiers, I believe, and many of my father's friends and colleagues.'

'I expect he will be wanting to find a suitable husband for you?'

Athena nodded.

'Ah, Mam'selle,' sighed the seamstress, 'then may I offer you a word of advice? There are so many at Court of whom you must beware. Names spring to my mind – self-seeking men who would give their eye teeth to get their hands on your fortune.'

'My fortune seems to be common knowledge,' said Athena, somewhat wryly.

'Fortunes have a habit of becoming so, Mam'selle.'

'Tell me the names of those fortune-hunters you know.'

'Well now,' Madame Le Brun began, 'the first name which comes into my mind is that of the Comte Mallière. He has buried two young wives already – both heiresses – and it is reputed that he is beginning to search for a third. If you ask me, his wives died from neglect and ill-treatment.'

'How terrible! Has no one done anything?'

'What can be done? He is a Comte and he is now immensely rich thanks to the past successes of his fortune-hunting. But he is insatiable. These things are a protection, a barrier between a man and rightful justice. There is another. He has no title. Engerrand du Ville; he is the heir of the Duc de Craille and I would not trust him, not with one small coin, and I would advise you to treat him the same. Those are the two who occur to me and who might mislead you, for their surface charms are great. You are very young, Mam'selle, do take care.' Madame le Brun pressed a hand to her lips. 'Oh, and there is another. I do not know whether I should warn you against him, for he is very close to the King and my words might be construed as treason. You will promise that you will tell no one?'

'I promise, Madame,' Athena said, all curiosity.

'His name is Hamish, Lord Mullally. Yes, I can see that you think that is a strange name for a Frenchman, but he is not French. Oh, I do not know the whole story, but some years ago in battle his father saved the life of King Francis's father – very bravely too, I believe – and when Lord Mullally was orphaned, Madame Louise brought him up as King Francis's foster-brother, so he and the King have grown up together and are very close.'

'What nationality is he, Madame?'

'Half English, half Irish. Now remember, you have promised that you will tell no one of my words, Mam'selle. Hamish Mullally has had everything he has ever wanted, he is thoroughly spoiled. He has been cossetted and indulged to a fault. He is one of those men who takes everything and gives nothing in return. Girls fall down at his feet, they worship him, and he expects it as his right. You must not be like them; you must remain aloof from his charms. When I think of Hamish Mullally, I think of Madame Louise's husband and what a terrible time she had with him. I would not wish such a husband on any woman; certainly not upon yourself, Mam'selle. Infidelity – pah! It sickens me.'

'Have you perhaps some experience of it yourself, Madame?'

'You could say that, Mam'selle. I had a fine young cockerel of a husband once, and he led me a fine dance, betraying me left, right and centre.'

'What did you do?' Athena enquired, unable to restrain her curiosity.

'I let him devise his own fate, knowing that his loose ways would bring their own punishment, and they did. He died of a disease of the parts of Venus – but I should not be speaking of such things to you, you so young and unwed. Forgive me.' The look of bitterness that had crossed Madame le Brun's face vanished as if it had never been there. 'Now, will you try on the pink brocade gown, Mam'selle, for I believe it is a little loose round the waist.'

CHAPTER THREE

Athena's French was progressing by leaps and bounds. She was quite a consummate conversationalist in that language now, much to the Comte's delight. Athena had shown him some of her new gowns and jewels, parading before him proudly. He had been overwhelmed by her beauty, by the picture of sweetness and elegance before him. One day she would be married to some powerful and wealthy man, but not yet, oh no, not yet. He could not bear to part with her. Seeing her so finely dressed, carrying herself so nobly, he could not envisage any husband sufficiently good for her. No, he thought, not even a King would be good enough for her. She deserved an empire, riches, blessings unlimited.

The Comte had given Athena a young hound pup, a dove-coloured creature with huge lolloping paws, floppy ears and great mournful brown eyes. She had named him Carol after the circular folk dances beloved by the peasants, for his favourite pastime was chasing round and round in circles after his tail. Carol soon grew bored with costume fittings, longing to escape into the summer sunshine in the gardens. Athena and the Comte would walk through the rose arbours and onto the chamomile lawns where the sweet, fresh scent soothed and refreshed them even on the hottest day as they crushed the herbs underfoot. Athena loved to sit in the rose bower, from where she could see a great deal of the gardens, all carefully designed and laid out by Signor Bernadetto, whom the Comte had hired for just that very purpose. Carol loved to lollop up and down on the chamomile lawns, sometimes pausing dramatically on finding a ladybird or beetle. He would snuffle cautiously at the insect as if pondering as to its identity and purpose in life. Once, he took a beetle into his mouth but it buzzed so loudly and frighteningly that he dropped it in shock, giving a yelp. Athena had rushed over to him, thinking that he had hurt himself, but she had seen the beetle scuttling away indignantly and gauged what had happened.

Athena and the Comte were sitting basking in the July sunshine in the gardens, a positive auriole of gold, some four days prior to the ball in Athena's honour. Athena was wearing a light gown of blue *toile de Paris*, but even so she was unbearably hot. A flat straw bonnet, similar to that worn by the peasants who worked in the fields, shaded her eyes. Despite the heat the Comte wore his usual array of splendid clothes: pink hose with pink and blue embroidered breeches, a doublet of deep pink satin with trelliswork of silver, and on his curly brown and grey hair a *toque à crenaux* of vivid crimson velvet decorated with golden brooches and a swirl of black feathers.

Thinking that he must be suffering from the heat, Athena besought him to remove his doublet and sit in his shirt of fine Paris lawn, but he was adamant that he was quite comfortable.

'Carol cannot remove his coat, why should I?' the Comte twinkled.

'Father, sometimes you can be very stubborn,' Athena laughed. 'Sunshine is good for you. I would like to see you benefiting from it instead of sitting in such a heavy doublet.'

'When you have stayed at Court as many times as I have, *mon trésor*, you will know that retaining your composure in hot weather is the least of your worries. I have sweltered in far worse heat than this at Fontainbleau or the Louvre with King Francis and his Court.'

'Perhaps we shall be able to use the gardens on the night of the ball, Father? I mean, for more than just stepping out for a breath of fresh air. The terraces are wide, could they not be used for dancing?'

'I do not see why not,' responded the Comte. 'The windows can be opened onto the terraces and people will be able to hear the music even from outside. We have done it before. I remember once, oh many, many years ago, before you were born, when your sweet mother was alive, God rest her soul –' the Comte crossed himself – 'we held such a splendid ball here. Everyone was dressed up either as a weird beast, strange animal or mythical figure. There were gods and goddesses galore. The old King attended, I remember. He was dressed as Zeus, the King of Gods, but his health was poor and he danced very little. He strolled out into the gardens and he sat upon this very seat where we now sit, surrounded by his courtiers of course – a King is never alone. I had walked out with him, and he turned to me and he said: "We need more festivities like this, old friend. Why do you not arrange a similar masque for us at Court? The Queen would love it. Wait until she has recovered from her confinement and then she will atend, I am sure." '

'And did you do that, Father?'

'Alas no, I never did, because the Queen, poor soul, lost her son within a few hours of his birth and the Court was plunged into mourning. She was soon confined again, and that child was lost also. But we do not want to speak of such dismal and unhappy things on this beautiful day, *ma petite*. We must think only of you and your happiness and the coming ball.'

Athena sighed impatiently. She could hardly wait for the four days to pass so that she could wear the beautiful rose-pink gown and the pink pearls to match, to hear the Château filled with lilting music, and to see all their guests garbed in brilliant finery, glittering with jewels. She would also have been filled with trepidation at the thought of meeting her possible future husband at the ball, had not the Comte repeatedly assured her that he had no intention of parting with her for a long time yet. He would pat her hand or stroke her cheek, telling her again and again that he loved her dearly, that she was his own sweet daughter, and that he relished her company above all things. Not for many years would he let her leave, he said.

'But what of my suitors? What of the men of whom you told me?' she had said, bewildered, for she had worked so hard to quell the combination of curiosity and excitement which had gripped her over the past weeks as she had thought of being wooed by ardent suitors. Despite her misgivings, she was determined to be a dutiful daughter, to acquiesce to whatever her father asked of her.

But the Comte had merely smiled at her and led the conversation into safer channels.

The following days were a hubbub of activity as the finishing touches were put to the preparations for the ball in Athena's honour. The preparations for the accompanying feast were extensive. There were meats in plenty – capon, crane, geese, ducks, pork, hams – with stuffings of garlic and cheese, purėed hard-boiled eggs, apples, nuts, spices, saffron and cloves. Swans and peacocks would take pride of place at the tables, having their plumage replaced after they were roasted as decoration. There would be Lombardy green tart made with soft cheese mixed with parsley and other herbs, to which were added beaten eggs, butter and saffron, all baked in a pastry case; venison pastry also, and veal, lamb and kid. To follow, there would be delicately flavoured custards and syllabubs, pies and almond pasties glazed with sugar, and sweetmeats in many different colours decorated with fruit and nuts and crystallized sugars. And to compliment each course there was a different wine, every one of the finest that French vineyards could produce.

The banqueting hall was decorated with hundreds of roses so that their scent would drown that of the many flickering tapers. The floors had been swept and strewn with fresh rushes, and scented with chamomile and other sweet-scented herbs. Cooks, valets, pages, stewards, had not had time or opportunity to relax for days now. It was the festive season all over again in the heat of midsummer. But there was not a moment to complain of the discomforts of the time of year. If backs ached, feet swelled, and clothes were drenched in sweat, that was just unfortunate. No one would rest, or even think of rest, until after the night of the Grand Ball.

And finally the moment was come. All the guests were assembled, seemingly in their thousands, for carriage after carriage had rolled up since early evening, and the Great Hall was crammed with gentlemen and ladies, all robed in their finest gowns, breeches and doublets. The scent of musk filled the air, along with a myriad of other perfumes – rose-water, violet-water, verbena, jasmine, Hungary-water. *Toques* dipped on carefully curled heads, feathers swaying and bobbing, golden brooches glittering. Ladies fluttered their lashes, simpered, pursed their lips, or avoided direct glances, according to their predilections. Throats blazed with gems; some throats slender and swanlike, white as Camellias, others short and plump, of a sallow colour, yet others ageing and wrinkled, but all afire with carcanets studded with jewels and pearls, richly decorated with goldsmiths' work, filigree and delicate scrolls. Stiffened skirts flared from the fashionable farthingale, nowhere near as wide and stately as it would later become but, nonetheless, earning its Spanish name of *vertugarde*.

Some ladies wore no headdresses but only an ornament of jewels, their hair tautly rolled back over a false hairpiece, giving the illusion of height, with curls carefully arranged at the sides and rear. Where headdresses were worn, they were heart-shaped or crescent-shaped, lending an air of innocent sweetness to the faces they adorned. No one could look worldly while wearing a heart-shaped headdress. Virginity had never been more in vogue, nor the look of virginal innocence more popular.

In her suite, Athena was putting the final touches to her

outfit. The pear-shaped pink pearl hung enticingly in the centre of her forehead, its twin dangling from her slender lily throat, her sumptuous, richly-decorated pink gown echoing the colour of the priceless pearls. She wore her hair loose, as befitted a maiden, wearing no headdress but the *ferronière* and a dainty gold *filet* like an angel's aureole around her head.

Her cheeks were rosy with excitement, her heart pounding unevenly. From her suite she could hear the hubbub of voices in the great hall, the sound of lutes and viols from the Minstrels' Gallery. She wanted so much to be a part of that brilliantly assembled company, but she felt a sudden attack of nerves. She was thinking of all eyes turned on her as she descended the beautiful onyx stairway to the Great Hall. What if they did not take to her . . .? What if the eyes were cold, unfriendly, the faces stern? Perhaps they would find fault with her French accent, remarking upon her English upbringing, consider her a foreigner? She pressed a hand to her heart. She had not thought of that. A foreigner – and simply because she had never been taught to speak French in her convent!

Madame le Brun, helping to dress Athena on this most important night, looked at the beautiful young girl standing before her. She saw the cheeks rose-pink with colour, then, as fears grew, a pallor setting in. The child was so nervous, so anxious, yet this should be the happiest time of her life.

'Oh Madame, my fingers are trembling.' Athena hooked her fingers together, trying to still their quivering. 'What shall I say to them? What shall I do? What if I am tongue-tied, what if I can think of nothing polite to say? Oh, what if they do not like me?'

'They are your guests, Mam'selle, and your father's guests. They have come freely to attend a magnificent feast and a Grand Ball in your honour. They would not be so ignorant and uncouth as to find fault with you and, indeed, if any should be so arrogant, then they are not worth caring about.'

'I am sure that you give me excellent advice, Madame, but all the same . . .' Athena swallowed, her throat constricted and dry.

'You will be the most beautiful young lady in the room, and I know that I do not boast when I say that your gown is superb, that it will outshine all others.' Madame le Brun simpered a little, for it had been her fingers which had worked the magic. 'They could not fail to adore you, Mam'selle. Indeed, I think it quite likely that you will find so many will adore you, so many will vie for your favours, that you will be quite overcome by their attentions.'

This was an aspect which had not occurred to Athena, and she put a hand to her lips in sudden alarm. 'You think I will be beseiged with admirers? Oh, Madame le Brun, if only that were so! Anything, rather than call down their ridicule . . .'

'What nonsense is this, Mam'selle? Ridicule –? There will be nothing but eulogies for you tonight. Prepare yourself for the praise, the flattery, the compliments which, I can assure you, will be excessive rather than lacking.'

'But, Madame, how do I gauge what is flattery and what is truly meant?'

'Instinct, Mam'selle. A woman's instinct is her greatest armour. Always trust it. If you have misgivings about a certain gentleman, then listen to it, listen to what it says to you, do not ignore it. God gave man a strong sword arm, but he gave a woman her intuition, and I know which I would prefer. Now, you remember those names, do you not? The men of whom I warned you. Especially that wicked Lord Mullally, that – that *womanizer*.' Madame le Brun's lip curled. 'When I think of the hearts he has broken, the way he has used so many fair young ladies for his own selfish ends. Oh, it would be a different story if he were not so close to the King, but he has immunity for that, you see. He truly believes that he is as good as the King, that he has as much right to do whatever he wills, to disregard the feelings of others. These are not qualities which I admire. A man should have his tender feelings as surely as any woman.'

Athena thought fondly of the Comte and agreed with Madame le Brun. How lonely and bereft she would have been without her father's tender feelings towards her, his gentleness and his loving care. How untenable life would have been if he were stern and grim and did not show his emotions. To be loved and cherished: it was her greatest need.

In the Great Hall, the English Earl of Faltringham, a drunkard and gambler who was in disgrace in his country and now lived in Paris, waited with his hand on the gilded and chased pommel of his sword. He was seething with impatience to see Athena, the daughter of the Comte de Deverelle, for he had received permission from her father to woo her.

The Earl's first wife had died in suspicious circumstances at his London house, the strength of the ensuing rumours driving him from England. It was said that he had helped her to an early grave. Behind his handsome exterior, with his curled yellow hair and pale blue eyes, he concealed a loathsome character. His very flesh crawled with lust at the thought of marrying a sweet and innocent young heiress who had been raised in a convent, for his perverted delight was corrupting the innocent. Word had gone round that the Lady Athena would not appear until the clock had struck eleven. He wondered if his patience would last out. Pacing up and down at the foot of the onyx stairway, he affected not to notice the crush of guests all around him.

The other suitor for Athena's hand was Claud, Comte Belleme, a young French nobleman who was given to falling wildly in love at first sight, for he possessed an ardently romantic heart which wallowed in dreams, fantasy and poetry. Belleme wore a doublet of cerise, gold-barred velvet with matching breeches, his *toque à crenaux* was of rich black velvet studded with golden brooches and ropes of pearls, his clothes and fingers were fluorescent with jewels. But he wore his entire fortune on his back. Apart from what could be seen he owned nothing. He and Faltringham were at daggers drawn; they had already exchanged baleful glances, and now they stood a few yards apart, at the foot of the grand stairway, glaring at one another in open hostility.

'You are wasting your time, Belleme,' Faltringham sneered. 'She will not be looking for a callow youth. She will want a man, a *real* man, like myself.'

'She is a young lady and fair,' retorted Belleme, 'and it is rumoured that she has a highly romantic heart. Will you be able to satisfy her longing for romance, Faltringham? You must be all of five and thirty.' (To the twenty-year-old Belleme that seemed a great age.)

'My maturity and experience will arouse her passions,' snarled Faltringham, 'and *I* shall be able to satisfy them. She would never look at you.' His cold blue eyes were venomous as a snake's.

Belleme stared back furiously, struggling to control a sudden impulse to strike his rival in the face. 'There is not much time before the Lady appears. We shall find out then whom she favours.'

'I fear that it will be an unfortunate time for you, Belleme. I will wager this ruby on my finger that she will choose me.'

'And I wager this sapphire on my bonnet that she will choose *me*!' Belleme thrust out his chin, which had a smooth egglike shape and surface, not one hair sprouting from it.

'Pah, you are an imbecile,' Faltringham jeered, turning on his heel.

'We shall see who is the fool, before the night is out!' Belleme called after him, cheeks flushed a bright pink, pearls of sweat bedewing his forehead.

It was at that moment that Athena began her descent down the onyx stairway, the light from a hundred tapers lending her skin an opalescent radiance as she glided down step after step with the utmost grace.

Faltringham and Belleme, after their first gasping reaction to such beauty, scuttled forward, digging their elbows into each other as hard as possible, each determined to be the one to lead the vision in to dinner. Weighing up the situation, with a suppressed smile playing upon her lips, Athena offered an arm to each of the men while the Comte de Deverelle, eyes glinting with laughter, watched the scene, then followed the trio into the dining hall.

Quail, peacock, lark, swan and great, succulent hams were laid out for the feast. Piquant sauces and sweetmeats of every hue and flavour to delight the palate, lampreys and huge tarts, jellies and custards, awaited the hungry guests. To drink there was Grenache, Loire wines, Burgundy and Hippocras.

With Faltringham and Belleme on either side of her, Athena attempted to enjoy the meal. But it was not easy with the poisonous glances which were flung across her from one man to the other. They effected charming, ingratiating smiles when they caught her glance, but when they looked at one another their faces were black with fury and hatred. She looked forward to laughing about it with her father when it was all over. Her eyes fell lovingly upon the Comte, who was being charmed by a beautiful, raven-haired lady who seemed to have attached herself to him. Athena's eyes swept up and down the table, taking in the guests. She wanted to see what her father's friends were like.

It was with a little start of something like shock that her eyes came to rest upon a man who was totally unlike the two fops vying for her attentions. He sat at the far end of the table, surrounded by ladies, all of whom were intent upon obtaining and keeping his attention. He was quite startlingly handsome, with silky black hair and brows, the planes of his face engagingly cut and shaped so that one's eyes were drawn back to them again and again. From this distance Athena could not see the colour of his eyes, but she felt a mysterious certainty that they were a deep, dark blue. She wondered who the handsome, dignified man was, with his aloof and compelling charm. Whoever he was, he must be conceited, she thought, if he was always such a focus of fervent attention from the ladies.

However, whether she liked it or no, her eyes would keep slipping back to the dashing, laughing man at the other end of the table. She did not dare ask his identity of the Earl of Faltringham or the Comte Belleme for fear that they would immediately draw their swords and attack the handsome stranger. The mood they were in, anything might be possible. Idly she wondered how the stranger would conduct himself in such a situation. Then she forced her thoughts back to her neighbours.

Faltringham was holding out a dish of sweetmeats for her to partake of one and Belleme deliberately dashed the platter out of Faltringham's hand, replacing it with another which he held under Athena's nose, begging her to take as many marchpane delicacies as she desired.

'I will have more wine please, gentlemen,' she said, gently pushing away the rudely presented platter of sweetmeats. Then she wished she had not spoken, for both of the men reached for the flask of Grenache at one and the same moment, the flask tipping and wine gushing out over the table.

'You mule-fingered clodhead!' cried Faltringham.

'How dare you, My Lord Earl! The fault was entirely yours.' Belleme rejoindered hotly, reaching for a decanter of Burgundy wine. Faltringham decided to do exactly the same, each man clutching the flask tightly, each refusing to let go.

Athena leaned back in her chair, weary of their childish duelling.

'Gentlemen, gentlemen,' called out the Comte de Deverelle from across the table. 'My daughter told me only this evening how she delights in good manners in men. Pray, gentlemen, control your hostilities a little longer.'

Belleme's hand fell away from the flask. Triumphantly, Faltringham poured out the Burgundy for Athena, pushing the goblet towards her.

Coldly, she thanked him, but did not take a drink. How bored she was with the two men's asinine behaviour; she wished that they would both go away and leave her in peace. Her eyes travelled back to the lower end of the table. The dashing stranger was laughing at something one of the attentive ladies had said. He had thrown back his head showing perfectly shaped white teeth. One tanned, strong hand was holding a goblet of Hippocras, the other was being clutched by a lady who appeared about to rain kisses upon it.

Athena looked away, as if she had burst in upon an intimate scene in a boudoir, then her eyes slid back. Was the lady really going to kiss the stranger's hand? Indeed she was. Kiss after kiss descended on the lean brown fingers, the back of his hand. Athena looked up at his face. He did not look in the slightest surprised, nor embarrassed. He seemed to be relishing every moment. How could he allow such bold and intimate behaviour in public? It was most unseemly.

The end of the meal was approaching, and the tables and benches were being taken away to make room for dancing. The minstrels had struck up a merry tune and the guests were assembling to do it justice.

Instinctively, Athena knew what was going to happen next. Faltringham and Belleme were going to fight over who should lead her onto the dance floor. With sinking heart, she watched their furious, flashing faces, the bulging, hate-filled eyes.

To forestall them, Athena said: 'Gentlemen, gentlemen, I shall dance with neither of you if you continue in this fashion. I think I shall select you in alphabetical order;

that means you first, Belleme, and then you, Faltringham. If that does not please you then I shall have to decline dancing with either of you for the rest of the evening and, who knows, perhaps for ever more.' She let the words fall idly from her lips as if she were overcome with ennui and could barely be bothered to speak to them. Her words seemed to have the desired effect, for Faltringham withdrew, his face ugly. Belleme led her onto the dance floor.

She had been well prepared for what would be expected of her, the Comte having taught her a number of dances which he knew that his musicians would be playing on the night of the Grand Ball. Having decided that Belleme's company was infinitely sweeter than that of the surly Faltringham, even if the former's smooth, immature face did have a habit of colouring in an unsightly fashion every time she spoke, Athena danced a number of dances with him, aware of the fuming Faltringham on the edge of the dance floor.

As the stages of the courtly and elegant dance progressed, Athena had plenty of time to look about her and to notice the handsome black-haired stranger again surrounded by attentive ladies, their faces uplifted to his as if transfixed. That section of the Hall where he sat with his *cortège* of women seemed by far the liveliest area, but Athena would rather have died than become merely another simpering female desirous of obtaining the stranger's attention. No, that was not for her at all; the man must always do the pursuing.

The stranger's lively face, tanned and expressive, was turning from one to the other of his companions, as if searching for someone worthy of his favours. Athena felt a pang of disgust. She would rather suffer than chase after such a man, such an odious, pampered philanderer.

She looked around for her father, to see him in discussion with a most attractive auburn-haired lady who seemed to be hanging upon his every word. Athena was delighted that he was enjoying the evening – and then she realized that she was enjoying herself, too. There had been no awkwardness with the assembled guests, no one had glared at her, though many had stared with open admiration. She had not mis-spoken her French or fumbled on the dance floor and forgotten her steps, nor had she spilled sauce down her gown, nor choked on a sweetmeat, all the things which she had dreaded doing on this most important night. She was not even nonplussed by the behaviour of her two suitors, finding herself able to view them in a most amiable light. Let them woo and ogle and pursue as energetically as they wished: neither of them would possess her, she was quite safe. And for that she had her dearest father to thank.

Lucien, Comte de Deverelle, was indeed enjoying himself immensely. The witless antics of Faltringham and Belleme were something that he would remember for months to come. What apes they were! He was remembering one of his other most successful practical jokes, which he had played on the Marshal of France some years ago. The Marshal had been a sombre, humourless man, his saturnine temperament only enlivened by his devotion to horses and all things equine. The Comte had begged the Marshal to come to dinner with him one day, and he had invited simultaneously a dozen of the Marshal's closest friends and colleagues. He promised them a magnificent feast, worthy of a king. Upon their arrival on the appointed day, the Comte had welcomed them warmly, but begged them to excuse him briefly while he attended to final preparations for the feast. He had then disappeared into the kitchens, the source of mouth-watering smells and the sounds of intense activity.

For half an hour, for an hour, for nearly two hours the Comte did not reappear. His guests by now were ravenous, their mouths drooling with anticipation. And finally he returned to them, red-faced as if through exertion, leading a procession of servants carrying platters laden with scores of crisp golden pasties, steaming hot and fragrant, spilling their aromatic juices and promising a feast fit for the gods.

But then the Comte had asked his guests' forbearance, saying that he had been called to attend upon the King, and that he must leave immediately – but that they, of course, must not be prevented from supping in his absence.

And with that he left them. He did indeed go to the Court, although he had not been summoned there. He had gone to tell the King about the joke he had played upon his guests.

For inside the pasties, wrapped in the light melting pastry and coated in the appetizing sauce, there was no meat, not even a particle of bone or gristle. The pasties were filled with an assortment of equine accoutrements – old leather straps, bridles, reins, bits of saddle, anything that could be minced up small enough.

How the King had laughed! And the Comte could hardly restrain himself from laughing now again at the memory. It had been one of his favourite pranks.

But suddenly the Comte caught sight of Athena, who was still on the dance floor, surrounded by a crowd of admirers. She was smiling bravely, but clearly growing weary. He excused himself to his dancing partner, and hurried over to her.

'*Mon trésor*, you are tired. You must not exhaust yourself. I will escort you to bed. First, would you say goodnight to our guests?'

'Of course, Father,' Athena smiled indulgently, doing as she was bidden, then taking her father's arm and going back up the onyx stairway. Her legs were aching from the unaccustomed dancing, but she knew that she would not forget this night. At the top of the staircase she turned her head once to look back into the Hall. Most faces had turned away from her by then but there was one who was looking up at her, directly into her eyes. It was the dark-haired stranger.

Before they had passed out of sight of the hall, Athena

asked her father who the man was, pointing him out with a discreet gesture.

The Comte looked back. 'Ah, *him*,' he said, mysteriously. 'Did he not ask you to dance with him during the evening?' Athena shook her head. 'Then I am extremely surprised, for he is a most forward gentleman.'

'Yes, Father, but who is he?'

'Hamish, Lord Mullally, the King's foster-brother and one of his closest friends.'

'Lord Mullally?' Athena gasped. 'Why, is he not – I mean, does he not have a reputation as an – an adventurer?'

'That is so. Yes, an adventurer, the very word.'

Athena's heart was sinking deeply. She was remembering Madame le Brun's warning. Did not the seamstress's words only tally with what Athena herself had conjectured during the evening, that Mullally was spoiled and pampered, living a life of idle self-indulgence, surrounded by ladies who fell at his feet at regular intervals? Surprisingly, she felt a little pain, as if she had been told some dreadful news, but she could not analyse why she felt thus. What was the man to her? Only someone of whom she must beware at all costs. But he was so handsome, so devilishly handsome, and he had such an aura about him . . . But she must put him out of her mind. A 'womanizer' Madame le Brun had called him, and Athena had seen the evidence herself. All the same . . . She glanced back to see if he was still staring up at her, but he had averted his head and was speaking to one of the sumptuously beautiful ladies sitting beside him. She felt again a pang of discomfort, as if a hand had squeezed her heart.

CHAPTER FOUR

The weeks following the Grand Ball seemed to be filled wtih an unending line of suitors, for now Faltringham and Belleme were not alone. Athena de Deverelle had been seen, inspected and approved of by all. They came laden with gifts for her, all of which she gently but determinedly refused, however dismayed her suitors might appear to be as a result. Men with red hair, with brown, with gold, with black, all plied their way to her door, eager to win the hand of the beautiful young heiress. To please her father, whom she would not have dreamed of upsetting, she let the men call upon her. However, she could not take to Faltringham at all, and she feared she would soon have to make this plain to him, for her carefully nurtured civilities could not last much longer in the face of his sometimes surly, sometimes peevish wooing.

There was something all-pervasive about his moods. If he arrived to woo Athena in a good mood then it appeared to put everyone else he met into a good mood, but if he arrived in one of his saturnine and snappish moods then it seemed that it put everyone out for the day. Athena could well visualize how life would be with him, the tentacles of his moods reaching out to envelop her, to crush happiness from her on his black days, to sweep her into sunniness on his good days. Who would want to live the life of a see-saw? Not she.

Belleme was a different proposition. Despite his callowness and the smooth, hairless, egg-like face, she felt that there might have been a chance for them. But daily she thanked God that her father was so enlightened, that he was not like others of whom she had heard, fathers who raised their daughters with one thought in mind and one thought only – to marry them off at the earliest possible age.

As for the Comte de Deverelle, he revelled in every second of the suitors' visits, discussing them afterwards with Athena, laughing at their courtly blandishments, sighing because she continued to refuse all the gifts offered to her and he could not persuade her to accept them. He thought of the furs and gowns, the satin slippers, the jewelled headdresses that might have filled Athena's wardrobe, that might have been sold for money to finance their costly way of life. But that, of course, was not a gallant thought.

He wished that he could say to her, 'Athena, my dearest, all this show, this panoply you see about you, is but a sham. I have barely two *sous* to my name. If you could but accept the gifts which are brought you in such good faith, then you would make my life that much merrier for, with the money from the sale of the jewels, I could perhaps pay off some of my debts.' But how could he say such words without alarming his beautiful daughter? And, above all, he wished her to live a life of blissful tranquillity, secure in her father's riches. The day of reckoning must come, but the longer he postponed it the better for them both, he was sure. Oh, how he loved her, how he revelled in her company! Her proximity was a delight: when her spring-like turquoise eyes turned on him he was transmuted, cast into a golden world of gods and goddesses, a world of everlasting youth and ambrosia. It was a world which he had longed for all his natural life, yet without knowing it until it arrived. And now that he had it, how could he bear to part with it? A fair daughter, a beautiful creature, golden-haired and turquoise-eyed, with skin of opalescent pearl, a dimpled smile and slender, dainty hands which moved as expressively as butterflies' wings. He knew that he did not deserve such munificence, such joy, but it blazed in his heart every day that his Athena was in his Château.

*

July sweltered into August and still the suitors came. Carol professed interest in one of the Comte's black bitches, and Athena spent much of her time wondering whether their pups would be like Carol or black and long-haired like the bitch. Many times, as she serenely greeted her *beaux*, Athena's mind was on puppies and their possible appearances. Had Faltringham known what she was thinking about, he would have snorted in outrage and flounced out in a huff.

The days were inordinately hot, much too much so, and Athena took to welcoming her visitors out in the garden, on the terraces or in the sheltered rose arbour. Beneath the veiling branches of a willow where coolness held sway, with Carol stretching out, panting, at her feet, she would sit, a young Diana, to greet the ardent hunters.

Belleme was the first to propose formally. They were alone momentarily and Belleme took the opportunity of sinking on one knee before Athena and pouring out his heart to her.

'Madame,' he began, 'your beauty surpasses that of the angels, your skin is like silk, your hair is purest gold, your eyes are like turquoises. I have no doubt that you are a goddess reborn. And if you would agree to becoming my Comtesse, then you would make me the most joyous man on earth.'

Pink rushed into Athena's cheeks. She looked round urgently for her father but he was nowhere to be seen.

'*M'sieur le Comte*, you must first consult with my father. You must first ask his permission to speak to me thus. That is the custom, Monsieur, and you must adhere to it.'

Belleme looked shame-faced. He begged Athena's forgiveness for his temerity, and she gladly granted it but repeated what she had said: her father must first be consulted. Then she said that she had a megrim coming on and that her head was beginning to hurt, at which Belleme jumped to his feet, bowed courteously, and begged her leave to depart. He then went in search of the Comte.

The Comte was sitting in the coolness of one of the courtyards, two of his hounds at his feet, their bellies pressed against the cool paving stones. Gulping, Belleme approached him and stood awkwardly, his hat in his hands.

'*M'sieur le Comte*, I beg leave – that is, I – *M'sieur le Comte*, I –'

'It is about my daughter that you wish to speak?' the Comte interrupted with a benign smile.

'Yes, that is so, *M'sieur le Comte*. I wish – I wish to have your permission to ask your daughter to marry me.'

The Comte leaned back in his chair, his smile even broader, his eyes twinkling. Had Belleme been older and known more of the Comte's reputation he might have been forewarned.

'And why do you wish to marry my daughter?' the Comte asked softly.

'Why, *M'sieur le Comte*, I think she is the most beautiful young lady I have ever seen! Her beauty dazzles me. I cannot be happy without her to share my life.'

'And would you feel the same way, Belleme, if you knew that she was not a great heiress?'

'Not – not an heiress?' stuttered Belleme. 'But surely . . . I mean – that is – *M'sieur le Comte*!'

'I speak the truth, man. My daughter is no heiress, she has not a penny to her name. Nor, if it comes to that, do I. We are paupers – yes, paupers.'

'But your Château, Monsieur? Your fine clothes, your servants, the Grand Ball you held in Athena's honour?'

'I am deeply and irrevocably in debt,' the Comte said, his voice sombre. 'If I live to be a hundred I shall never be able to repay my debts.'

'This is the truth –?' Belleme squeaked.

'Why would I lie to you?' The Comte shrugged.

Outrage was beginning to replace Belleme's first shock. 'But Monsieur – how could you allow me to pay court to your daughter in this fashion, knowing what you know?'

'You mean that you do not want to marry her, Belleme? You mean that you no longer love her now that you have found out she is a pauper? But why should I prevent you from courting her because she is poor?'

'Monsieur, you must know my situation! I, too, am desperately poor; I have no money, no property, nothing. I *need* a rich wife.'

'You have just said that you could not be happy if you did not share your life with my daughter. Am I to understand that you have now changed your mind, and in such a short time?' Now the Comte was starting to enjoy himself again.

Belleme's cheeks were the colour of raspberries. For no particular reason, the Comte noticed that although Belleme had not one hair on his smooth chin, he had a great excess of them sprouting out of his nose, all fine and golden, but excessive nonetheless.

'Monsieur, you are baiting me! I protest, I protest, Monsieur! This is no way to treat a gentleman.'

'But my daughter is still there, she is still marriageable. Do not let me stand in your way, Belleme.' The Comte leaned down to pat one of his hounds, hiding his mirth.

Realizing that he could say no more, do no more, Belleme flung back his shoulders in vain pursuit of dignity, turned on his heel and stormed away.

The Comte chuckled heartily. He found practical jokes the best restorative, and it had been a long time since he had executed such a superb jest as this one. If he had gauged Belleme correctly, the youth would not have the courage to spread the word around that Athena was no heiress, that he had been successfully duped. So the joke would not be spoiled for the Comte; there would be others who would come to beg for Athena's hand, and who would each become victims of the prank. Most of all, he was looking forward to Faltringham coming, for the Earl was a supercilious bore at the best of times and his temper short. In his mind's eye, the Comte could see him apoplectic with rage, his pride crushed, the glittering jewel that had been Athena snatched from his impatient grasp.

'Father, Belleme has not been to see me for over a week now. Do you think that he is ill?' Athena looked up at the Comte.

'Ill? Why no, *mon trésor*. He came to ask me for your hand and I told him that he could not have it.'

Although she had been fully prepared for this eventuality, Athena felt a pang of pity for poor Belleme. 'Oh Father – he meant no harm.'

'Anyone who takes my daughter from me means me harm,' the Comte smiled, but his eyes were momentarily cold.

'Did he take it badly?'

'He was not emotionally upset, if that is what you mean. He bridled, he ejected some words of wrath.'

'And then?'

'And then he flounced away.'

'And he has not been back.' Athena sighed. 'I rather liked him . . .'

'A man not even mature enough to have grown a beard?' teased the Comte.

'I hardly noticed that. He was very gentle and attentive, so different from Faltringham.' Athena shuddered at the thought of the English Earl.

'Ah yes, Faltringham. I do not like the man either.'

'Then why encourage him to court me, Father?'

'I do not think that I have encouraged him, *ma petite*. All the encouragement he needed was the thought of your fortune.'

'Is my fortune very large, Father?'

'Very.'

'And it was left to me by my grandmother?'

'That is so. She lost three husbands, and all of them left

her with great wealth. You were her only grandchild. But you have seen the portrait of her in the Gallery.'

'Yes, she looks a handsome woman with a strong character. I would have liked to have known her. Oh, I wish that I could remember more – that is, if only I could remember *something*! Every time I try to recall my past, there is just this grey blank. It is very frightening.'

The Comte leaned forward, taking her hands in his and patting them gently. 'I know, I know, but we have discussed this before. Loss of memory like this does sometimes happen after a blow to the head. The physician told you that you must be patient; fretting and straining to remember will not do you any good at all.'

'I know, Father, I have not forgotten what he told me. Oh, but it is so difficult.'

'I am here to tell you everything you could possibly want to know, *mon trésor*.' The Comte's kindly, much wrinkled face had never looked more benign, his brown curls more shining or more boyish. Who could suspect him of deceit or perfidy? Certainly not the girl who doted on him and had no reason to suspect him of any double-dealing.

'Father, can you really imagine what it is like to live in a – well, in a void, with no past to look back into, no memories? If only I could remember the nuns, the convent, England, the stories of you and Mother which they surely must have told me.'

'I will fill that void for you, my sweet Athena. Have I not already made that clear to you? I would be frantic if any further harm befell you because you insisted on searching your mind. Your body is strong and healthy now, you do not even have a scar to show for the accident. Do not tempt the Fates, my dearest daughter; you could have been so much worse.' In his mind's eye he saw Athena lying sprawled on the London cobbles, her golden hair streaming out around her, her body inert and still, a pool of blood spreading from her head wound. He almost believed she really was his daughter, and not the pauper girl whom he had rescued to fashion into a new Athena. These days he hardly ever remembered that girl in the tattered, muddy shift; by now he had almost convinced himself that she was his true daughter, the child of his body, Athena, as if she had never died of a fever when she was sixteen years old. But he had not entirely lost all caution. He knew that there was a danger, a terrible danger, in his new Athena remembering the truth about her past. If she did, she would know that he was not her real parent, she would see him for what he was: a sham, a trickster. How would she react to that piece of information? He shuddered to think. Oh, he could bribe her with clothes and jewels but it would not be the same. She would look at him with stark knowledge in her eyes and the beautiful but tenuous bond between them would be riven. He knew that he could not survive that: losing his daughter twice over. It would kill him.

'I will try to do as you say, Father, but it is not easy.' Athena looked down at his brown crêpey hands, at the brilliant green emerald which winked on his forefinger, the neat square, white-tipped nails which always looked freshly scrubbed. She wanted – needed – so much to please him; she could not bear to see pain in his eyes. Because she loved him she would try her utmost to obey him.

The Comte had been correct in predicting Belleme's reaction. The young man did not broadcast his experience throughout Paris. Instead, he retired from life for some time to lave his wounds, while Athena's other suitors continued to call on her.

In truth, she was wearying of them, especially of Faltringham, who would insist on bringing her jewels although she had begged him not to, saying that she would only accept such precious tokens from the man she intended to marry.

'Then marry me, my Lady,' he had said, his dark eyes acquisitive, his fingertips twitching with desperation to encase her in his arms. His little convent-bred virgin – he would soon show her what life was all about, what happened between a mature man and woman in bed together. He dreamed of her innocent face, waking from his dreams drenched with sweat to toss and turn in his bed, his every pore aching to possess her. How much longer would he have to wait for her to acquiesce? The thought that she would not agree to become his wife never entered his arrogant head. Had it done so, he would not have got himself so deeply into debt purchasing gifts for her. Jewels to catch a jewel, he had thought, more impatient for the kill than for the chase. He could not remember ever having lusted after a woman at so high a pitch. It was the innocent look which did it, the wide turquoise eyes unshadowed by wordliness or carnal knowledge. The fact that she would come into money, too, was an added – but essential – fillip.

His first wife had loathed sexual contact with him. Having the mind of a nun, she had done her utmost to rebuff his advances even after they were married. Her behaviour he had found highly titillating, her reluctance spurring him on to a greater sensuality. He had made use of her body repeatedly without there being one iota of affection involved. By way of reward, she had grown pale and thin, then she had miscarried of their son; this had infuriated him and he had beaten her, leaving her a pulpy mass of blood-covered bruises. She had suffered some kind of brain damage from the beating and had not recovered her sensibilities, save to scream whenever she saw him approach her. He had gone on using her body, fully aware that babies were not conceived in the mind and that even if her mind had gone she might well still bear him the son he desired. She had miscarried again, however. Three days later her body had been found at the foot of the winding spiral staircase in his London home. She was dead.

Having found it so easy to dispose of one unwanted wife, the Earl had taken a second bride, a young girl of fourteen whom he had awakened to the delights of sex. She had proved a most willing partner, always ready to accommodate him. The years had passed and she did not conceive, until finally Faltringham realized that his labours were never going to bear fruit, for she was barren – her fault entirely, of course. How dared a woman withhold a son from her husband? Was it not the most heinous crime? He instructed her to provide him with a son and when a few more months had passed and she did not, he had beaten her for her insubordination. To see a woman weeping, subjugated before him, never ceased to excite him, and so the beatings became a regular part of their life. He broke her arm; it healed crookedly. He broke her jaw, and then her nose. Soon she was no longer physically attractive to him, nor did his much-wanted son put in an appearance.

One wife had been so easily murdered: what was one more? The second wife drowned in her bath, Faltringham's alibi to have been his attendance at the Crumley Hunt. He had dismissed all his servants for the day to go to the local fair, but one, his steward, had been taken seriously ill and was brought back to the house by two of his friends. Faltringham had been spotted creeping guiltily out of the rear of his house. Moments later, his wife's drowned body had been found. The uproar had been tremendous. All London was in a frenzy to catch and punish the murderous Earl. He had fled to France, to Paris, with his wife's jewel cases. Now, here he sat in the gardens of the Château de Deverelle in close proximity to the most divine young woman he had ever met. Everything about her was perfection, from the demurely downcast eyes to the dainty tips of her jewelled slippers. He would ask for her hand today!

The Comte was in the library, writing the day's entry in his diary. At Faltringham's arrival, he started, for he had been about to write what he would say to the Earl when he came to ask for Athena's hand. It looked as if the hour had come and sooner than he had thought.

'*M'sieur le Comte*,' the Earl gave his most bland smile,

'might I make a request of you? Your daughter, the fair Athena – do I have your permission to ask for her hand in marriage?' The Earl waited, for the Comte's face had frozen. Then the twinkling brown eyes became themselves again, and a dimple appeared in each wrinkled cheek, the ivory-nailed hands coming to rest on the satin-clad knees.

'You are in love with my daughter?'

'Indeed I am, most definitely so.'

'You have spoken with Belleme of late?' the Comte asked, although he knew that had Faltringham done so he would not be here now.

'Spoken with Belleme? Why no, sir. Why do you ask?'

'Oh nothing, mere curiosity.' He settled himself in his seat, leaning forward a little, the dimples becoming deeper. 'You believe that my daughter is a great heiress, do you not, My Lord Earl?'

'I do.'

'What would you say if you were told that she is not, that she has less money even than yourself?'

'But that would not be true, sir – you would be jesting with me.'

'What makes you so sure?'

'But everyone knows that she is a great heiress. Her grandmother's inheritance . . .' The Earl's voice trailed into silence.

'Who says?'

'Why – why, you do!'

'Can you trust me?'

'I have no reason to doubt you, sir.'

'Have you not heard of my reputation?'

'Your reputation –? But I do not understand. Your reputation for what?'

'For practical jokes, My Lord Earl.' The Comte leaned back, grinning happily.

Faltringham had no sense of humour at the best of times, and he was usually slow on the uptake, especially where his pride was concerned. It was easier to keep his pride intact than to see what the Comte was getting at.

'You have been tricked, My Lord. Athena, my daughter is no heiress, not even of the most minor variety. I myself am virtually penniless, and her grandmother did not leave her one sou, nor did her grandfather, nor did any other of her relatives. She has nothing. Now do you still love her, my Lord Earl of Faltringham?'

Faltringham had gone ashen white and then a violent purple while the Comte was speaking. His face looked as if it were about to burst, his eyes bulged; he gave the appearance of one who was about to have an apoplectic fit. He opened his mouth once, twice, three times, but no words came out. Then, finally, he managed to speak.

'You cur, you vile knave! You deserve to be horse-whipped! I – I shall speak to the King! You will be put in irons, you will be put in the lowest *oubliette*, in the dankest, most desolate prison possessed by His Majesty! You will never be let out, *never*!'

The Comte began to chortle, and once he had started, could not stop, the chortling growing louder and louder until it was great guffaws.

Faltringham continued to grow more and more purple, more and more enraged. He looked as if he were about to strike the Comte, and he did indeed advance upon him, at which the Comte shouted immediately for his servants, who hastened into the room.

'You coward! I challenge you, I –' Faltringham remembered that he was useless with swords and even worse with firearms. He stepped back, drew a hand across his mouth as if wiping saliva from it. Then he gave a shudder as if racked with invisible pains, before turning on his heel and, with a semblance of dignity, vacating the library.

'You are all right, *M'sieur le Comte*?'

'Yes, Lazare, thank you. Now, if you will bring me some wine and cakes and request the lady Athena to join me.'

When Athena arrived she kissed her father on the

forehead, smiling at him. 'Has Faltringham declared himself, Father?'

'He has, my treasure.'

'And what was the outcome?'

'For some strange and inexplicable reason he changed his mind.'

'Changed his mind?' Athena said, astonished. 'So you did not have to tell him that you had no intention of parting with me?'

'Have a cake, *mon trésor*,' the Comte said airily. 'No, I had to say very little to him, in fact.'

'Father, are you quite sure that he changed his mind just like that? As I was coming into the Château I saw him riding out on his horse. He looked a very peculiar colour, as if he had become exceedingly angry. I called out to him but he did not so much as look in my direction.'

'Is that so? Strange indeed, daughter. Perhaps it was part of the change which came over him during our discussion.'

'So you had a discussion? But you said that you did not have to say very much to him,' Athena pressed.

'Oh, it was only the tiniest of discussions . . .'

'Father, are you sure that you did not tell him that he could not marry me, and that is why he was looking so distressed?'

'Quite sure.'

'It is very odd.' Athena bit into a cake, sipping at her wine. She had noticed the Comte shutting a leather-bound book as she came into the library. She had not missed the surreptitious look on his face, as if he had been caught out. And then there was the triumphant gleam in his eye. He was up to something and she wanted to know exactly what it was. She could not imagine the Earl of Faltringham changing his mind so swiftly, not when he had been so ardent in his pursuit of her. But why should her father lie? Now she felt sorry for Faltringham for no explicable reason, and yet she had not liked the man, he made her flesh creep.

Now if only he had been Lord Mullally . . . She caught herself up suddenly. What had made her think of that pompous, conceited adventurer? She did not even want to go near the man, let alone think of marrying him! Was he not surrounded by bevies of ladies who would prostrate themselves at his feet at a moment's notice? A man used to such acquiescence from females was not the kind of man she had in mind to marry, no indeed. She was not going to forget Madame le Brun's warning, nor what she had seen with her own eyes on the night of the Grand Ball.

That night, as Athena lay in her ivory and eau-de-nil bedroom, she found her thoughts drawn backwards repeatedly to the guilty movement her father had made earlier when she had gone into the library. Had he been hiding something in that leather-bound volume on his desk, the one which he had shut with such haste on seeing her? The thought came into her mind that perhaps her father had paid Faltringham to go away, to leave her in peace, and if that were so then she wanted to know the truth of it. Why should her father part with his gold to keep her with him when she would stay with him freely? She had never really understood anyway why he set so much store by her having suitors and encouraging them, when, as he had so frequently told her, he did not intend any of the men to marry her. She had wondered if it was a matter of his own pride: his wanting his daughter to be seen to be highly desirable. Whatever it was, she felt that she had allowed herself to drift along too blandly in the past months, accepting unquestioningly, being altogether the obedient and dutiful daughter. She put down much of it to her accident, for since that time she had tired easily, thinking too hard gave her a splitting headache, and for weeks she had had to rest frequently. But that time was over now, and much of her former spirit returning.

What had her father been hiding as she entered the library? She had to know.

The dark Château was silent and almost eerie as she opened the door of her bedchamber and crept cautiously out; along corridors, down stairways, along more corridors, and there was the library door before her. Gently she opened it and slipped inside the room. An oblong of moonlight illuminated her father's desk. There was no leather-bound volume to be seen. She lit a branch of tapers and slowly walked round the library, looking at shelves, book after book. So many were leather-bound; it would take her days to find the one she sought. She remembered the drawers in the desk and began to open them, one after another. Nothing, just papers and parchments, notebooks and other oddments. And then, hidden beneath a pile of papers in the bottom-most drawer, she found what she was seeking.

Drawing out the leather-bound book, she lifted it up onto the desk. It was quite heavy, heavier than she had anticipated, and the effort made her gasp a little. Quickly, she opened the book and turned the pages, searching for some scrap of parchment, some note, or other betraying paper. Was it a household account book? Would she see an entry saying *Paid to the Earl of Faltringham a certain sum on the fifteenth day of August 1518*?

But no, it was not a household account book, which became clear as Athena turned page after page. It was a diary, each entry carefully allotted its own space and written in the Comte's own large and generous handwriting.

The entry for the fifteenth of August 1518, read:

'Faltringham was here, suing for Athena's hand. What a dastard he is, what a scoundrel. I would die before such as he got his hands on my fair daughter. When I told him the truth he looked as if he were about to explode. I do not think that I have ever enjoyed a jest so greatly in my

entire life. That man is a venomous knave and he deserves to suffer. The poltroon actually began to challenge me to a duel, and then he remembered what I had already heard: that he is clumsy and inept with both sword and firearms. I shall remember the expression on his face for the rest of my days. What a comfort that memory will be to me. I think that I have surpassed myself this time.'

Athena placed a trembling hand to her mouth. What did the entry mean: 'the truth'? When her father had told Faltringham *what* truth? The Comte was certainly up to something and she must know what. This could not go on. She had a right to know everything. Perhaps if she looked back at earlier entries she would find out more, so she turned back the pages, skimming her eyes over various paragraphs. There was a similar account for the interview with Belleme, her father writing of how he had laughed to himself over Belleme's discomfiture on being told the truth. Always that phrase: 'the truth'. She must find out what it meant. Could it refer simply to her father telling the men that his daughter was not to be married to either of them after all? But no, she felt that it had a deeper meaning. First thing next morning she would ask her father and she would not rest until he had explained.

She yawned. It was very late. Had she turned back a few more pages she would have read an account of how she, a strange pauper child in London, became the adopted daughter of the Comte de Deverelle, but she had closed the diary and replaced it and was soon on her way back to bed.

Next morning, she rose and dressed with purpose. Seeing that she was in no mood for light conversation, her *femme de chambre* said very little. When Athena joined her father in the Great Hall to sit down opposite him at table, she had determined that she would not leave that table without having made her father answer all her questions fully.

As valets served breakfast, sops in wine, fresh bread with butter and honey, a haunch of rose-pink beef dark brown at the edges, Athena caught her father's eye.

'What is it, *mon trésor*?' he asked. 'You look very serious this morning.'

'Father . . . Father, I must know the truth.'

'The truth about what?' The Comte's smile had never been more blithe.

'I have a confession to make, Father. Last night I went into the library and I read your diary. Oh, not all of it. I turned to yesterday's entry to see exactly what had happened between you and Faltringham. I had to know, Father.'

A clammy coldness had settled around the Comte's heart. He fought for breath while appearing to be nonchalant.

'So you read my entry for August the fifteenth . . . Has that not satisfied you?'

'No, Father. You spoke of telling Faltringham – Belleme, too – the truth, but you did not mention in your diary what the truth was, and I want to know. It concerns me very closely, you must admit that.'

'Why, the truth was that you were not available for marriage.' The Comte sipped some wine, struggling for composure, trying to keep his brow smooth, his mouth from quivering.

'I am sorry but I do not believe you, Father. There is something much deeper behind all this and I insist on knowing it.'

'*Ma petite*, I do assure you—'

'No assurances will pacify me. Indeed, I have been suspicious for more than a little time. Things do not quite seem to tally as they ought.'

'What things?'

'Oh, many things. Why all these suitors if I am not to marry as yet? How can you bring yourself to tell each one of them that I am not available for marriage? It cannot be an easy task, and yet you appear willing to take it on.'

The Comte had the grace to blush, a reaction which Athena did not miss.

'You see, Father, there *is* something amiss. You must tell me, truly you must!' She leaned forward. 'Otherwise – otherwise, Father, I shall be deeply unhappy, at the thought that there is some secret between us which I do not share.' She turned her head away, mouth trembling slightly. There was pain in her eyes.

'I will tell you the truth,' the Comte said huskily, unable to have his beloved Athena suffer for an instant. 'You must prepare yourself for a shock.' Now that he had begun, the words rattled out of his mouth. 'Faltringham and Belleme would have been no good for you as husbands. The moment that they knew the truth concerning your lack of fortune they scuttled away like rats pursued by terriers.'

'My – my *lack* of fortune? What do you mean?'

'I made it up, Athena, I made up the story about your fortune. I – I have a reputation for playing practical jokes. This was to have been my most supreme jest.'

'You held me out as bait to those poor men? You led them on, letting them think that I was a great heiress? And you let *me* believe that I was a great heiress – and it is not true?' Athena jumped to her feet, hands clenched at her sides. 'Father, how could you do such a thing? To take advantage of my loss of memory after the accident – to trick me as you tricked those poor men. . . .'

The Comte hung his head, unable to look Athena in the eyes, shame rolling over him. 'Forgive me,' he whispered, 'I have been cruel and thoughtless. I should never have done it. I have no excuse.' A tear rolled out of the corner of one brown eye.

'Oh, Father,' Athena hurried round the table to him, 'you must not weep. I will try to understand, but I feel so sorry for those poor men.'

'Poor men?' sniffed the Comte, recovering his composure. 'Immediately they knew you had no inheritance they lost interest in you, Athena. They showed themselves for what they were: fortune-hunters. Had either of them truly loved you they would have insisted on marrying you despite your lack of money.'

'I suppose you are right,' she admitted. 'But why did you do it, Father? Why did you involve me? Me, your own daughter – the innocent victim of one of your jokes.'

'Forgive me, please forgive me!' As he spoke, the Comte thought of his diary. How could he have been such a fool as to leave it where Athena could lay her hands on it? The very first moment he got he would destroy it.

'I forgive you, Father, but this must never happen again. You do promise me that, do you not?'

'I promise you, daughter.' The Comte paused for a moment, then said, 'The diary – did you read any more of the entries?'

'A few.'

'Are there any other questions you want to ask me?'

'No, Father, I think that is everything.'

The Comte looked deeply into her wide, turquoise eyes and thanked God and His Blessed Mother that she had seen nothing else, nothing which would have shocked her even more. If she had found out that she was just a simple pauper girl whom he had found on the cobblestones in a London alley, what would she have thought of *that*? She had every right to look perplexed. Why should she take the trouble to understand him, a foolish old man who played silly pranks on people? How could he hope such a tender and sweet young girl would comprehend his motives, when he did not understand them himself? He must thank God that she loved him; she was his blessing and nothing else mattered.

'Father, before anyone else comes to ask you for my hand, we must let it be known that I am no longer available for marriage. *That* I insist upon.' Her head rose high. 'I have tried to be a dutiful daughter and, in truth, have not found it difficult, but I do not wish to be a party to any further deception. Those poor men—'

'You imagine them with broken hearts?'

'I would not be so arrogant as to think that, Father. Undoubtedly some of them will be fond of me, or else they would not be paying court to me. But as for broken hearts, that I think not.'

'Paying court to your money, *mon trésor*. That is why I invented your fortune.'

'Is that not being cynical?'

'Realistic, my daughter. Allow your old Father to know a thing or two about the world and those who people it.'

Athena sighed. She still felt pity for poor Belleme but not for Faltringham, however. He could well survive alone, she felt.

She voiced her feelings, at which the Comte said, '*Poor* Belleme, is it? But where is he now? When he found out that you had no fortune coming to you he vanished like a puff of smoke in the wind.' The Comte could not conceal the glint of amusement which appeared in his eyes for a few moments.

'Father, you have had your amusement, now we must be serious. I have every right to be deeply hurt that you misled me regarding my fortune. You should have told me the truth from the start.'

'Ah, but then the joke would not have been so funny, my dearest. I feared that you would give yourself away by some word or action. Also, you would have had to lie, and I do not imagine that you would be content with such a state of affairs.'

'No, that is true, Father. All the same, I wish that you had been honest with me, but I see now that you could not be honest and also play your jest as you wished, and therefore you should not have played it.'

'I am most humbly sorry, my dear, and I will endeavour to make it up to you in some way.'

'I do not see how it can be made up to me. I thought I

was an heiress and now I find that I am not, that a cruel jest has been played upon me, too.'

'Oh, never say that, dearest daughter! I did not for one minute envisage making you unhappy or tricking you in any way, indeed no.' The Comte looked askance. I *will* make it up to you!'

'I do not see how you can, Father . . . it will take me some time to get over all this.'

'And how would a visit to Court help you over it?' The Comte's eyes twinkled.

'To Court?' Athena gasped. You mean, to the King's Court in Paris?'

'I do.'

'Would I meet the King and Queen? Would I meet the Royal Family?'

'Indeed you would.'

'That would be absolutely wonderful.'

The Comte relaxed somewhat, the awkward moment over, so he hoped. But now he had got himself into an equally difficult predicament. He had been banned from Court a year ago after playing a practical joke on the courtiers. He had hired an actress-whore to dress up as Louise of Savoy, the Queen Mother. The woman had done her work well: she had acted and looked every bit like the haughty and high-handed Louise, and many people had been taken in. Strutting up and down in a gown and headdress similar to that of the Queen Mother's, the whore had issued a stream of inane orders and commands, many of which had been obeyed. The Court had been in uproar before the Comte's jest had been discovered and the Queen Mother, furious and outraged, had banned him from Court. She was a proud and strong-willed woman, and the thought of being impersonated by a whore – and successfully at that – had insulted her to the core. Others who had offended her in far more minor ways had been out of favour for much longer than a year, and the Comte wondered how he was going to get round this problem so that he could present Athena at Court.

As preparations for the visit to Court got underway, Athena was filled with the eeriest sensation: it was almost *déjà vu*: a feeling that she had prepared for just such an occasion before. But how could she have done, she asked herself? Yet, nonetheless, the sensation remained and strongly, too, haunting her as she sorted through her gowns and jewels, deciding which she would take with her. She pictured the King and Queen of France in her mind's eye, but their images seemed to distort. Instead of a tall, handsome King Francis with his dark auburn bobbed hair and long foxlike nose, she saw a King with russet hair and a fair complexion. Instead of petite Queen Claude with her deformed hip which gave her an ungainly limp and her red-tipped nose, she saw a small, plump Queen with long, red-gold hair and deep blue eyes. She tried her utmost to clear her mind, to visualize the King and Queen of France as her father had described them, and finally she succeeded.

Meanwhile, the Comte dreamed of returning to Royal favour once more, knowing that much of this would depend on how the Queen Mother reacted to his return. Louise of Savoy was the uncrowned Queen of France, her son listened to her advice and was greatly influenced by her. If she continued to reject the Comte then it was most likely that the King would do the same.

Finally, the Comte decided that he must give the Queen Mother a gift, something that would make her hostility evaporate. It would have to be something befitting a Queen Mother and great Lady, but the bills for Athena's gowns and jewels had not yet been paid and the merchants were growing restive. He knew that Louise of Savoy had a predilection for rubies, and he decided that he must find her a set so rare and beautiful that she would forget her anger towards him.

The rubies must be both exceptional and to be found at a merchant's who had not done business with the Comte before, and so would not know of his dire financial straits. The Comte travelled into Paris a number of times in pursuit of such rubies, and he finally found them at a goldsmiths in the Rue des Anges. One central, pear-shaped ruby was surrounded by a galaxy of smaller rubies, each one a blazing fire, the whole suspended on a chain of delicate goldsmiths' work. The Comte rode back to the Château feeling extremely pleased with himself, the rubies in a leathern pouch at his waist. He showed them to Athena, who exclaimed with delight at their fiery lustre, holding them against her white throat.

'The Queen Mother is a proud woman, Athena. If one is in favour with her, one is in favour with the entire Royal Family.'

He had explained to his daughter about his outrageous practical joke on Louise of Savoy, and she had clapped a hand to her mouth, looking at him with round eyes at his temerity. Now, so that he could go back to Court, he had to bribe the Queen Mother with an expensive gift, for bribery it was, even if called by any other name.

'She cannot fail to adore these on sight,' Athena said, touching the glowing stones admiringly.

'They're the best I could find in all Paris.'

'I can believe it; they are superb. You will be welcomed back to Court with open arms.'

'I only hope that that will be true, *mon trésor*.'

'You are so generous to do this just for my sake, Father, and I do appreciate it.' Athena lightly kissed her father's forehead.

'You are a dear, sweet child, and I am very fortunate,' the Comte beamed. He had not told Athena that he had other reasons for returning to Court, that he desperately needed the reinstatement of his annuity from the King and the opportunity of gambling with the wealthiest Lords who flocked to Court. For fortunes could be made in one night of gambling, more rapidly than in any other way.

*

The day came when the Deverelle carriage was in readiness for the Comte and Athena to depart for Paris, and again Athena was stricken with the powerful feeling of *déjà vu*. Had she not done all this before, exactly like this, set off in a carriage to go to the King's Court? She was almost certain that she had. But no – she must dismiss her notions for the nonsense that they surely were.

The French Court was in its last weeks at the Louvre before the ever-increasing heat drove them to one of the summer palaces. Athena thought the architecture of the Louvre somewhat disappointing: it was flat and square, too sturdy for beauty to her mind. But the inner rooms and corridors and halls were sumptuous, totally dazzling, and she was overawed by everything she saw.

First, before they did anything, the Comte had to beg an audience with Louise of Savoy to give her the rubies and to ensure she would not actively prevent their taking up residence at Court. He instructed Athena to wait in one of the ante-rooms while he took his place in the Queen Mother's audience-chamber and waited on her pleasure.

The Queen Mother had the most regal bearing in all of France. She had raised her son and daughter single-handed, never doubting for one second that one day her son would be King. She was acutely intelligent, sagacious, indomitable, and never forgot a slight. The Comte was very much aware of all these qualities as he knelt before her, his face displaying the most respectful expression he could muster.

'Madame,' he began, 'I humbly present myself to you and beseech you to bear with me for a little while. I deeply and bitterly regret the outrage I committed upon your most *haute* and Royal personage. I cannot think what made me do such an appalling thing, and I have regretted it ever since. If Your Royal Highness could see fit to forgive me I would be the happiest man on earth.'

Having said that, he drew out the velvet-lined box

containing the rubies and presented it to the Queen Mother, begging her to take this gift from him.

Curiosity narrowing her dark eyes, slender white jewelled hands came out to take the box, to open it. She gazed inside at the rubies in silence, not betraying her reaction by one flicker of movement in her face. Long seconds elapsed and still she gazed at the rubies.

I have failed, thought the Comte, his heart plummeting. Everything is lost, we shall not be able to live at Court. I might as well leave gracefully now . . .

The dark, hooded eyes in the broad, strong-boned face flicked up from the rubies to look at the Comte.

'How long is it since the disgraceful débâcle in which you dared to involve my name?' the Queen Mother asked.

'Exactly one year, Madame,' said the Comte hoarsely, his heart giving a painful jolt.

'One year, hmm, twelve months. You say that you are penitent?'

'Oh, assuredly, Madame, *most* penitent. Never have I been more penitent in my entire life. I am truly and humbly sorry for what I did.'

'An entire year banned from Court; you must have suffered appallingly *M'sieur le Comte*.' A slight smile curved the Royal lips.

'Oh, I have, Madame, terribly. I have not slept, I have barely eaten.'

'Then you look remarkably fit,' the Queen Mother responded dryly.

'The only thought which sustained me, Madame, was that I might one day be able to return to Court, to beg your forgiveness.'

'I see.' Again the dark, hooded eyes returned to the rubies, the Royal knuckles whitening slightly as they increased their grip upon the trinket-box.

I have won! thought the Comte exuberantly. But then the Queen Mother snapped shut the lid of the box and made as if to return it to him. His joy evaporated as swiftly as if he had been doused with cold water. He reached up to take the box. It was almost in his palms when, to his utter relief and elation, the Queen Mother apparently changed her mind, for she retrieved the box, clamping it tightly in her grasp. Again long seconds elapsed while the Comte waited, his heart hardly daring to beat. And then Louise of Savoy gave a slow, tight smile.

'You are forgiven, *M'sieur le Comte.* I will accept the rubies,' she said.

There was to be a masque that night when the entire Court would be dressed as gods and goddesses, nymphs and satyrs. As everyone's outfit had been made, Athena had the choice of the seamstresses.

'I want something quite different,' she told the woman she selected. 'I do not want to be another Diana, nor a Venus, nor even a Pallas Athena,' she smiled at her own parody.

'Very wise,' the seamstress beamed. 'I have made a dozen outfits for those who will all be dressed as Venus tonight, six for Dianas, and four for Pallas Athenas.'

'But it will not be easy to decide what I shall go as,' Athena said thoughtfully.

'I feel that a simple outfit would be best, My Lady. A robe of *toile de Paris* barred with silver fretwork and caught across the breasts with silver cords in the Grecian style. My Lady's hair is admirable for that style; it can be looped and coiled also in the Grecian style, and caught with white silk roses and pearls. Might I suggest that Your Ladyship goes as Helen of Troy, whose face launched a thousand ships?'

'Helen of Troy,' Athena mused. 'But is no one else going as that lady?'

'No, the suggestion has just come to me. It is My Lady's colouring which made me think thus: such beautiful silver-gold hair.'

'Then Helen of Troy it shall be,' Athena smiled.

Measurements were taken and the seamstress had the first fitting ready in three hours. She had worked non-stop but with great skill, and she was very pleased with the result, as was Athena. The material was fine and light, giving the suggestion of transparency and yet, in fact, it was safely opaque. The outfit was finished three-quarters of an hour before the masque began.

The Comte had been busy attiring himself as Poseidon in the costume which he had worn once before for a Court masque. He did not consider himself sufficiently important to have a new costume, nor was he overly delighted at having to dress up. But he tapped at Athena's door promptly to escort her to the masque, smiling self-consciously and looking most apologetic.

Athena smiled broadly when she saw her father. She told him that he looked splendid, which she believed he did, and he warmed to her praise.

'I find these Court frolics immensely tiresome,' he said, 'but they must be borne for the Royal Family relish them highly. *You* look superb, and in so short a time! I vow that all eyes will be upon you.'

'I am sure that there will be far greater beauties than I to be seen tonight,' Athena said demurely, tucking in a stray curl before taking her father's arm and following him to the ballroom where the masque was to be held.

As they entered she was momentarily dazzled by the lights and the colour, the noise of minstrels playing energetically. It seemed that a thousand tapers had been lit to illuminate the scene, that everyone was robed in brilliant-hued silks and garbed in dazzling diamonds.

'Now, do not forget,' the Comte whispered in Athena's ear, 'you must, of course, be reverent to the King and Queen, but it is Louise of Savoy who is the power behind the throne and she has been very benevolent to us.'

'I shall not forget it, Father. Do not fear that I shall let you down.' Athena squeezed his arm.

They found seats for themselves and sat silently while a young troubadour sang a passionate love song to the assembled company. There were sighs of appreciation from the ladies, and somewhat languid, bored expressions on the faces of the men, but the singer was loudly applauded when he had finished.

'He is a great favourite at Court,' whispered the Comte. 'The Queen Mother likes his voice very much, so of course everyone else does, too.'

A troupe of acrobats were next, their skilled exertions drawing gasps and oohs and aahs from the audience. They leapt and tumbled, flinging themselves through the air as if they had wings. Then, having completed their act, they bowed and withdrew to tremendous applause.

Athena was open-mouthed at the daring exertions of the troupe, but her eyes could not help sliding round the room. She wanted to see the King and Queen and Louise of Savoy. She wanted to see what everyone looked like, what costumes they were wearing, the expressions on their faces, the way they sat and held themselves. There was so much to see.

Applause was ringing in her ears as her eyes locked with those of the man sitting across the room, near to a handsome jewelled figure who must surely be the King. Lord Mullally, again surrounded by a bevy of beautiful courtesans. Ladies were sitting on either side of him, holding his hands. He sat with a nonchalant and assured grace, his powerful, virile body relaxed. Yet there was an air of coiled tension about him, like a tiger in readiness to spring. His black hair gleamed about his ears and was encircled by a ring of vine leaves, for he was dressed as Dionysius, the god of feasting and celebration. He *would* be, thought Athena; nothing more serious has ever entered his handsome head than how to pass his hours in self-indulgent entertainment. Yet she could not draw her eyes away from him; his coiled, tiger-like grace was eminently compelling and she found herself wishing that she was one of the ladies sitting at his side holding his hand. She imagined the feel of his hand in hers, smooth yet powerful. An excited shiver coursed down her spine, colour staining her cheeks. But she must not think like that: the man was an adventurer, a good-for-nothing. He was not worthy of her interest. Reluctantly, she drew her eyes away from him to find the eyes of the King directly upon her.

King Francis was also powerfully built, and handsome. Naturally, he was attired as Zeus, the King of the Gods. His slender, but shapely legs crossed at the ankles, Grecian sandals on his feet, he wore a short white toga studded with diamonds and a gold coronal on his gleaming dark auburn hair. There was a lascivious expression on his face and his eyes smouldered with sensuality. Athena found herself transfixed by his gaze, fresh colour flooding into her cheeks.

'That is the King,' the Comte whispered. 'It seems that he has taken a liking to you. No doubt he will ask you to dance.'

'Will the Queen not be jealous, Father?'

'Jealous, my dear? She would think the world was upside-down if her husband did not dance with every beautiful lady in sight. She quite expects it, she is resigned.'

'Poor woman.' Athena felt a wave of sympathy for Claude of Brittany.

'She will leave early, she rarely stays very long for these entertainments. Besides, she is with child again.'

As if she had heard the Comte speak, at that moment the Queen rose from her seat and left the room, followed by her attendants. Athena saw how badly she limped, one leg being shorter than the other. How dreadful for a Queen to have such a deformity, especially when there were so many beautiful ladies at Court.

The minstrels had struck up dance music, and within a few moments the King was at Athena's side, the Comte introducing them to one another.

At close quarters King Francis was quite overpowering.

His dark eyes burned with unspoken passions, his mouth was thin but sensual. As he swept Athena onto the dance floor, she knew a moment's panic. She had expected anything but this, and here she was being escorted by the King of France himself. She hoped that he would not find her too wooden, too inexperienced, on the dance floor. The King's charm, however, soon overcame her misgivings, and she found herself warming to him. He asked her many questions about herself and she tried to answer them as naturally as possible, although her throat was taut and dry with excitement.

'I believe that you spent your childhood in a convent in England, is that correct?' the King asked.

Athena nodded. 'Yes, Your Majesty. I have only recently arrived in France.'

'Yes, I know.'

'You know, Your Majesty? I did not think that I would be of sufficient interest for Your Majesty to know my activities.'

The King smiled lazily. 'Do not imagine that anyone is so insignificant in my Kingdom that I do not know what he is doing. And where such glowing beauty as yours is concerned – well, I make it my pride and my pleasure to know every movement.'

'Thank you, Your Majesty,' Athena whispered, waves of colour flooding into her cheeks.

'It is too long since such sweet and fresh beauty has graced the Louvre. If I had known Deverelle's daughter was so charming, I would have insisted that she be brought here much sooner.'

'Your Majesty is too kind to me.'

'How could I ever be kind enough to such an adorable young creature as yourself, my dear? The King's hand squeezed hers in an intimate gesture.

'I hear that the Queen is not very fond of such entertainments as these,' Athena stammered, wishing to change the conversation.

'The Queen likes very little except saying her prayers, going to Confession and hearing Mass, my dear, as you will find out when you have been a little longer at Court.'

'Then Her Majesty is pious?'

'Extremely so.'

'That is a great virtue in a woman.'

'To the exclusion of all other virtues, my dear,' the King said, somewhat cryptically.

'I meant no criticism of Her Majesty.'

'Of course not, my dear, I did not take it so. But shall we not change the subject? Your gown is most becoming. You are dressed as . . .?'

'Helen of Troy, Your Majesty. It was the seamstress's idea.'

'Admirable, admirable. The face that launched a thousand ships. Such sumptuous hair, such unusual eyes . . .' The King's dark, slumbrous gaze fixed on Athena. She did not know whether to blush anew or shrink from his determined flattery. Fortunately the dance ended there, and the King returned her to her father, but he said that he would be back again for further dances during the evening.

The Comte looked delighted. 'The King likes you! That is marvellous. I had not hoped for such good fortune.'

'You have not told him that I am a great heiress, too, have you, Father?' Athena twinkled.

'He is not interested in a lady's money, far from it. It is her womanliness which attracts him most of all.'

'You told me that he has many mistresses.'

'That is so, but while a woman is his mistress she holds great power at Court and she can win great favours, jewels, gowns, gifts from the King, and he is quite likely to pension her off with a generous annuity when he loses interest in her.'

'I see,' Athena said thoughtfully, narrowing her eyes at her father. What was he up to now? Why was he looking so pleased at the King's interest in her?

'Now, I must present you to the Queen Mother, *mon trésor*. Remember to be on your best behaviour.' The Comte's voice interrupted her train of thought. He took her arm and led her across the room to the Royal dais, and there Athena was presented formally to Louise of Savoy, the Queen Mother's shrewd, hooded eyes fixing on her intently.

'Your daughter, *M'sieur le Comte*, she is very fair.'

'Thank you, Your Highness.'

'You think you will like our Court?'

'I am sure I am going to find it quite delightful, Your Highness,' Athena said. 'This room is so beautiful and the music is entrancing. And all these vivid costumes, I have never seen such beauty. It is so very kind of Your Royal Highness to allow me to stay here and I am extremely grateful.'

'That is good to hear, my dear. I do not like ingratitude.' The hooded eyes flickered momentarily in the Comte's direction. 'I trust that you will find great happiness here and that your visit will be a memorable one.' The Queen Mother removed her gaze from Athena, which was a sign for her to give a second deep obeisance before taking her father's arm to return to her seat.

They had to pass Lord Mullally and Athena tried to keep her gaze averted, but it was extremely difficult. She heard his voice, rich and deep, as he spoke to one of his fair companions and she longed with all her heart to look up, to see the colour of his eyes, to exchange a glance with him. But no, she must not, her heart must not betray her . . .

Fate had decreed that she was not to pass Lord Mullally unscathed, for his rich, drawling voice called out the Comte's name.

'Are you not going to introduce us, *M'sieur le Comte*?' he said. 'This is your daughter, I believe. I did not have the pleasure of meeting her at your Château.'

'Then that unfortunate lack must be corrected, My Lord,' the Comte smiled, drawing Athena forward.

She came reluctantly, a turmoil of emotions seething within her. Lord Mullally rose to his feet. How tall and strong he looked. She gazed into his face briefly before he bent over and kissed her hand in the most graceful fashion. At last she saw the colour of his eyes: dark blue, as she had guessed; she felt as if she were dissolving in their depths.

'So young and so fair,' Lord Mullally smiled.

'Do not let me distract you from your companions,' Athena said stiffly.

The blue eyes narrowed slightly, black brows arching a little. 'My companions are accustomed to waiting.'

'I have no doubt of that,' Athena said, fighting down the waves of attraction which she felt towards this spoiled and insufferable man.

Lord Mullally's face hardened somewhat and he let Athena's hand go. She was conscious of a feeling of loss as the contact between them was broken.

'Pray do not keep your ladies waiting one moment longer,' she said, head high, at which he gave a curt little bow before returning to his seat.

She was stricken by the most profound feeling of disappointment. The brief dialogue had been barbed, but his proximity was lively and exciting. If only he were not an adventurer, and a pampered idler . . .

'Well, that did not go very well,' said the Comte wryly. 'Come, let us return to our seats, my dear. Mullally is a strange man. He seems determined to outdo the King with his mistresses. I have never known any man to work so hard at his pleasure.'

'That is exactly the opinion I have formed of him, Father,' Athena said, striving to keep her tone light.

'But one must be careful what one says about such activities, for what the King does must not be questioned. You understand, *ma petite*?' Athena nodded. 'The King is the King, which gives him *carte blanche*. He is seen to rule, to govern, however many hours it appears that he spends indulging in vain and empty pastimes.'

At that moment, the King appeared again, bowing elegantly before Athena and asking her to dance with him. Smiling up at him sweetly, she took his arm.

The Comte gave a happy little smirk to himself as he watched the two dancers on the floor. Such a splendid couple they were, so handsome, so composed. His beloved Athena and the King of France . . . If she were to become the next Royal mistress all his troubles would be over. The King was generous with his gifts; nothing was too good for those he favoured. One of his ex-mistresses was now the possessor of a fine château in the country and her illegitimate son had received a title. If Francis took Athena to his bed, he, the Comte, would not lose his daughter. It would not be the same as if she were married to someone who might take her away from him: she would be at Court with the King and so would he. Excitement coursed through him at the vistas opening before him.

His daughter, Royal mistress. Himself the father of the *maîtresse en titre*: what glories would follow! Wealth, power, all his bills paid. He would be beyond the reach even of Louise of Savoy, for the King would brook no interference with his lovelife, nor would his mother dare to attempt such a thing. It was the one sphere where she had no authority whatsoever.

The Comte watched his daughter and the King responding to the lilting minstrels' music. His were not the only eyes affixed on the couple. It seemed that many courtiers were watching closely, weighing up the situation. Was this a new favourite, for the King had danced with her twice now? If she were, then approaches must be made to her; she must be won over to various causes and projects which would flourish with her backing, for whatever the Royal mistress was interested in, so was the King.

Athena was quite overwhelmed by the King's proximity. He was at his most charming and elegant, full of praise for her beauty and for her skill on the dance floor, although she was quite honest with him, telling him that she had done very little dancing in her lifetime.

'We must amend that,' he had said, squeezing her hand tightly. 'You must expect to dance every night at Court. I shall make sure of that.' He had given his lazy grin.

Athena had blushed, which was something she seemed to be doing regularly while in the King's company. She had never known a man exude such virile, dazzling masculinity, and yet he had as many jewels on his masque outfit as any woman. His artistry in the dance was consummate, and Athena would have floundered had he not been so patient, so admiring of her technique.

'Your father intends to stay at Court?' the King asked, knowing full well that the Comte preferred the Louvre to anywhere else on earth.

'I think so, Your Majesty. He tells me that he loves Court life immensely, that he has missed it greatly during the year he has been absent.'

'Ah yes, he did a very foolish thing, playing a trick on Madame, my mother. She has no tolerance where her pride is concerned.'

'Oh, I do agree, Your Majesty, it was very foolish. I know that he has deeply regretted it. I am sure that such a thing will never happen again.'

'It certainly must not. Perhaps you will make sure of that. I do not want you or your father out of favour with my mother, for that would only make things more difficult.'

Athena wanted to ask what things, but she dared not question the King.

'What do you think of the Court, my dear?'

'I am enthralled by it, Your Majesty; such colour and beauty, such magnificent décor, so many beautiful women, so many handsome men, and the minstrels playing such sweet music. It is so exciting to see all these famous and important people.'

'Like your King?'

'Oh, most certainly that, Your Majesty. I never expected to be dancing with Your Majesty tonight.'

'I am not immune to beauty, my dear.'

'Your Majesty is very generous with his compliments.'

'Only where they are deserved.'

There the dance music ended, and the King led Athena back to her father.

'*M'sieur le Comte*, we command that you and your fair daughter remain at Court at the Royal pleasure. There will be no nonsense about your leaving without our permission, and that is unlikely to be given for some time.'

'Yes, Your Majesty. As you say, Your Majesty.' The Comte could not conceal his delight.

When the King had gone to dance with one of the courtesans, Athena turned to her father.

'So, we are staying here?'

'Yes, my little one, that is what I intended. Did you not realize that we had come to stay?'

'But the way the King spoke it sounded as though we were here whether we liked it or not, as if we had no right to leave.'

'Why should we leave? Everything here is free, the food, the entertainments, all are given generously by the King, and in return we do various tasks for him, whatever he asks of us of course, but mainly he demands that we entertain him with our company. It is really very easy, little one, and I have done it all before.'

'What if I should want to leave? What if I should want to go back to the Château de Deverelle? I would like to see Carol again.'

'He can wait. He is quite happy at the château and well cared for; there is nothing for you to worry about. Meanwhile, I can attend to my fortunes while we are here, and, believe me, my treasure, they are desperately in need of attention. I do not think you quite understand what desperate straits I have been in of late.'

'Because my fortune disappeared overnight?' Athena said, somewhat tartly.

The Comte gave a wry little smile. 'No, not that, my treasure. It is the fact that my fortunes disappeared overnight some time ago. One year ago, in fact, when I was so foolish as to annoy the Queen Mother. She immediately had my annuity stopped, and that was all I was living on at the time. After that there was nothing and now I have coffers full of debts but little else.'

'It is as bad as that?'

'It is worse. At Court I can mingle with wealthy nobles and gentlemen and we gamble, play dice, cards. I am not unskilled in such pastimes; I have been known to win quite large sums of money, in fact, and I know that I can do it again if I am given the chance. If we are here at Court I can do that and begin to amass my fortunes again.'

'What is the alternative, Father?'

'Total ruin.' The Comte sighed.

Athena digested this information silently, momentarily oblivious to the swirl of colour and noise surrounding her. It was obvious from her father's face that he was not jesting, nor exaggerating the situation. He had been so good to her, so gentle and generous and kind; how could she let him down? He desperately needed to remain at Court and she would of course be with him – and at Court was the King, who had already shown a more than cursory interest in her. She began to understand what her fate might be and she felt a shiver of apprehension, but also of excitement. Herself and the King of France – together.

She had not, as yet, had time to think of the physical details, of what it would truly mean to be Royal mistress, sharing the Royal bed. Later, when she considered it, she wondered if she would be able to overcome her fears. Had she sufficient courage to allow the King to take her virginity, to let him make love to her? But again the Comte spoke to her about their desperate straits and how he needed her co-operation. He explained to her how the

Royal mistress would be generously treated with gifts and jewels and presents, and how the relatives of the Royal mistress also benefited. He spoke of growing old, of fearing the passing of the years, of poverty staring him in the face. He said repeatedly that there was no disgrace in being a Royal mistress, only glory, and that it would enhance, not destroy, Athena's reputation.

'Great lords will leap at the chance to marry a woman who has been the Royal mistress,' he told Athena. 'Even after the King has tired of her she will still have authority, greatness, allure.'

'So the King always tires of his mistresses?' Athena asked.

'Always, I fear. But what is important is what one makes of the time one is *maîtresse en titre*, and there is always the possibility that the King will become totally faithful to you and that you will remain in favour for longer than any other. It is a gamble, like so many things in life.'

'You like gambling, Father, but I do not. I fear that it is not my nature.'

'But I shall be there beside you, *mon trésor*. I shall guide you and help you. And the King will make everything very easy for you. He is not a hard task-master. The one you must beware of always is his mother. Please her and the world is your oyster, but displease her and she can make your life hell.'

'But not if I am the King's favourite, Father?'

'No, then you would be immune, which is another reason why you must consider forming an alliance with His Majesty. Then we both shall be immune, you and I, quite safe. A marvellous thought!' The Comte sighed in happy anticipation.

'Oh Father – if only you had not angered the Queen Mother a year ago! How could you have been so foolish?'

'I do not know. At the time it seemed a marvellous jest; people expect much of me in that way, you know. Once one has a reputation for a certain thing, then one feels obliged to maintain it. I know that I should never have done such a thing. It was asinine and dangerous. If I had foreseen the results, I would never have indulged myself.'

'Is the Queen Mother still angry with you, Father, is that it? And you will feel safe if I am in the Royal favour?'

'Yes, that is it. She still looks at me with those cruel, hooded eyes of hers and I can see thoughts brewing in her head. I am sure she is determined to have her revenge upon me and that is probably why she has allowed me to return to Court, because it would be hard to get her revenge while I am far away. I confess that I am afraid of her vengeance.'

'Afraid, father? Are you truly?'

'Everyone in their right mind is a little afraid of the Queen Mother, and those who have displeased her are *very* afraid of her.'

'I see.' Athena looked down at her linked hands. She did not want her father to be afraid, nor to be in danger. She wanted him to be content and happy. She did not want him to be a pauper in his old age, and she now knew that the instrument of his delivery was in her own hands. She would take time to adjust to the thought of it, however – if only the King would give her time. Somehow she doubted it. His attentions were pressing and ardent, and the lady who had been attracting his favours until Athena's arrival at Court spent much of her time darting venomous glances at Athena, which meant that *she* knew, even if Athena had not yet come to accept it, that the King intended to make her the next Royal mistress.

A few days later Athena was shown to a magnificent suite of rooms, three times larger than the one she had occupied on first coming to Court. This was the suite which the King had given her to show publicly what his feelings were.

Athena had the feeling of being swept along helplessly

by fate. Events were proving too strong for her. There was so much she longed to say. She wanted to protest, to demand more time, to say that she had not been given occasion to think out matters at a genteel pace. But she was being pursued by a King, and an impatient King at that. What was her opinion by comparison? As nothing.

She tossed and turned in bed that night, thinking of the disgrace, the uproar, if she should refuse the King's attentions. Her father's unhappiness would be too much for her to face. It would not only be his unhappiness but his disgrace, a worse disgrace than that he had incurred by insulting the Queen Mother a year ago. To offend the King of France himself – who would have the courage? Certainly not she.

She had barely been settled in her new rooms for an hour when two ladies-in-waiting arrived, saying that they had come to dress her for the King's visit. She was told that she had one hour to prepare before he arrived.

Immediately her heart started thudding, her legs turned to paper. She wanted to cry out: No, no I cannot do it! but she knew that such a reaction was totally impossible. She tried to think of the King as he was in public, when he courted and flattered her, of his slumbrous dark eyes and sensual features. He was a most attractive man, she could not deny that. Under any other circumstances, without this haste, she might soon have warmed to him; but Kings did not wait, nor would they be kept waiting, certainly not the pampered and indulged Francis the First.

The ladies-in-waiting were in light-hearted mood. They chattered and giggled and seemed to think that Athena was the most fortunate woman in France. One even said that she would give anything to exchange places with her. Athena did not reply. Her personal feelings regarding the King's suit must remain personal. It was not for her to tell anyone how reluctant she was. The Comte had warned her that the Queen Mother had spies everywhere, that she must not confess her emotions or reactions to anyone, and that she must always guard her tongue, even with the King. Besides, she had no intention of being outspoken or indiscreet; that was not in her nature.

Athena had the ladies robe her in a gown of turquoise-blue silk in the Grecian style, minus cumbersome corseting. Over this she wore a peignoir of deeper blue velvet, fastened with cerise velvet bows. When the ladies had dressed her hair and she had applied a perfumed oil, a mixture of roses, jasmine and lavender, to her wrists and throat, she dismissed the women and took a seat on the carved bench at the foot of her bed to await the King's arrival. She was too tense to relax into a softer chair and she sat stiffly, her back ramrod-straight, hands tautly clasped in her lap. She felt like the sacrificial lamb awaiting its agonizing fate. She had been told only the bare facts about the physical side of marriage, and the thought of undergoing this with a virtual stranger filled her with fear and revulsion.

Her palms were damp and her robe felt clammy. She would have liked to remove it and bathe all over again, but she knew that she did not have the time. He would be here any minute . . . She breathed deeply, trying her utmost to relax, but she did not succeed. Then she heard movement outside in the corridor, and she tensed all over again, looking aghast at the door, trying to control her features so that she would not look like a little terrified creature waiting for the knife.

The door flew open and King Francis stood there. He wore a brocade robe edged with marten, and he looked taller and more overwhelming than ever. He smiled broadly, coming forward, hands outstretched to take her hands. She gave a deep obeisance, from which he immediately raised her, telling her that she must not bow down before him, for it was not a formal relationship which he required with her.

'I can have a formal relationship with any one of my

courtiers, my dear. That is not what I wish to have with you,' he said, still smiling genially.

'I am sorry, Your Majesty,' Athena whispered, her throat dry.

'Please – call me Francis.'

Totally overcome, her throat even drier, Athena merely whispered, 'Yes, Francis,' stunned that she should be standing there, being asked to call the King of France by his Christian name.

Behind the King was a valet bearing a silver tray on which was a flask of wine and jewelled goblets. When the valet had deposited the tray the King snapped his fingers at him in dismissal, and he himself filled the goblets of wine, handing one to Athena.

'Now we must drink to our relationship, my dear, and trust that it will be both happy and rewarding.' The dark eyes flashed.

Obediently Athena raised her goblet and they drank. The wine was strong and heady; she knew that if she had a goblet-full she would feel light-headed, so she took only sips. She tried not to meet the King's eyes, for every time she did so waves of crimson flooded her cheeks. He, however, did not seem at all nonplussed by her embarrassment and shyness. In fact, he seemed to find both acutely alluring, and very soon he had drawn her to the bed and was sitting down beside her, his arm round her shoulders. When he dropped a kiss on her cheek she shrank inside, wanting to protest yet not daring to stop him. But then he was kissing her lips and, despite herself, she felt some reaction. She could not at first tell whether it was pleasurable or just the opposite, for the tension was distorting her emotions. Strangely, a face swam before her closed eyes, and to her amazement she identified it as that of Hamish, Lord Mullally. She found herself yearning for the man whose arms were around her to be Lord Mullally. But how inane that was. He, of all people, was no different from his foster-brother, the King. Were they not two of a kind? But, said a little voice in her head, if you must be seduced by one of them then it should be Lord Mullally, for it is he . . . She could not finish her thought, for the King's arms were clamped tightly round her, caging her, and his lips were kissing hers with enveloping passion. She could not breathe. She wanted to struggle, to gasp out: Let me go, let me go! but she had not the breath to do so, nor the courage. Her father was depending on her. So much lay in her hands.

'You are adorable,' she heard the King say, 'quite, quite adorable. I cannot imagine why your father has kept you hidden away from me for so long, you should have been at Court months ago.'

'I was not in France, Your Majesty – Francis, that is,' Athena stammered. 'I was in England, in a convent, until quite recently.'

'*Nom de Dieu*! You were brought up in a convent?' the King exclaimed. 'And how did a convent-bred girl learn such graces, such allure?' His kisses rained down upon her lips, her breast, her shoulders, the palms of her hands.

Then, pressing his mouth to her ear, he whispered, 'I have always believed that the fairer a lady the better she looks without her clothes . . .' His fingers reached for the fastening of her gown, and to her acute embarrassment she felt his practised touch loosening her robe.

His kisses travelled down her throat to her shoulders and the upper halves of her breasts, strong brown fingers caressing where the lips had travelled.

Despite herself, Athena felt a thrill of excitement. After all, this was the King of France and he wanted to hold her in his arms, to kiss and caress her: it was very flattering. If only he loved her . . . But, of course, she was being impractical, romantic.

The King pressed her back, unresisting, against the pillows. Lying down beside her, he ran his hands over her breasts, pulling her gown lower for easier access to her soft flesh. He palmed each breast gently, coaxingly, whispering into her ear that she was very beautiful, that she roused him, that he longed for her.

She was enduring a conflict of emotions, excitement vying with reluctance and anxiety. This had all happened so very quickly: she was unprepared in every way, most especially emotionally. And she could not forget her sight of the Queen limping painfully out of the Great Hall on the night of the masque. Poor Queen Claude. Did she know what her husband was, did she know what he was doing?

The King now had Athena completely disrobed, and he was looking down at her body with an almost stunned expression on his slumbrous features.

'Such beauty . . . An angel,' he said, his voice thick with passion. 'Ah *chérie*, you make me so happy . . .' Hastily he began to undress, and soon he was lying naked beside Athena. He kissed her again, holding her close, smoothing his hands over her breasts and hips, touching the silver-gilt triangle between her thighs so that fierce jolts of feeling coursed through her body. And then he was climbing on top of her, pressing open her legs to guide himself inside her body.

So this is how it happens, she thought, this is how a man makes love to a woman. How strange, how clumsy and cumbersome . . . She could feel him growing more and more excited, thrusting against her body – but then, to her astonishment, he suddenly stopped, cursing out loud.

'*Nom de Dieu*, I cannot understand it! This has never happened to me before.'

'What is wrong, Francis? Please tell me! Oh, what is wrong?' Athena looked up at him, stricken. He seemed distressed. His cheeks were flushed, he had rolled away from her.

'I do not wish to speak of it. Doubtless it will not happen the next time. I am a little tired tonight, it is true; perhaps that is the reason.'

She wanted to ask him why he had stopped, but she

dared not. Something had angered him, something had halted his lovemaking. He had barely begun and yet already it was over. He got up, walking naked and unselfconsciously across the room, fetching the tray of wine and bringing it to their bedside. He poured wine for her and for himself and they drank deeply, Athena waiting for him to say more about what had happened, but he did not. He poured them second goblets of wine, drinking his in two or three deep gulps while Athena sipped at hers. He did not look angry, yet he seemed a little embarrassed. She hoped with all her heart that she had not displeased him, that he would not take out his displeasure on her father. She reached out cautiously to touch the King's arm.

'If I have offended Your Majesty in some way . . .' she began.

'Offended? Of course not, *chérie*, and I told you to call me Francis, did I not?' He grinned. 'How could an angel offend me?' He reached out and cupped her chin in his palm, dropping a kiss on her forehead, then a soft, velvet kiss on her lips. 'We will try again, never fear, *chérie*, and as soon as possible, but for now I am tired; I will leave you to sleep. Should you wish anything of me, you have only to ask it. Goodnight, *chérie*.'

'Goodnight, Francis.'

A few seconds later she was alone, doubting that she had ever been in such intimate company with the King of France himself. It had all seemed like a dream, a strange and disturbing dream.

She was preparing for sleep when a servant brought her a message from the King. Opening it, she read:

> *'Say nothing of what has happened between us. I swear you to secrecy. Francis.'*

She got into bed thoughtfully. The King's pride – of course it must not be attacked in any way, she had known that without being told. He had failed to consummate his lovemaking with her. She had no way of knowing whether this was a regular occurrence with him and his mistresses or whether it was a new experience for him. She tried to imagine how she would feel if she were a man and it had happened to her: she thought that she would be greatly alarmed. But perhaps to a man of Francis's great experience it meant little. She wondered if it had brought an abrupt halt to her career as Royal mistress, and that was what perturbed her the most, for she had her father to think of and his impecunious state. She felt sad at having let him down – if, indeed, she had. If her sudden, meteoric rise to fortune were over, it would be a tremendous relief to her, but she knew that she had others to think of besides herself: her beloved father who had been so good to her and whose future she could make so splendid if she stayed in favour with the King.

She pulled the coverlet up to her shoulders, tucking one hand comfortably beneath the pillow and resting the other near her chin. Staring into the darkness, she relived the scene with Francis, trying to reconstruct it so that she could see what had gone wrong: what could be wrong with *her*. She thought of the other Royal mistresses she had seen around the Court, women who at one time or another had met with the King's approval and of whom he had tired. They were all handsomely built, dark-haired creatures, with far heavier features than her own, and one or two were positively overweight. She realized that she was in a very different mould from the usual Royal mistress. She was aware that men were attracted to certain types of women and vice versa, and she wondered if she were so unlike the usual pattern of women preferred by Francis that this had been an active deterrent to the consummation of their relationship. If so, it boded no good for its future.

But perhaps she was merely making too much out of nothing. Perhaps, after all, he had merely been tired, in which case he would return to her again. If only she knew now, tonight, what the future held. Not knowing was intolerable, and she found herself yearning for the peaceful, tranquil and predictable existence at the Château de Deverelle, longing, too, for Carol's rumbustious company. There were hounds about the Court, but they seemed silent, bovine creatures compared to her own beloved dog.

Next morning the Comte de Deverelle was Athena's first visitor. He entered her suite with an almost tremulous expression on his face. He looked hesitant and yet eager, at one and the same time, and he hurried towards her to plant kisses on her cheeks before stepping back to view her, as if he thought she might have changed overnight.

'Everything went well, *mon trésor*?' he asked, his voice husky. 'Did – did the King seem content?'

Athena bit on her lip, wondering what to say, how to tell her father. Then, the King's own words came to her rescue.

'The King besought me to secrecy, Father. He said that I must not discuss it with anyone, even with yourself. I am sure that you will understand.'

'Understand? Of course I do! Oh yes, yes, indeed I do.' The Comte beamed, longing to know everything that had happened to his daughter the previous night. Must he wait to hear it from the lips of courtiers, strangers? He struggled with an overwhelming desire to demand more information from Athena, to set his nerves at rest. If the King were displeased with her . . .

'Father, do not look so anxious.' Athena rested her hands lightly on his shoulders. 'I did my best under the circumstances.' She shrugged, wishing that she could give a glowing account of what had happened, wishing in fact that something glowing had happened. Her poor father, how he must be suffering: to have cast the dice and not to be able to read the numbers which came uppermost. What a quandary he must be in – what a quandary *she* was in . . .

At that moment a tap came at the door and a young page stood there bearing a small, carved casket on a silver platter. A gift for Athena from the King. She opened it with trembling hands. Inside the casket lay a rope of pearls, coiled in serpentine fashion. They were small but exquisitely fine and perfectly matched. The card with them read, '*For a pearl amongst pearls*'. Pink-cheeked, Athena allowed the Comte to slip the pearls round her neck, and she stood admiring herself while he held a hand-mirror aloft to catch her reflection.

'You have done well, *mon trésor*; the pearls are splendid. It is obvious that the King is highly pleased with you.'

'That may be so, Father.' Athena was trying to hide her sinking heart, for she believed the gift to be a farewell present from the King – or, worse still, a gift to keep her lips sealed. Either way, the reflection on her character was as nothing compared to the reflection she saw in the hand-mirror. Did the King think that he must bribe her to keep quiet? If so, he did not know her! She would never dream of betraying his confidence. She tried to visualize a man, who, all his life, had had to buy what he wanted, more especially now that he was King. Nothing given him free without thought of the cost. But, because he was the sovereign, all-powerful, immensely wealthy, always he must pay for what he received. She found it a chilling thought, and a sudden wave of pity for the King coursed through her. Even his own mother had dreamed of him becoming King for the power it would bring her as Queen Mother. On what a lonely pinnacle the King sat, no one approaching him unless it was with thought of the payment they would receive for whatever they brought, their interest, their favours, information, company, entertainment. Yes, the King would pay dearly every time. But she did not want him to see her as somebody who must be bought: that quality did not exist in her character. She vowed in that moment that if she could help in any way, however small, she would do so. Unless the pearls were a farewell gift.

Athena caught sight of the Comte's face: it was glowing

with happiness. He believed that what he wanted was already within his grasp, and after so little effort, merely because of the night she had spent with the King. In his brown, twinkling eyes there was hope and exhilaration, and also gratitude.

'My fair daughter,' he caught her hands, 'you have no idea how joyful I feel at this moment, to know that I am back in Royal favour and because of you, because of your beauty, your charm and sweetness. I cannot find enough words to thank you, but you know you will have my eternal gratitude.'

'Really, Father, I did nothing,' Athena said uneasily. 'You know that I would do anything in my power to help you.'

'You are not – you did not find last night distressing in any way, my daughter?' The Comte's brow wrinkled with anxiety.

'Distressing, Father? Why, no, not at all.'

'You are quite sure, *mon trésor*? It has worried me, you know, worried me greatly. To sacrifice my fair daughter to the lions, so to speak.'

Athena forced a smile. 'There were no lions, just a young King. Truth to tell, I found him intriguing, captivating.'

'Did he give you any idea of what he really felt about you? Did he lead you to believe that there would be a future in your relationship?'

'No, Father, but it is far too soon to tell such things. I doubt whether he knows his own mind as yet. We have spent but one night together so far.'

'Do you not think the pearls are a sign of his great delight in you?'

'I cannot say . . . I would imagine so.' Athena saw the anxiety which lay behind the Comte's questions. He desperately wanted to know it all now, before anyone else. She wished that she could tell him, that she could reassure him, saying that the King adored her, that she was going to be Royal mistress for a very long time and that all would go well for the Comte's fortunes. But, of course, she could not. She dropped a kiss lightly on the Comte's forehead, squeezing his hand.

'You must be patient, Father. Who knows what the future will bring? But whatever happens, the King cannot marry me, so you are not going to lose me yet.'

'I comfort myself with that thought, *mon trésor*. Oh, you have no idea what a comfort it is to me. I would rather you were the King's mistress than taken from me by some selfish young husband who had his own plans for you which excluded me.' The Comte shuddered at the thought. 'I will leave you now to dress. We shall meet tonight at the feast.'

'Yes, Father, I will see you then.'

CHAPTER FIVE

The feast was being held by Marguerite, the King's sister, who had recently completed a book of poetry and wanted to celebrate this fact. She wrote love stories and poetry constantly, and Athena was told that there were at least four celebrations a year to welcome the various works of the Princess's.

There would be a dancing bear, a troupe of acrobats, wrestlers, jugglers, and a group of travelling minstrels who had arrived at the Louvre that very day and who were to sing the very latest Provençal love songs, much to the Princess's delight. During the evening she herself would read out some of her poems.

Athena was a little unsure what would be expected of her that evening. She did not know whether she would be attending the feast merely as the Comte's daughter, mixing with the rest of the Court, or whether the King would want to single her out. No further word had reached her from him that day, so she had no idea of the outcome of the evening. She dressed with especial care in a shimmering white gown, with an underskirt of scarlet and gold silk embroidery so stiff that it would stand up on its own, unsupported. She would, of course, wear the King's pearls, and they glowed warmly, with a sheen that matched the white gown.

Then, Athena found herself in a quandary. As a virgin she could wear her gold hair loose and flowing down her back, but, to all intents and purposes, she was no longer a virgin. Did such things matter at Court, however, or was she being old-fashioned, narrow-minded? Normally, as soon as a girl was married she bound up her hair and covered it with a hood. She tried hard to think of what she had seen on the other nights at Court. At the masque, many had worn their hair loose in the classical style, but that might have been just for that evening; she could not tell. She wished that she could ask someone's advice, but believed that to do so would be a sign of unsophistication, almost of ignorance: a lack which she would want to hide from anybody. A Royal mistress who was both ignorant and unsophisticated – whatever next, she thought to herself, as she viewed her reflection.

Finally, she decided upon a coil of gold netting oversewn with seed pearls into which she tucked her hair so that it was, to all effects, bound, and yet partially loose inside the coil. It looked very becoming, and she was pleased with her decision.

At eight a young page tapped at her door. She had not been expecting him, but he wore the King's livery with the salamander embroidered on his chest and back.

'His Majesty requests the pleasure of your company at the feast tonight, Your Ladyship,' said the page, bowing.

'He is waiting for me now?' Athena gasped.

'That is so, Your Ladyship. He awaits you in the Great Hall.'

Thank heavens she was ready! What a thought – to keep the King waiting. Hurriedly, she took one last look at herself in the mirror and then followed the page through the door, down long corridors, towards the Great Hall. Strains of music came to her ears, lilting, romantic music from the passionate Provençal area of France. A sweet, tremulous voice was singing of the agonies of unrequited love, and, as Athena and the page neared the entrance to the Great Hall, she smelt again the exciting and evocative scent of a myriad lighted tapers mingling with the odours of many different perfumes and oils. As before, the dazzle and glitter of jewels and sumptuous gowns was almost blinding, illuminated as it was by the glowing tapers.

It was a fairytale world, a magical cave of jewels and riches beyond dreams. Athena walked towards the Royal dais where the King sat, resplendent in gold satin and emeralds, his mother on one side of him, his sister on the other side. The Princess Marguerite was robed in tissue-of-silver barred with gold, and the Queen Mother wore a gown of deep, rich wine brocade. Rubies blazed like a fire at her throat, and Athena recognized them instantly as the ones she had received from the Comte; she suppressed a smile.

On seeing Athena, the King rose, stepping down from the dais and taking her by the hand. There was a space and a small chair placed between the King's throne and the place where the Princess Marguerite sat. Still holding onto her hand, the King led her to this seat and gestured to her to sit down. Her cheeks pink, she obeyed. It seemed to her that a murmur of voices billowed through the Hall as everyone noted what had happened and commented upon it, and then the singer was finishing his song and there was loud applause before the next singer took his place and began to strum his lute, which was decorated with silken roses and ribbons.

'These Provençal love songs are very moving, brother,' the Princess Marguerite said in her languid, cultured voice, totally ignoring the proximity of Athena, who watched her as she spoke. The Princess had very strong, aquiline features; her nose was very like that of her brother and for a woman a little too pronounced for beauty, but her almond-shaped rich brown eyes were most attractive, and her brows were slender and arched. A pear-shaped sapphire hung round her throat and her lustrous, dark russet hair was coiled with ropes of pearls, on top of which lay a silver coronet sparkling with diamonds and sapphires.

'One needs to have one's lover close by at such times,' the King smiled broadly, glancing at Athena and then at his sister, who pursed her lips slightly as if annoyed at being separated from her adored brother.

'You always have a lover close by, brother,' the Princess said somewhat tartly. 'I have yet to see you without one.'

Francis grinned, seeming not at all put out by the

comment, much to Athena's surprise. She felt the King's warm hand coil round hers and squeeze it. It was obvious that he had not sent her the pearls as a farewell gift and that he wished their relationship to continue. But again that thought came into her head: was he merely elevating her to keep her lips sealed? Only time would give her the answer to that question.

The Queen Mother had said nothing, nor did she speak for some time. She seemed fully attentive to the singers and to the performers and entertainers who followed them. She ate slowly and delicately, as if the food bored her. She had long, thin fingers, like spiders' legs, which were heavily encrusted with rings of every hue, rubies predominating. Compared to her daughter's gown, her outfit was somewhat sombre, almost like a mourning robe, and her headdress was cut in a simple heart-shape, her hair completely concealed. Athena knew that she would never dare speak to the Queen Mother unless she was spoken to, and even then she was sure she would tremble the entire time. There was something about the powerful hawklike features, the proud nose and severe bone structure which filled her with trepidation – and she knew how much the Comte had regretted incurring the Queen Mother's wrath. He had said many times that her vengeance was to be feared and that she must be placated at all costs. Athena had no difficulty in believing this.

The evening wore on, and the King spoke to Athena constantly, putting her at ease. He asked her how she was enjoying the feast, was the food to her satisfaction? He even wanted to know what were her favourite foods so he could make sure they were served on future occasions. She told him that there were very few foods she did not like, but that she could not abide strong wines.

'So a man must depend upon the arts of seduction and not those of oblivion, my dear?' the King smiled, making Athena blush anew.

The Princess Marguerite gave a throaty chuckle.

'Always a lover first, eh, brother? And then perhaps third or fourth a King, is that not so?'

'It depends upon the occasion, sister. Now, are we not to hear some of your verses?'

The Princess reached for a leather-bound book at the side of her plate. 'I could not decide whether to speak them before or after the dancing bear.' Her narrowed eyes were filled with humour. 'If I came on before the dancing bear, everyone would be bound to think on reflection how slender and graceful I looked by comparison; but if I came on after the dancing bear, I thought my verses might be robbed of some of their impact.'

'I think, with such a difficult choice to hand, I would have dispensed with the dancing bear altogether,' the King grinned. 'Now proceed, sister. Can you not see that the entire Court is awaiting your recital with baited breath? I do not know how they have survived the last four months since your previous book was finished.'

Athena was astonished at the sarcastic, almost cutting way in which the brother and sister spoke to one another, yet she could see that their eyes were filled with glittering humour, that their mouths were fighting to repress smiles all the while they conversed, and she realized that they doted on one another, that this form of banter was one way of expressing that love.

As the Princess rose, a hushed silence fell on the Hall, the music dying away. With great dignity, she made her way to the centre of the floor, where a chair was brought for her to sit upon. Sitting there, facing the Royal dais, she began to read from the book in her hands. The poems were all of deep and undivided love, of the fusion of spirits which only took place during true love and all its varied experiences. During the recitation, the King frequently squeezed Athena's hand and glanced at her sideways, his russet-brown eyes slumbrous with passion. She guessed that he intended to visit her room again that night and the consequent onrush of emotions which she felt at that prospect was confusing. Again, she had the feeling of being caught up in something she could not control, and yet when she glanced across the room at her father, who was sitting beaming so happily, looking so pleased with himself, she could no more have attempted to deny the King than to tell her father she did not love him. All these months he had cared for her so devotedly, nursing her when she was recovering from her accident, giving her so many gifts and jewels, revelling in her company, in every way being so kind and gentle and indulgent with her. No, she could not fail him now.

There was riotous applause for the Princess's rendition. Looking immensely pleased with herself, she returned to her seat on the dais to shouts of *Encore!* But she had no intention of reading out any more verses. She gestured to a valet to pour her more wine and then she leaned back, relaxed and comfortable, to sip at her jewelled goblet of Burgundy.

Louise of Savoy spoke then, somewhat startling Athena. Her voice was deep and rich and melodious but Athena could well imagine its tone growing harsher, rasping even, when she was angry.

'Congratulations, my daughter, you have done well, as always,' she said, smiling across at Marguerite.

'Thank you, Mother, you know how I esteem your praise,' Marguerite smiled back.

There followed an hour of drinking and eating and incessant conversation. Even the indomitable Louise of Savoy had stifled a yawn or two when the King whispered in Athena's ear:

'I will come to your room in thirty minutes, my sweet.' His voice was velvet with desire.

'Yes, Your Majesty,' Athena whispered back, forgetting to call him Francis, but he did not seem to notice: perhaps he wished to be called by his full title in public. She rose slowly, gracefully, curtseying low to the Queen Mother and the Princess and bidding them goodnight. Neither of them spoke to her but merely inclined their heads graciously. Then she withdrew, the little page appearing as if from nowhere to lead her back to her room. She had less than thirty minutes to prepare. A *femme de chambre* arrived to help her undress, for which she was immensely grateful. The King really was very thoughtful. Soon she was standing still while the woman slipped a lace nightrobe over her head and helped her into a satin peignoir, edged and ruffled with lace. The woman brushed out her hair until it gleamed and then she bobbed a curtsey and withdrew silently.

Athena climbed into bed and sat there, leaning against the plumped-up pillows, waiting. Her heart was beating almost painfully and her palms were clammy. Her previous night's experience had not in any way tempered her nerves: she felt just as anxious, just as panic-stricken, as the night before.

Would she be able to go through what would, undeniably, be an ordeal? And again, what if she disappointed the King, what if tonight was as great a failure as the previous night? She was not equipped to deal with such a possibility, being totally inexperienced. Would her sympathies, her attempts at consolation, be enough? How inadequate she felt.

The King's arrival was a whirlwind of jewels and colours, his vibrant personality filling the room. He took her hands, kissed her on both cheeks, and dismissed his valets for the night. They closed the door and trooped away, leaving Athena alone with the King.

'You look like a beautiful carved doll sitting in that bed with your hair loose,' the King smiled, touching her hair, lacing his fingers through it gently. 'You look so fragile, so delicate: it almost makes me think that you would break if I touched you.'

Athena smiled. 'I will not break, Your Majesty.'

'There you go, calling me by that stiff and formal title. Have I not told you to call me Francis? After all, that is my name, the name with which I was christened before God. I was not christened "Your Majesty",' he grinned boyishly.

'You must forgive me for forgetting, Francis.'

'I could forgive you *anything*, my dear.' He lifted her hands to his lips again and she felt the warm, velvet pressure of his mouth against her skin and knew a sensation of deep excitement. Then the King flung his arms around her, pulling her close, his crimson and gold nightrobe falling open to reveal his nakedness. His body was swarthy and muscular, there was not an ounce of spare flesh on him. He had strong, smooth thighs, narrow hips, a broad solid chest.

Next moment he was in bed with Athena, thrusting kisses against her face and neck and breasts, pulling aside her nightgown almost roughly and murmuring endearments, a running commentary on her beauty.

She sought for words with which to respond, but was tongue-tied by his passion. Anything she might say would appear a trite and insincere response to his approaches, and she did not wish to appear sycophantic. She knew that the King was surrounded by enough toadying courtiers already.

She remembered her experience of the night before and how she had seen an image of Lord Mullally's face so clearly in her mind, and with that remembrance his face appeared again as brilliantly etched and coloured as if he were standing before her. Her reaction was one of anger: how dared he interfere, even if it was only in her own imaginings! How dared he interpose himself between her and the King!

Her thoughts were brought back sharply to the present by the King uttering an oath. His hands had been palming her breasts, curving over her hips and over her flat stomach, probing gently between her thighs, but now he fell back from her, uttering a second expletive as if infuriated by events. He leapt from the bed, walking across the room to the platter of wine and cakes which one of his valets had brought. He poured wine into the jewelled goblets, bringing one for Athena and one for himself, then he sat on the bed, looking at her closely.

'You are exquisitely lovely, radiant, like a young virginal angel,' the King said in almost wondering tones. 'I wonder if it is that which. . . .' He paused and sipped at his wine thoughtfully.

'Which what, Francis?' Athena asked.

'You will have noticed that I have not been able to—' again the King paused, scarlet flushing through his cheeks – 'that I have not been able to make love to you.'

'Oh Francis, whatever you do will make me happy. Your cares of state weigh heavily on you, I understand that. If you are tired, then there is no need to do anything but lie here in my arms and I will try to soothe you, to comfort you, if it is in my power.'

'You are very sweet, my dear.' The King sighed heavily. 'Cares of state? You are right about those, and I suppose that I *am* tired, although I try to fight it. I have a long day, and then there is merrymaking every evening until late, but I always tell myself that I am young, that I should be able to cope with it all without getting tired.'

'But Francis, I too get very tired at times, yet I am but sixteen and I do not have the cares of state which fall on you.'

The King took her hand. 'How different you are from all the brash courtesans I have known in the past. I wish that things could be different between us. I wish – I wish that I could possess you, for I dearly want to; I think that I want it more than anything else in my whole life at this moment, but it seems that Fate is against my desire.'

'Time will change things, Francis, I am sure of that. Our relationship is very new.'

'You think so, you think that is it? I hope that you are right. But do not think that I am going to desert you because of this – far from it. I feel a great warmth towards you and despite what has happened – or should I say, what has not happened – I want our relationship to go on, to progress, to strengthen. Besides, if I decided you were not suitable to be my Royal mistress, Court tongues would be very cruel and malicious. It would be unforgivably cruel of me to drop you after a mere two days of interest; I fear that your reputation would not recover. And besides, it is all too obvious that there is nothing wrong with you in any way, so people would look to me and think what is wrong with me that I have dropped you so speedily. I shall behave towards you as I have done towards my other special favourites, do not fear that; and neither need you worry that your father will be dropped from favour, for he will not. I think he has suffered enough punishment for upsetting my mother.' The King's lips twitched. 'A year away from Court – what a hellish punishment that must have been!'

'Oh, he has suffered, Francis, terribly. I have watched him suffering and longing for Court life, to be back close to you and the Royal Family and all his friends. . . .'

'Then we shall say nothing about this, my dear. We shall go on as if all is well between us – which it is, but for this damned body of mine which will not react when I want it to, and that is no fault of yours. Now, drink your wine and let me pour you more. And one more thing, you will promise not to speak of this to anyone?'

'Of course I promise, Francis. I would not dream of revealing what happens between us to anyone at all, you can be assured of that.'

'I was right, you are a sweet creature, and I do not think that I deserve you.' He took her gently into his arms and kissed the top of her head.

Later, when the King slept beside her, Athena lay thinking into the night. She had no past experiences to compare with this, but she knew of the King's reputation as a great lover. Could the fault lie with her, could there be something wrong with her which made the King's love-making fail each time? But he had assured her that there was nothing amiss with her and she must accept his word, for he knew more about it than she did. Mostly, she was immensely relieved that his lovemaking had come to nothing and that she was still a virgin. Yet, there was a little wisp of disappointment inside her. She supposed that it would have been an unforgettable experience to be made love to by the King of France; she imagined that it would have given her an added sophistication to carry her through Court life, to arm her against the rivalry and envy all about her now that she was Royal favourite. She saw herself sitting on the heights, but what unsteady heights they were; she could topple at any moment. There was little to hold her to the King except his benevolence towards her. To her shame, he might have dropped her after showing a mere two days' interest in her physical charms, and then she would have been like a leper about the Court – as would her father. How would Louise of Savoy treat a girl who had failed to continue to interest her son? And what of the girl's father, who had angered her once already? Their names would have been blackened, their reputations ruined.

Ascending to the heights had been so easy, so unexpected, but now she was there she was filled with trepidation. She felt so helpless, so unsure, but for her father she must try her best: there was no other course open to her, she could not see him ruined.

The following weeks were filled with banquets and feasts in Athena's honour. The King certainly intended to keep his word and he was treating her as well as he had many of his other favourites, if not better. As it became obvious to others about the Court that Athena was not avaricious or grasping, she began to be accepted more readily by those who would normally have been her enemies or at least her rivals. Some said that it was a change to have a golden-haired Royal mistress when all the others had been stolid women with jet-black hair and heavier features: women who had set about making their fortunes by leeching all they could get from the King and the Royal Treasury.

The Queen, Claude, began to show friendship towards Athena, much to the latter's surprise. She still felt immensely sorry for the poor Queen, with her deformed hip and painful limp. The Queen seemed to have no advantageous qualities save that she was extremely pious: she was not in any way pretty, nor could she be called attractive, and she had an irritating permanent snuffle. What was more, she constantly suffered from some pains or illness, undiagnosed by her physicians. She was always trying out some new herb or posset or potion which was supposed to bring eternal good health or freedom from megrims or whatever ailed her. Her latest complaint was backache, and as she sat talking to Athena one day she constantly thrust her balled fist into the small of her back and sighed loudly.

'Oh my dear,' she said to Athena, 'if only my husband would now abandon the avaricious women he normally favours and keep to such a sweet, unselfish girl as yourself, then I would be truly happy.' The Queen sighed. 'I have watched him with his women. Oh, I know that he is a King and he has great appetites, but I have the comfort of my God and His mother, the Blessed Virgin, and I pray to them constantly. Now it seems that my prayers have been answered, for you are here and it is obvious that my husband dotes on you. Oh, I am not jealous, my dear, do not think that, for I am his wife and the Queen and nothing can alter that. Besides, I have given him a large family and he adores his children. I can see that you look embarrassed but there is no need to be, my dear, for, as I have said, I am not jealous. In fact, I am pleased that my husband now looks to you. Can you imagine how I have felt when I have seen his earlier mistresses decked out in emeralds and rubies and diamonds, women who have demanded titles for themselves and their fathers, titles for their bastards, titles for their cousins and second cousins, third cousins? My husband is a generous man and I fear that he has given too much to the wrong sort of women. You have asked for nothing when it is obvious from his behaviour towards you that you could have had more than all the others put together.'

'I want nothing, Your Majesty.' Athena gripped her hands together, feeling even sorrier for the poor Queen. 'That is, I want nothing except to be able to make His Majesty happy, if that is within my power.'

'It is obvious to me that he has been much happier since he met you, my dear.' The Queen took out a large lace kerchief and blew her nose noisily once, and then a second time; but even so, she continued to sniff between very third or fourth word. 'He seems to have more tranquillity, and more tolerance: these are qualities which I have prayed he would acquire one day, so you can imagine how happy I feel myself. What can be more joyous than to have one's prayers answered?'

'I am delighted to hear this, Your Majesty, and it is very kind of you to tell me.'

'I believe in praising where praise is due. I only hope—' the Queen paused, sniffed, and blew her nose again, Athena waiting patiently for her to continue speaking. 'I only hope that the King, my husband, does not grow restive. He has such a reputation for changing partners almost quicker than one can count.'

'I will do my best to hold him, Your Majesty, that is, if it is in my power.'

'He has a mind of his own, *Ma Dame*; he is a very strong and wilful man. It is not apparent in the early stages of his wooing, as I know from my own experience, but eventually it will display itself, sometimes to the extinction of all else.'

'He is the King, Your Majesty.'

'I know. I am a King's daughter as well as a King's wife, and therefore my knowledge of Kings is wide. My father was totally faithful to my mother; they were a devoted couple, their only sadness being that they lost so many sons. I was not raised to the sort of life I have to lead now.'

'You have adjusted admirably, Your Majesty.'

'With God's help, *Ma Dame*, only with God's help. I could not have done it alone. I have a great cross to bear, you understand.' The Queen sniffed loudly. 'Sometimes I feel as burdened as Jesu carrying His cross towards Calvary. But with God and His Blessed Mother's help I stay on my feet.' The Queen laced her hands on her lap. They were small, delicate hands and they trembled very slightly. 'Now remember what I have told you: you have made the King happy. With God's benificence this state of affairs will continue. Remember that while you are Royal mistress you exclude others who would be far less suitable than yourself. I shall pray that my husband's interest in you continues.'

Queen Claude lifted a hand, gesturing to one of her ladies-in-waiting, and Athena realized that she was dismissed. Making a deep obeisance, she left the Queen's presence, feeling somewhat moved by the audience. She felt humble, too, for she had not seen her role as of such importance to the King and Queen. She knew that there had been a bevy of Royal mistresses: she did not think that to be merely another was of such great value. Nor had she visualized herself as better than others – but if the Queen thought so then she must try to live up to it. Not for the first time, she felt a tremendous wave of empathy for Queen Claude; in her own way, she was similarly inclined towards the King. To be compelled to infidelity – what a tragic condition that was: an imprisonment. She was sure that if the King showed more interest towards his wife, the Queen's sniffles and her illnesses would vanish.

As a Royal mistress must be seen to be sexually desirable, the King continued to visit Athena in her suite of rooms. However, he was no more successful with his lovemaking than before, and they frequently spent their time merely talking or playing cards.

'The world shall not know our little secret, eh?' the King would smile as he shuffled the cards. 'They think we are concerned with amorous activities in here, but we know better, do we not?'

Athena smiled. She did not question why the King still visited her even though he had failed to consummate their relationship. He seemed to find a genuine delight in her company and she liked to think that this was the reason for his visits, rather than that he continued to woo her to keep her quiet about his failures. Did he imagine that if he suddenly dropped her she would tell the entire Court that he had been unable to make love to her? Perhaps he truly thought that, although she did not really think so. It seemed to be just as the Queen had said: that he did relish her attentions, that he found her companionable after the steely, avaricious courtesans whom he had previously wooed.

She enjoyed the King's company far more now that there was no physical threat. She found conversation and card-playing far easier to tolerate and enjoy than embarrassing fumblings in bed.

Things were going well for the Comte, too. He had had his annuity restored and it had even been known for him to receive a wintry smile from the Queen Mother herself. Who knew what honours he would reap now that he had accomplished the impossible? He spent much of his time dicing and gambling with the noblemen who flocked around the Court, and he was enjoying more success in that line than even he had anticipated. Athena knew that the sacrifice of her reputation had not been in vain – which was some comfort.

One evening, as if he had been reading her mind, the King leaned forward.

'Are you content with Court life as your father seems to be, *chérie*?' He tilted her chin with his forefinger. 'Now *there* is a man who knows how to abandon himself to the life of a sybarite, and for that I have to admire him. His gambling successes are the talk of the Louvre.'

'He has had an extraordinary run of luck, Francis.'

'Let us hope that it continues, but luck is a fickle jade at the best of times.'

The King was right. The Comte's run of luck evaporated a few days later. Shortly, he had lost all the money he had won on earlier occasions and was looking mournful and hollow-eyed as he went about the Palace. But at least his annuity had been restored, so he had some money for day-to-day expenses.

Weeks passed and the Comte's fortunes did not change. He was now into a run of bad luck, he told Athena airily, although she could tell that he was deeply worried. He had not come to court to become even more destitute. Finally, he admitted that if things continued as badly he would have to sell the Château Deverelle and depend eternally upon the King's good nature.

Athena's heart sank. She had done everything in her power beyond becoming yet another avaricious Royal mistress and extorting money from the King. She had no wish to do that, nor could she even imagine herself in such a role. She spent the following weeks struggling to think of a solution, but when it came it was not of her own volition.

The King was growing restive. He was a man of uncontrollable passions and his unaccustomed celibacy with Athena could be borne for just so long – though long enough for her to have had a gratifying amount of time as *maîtresse en titre*. Besides, the King had no intention of discarding Athena dishonourably, nor of allowing anyone to think that she was unworthy. He was going to dispose of her in the time-honoured way: in marriage.

For her, he had chosen a husband who would make her almost one of the Royal Family herself. Undoubtedly she would be overwhelmed and immensely grateful at the honour done her, and at the King's untold generosity, accepting the offer for what it was: payment for keeping her mouth closed about the King's failure to consummate the union.

When the Comte was told, he was stunned – speechless from joy. How could he thank the King for such munificence? His daughter married to one of the premier Lords at Court, her future assured forever, since the man selected to be her husband could afford to keep a bevy of wives and fathers-in-law.

'Your Majesty,' the Comte fell to his knees before the King, 'you have honoured my daughter far more than I had dared hope. How can I express my gratitude to you? She will be delighted, I know – when I tell her she will want to hasten to Your Majesty's side to kiss Your Majesty's hands.'

The King looked down at the Comte's brown curly head, noting the lavish threads of grey amongst the brown. He thought he had dealt rather well with the whole business. It was time his foster-brother settled down and took a wife, for he had been unable to choose amongst the coterie of ladies who constantly thronged around him. They would make a handsome couple, and his foster-brother could well afford to keep both Athena and her father, however destitute the Comte's fortunes were at this moment. It would solve a double problem for the King: that of what to do with his discarded mistress and her poverty-stricken father. The King's fickle eye had fallen upon the Dame de Beauvière, a dark-haired, handsome and robust lady. Now he wanted Athena safely out of the way before he began wooing the Dame de Beauvière.

For his part, the King's foster-brother, Hamish, Lord Mullally, intended to obey the King implicitly as ever. He owed King Francis and Louise of Savoy an inestimable debt for having raised him when he was orphaned, and for ensuring that his fortunes were not misappropriated by the unscrupulous. He had always been totally obedient and loyal to the King in every way, and he would continue thus even if it meant having to marry a discarded mistress of the King. He would do it; yes, even that. Many rumours had come to his ears about the origins of Athena, Lady Deverelle, none of which he had heeded, for he was not a man to listen to gossip. He could see with his own eyes that she had great beauty, great gentility. He had even heard it said that she was baseborn, not the Comte's true daughter at all, but he had dismissed that rumour as highly unlikely. Even if it were true, his father and grandfather before him had both married lowborn girls and it had not done the Mullally line any harm. Indeed, it had even seemed to strengthen the blood line and certainly there was nothing wrong with *him*. Yes, he would take the girl as his bride and gladly, for it would help his foster-brother out of an awkward situation and repay in some small measure the great debt he owed him.

No one asked Athena her opinion of the marriage. She heard of it from her father and was so astonished that she could not speak. She stood as if frozen to the ground, her eyes dilated. Then she gasped:

'Marry that effete, good-for-nothing adventurer? *Never!*'

The Comte went a sickly white. 'But, *mon trésor*, it is the King's will.'

'King's will or no, I shall never marry that knave! I would rather die!'

'Oh my treasure, my daughter! You *cannot* disobey the King!' The Comte's voice rose to a squeak.

Athena gripped her hands together, turning her back on him, her mouth quivering. Marry that lazy, self-indulgent lecher, Lord Mullally? Marry that poltroon? She would die first.

'Father, you promised me that I need marry no one, that you would keep me with you. . . .'

The Comte went even paler. 'I know, *ma petite*, I know, but this is the King's decision and I have no part in it. He thinks he is doing you a great favour – and he is, he is. His own foster-brother, one of the greatest catches in France! He is immensely, immeasurably wealthy, my dove. You need never worry for money again.'

'It will solve your financial problems, too,' Athena said, her voice toneless.

'Yes,' he admitted, somewhat shame-faced.

'So you would marry me to a man I loathe to pay off your debts?'

'Oh, it is not like that at all! No, no indeed. This is the King's doing. No one can deny His Majesty's wishes.'

'Father, have I not done everything you wanted? Have I not compromised my reputation in order to improve your fortunes?'

'Oh yes, my daughter, and I am eternally, infinitely, grateful, you know I am. Just do this one more thing for me, *mon trésor*, I beg of you.' Tears glimmered in the usually twinkling brown eyes.

Slowly, Athena turned to face her father, seeing his tears but deciding that she would not be moved by them this time. She told him so, at which he took her hands in his and let the tears roll down his cheeks.

'Daughter, you will ruin me! I shall be banished from Court, I shall never be allowed back again.'

'Then so be it,' Athena said firmly. 'I am not a puppet. I have a mind of my own, and I will *not* be married to that lecher. My life will be as intolerable as that of Queen Claude, who has to watch her husband with his many mistresses and can say and do nothing.'

'Hush, hush, child, you must not speak thus! It is treason.'

'It is treason to marry me to a man I do not love, nor ever can love – the most loathsome man at Court!'

'Oh, he is not that, my daughter. You will grow to love him. He is a striking figure of a man. . . .'

'And that is all, for everything he has lies in his looks. I doubt he can move without a dozen ladies in attendance upon him.'

'He is ardent, as young men are,' protested the Comte. 'It is no crime to take mistresses.'

'Maybe not, but it is a crime to marry such a man to a young bride – and an inexperienced one at that.'

'How can you say that, my daughter, when you have been the Royal mistress all these weeks?'

'Oh father—' Athena would have said more, but knew that she must hold her tongue. The King's secret was safe with her. She went on. 'I have had only one lover. Lord Mullally must have had dozens.'

'It is only right that a man should be more experienced than his bride. Would you bed a callow youth?'

'Yes, if I loved him.'

'Oh Athena, what are we going to *do*?' The Comte sank down upon a bench, his head in his hands. 'If you refuse to marry Lord Mullally I shall be ruined, banished from Court forever, there will be no second chance for me. What shall I do, what shall I do?' He rocked his head in his hands.

'What has Lord Mullally said about all this?'

'He is obedient to his foster-brother's wishes, of course. There is no doubt about that.'

So she had no ally, not even in Lord Mullally himself. He would obey the King unconditionally. Athena saw that there was, in truth, nothing she could do. She was trapped.

She went to the Comte's side and sat down beside him, taking one of his hands in hers. 'Father, what will become of us?'

'Why, you will become Lady Mullally. Bride to the King's foster-brother. A glorious role. You will have jewels and gowns and furs beyond imaginings, and I shall have enough money to pay off all my debts and to live in comfort.'

'Is that truly how it must be, Father?'

'Truly, *mon trésor*. There can be no evasion of the Royal will.'

'None?'

'None whatsoever.'

Athena was close to despair. 'Then so be it,' she whispered, and hid her face against his shoulder.

CHAPTER SIX

Lord Mullally's face was darkly mocking, vibrantly handsome, as he bent the knee to Athena, taking her small white hand and pressing it to his lips.

'I hear that we are to be married, My Lady. I find it excellent news.'

Athena felt his midnight blue eyes searchingly upon her face. What could she say? She felt unutterably trapped, and yet there was a thrill of excitement deep within her. She could not deny that he was the most attractive man she had ever met, moving her in a way in which the King had failed to do. There was humour and discernment in his eyes and something else which she could not, at this moment, identify. Her voice was low and husky as she whispered that, yes, she had also heard that they were to be married. She felt almost disembodied as she spoke, as if someone had control of her voice, her mind.

Lord Mullally continued to look at her admiringly. He did not release her hand, and long moments passed, during which she was conscious of his fingers burning against hers, searing through her palm, a flush of heat coursing through her body by way of response. His hair was so very thick and black and luxuriant, his face so tanned, his eyes such a deep, rich blue. She could not imagine how he looked so healthy, considering his pampered indoor existence, his life of selfish indolence. Yet he did; there was no doubt of that.

She wished that she could cry out: *I will not marry you! I shall not, no one can make me, not even the King!* But she knew that she was helpless. Her father would be crushed, heartbroken if she made a great scene; he had intimated that he would have no desire to live should she bring disgrace upon him by attempting to fight the King's command. He had said that his life would not be worth living if she did not comply. So she was totally trapped, ensnared by Fate. There was no way out. She tried to console herself with the thought that she was fortunate: whatever his proclivities, at least Lord Mullally was attractive physically; he might have been a dotard, fat and balding, toothless, wrinkled. At least she had something to be thankful for.

'You are very quiet, My Lady.' The rich low voice broke into her thoughts. 'Does this marriage not meet with your favour?' The lean, hard fingers pressed against her palm, searing her flesh.

'It is the King's will,' she said tonelessly.

'But is it not My Lady's will?'

'It is not for me to question the King's command,' she answered coolly.

'So the marriage pleases you?'

Swallowing, Athena said, 'It does.'

'That is all I wish to know. Nothing would make me rebel against the King's wishes, but I realize that my bride-to-be might have other thoughts on the matter.'

'I have said all that I am prepared to say, My Lord. The King wishes us to marry and no one questions the King's will.'

'Your loyal obedience to our King delights me, My Lady. I feel exactly the same way.'

'Then we are agreed. The marriage shall go ahead as the King ordains.'

'The ceremony is to be in the Royal Chapel of the Louvre. The Royal Family will be present.'

'I am honoured, my lord.' Athena's voice was a whisper. If only these had been different circumstances, if only she loved Lord Mullally, how joyous she would have been to have heard the news he had just given her. The Royal Family at her wedding! She was deeply gratified.

'The King wishes us to marry as soon as possible. But,

of course, My Lady will want time to prepare her trousseau, her wedding gown.'

'That is so, My Lord.' She tried to pull her hand away from his, for her skin was burning. Reluctantly he freed her fingers and she clasped her hands together in her lap, a wave of heat coursing over her so that pink rushed to her cheeks. She was thinking of all the women he must have bedded: dozens of them, one after the other without a thought for their emotional needs. What sort of life was she going to have as his wife? She was sure that she would be just another female to bed, to ignore when he chose. How could such a promiscuous man settle to loving just one wife? It would be impossible.

Lord Mullally bowed gracefully and bade her goodbye, adding that he would see her again shortly. She inclined her head, whispering goodbye to him, watching him leave the room. For a self-indulgent man he displayed great physical strength, an aura of power and authority, she thought, as the door closed behind him. He looked like a man who spent his days in arduous activity, not one whose only exercise was taken in bed.

A flush stole over her cheeks as she thought once more of Lord Mullally in bed with one of his many mistresses. She imagined their bodies coiled together, his dark and lithe and tiger-like, hard muscles beneath smooth, tanned skin, hers soft and velvety and pallid. She pressed a hand to a burning cheek. This man, this sybarite, was going to be her *husband*. How could she bear it? How could she go through with it? She saw a life of desolation lying ahead, herself neglected, ignored, cast aside for other women. Her shoulders slumped. If only he were not so attractive she thought that she could stand what lay ahead, but, from the very first, even as she had hated him, she had been drawn to him. He was the most attractive man at Court, eclipsing even the King. Even as she despised Lord Mullally, hating everything he stood for, she felt powerless to resist him.

If only this were a love-match and not a Royal command;

if only there were some feeling in it—! But there was not. There was nothing but ice and pain.

Queen Claude pressed a hand into the small of her back and grimaced. She was very heavily pregnant, suffering even more than usual. She bade Athena rise from the deep obeisance she was making before her, and gestured to her to take a seat, which Athena did.

'So, it did not last, *Ma Dame*. Well, I had foreseen that. It is *tragique* but it is destiny. My husband will not alter: no, not ever. So you are to marry Lord Mullally? His attributes are many, *Ma Dame*. He is faithful to the King, he is grateful for having been raised by Madame Louise. There are few at Court more loyal than he.'

'He has many mistresses, Your Majesty,' Athena said, her voice low, controlled.

'Ah yes, but so has the King. So have many men about the Court. Men must prove their virility; is it not part of their attraction? Should we not be very bored by a man who doubted his masculinity? These men have no doubts. You think that he will discard you, that he will tire of you? Ah no, *Ma Dame*, you need have no fear of that. You will be his wife: a wife holds a special position. You will be the mother of his sons, his legitimate sons, and in that you will be quite unique.'

'There is no love between us, Your Majesty.'

'Love, love?' cried the Queen, throwing up her hands, forgetting for a moment the pain in her back. 'You wish to have the moon and the stars? This is the King's own foster-brother of whom you speak, a man who has been raised as the King's brother. It is a great, a magnificent, honour for you to be married to him, *Ma Dame*. Whether love is involved or not has nothing to do with it. You are truly fortunate. You will have everything you desire; you will never have to live the uncertain, doubtful life which your father compelled you to live.' Queen Claude gave a slight, apologetic smile. 'You will live like a princess, a great princess. Lord Mullally has so many estates: in France, in Ireland. You will visit them all; you will see the world! Whereas I, the Queen of France, rarely see beyond the bounds of Paris itself: always I must be *enceinte*, always I must be producing Royal children to strengthen the Throne, the Crown, you understand. You will have time to enjoy your existence, to travel. I think you are very fortunate, *Ma Dame*.'

Queen Claude leaned back, reaching for her lace kerchief and blowing her nose loudly. She looked very pale today, which made her pink-tipped nose seem all the more rosy. Her eyes were red-rimmed, too; she looked as if she had not slept properly for days. Athena felt a surge of sympathy for her.

There was nothing more that could be said during the interview. The Queen wished to retire to her bed to rest, and Athena curtsied and thanked her before leaving her to her ladies.

The Comte was genuinely stricken by Athena's pallor, her lack of spirit since she had heard of her enforced marriage to Lord Mullally. He believed that there was one way out of the problem. If he went to Lord Mullally personally and told him the truth about Athena, surely the man would free her of her obligation? And so the Comte begged a private audience with the half-Irish Lord to tell him the entire truth.

'My Lord,' he began, 'there is something vitally important which I must tell you about my daughter – that is, about Athena, the lady whom you have been commanded to marry. She is not – she is not, in fact, my true daughter. She is not the child of my blood . . .'

Lord Mullally's dark eyebrows raised but he said nothing, waiting for the Comte to go on.

'Many months ago when I was in London, about to take

ship for France, as my carriage was travelling towards the docks, I saw a poor beggar-girl lying on the cobbles. She had been cruelly beaten about the head and was in a very weak state. She had long, fair hair streaming out on the cobbles around her and I was immediately reminded of my own sweet daughter, Athena, who died of a fever some years before.' The Comte paused, swallowing, knowing that he was bringing his world crashing down in ruins about him. 'I and my coachman lifted up the girl. We wrapped her in furs and cared for her. I brought her back to France with me. I told everyone that she was my daughter, Athena, who had been raised in a convent in England.' He stopped, feeling as if the words were strangling him.

'She is the Lady Athena whom I am to marry?' Lord Mullally's voice betrayed no emotion.

'Yes, My Lord. She is the Lady Athena. She is nothing more than a beggar-girl, the lowest of the low.'

'Does she know this?'

'No, indeed not, My Lord. The blow to her head destroyed her memory: she remembers nothing of her former life. I have told her that she is my true daughter and she has believed me all along.'

'An extremely dangerous game for you to play, *M'sieur le Comte*. What would you do if her memory returned?'

'I have not thought of that day. I thought only of the joy of possessing my beautiful daughter Athena again. A second chance, that is how I saw it.'

'And you say she is a beggar-child, rescued from the slums of London?'

'That is so, My Lord.'

'A beggar-child,' Lord Mullally mused almost to himself, eyes half closed. 'But she is very beautiful, she looks a true Lady. Her skin is soft and velvety, her hair is like the moonlight's glow, like pure silk. She has such small, soft white hands.'

The Comte listened, realizing that Lord Mullally was

more involved with Athena than he had guessed. 'You – you have some feeling for the Lady Athena?' he asked hesitantly.

'I cannot deny it; I am greatly attracted to her, *M'sieur le Comte.*'

'But my lord, I thought that you were agreeing to marry her only because the King, your foster-brother, commanded it?'

'That has a lot to do with it, *M'sieur le Comte*, but there are also other things involved. From the first moment that I saw Athena I have found her to my liking.'

'But what of her baseborn origins, her peasant blood?'

'My grandfather and my great-grandfather both married baseborn women,' responded Lord Mullally. 'Have you not heard of my great-grandfather, Dirkgado the Black Blade – the pirate who commandeered the English Channel during the Wars of the Roses? He married a gypsy girl, my own great-grandmother – a *gypsy* girl, you understand. I cannot see that it has done us any harm: in fact, I would say that the peasant blood has strengthened us in every way.'

'So you have nothing against the Lady Athena's lowly origins, my Lord?'

'None whatsoever.'

'I see.' The Comte felt that he had failed Athena totally. He had come here prepared to tell the whole truth to Lord Mullally and in telling it he had found that it was not enough to change his mind, to avert the coming wedding. All was lost. He fought back tears, his lower lip quivering. Hastily, he begged leave to withdraw, and scuttled out of Lord Mullally's suite of rooms, down the corridors of the Palace towards his own apartment. So much invested in Athena, so very much: all his love, all his feelings and emotions and tender care. And yet there was nothing he could do to prevent this marriage between Athena and a man whom she did not love, a man who said he had no objections to making a peasant girl his bride. What manner of man was that?

Shut in his apartment, the Comte let the tears flow. They were noisy, gusty tears and he was thankful that he was alone. When he had finished weeping, he blew his nose and wiped his eyes, but he felt no better. There was a great, crushing weight hanging upon him. He saw Athena lying on the sacrificial altar, wrapped in a snowy white robe, and, standing over her was the High Priest, his hands raised with a great curving blade in them to bring it down directly between her breasts. And there was nothing, absolutely nothing, he could do to halt her destiny.

In his suite, Lord Mullally sat thoughtfully. So his future wife was a beggar-girl rescued from the London streets by the Comte de Deverelle? He found it difficult to believe that such gentleness and beauty could have had such a vulgar beginning, but if the Comte said that was how things were, then that was how they must be. It did not change his feelings towards her in any way whatsoever. Her health was good, she would bear him the sons he needed to continue his line, sons who would rule his estates in France and Ireland, who would carry on his family name. He realized that she was reluctant to become his bride, and that seemed to be the greatest hurdle. However, if she should prove difficult to handle, surely all he had to do was to reveal her peasant origins, tell her that she was a beggar-girl from the streets and not a true Lady at all, and she would be chastened, humbled, grateful to him for making her his wife.

He foresaw no serious problems with their marriage. Immediately the ceremony was over he would take her to Mullally Hall in Muldara in Ireland, and there she would be introduced to his Irish friends and relatives. The sooner she understood the extent of his wealth and power the better. So far, she had only seen him about the Court in an indolent capacity. Well, if she had secrets, so had he, but not ones which he was willing to disclose.

He had not told the Comte everything of his feelings for the Lady Athena. The truth was that he found her inordinately attractive, had done so from the first moment he had seen her. Baseborn peasant girl she might be, King's ex-mistress she might be, but her air of innocence and sweetness was overriding. He longed to possess her, to make her his own in every way. As he thought of that prospect – of taking her to bed with him – he experienced a spasm of sheer sensual delight. He knew that it would be an unforgettable experience – for her too, he hoped.

He sat for a long time thinking of making love to the Lady Athena. It was a highly pleasurable time. Later, he went to a secret cupboard behind a portrait in his apartment and drew out a tooled leather box. He opened its lid and looked inside with quiet satisfaction. Then he summoned his manservant and bade him deliver the box to the Lady Athena with a message that it came from Lord Mullally.

Athena opened the box and gasped out loud. Enormous, blood-red, fiery, the rubies gazed back at her. The Queen Mother would die of envy when she saw them round Athena's neck! Thanking the manservant and dismissing him, Athena hurried to a mirror and fastened the ruby necklace round her throat. The stones were enormous, the central one being the size of the hollow in the palm of her hand. The others were perfectly matched, flawless, glowing like drops of freshly shed blood.

Later, when Athena showed the rubies to her father, he was stupefied.

'The Trastamara rubies!' he choked. 'He has given you the Trastamara rubies! I can hardly believe it.'

'What are they, Father? What are the Trastamara rubies?'

'You have heard of Queen Katharine of Aragon, the wife of King Henry the Eighth? Well, her parents, Ferdinand and Isabella of Spain, gave these rubies to Lord Mullally.'

'Why?' Athena frowned.

'Apparently Lord Mullally discovered a plot to assassinate King Ferdinand and brought the plotters to their just punishment. He was rewarded with the rubies.'

'Lord Mullally discovered a plot to assassinate the King . . . *He* brought the plotters to their punishment, Father?' Athena found this difficult to believe. Could this be the same man she had seen lounging about the Court with his mistresses?

'Yes, *mon trésor*. Lord Mullally saved the life of King Ferdinand. The story is true, absolutely true, there is no doubt of it.'

Athena looked again at the rubies in the mirror. She had to confess that she had very strong feelings about her future husband, but exactly what they were she could not say. One moment she raged inwardly at him, hating him and everything he stood for; the next she found herself compelled to dwell on his handsome, mocking face and superb physique. Now he had given her the Trastamara rubies . . . rubies gained when he had saved the life of the King of Spain. It sounded an incredible tale, and she just could not visualize her future husband in such a daring and dangerous role.

'Well, Mam'selle, so you did not heed my warning,' Madame le Brun said as she pin-tucked the waistband of Athena's silver tissue wedding gown. 'But then, you seem to have had little say in the matter. When the King commands, his subjects must obey.'

'That is so, Madame.'

'But to have landed in the very clutches of the man I warned you about . . .' the seamstress tut-tutted.

'Perhaps it would have been better if you had not warned me, Madame.'

'Why, then you would have been an innocent, Mam'selle, knowing nothing. The shock—'

'I imagine that there will still be shocks after my wedding, Madame, whether I am warned or not,' Athena said wryly. 'Even if you had not told me something of Lord Mullally, I would have seen for myself when I came to Court. Some men have great taste, he merely has great appetites.'

Madame le Brun pinched her lips together. 'Men are men the world over but he – well, he and the King, they make a fine pair. So alike in so many ways. If anything, I would say your future husband has more attraction for the ladies than the King, for he has no Crown and yet the ladies flock to him as if worked by strings.'

'I have only once seen him not surrounded by a gaggle of courtesans,' agreed Athena.

The seamstress hunched her shoulders and put her head on one side. 'Marriage is a great adventure, Mam'selle, and like all adventures it has its ups and downs. Sometimes you will be high in the clouds and so happy; at other times you will be lower than the earth and as miserable. With Lord Mullally I imagine that the latter occasions will be more frequent. But no, I should not be depressing you. It is unkind of me, thoughtless. You are young and very beautiful. Who am I to say that this will work out worse than any other arranged marriage? Sometimes they are highly successful, sometimes more rewarding than true love-matches, for they also have their flaws. Men and women brought together in a great rush of passion often have little else to hold them together and the passion soon fades, leaving them with nothing.'

'At least that cannot be said of Lord Mullally and myself,' Athena turned round so that the seamstress could pin-tuck the back of her gown. 'The only rush of feeling I experience about him is trepidation. Incidentally, Madame, do you know anything about the Trastamara rubies?'

'Trastamara rubies? No, I do not think that I do,' the seamstress answered. 'What are they?'

'Oh, a gift from my future husband. Rubies which were given to him by King Ferdinand of Spain.'

'No, I know nothing about them, Mam'selle, I am sorry. What did you want to know?'

'The true story behind the reason for King Ferdinand giving the rubies to my future husband, that is all.'

'No, I cannot help you there, Mam'selle.' The seamstress shrugged again. Plainly, she knew nothing of Lord Mullally's earlier life. For the moment Athena would have to be content with what she had heard from her father.

Her wedding gown was sumptuous: cloth of silver tissue, fragile and gleaming, a faerie queen's robe, with underskirts of rich and delicate ivory lace starred with diamonds. Her slippers were ivory satin with diamond-studded toes and heels, and her sleeves were cut and slashed to reveal ivory lace inner sleeves, decorated with pearls. Her headdress had been sent to her by Queen Claude: it was ivory cloth of silver, beaded with garnets and seed pearls, and ornamented with silver-embroidered lace. Against this delicate and glistening pallor, the Trastamara rubies would blaze like flaming drops of blood. She hoped that they would not be an ill omen on her wedding day.

Madame le Brun had finished pin-tucking the waistband, and was now evening the lengths of the sleeves.

'Of course, you might find it difficult to deal with such a handsome husband,' she suggested sympathetically.

'I shall treat him as he deserves, no matter how handsome he is.' Athena tossed her head.

The wedding ceremony was a quiet affair, its only grandeur

deriving from the presence of the Royal Family. The Queen Mother, regal in plum brocade barred with gold, so far forgot herself as to shed a quiet tear when her foster-son declared his marriage vows. Queen Claude, diminutive and self-effacing in green and gold satin, sniffed throughout the entire time, but there were tears in her eyes too, so Athena forgave her. (Whether the Queen was tearful because her husband was losing an approved mistress or because she was genuinely moved by the marriage, Athena could not say.)

The King was a Sun God in dazzling yellow satin dewed with emeralds and diamonds, his outfit more befitting the groom himself than a wedding guest. He and the Queen had given the couple a pouch filled with starry diamonds for them to share, the diamonds to be made up into whatever jewellery they each desired.

The Comte was red-eyed and pale, but he managed a tremulous smile whenever Athena looked at him. He wore dark blue velvet trellised with silver-work. His hair had been carefully curled and arranged, and his fingers were heavy with rings that he had been able to reclaim since it had become known that he was to be Lord Mullally's father-in-law.

Athena was a vision of delicacy in her silver wedding gown, but her back was stiff, her face tightly controlled, as she stood beside her new husband at the altar. She risked a brief, sideways glance at him. His rich dark blue eyes were fixed upon her in glowing admiration, his mouth curving, slightly mocking. His hand when it took hers seared through her flesh. He wore snow satin, trimmed with moonstones and pearls, and against its stark whiteness he looked doubly dark, doubly tanned and virile.

The ceremony had passed without a hitch. When the Bishop of Argentière had finished speaking, Lord Mullally put out his hands and caught Athena by the arms, pulling her close to him and planting his hard mouth on hers. The chapel and all its occupants receded, vanished. She was alone with her husband, spinning through space, encapsulated by an emotion she had not known existed. Her breathing seemed to stop; she felt that she would not be able to survive the kiss without fainting. But then her husband drew his mouth from hers, looking down deeply, fervently, into her eyes. Had he not still supported her with his arms around her waist, she was sure that she would have fallen. She had not thought that a kiss would be so moving, so rivetting, and she was stricken by a feeling of bleakness as his arms loosed themselves and he stepped back a little, a mocking smile on his lips.

Yes, she thought, it has meant nothing to him, that kiss. I am just another of his many mistresses to him, and how many hundreds of times he must have kissed them in just this way. A twist of anger, and also of bitter disappointment, speared through her.

After the Mass there were hasty preparations to be made for the couple's departure to Muldara and Mullally Hall, in Ireland. The tide was right and they were setting sail immediately.

Even though Athena had been prepared for this, had said her goodbyes repeatedly during the past few days, she felt bereft as she climbed into the coach beside her new husband. The entire Royal Family waved goodbye to them, but it was on the Comte's face that Athena's eyes rested until he was so far distant that she could see him no longer. She swallowed bitter misery. It was not as if they were going to Ireland forever, only for a visit. They would be back. She would see her father again. Nonetheless, she felt desolate.

Her husband's eyes were upon her as the carriage lurched along, but he said nothing and for that she was grateful. If he had spoken words of tenderness she knew that she would have burst into floods of tears. But what was she thinking? Words of tenderness from Lord Mullally? What made her imagine she would ever hear those? Theirs was a marriage of convenience, nothing else. Arranged for them by the King so that he could dispose of his ex-mistress and see his foster-brother settled at the same time.

Ex-mistress, she thought bitterly. If only they knew. Still a virgin – yes, still a virgin, and yet here she was sitting beside the most experienced man at Court: a man who thought that she was the discarded lover of the King. It made her feel almost a hypocrite, for she certainly was not what events had forced her to pretend to be. She knew that she was being foolish: it was far better to be pure than impure.

She was conscious again of the rich dark blue eyes of her husband surveying her, and a shiver of apprehension trickled down her back. She was alone with him, a man she barely knew, and one she had instinctively abhorred, an indolent, self-indulgent libertine. And he was her husband! Fresh waves of doubt assailed her. When she thought he was not looking at her, she examined him furtively, noting his tiger-like grace, the air of coiled tension about him. She tried to imagine him scenting out a plot to murder the King of Spain and bringing the plotters to justice. Could that man and her husband really be one and the same?

The carriage lurched on and her trepidation grew. She was so alone: so very alone. With all her heart and being she longed for her father.

CHAPTER SEVEN

A wild summer storm blew up in the Channel and Athena began to feel very ill indeed. The heaving and rolling of the ship seemed to echo the churnings in her stomach, and very early on she took to her bunk, lying ashen and still in between bouts of vomiting.

Preoccupied by her sickness, Athena barely noticed the care which her new husband gave her. Instead of abandoning her to her illness, he sat beside her, holding the bowl when she vomited and mopping her brow. He chafed her wrists and bathed her face and spoke marvellously soothing words to her. But she had not the strength even to wonder at his surprising kindness.

The hours wore on, but his ministrations continued as tenderly as at the beginning. There was no sign of his wearying of her sea-sickness, nor of his neglecting her. The storm seemed to go on for an eternity. She was prepared to die, she felt so wretched; death would have been a release. When the lashing seas finally began to abate, Athena was able to forget some of the desperate misery she had endured and look at her husband with new eyes. He had cared for her every bit as tenderly as her father had done after her accident, and yet this man barely knew her and he was no blood kin of hers. What possible reason did he have for nurturing her so tenderly? She could think of none. And his ministrations certainly did not comply with her image of him. Where now was the selfish, indolent libertine?

Unfortunately, no sooner had Athena begun to recover from the first storm than a second began, even worse in its intensity. It raged all through the first night and much of the next day, blowing them off course so that their journey, of necessity, was prolonged.

At some point during the torture, Athena remembered whispering her husband's name: Lord Mullally.

She remembered him replying. 'I am not a stranger, I am your husband. My name is Hamish, call me by that name, for you are now my wife. . . .' His words brought her a measure of comfort, as did his actions.

When she thought tht she was about to die all over again, he assured her repeatedly that she would survive, that he would look after her. She heard his voice against a background of creaking and straining timbers, the shouting of sailors' voices, distorted by the violence of the wind.

'Everyone is seasick at one time or another,' he told her soothingly, 'and everyone survives. The storm is already beginning to die out.'

'I cannot believe it,' she whispered. 'The storm goes on forever.'

'It is dying out,' he repeated. 'The wind is dropping this very moment. You will see that I am speaking the truth.'

He was. Soon after, they were back on course for Southern Ireland. But Athena was now so weak and disorientated that she could do little more than lie in her bunk and moan. Hamish never lost patience with her. He helped her out of her soiled clothes and into a clean robe, he bathed her face for the dozenth time, and consoled her with the thought that they would soon be on land.

'A coach will be waiting for us. I should imagine that they will be growing pretty restive by now, for we are nearly a day late. You will love Mullally Hall: Muldara is the most beautiful county in Ireland, so verdant and gentle.'

A picture came into her mind of another verdant county, rich with trees and foliage, emerald hills and fields. Then the thought was gone as swiftly as it had come. Muldara: it had a beautiful ring to it. She knew that she would be able to feel more eagerness when she had recovered, but she still felt feeble.

Her husband smoothed back her straggling silver-gilt

hair with a gentle hand. 'You do not have to worry about walking; I shall carry you to the coach,' he said. 'Now, had we better not see that you are properly dressed before we disembark?'

Hamish did as he had promised, bearing his wife in his arms as if she weighed no more than an infant and carrying her off the ship, across the quay and into the Mullally coach which awaited them on the quayside. Athena tried once to look out of the windows of the coach to see the passing scenery, but her head swam so much that she shrank back in her corner, breathing deeply and slowly until the spinning ceased.

'Give your stomach time to settle,' Hamish said, smiling. 'After a day or two in bed you will feel yourself again, I can promise.'

Mullally Hall was built in the French Gothic style. It had been begun by Hamish's great-grandfather, Dirkgado the Black Blade, and had been added to by each successive generation of Mullallys. The earliest buildings were simple and low-slung in the Irish style, but the newer façade and main buildings were tasteful and elegant, if small by comparison to the Louvre. However, Athena saw little of the outside of her husband's Irish home for she was still feeling weak and he carried her into the house and straight up to the room prepared in readiness for them.

The bedroom was glowing with yellow brocade bedhangings and green, blue and gold tapestries on the walls. There were sweet scented rushes on the floor, sprinkled with chamomile herbs which gave a fragrant odour like new-mown hay.

Having deposited his bride into the comfortable half-tester bed, Hamish told her that he would sleep in the room next door until she was feeling better. Despite her enfeebled condition, she felt a moment of acute disappointment. Because of their speed of departure in leaving the Louvre and the ensuing storms at sea, they had not yet bedded together. She had known only relief at first, but now she was not so sure. The husband with whom she had dreaded intimacy had proved to have another side to him, altogether more appealing.

Because of her illness, the servants' welcoming line-up had been postponed until another time; she had glimpsed only one or two curious faces as her husband had carried her through the hall and up the great winding staircase. She felt bone-weary, strangely unsettled, and yet too unnerved to relax. Having seen that she had everything she might want, Hamish left her alone to sleep and she lay for a time staring round at the beautiful golden hangings, the elegant French tapestries on the walls depicting the gods and goddesses of ancient Rome. There was a tapestry too, of Adam and Eve in the Garden of Eden; they were clothed in bright green leaves and coiled between them was an evil-looking snake. Thinking of the Biblical couple led Athena's thoughts to original sin and from there to the consummation of her marriage. But, before she could enlarge on her thoughts, she fell into a sound sleep.

She woke the next morning to see a broad-faced, motherly woman dressed in Irish green with her brown hair tucked into an old-fashioned gable hood.

'Ah, and so ye are awake, alanna,' the woman said, beaming broadly, hands crossed on her ample stomach. 'I'll have your breakfast sent up to you in just a few moments. Hamish says you had some bad storms at sea and they made you very ill. When the carriage did not come back at the time we expected we were all praying for you to the Blessed Virgin, and now we shall all be giving thanks to Her and to Her Son for delivering ye safely.' The woman crossed herself, then went on: 'I am Hamish's Aunt Kathleen – perhaps he has spoken of me? I am the second wife of his uncle Liam, who died three years ago, God rest his soul.' Kathleen crossed herself again. 'Has he told ye all about us?'

Athena felt besieged by the woman's rapid but kindly mode of speaking. Without appearing rude, how could she tell her that Hamish had said not a word of his Irish relatives? She struggled to sit up against the pillows but still felt weak and dizzy. Kathleen immediately rushed forward, helping her into a sitting position and plumping up the pillows behind her.

'You poor lass, ye don't look well at all. But ye don't have to think about getting up, just stay in bed and we'll take care of you, alanna.'

Kathleen's onrush of warmth had got Athena out of one tricky moment. She would never have found words to tell the kind-hearted woman that her nephew had said absolutely nothing about her or anyone else in Ireland, but had spoken only of Mullally Hall itself and Muldara.

Breakfast arrived, brought by a stalwart young serving-maid, her eyes round with curiosity about Athena. The tray she brought held freshly baked bread, a pot of honey, six slices of thinly cut roast beef, and a mug of fresh creamy milk.

Athena looked at the tray of food which, under any other circumstances, she would have attacked hungrily. She gave a little groan. The mere sight of food nauseated her. She tried to sip at the milk, but after a few mouthfuls her stomach rebelled and she told Kathleen that she still felt ill and could not manage the food.

'Never mind, alanna, ye can eat all ye need to when ye are recovered. Pat and Joseph in the kitchens will soon finish this off.'

When the maid-servant had taken away the tray, Kathleen spoke conspiratorially to Athena, leaning forward slightly, her grey-blue eyes bright.

'Sadly, I never had any children of my own, although I always longed for some. When Hamish wrote saying that he had married he told us very little about you, but enough to make me think that ye would be like a daughter to me. I hope that will be so. I know that ye feel ill now, but we are all waiting to meet ye when ye are better; we are looking forward to ye joining our family. You will find us a kindly lot, and welcoming. I have prayed long and hard to the Virgin to see Hamish settled down, and now I am happy to see that She has answered my prayers. But that is enough of my chattering, alanna. I am going to mix ye one of my potions to soothe upset stomachs and I am sure that, with the Blessed Virgin's help, ye'll soon be yourself again.' Beaming, Kathleen swept out of the room.

A ray of light seemed to have left the room. Even in the short time Athena had been in her presence she had warmed to her motherly chatter. However, Kathleen was soon back with a flask containing her own home-made tincture. It looked murky and it smelled even worse than it looked; it took Athena all her willpower to sip it down but she did so, rather than offend the woman who stood watching her, smiling broadly, hands laced across her stomach. It was true that she did feel a little better after drinking the mixture, and she asked where Hamish was.

'Out riding, alanna. How he loves the horses! And Muldara is made for such pursuits: acres of beautiful green land which pull at the cords of your heart so you can never forget them but long all the time to see them. I guarantee Muldara will have the same effect on ye – that is, when ye're well enough to go out and view it.'

'I hope that will be soon.' Athena paused, not sure what to call Hamish's aunt, but she was soon fully informed.

'Call me Aunt Kathleen, alanna, for now I am your aunt too.'

'Thank you, Aunt Kathleen, you are very kind to me.'

'What else would I be to a sweet young girl like yourself, and you Hamish's bride? I'm thinking that ye'll need all the coddling ye can get.'

'It is true that I am feeling rather homesick, Aunt Kathleen. I miss my father very much.'

'No one can replace him, of course, but we shall all try to be your family here, alanna. Homesickness is a terrible blight, and I'd not be wanting ye to suffer from it under our roof. Now I expect the potion will make ye sleepy in a little while. Just go off to sleep when ye feel like it; don't worry about me sitting here chattering. I'll tiptoe out and not wake ye, and I'll warn that husband of yours not to burst in while ye're resting.'

'Thank you, Aunt Kathleen,' Athena murmured, already beginning to feel sleepy.

When she woke it was late afternoon. She had dreamt that somebody was leaning over her, staring hard at her face. She could almost feel the dark shadow falling across her. But when she opened her eyes no one was there. It had been a strange dream: she was going to Court to meet a king and queen, but they were not the King and Queen she knew in Paris, and there was a little girl, a princess she thought, dancing in a beautiful gilded dress. It could not have been one of the daughters of King Francis for they were much younger than this Princess. She woke with a feeling of sad remembrance, as if there was something she must recall, something vitally important. But she could not bring it to mind.

She did not see Hamish until late that evening. He came silently into the room, yet nonetheless he filled it with his powerful presence. He said very little; in fact, afterwards, she could not remember what he had said at all. She just remembered watching his face, watching the nuances of expression, waiting to see the light of tenderness in his deep, dark blue eyes, the light which had been ever-present during the sea voyage. But it did not appear; he seemed almost offhand with her, withdrawn, taciturn. She wanted to ask him if something was wrong but she dared not. Perhaps he had found things not to his liking at Mullally Hall; perhaps the servants had been neglecting their duties, or the farm was not being run as he wished. So many things could be wrong after his long absence. Something certainly seemed to have put him in a dark mood.

After he had gone, she thought: *What if he is regretting our marriage?* Perhaps he no more liked being forced into this marriage than she did; perhaps he resented her for it. His loyalty to the King would ensure that he did as he was commanded, but what if – and the possibility suddenly occurred to her – what if he had been in love with one of those women who flocked around him like gaily coloured butterflies? If he were missing his lost love in Paris that would be more than enough to make him gloomy. To her surprise, the thought dismayed her. To be torn from one's love: it was an agonizing thought. She shuddered. But even if it were not so, he had been forced into marriage by his foster-brother's command. There had been no escape for him, just as there had been no escape for her.

She sank back into the pillows wearily, her thoughts in a jumble. Kathleen appeared with another of her soothing potions and Athena swallowed it more readily this time, welcoming the sleep that it brought.

Hamish had so many Irish relatives that Athena felt sure she would never remember all their names. Two days after their arrival, she was much recovered from the sea voyage but still pale and easily tired. Kathleen had helped her to dress in a blue velvet gown, and led her downstairs to meet Hamish's family.

When she was seated, throne-like, at one end of the long salon, the family filed in. There seemed a never-ending stream, all with the same broad, smiling faces, rosy cheeks, grey-blue eyes and sturdy build. The girls, too, were of a stolid frame, strong and robust-looking. Athena felt very pallid and slight beside them, and she imagined that they thought the same.

During the welcomings Hamish sat nearby, saying nothing, two hounds lying at his feet. He wore the same saturnine expression of the night before: even his usual mocking grin was absent.

'Will ye not be speaking to your kin, Hamish?' Kathleen said after a while, her face quizzical.

Hamish looked up slowly but said nothing. Bending his head, he stroked the heads of the two dogs.

'Well, and this is a fine show! All these relatives come here to greet your bride and you not speaking to them.' Kathleen put her hands on her hips, her cheeks more flushed than ever.

'As you say, Aunt Kathleen, they have come to see my bride. They have seen me more then enough times before.'

Kathleen tut-tutted loudly, then introduced a further handful of cousins to Athena. Afterwards, the family sat round her chair, all of them sipping wine and eating honeyed cakes and questioning her about Paris and the King and Queen of France. She looked at their strong-boned cheery faces and marvelled that all these people were now related to her by marriage. How different they were from the overfed, elaborately dressed courtiers in Paris; their clothes were far simpler – their natures, too, she suspected. They were garrulous and uncomplicated, and for that she thanked God.

After a while, when they had exhausted their supply of questions, at least for the moment, Kathleen presented a young boy of about fourteen to Athena.

'This is Connell O'Flaherty who is to marry one of Hamish's nieces in the near future. He has some verses to say to you. He has been practising long and hard and he does not want to waste the moment by going away without them said.'

'I should be delighted to hear them, Connell. Please, carry on.'

Connell was very red in the face. He stood first on one foot and then on the other, then he began in a husky, uncertain voice which grew more powerful as he went on:

'Tell him the thing is a lie;
I love him as much as my life.

He needn't be jealous of me:
I love him and loathe his wife.

If he kill me through jealousy now
His wife will perish of spite;
He'll *die of grief for his wife –*
That's three of us dead in a night.

All blessings from Heaven to Earth
On the head of the woman I hate.
And the man I love as my life –
Sudden death be his fate.'

Connell bowed first to Athena then to the left, then to the right, loud applause greeting his offering. Athena applauded him too, smiling at the rumbustious Irish humour of the verses.

Seeing how much attention Connell was getting, another young boy stepped forward and whispered in Kathleen's ear.

'No, *no!*' Athena heard Kathleen cry. 'Ye'll not be telling the new mistress the story of Who'll carve the pig! It's blood-thirsty and quite unsuitable for a day like today.' The boy retired, crestfallen.

More spiced cakes and almond sweetmeats were handed round now, and the wine cups replenished again. As Athena saw interested faces turn to her, she realized that she was in for another bout of questioning; she smiled to herself but wished that she felt stronger.

Connell wanted to know if the Queen of France wore rubies and diamonds every day, Donough wanted to hear about the Royal Palace in France and if it was hung with jewels and cloth of gold, Lucan wanted to know if the new mistress was going to show them all how to dance in the Parisian fashion – but here Kathleen interjected again, waving her hands up in the air.

'Boys, boys,' she cried, 'can ye not see that the new

mistress has had an ordeal coming across the waters and is likely to collapse if she starts showing ye how to dance in the French style? Ye'll have to wait till she's better.'

An attractive dark girl with long streaming black hair and light blue eyes presented herself to Athena with a curtsy.

'I'm your new cousin Maeve, by marriage, and I'm wanting ye to know that I think ye're a beauty. Would ye be after letting me touch your hair, Lady Mullally?'

'Go ahead, touch it, Maeve,' Athena said, moved by the young girl's words. What natural, straightforward people they were; she knew that she could easily get to love them. Maeve's fingers ran lightly through her hair, gently touching, and then withdrew, at which Maeve curtsied again and stepped back.

Shortly, it became obvious that Athena was growing very tired and when she tried to stifle a yawn, Kathleen began to shoo the family away, saying that they could meet Athena another day, that there would be plenty more days for them to feast and chatter to their hearts' delight.

'Now, I'll take ye up the stairs and ye must have a nap,' Kathleen said, taking Athena's arm and leading her out of the salon to the staircase. They had gone up only two stairs when Athena realized she had lost her necklace, her favourite pearls, a gift from her father. Immediately, she told Kathleen and they returned to the salon to see where she had dropped them. She could not see them by the chair where she had been sitting, so she walked round slowly, looking at the floor wherever she had moved about earlier that day. Then she heard the words coming from the window embrasure set in the wall, the disembodied voices floating out to her. One of her many new cousins by marriage, no doubt – and her husband. They were speaking about her.

The cousin's rich, lilting tones were saying:

'She is a pallid little thing to my way of thinking. A gust of the breeze would blow her down. Are ye hoping for sons, Hamish Mullally? For if it's sons ye are wanting methinks ye have the wrong woman.'

Prickles of icy cold scoured Athena's skin as she listened, unable to move, paralysed by the words. She waited, not daring to breathe, for her husband's response. Would he agree that she was 'the wrong woman'?

'That's as may be,' Hamish was saying, 'but it was the King's command. I had no say in it, no say at all. When my foster-brother orders, I obey.'

Athena felt as if her heart had been crushed. She could feel it being squeezed inside her, the pain was choking her. *The King's command . . . When my foster-brother orders, I obey . . .* What cold, emotionless sentences. Silently she moved away from the window embrasure, looked again in the chair where she had been sitting, and saw that the pearls had slipped down the side of its velvet pleating. Rapidly she snatched them up and rejoined Kathleen, who had been waylaid on the stairs by young Connell.

Thank Heavens Aunt Kathleen had not heard what was said! She would have been mortified to know that one of her own relatives had made such critical remarks of the new bride. Athena tried to steel herself against what she had overheard. Had she not known all along that her husband had married her because King Francis had ordered it? Why, then, should she find his words so hurtful? She must not let it affect her, she must not show that she was broken by it!

As Kathleen settled her cosily in her bed, she thought of Hamish's tender ministrations during the Channel crossing. For a while she had felt more hopeful, wondering if he had some feelings for her after all; but now he was dark and moody, behaving as he had never behaved at the French Court. He had sat lowering in a corner the whole afternoon while his relatives spoke with the new bride. Had he been jealous of the attentions she was getting, or bored, or both? She understood now that he was a man of many moods, of a variable nature. In Paris she had seen him intent upon self-indulgence; on the boat she had seen him more attentive than any physician; now she had seen him scowling and dissatisfied. Undoubtedly, that dissatisfaction was with *her*, his chosen bride, chosen not by him but by the King. Unaccountably, she felt grimly depressed by this knowledge. A sudden wave of homesickness washed over her; she longed to see the Comte's cheery face and twinkling eyes.

If only theirs had been a love-match and not an arranged marriage; if only she had some loving warmth to comfort her. But she was not going to take the criticisms without complaint, oh indeed no. Pallid and weak and unlikely to bear children, was she? Well, the pallor was due to her illness, and as for her chances of bearing children – well, time would show. She would surely be able to prove that she was capable of having sons as soon as her husband came to her bed and consummated the marriage.

CHAPTER EIGHT

Athena's homesickness did not decrease despite Kathleen's warm kindliness, and although she fully recovered from the sea voyage, Hamish did not come to her bed. She did not know him well enough to broach the subject, to ask him why he did not come and, indeed, it would have taken a greater courage than she felt she possessed at this moment to have raised such a subject, for he went about Mullally Hall with a face black as thunder. His voice frequently was heard raised in anger or complaint. Nothing seemed to meet with his satisfaction, Kathleen being the only one who dared stand up to his mood: she thought nothing of telling him what she thought of him in brusque tones.

Athena marvelled at the way Kathleen dealt with her nephew, wishing that she could do likewise. Days passed and still Hamish did not come to her bed. He must deeply regret having been forced into marrying me, she thought. He must hate me, loathe the sight of me; he must be thinking of his lost love in Paris and wishing I were she . . .

Beside these two difficulties, Athena had another: her dreams were growing more disturbing. She felt that she might have been able to cope with them had she been able to remember what they were when she woke in the morning, but all memory of them faded immediately she opened her eyes, leaving her with a jumbled sea of faces, a barrage of sounds and voices, all mixed together. She was beset by the feeling that she had something vitally important to remember, but she could not think what it was, and the feeling haunted her both day and night.

Muldara was beautiful, and Athena loved its emerald pastures, the purple-blue hills. She loved the ivory dawns, crystal clear, each one waking the day as if it were for the very first time in eternity. The mauve and dove-grey shadows of gathering night were as beautiful. She knew that if she could only remember what was at the back of her mind she would feel much happier. She barely saw her husband, for he was out riding, supervising the estate and the farms and the cottagers who were his tenants. She knew that he was very busy, that this was mainly the reason he had come to Ireland, but all the same she felt that he should have found some time for her. Each day when he chose to go out riding around his land rather than stay and spend some time with her was a fresh pain, a fresh bitterness. Every morning she stood in her window watching him ride off, handsome and virile in grey or russet doublet and breeches, the late summer breezes whipping up his glossy black hair so that it blew across his forehead, making him look like a young boy. She ached for him to turn his head, to wave up at her window, to call goodbye to her, but he did not. Perhaps he never even knew that she was standing there. Eventually it became too much of a torture for her to watch him ride away and so she stopped, then found that it was an even greater torture not to do so.

Kathleen noticed that, after making a rapid recovery from her seasickness, Athena was beginning to look pale and wan again. Thinking the new bride was already with child, she broached the subject when they were alone together one morning. She was astonished by her niece's reaction, for Athena immediately burst into tears.

'Hush, hush, alanna,' she comforted, taking Athena in her arms and patting her on the back. 'So ye're not with child. Well, and there's no need to be crying. Ye'll have children one day –'

'No, not ever,' Athena wept. 'I shall not, I cannot!'

'You *cannot*? There is something wrong with you?' Kathleen gasped.

'Oh no, no, I did not mean that. Do not ask me any

more questions, Aunt Kathleen, please, I beg of you. It is too upsetting.'

Kathleen sighed, wondering what was wrong with the newly-married pair. She, pale as an icicle; he, black-faced and glowering. She very much wanted to speak out to Hamish, to rebuke him for allowing his bride to become so upset, but she knew that it was too delicate a matter for such harsh tactics. She would have to bide her time and watch over them, and if she could discreetly mend their relationship then she would do so. They would not be the first married pair that she had helped in her time.

One day in early September some unexpected guests arrived: English cousins of the Mullally family. Marvelling at the number of cousins possessed by the Mullallys, Athena found herself being introduced to a friend whom they had brought with them. His name was Paul, Lord Marningham. Blond and blue-eyed, with a pleasant face, he was elegant and attractive, and he seemed to possess a very equable temperament, totally unlike Athena's brooding husband. She took to him instantly, and he to her. (That he was, in truth, her blood-brother she did not know. Paul, having been raised in France since the age of seven, did not recognize his younger sister, nor would he have expected to see her in such surroundings, married to Lord Mullally. The disappearance of his sister had been a deep sadness from which his family knew they would never recover, however many years passed. Paul and his father had returned from France to find her vanished without trace. They had scoured London for her, paid messengers to travel the length and breadth of England, but she had disappeared as if she had never been.)

The days that followed were exceptionally pleasant ones for Athena. Paul, Lord Marningham, frequently played the lute for her and sang her romantic songs which she loved. When the Mullally family gathered together in the evenings to drink and talk, to tell stories and recite verses, she and Paul would dance together while one of the Mullally cousins played his lute.

Athena affected not to notice her husband's furious glares. Why should she care what he thought? He had taken no notice of her since they had arrived in Ireland; why should she hide herself away and not make friends who cheered her life so much, as Paul did? Let Hamish glower and sulk all he liked, she was not going to shut herself away to please him or anyone.

It was on one of these evenings that Connell recited another verse, and as the last few lines rang in Athena's ears she knew a moment of acute anguish. How well it seemed they applied to her situation.

'Too few, too fleet,
The hours I rested at his side;
With him the passionate hours were sweet.

Woods woke
About us for a lullaby
And to the blue waves in music spoke.

And now, too late,
More than for my sins I grieve
That I turned his love to hate.

Why should I hide
That he is still my heart's desire,
More than all the world beside?

A furnace blast
Of love has melted down my heart.
Without his love it cannot last.'

'*Why should I hide that he is still my heart's desire, more than all the world beside?*' The words spun round and round in

Athena's head. Had she turned Hamish's love to hate, was it really too late for them? She wished that she knew. There was a wealth of feeling in Irish poetry and she responded to it wholeheartedly.

It was at that moment that Denis struck up a slow dance tune on his lute, and Paul offered his hand to Athena, who took it gladly. He led her out onto the floor, followed by other couples, and they danced one dance after another throughout the rest of the evening. By bedtime Athena was tired but happier than she had been for some time. She retired to her bedroom smiling to herself and was halfway to the bed, her fingers on the ribbons of her gown, when she realized that she was not alone.

Her husband sat, legs outflung, in a chair by her bed. She had never seen him looking so enraged, and her heart sank.

'You have enjoyed yourself this evening?' he demanded in clipped tones.

'Yes, I have,' she answered defiantly, squaring her shoulders and tilting up her chin.

'No doubt you will be wanting to enjoy yourself similarly tomorrow evening and on other future occasions while Lord Marningham is staying with us?'

'You have guessed right, I shall.'

He was out of the chair in one tiger-like bound, gripping her wrist in a vice-like hold. 'You are my wife and do not forget that! *I* have married you, not that popinjay downstairs!'

'I know it,' she hissed, trying to drag her wrist away but finding it impossible.

'But it seems that I have to remind you, mistress.'

'How could I ever forget?' She flung back her head, staring him straight in the eyes. Already her wrist was beginning to feel bruised, half-broken, and she could feel tears pricking behind her lids. But she would not weep in front of him; she would not give hin that satisfaction.

'I have watched you with that popinjay. You think to

cuckold me! No doubt you think you can bring your immoral behaviour into my household as you did into the Court of France, but I am not my foster-brother, I am your husband.' He thrust his face closer to hers, glaring furiously at her. 'I am your *husband*, and I am not going to let you forget it.'

'You *think* you are my husband,' Athena said scathingly, 'but I have had no proof of it.' Instantly she knew that she had gone too far, for a flash of fury sped across his features.

'So it is proof you are after? And I can give it to you, mistress, believe me.'

He twisted her from him, flinging her down onto the bed so that she fell heavily, awkwardly. He strode to the door and locked it, then turned to face her. She knew immediately what he intended, and she did not know which was worse: the fear in her heart or the pain in her wrist.

'So you want proof that I am your husband?' he said again, and before she could reply, he had torn off his doublet, breeches and hose and had flung them aside. Next moment he was advancing upon her meaningfully.

She cowered back against the pillows. 'No, no, not like this,' she sobbed. Then he was upon her.

The next moments were a nightmare. He gripped the neck of her gown and tore it from breast to ankles, ripping open the underskirts which lay beneath. His passion was so strong that he was beyond the reach of any pleas she might utter, but she kept crying out, over and over, 'No, please, not like this!'

He ignored her protestations. His lips were clamped on hers, crushing and bruising them. She felt his tongue probing beneath her teeth, searching her mouth. His hands were on her breasts and stomach, between her thighs, roughly and without tenderness. She gasped from pain. But that was nothing to the onslaught of his body as he forced open her legs and crushed himself between them, entering her body in one harsh, scything movement.

Clamping his hand over her mouth to quiet her screams and now totally overwhelmed by desire, he continued to rape her mercilessly.

When he had finished, he lay panting on his side while she thrust her face into her hands and curled up away from him. She felt bruised and wounded. This, then was the 'lovemaking' which brought a husband and wife together. This was the consummation of the marriage which she had thought about so much – this terrible, angry and painful ordeal . . . She never wanted it to happen again. She was too shocked even to weep.

'Why did you not tell me?' he asked suddenly, his voice gruff.

'Tell you what?' she whispered.

'You are a virgin, are you not?' He sounded stunned, as well he might, for she had been the King's mistress – and yet she was still pure. He thought he knew now why the King had chosen him as her husband; Francis would have known that he could bank on his discretion. What, then, had been the strange charade between King Francis and the woman who now lay beside him looking white and cowed? Not for one moment could he imagine what had gone on between them, so he said again, his voice more insistent:

'You are – you were a virgin. Why did you not tell me?'

'You did not give me time.'

'All the same, you should have said. I would have been more gentle.' He thought of all the strange stories he had heard about Athena, about her having been a common strumpet before she was rescued in the London streets by the Comte de Deverelle. For the first time in his life Hamish was at a loss with a woman. He did not know what more to say, what more to do. He was inclined to suspect some trickery, but he could not be sure. But one thing he did know: his passions were rising again as he surveyed his beautiful naked wife beside him. He kissed her shoulder, curving his arm round her waist and pulling her against him. Seconds later, he was coupling with her again while she lay mute and unaroused beneath him, biting on her lips.

If this was marriage then she wanted no more of it. She just wanted to be left to sleep in peace and quiet. His deep kisses did not inspire her, not did his questing hands and when, after a time, he finally slept, she knew an intense relief. But it was almost dawn before she managed to sleep herself and then, what seemed like only minutes later, he was waking her again, his kisses scorching her bruised mouth, his body assaulting hers. She ached all over, she felt bruised, ill. Would this nightmare never end? When he finally slumped over her body, she thought she was suffocating. But, after a little time, he got up, snatching up his clothes from where he had flung them on the floor, and hastily dressed himself. Then, without a word, he was gone.

She lay in bed, stunned and miserable. He had said that if he had known she was a virgin he would have been more gentle, and then he had proceeded to be as lacking in gentleness as the first time. How could she have longed for the consummation of their marriage when it would be like this? She could not understand what all the furore was about. How could anyone, male or female, relish this angry, painful coupling? It was brutal, inhuman. She pressed trembling fingers to her swollen lips. If this dreadful, wretched act was to become a regular part of their relationship she did not think she could bear it, but how would she evade it? He was her husband and she his wife before God.

Eventually she fell into an uneasy slumber, the usual jumbled and frightening dreams haunting her.

CHAPTER NINE

Paul had elected to teach Athena to ride and, with this in mind, a sweet-tempered mare had been provided for her. However, she found that once in the saddle she either had a natural aptitude for riding or else, at some time in her life, she had learned how to master and control a horse.

All around them stretched many miles of heath, some of it lacquered with the rich purple of bell heather, some with the glowing gold of dwarf furze. In the distance were yew trees, oaks and larches; proud-spined harebells begemmed the grass, with here and there a cluster of dainty violets. Cautiously Athena and Paul skirted the peat bogs, black and evil-looking, nurturing cotton grasses with their flimsy flaxen heads, the shrubby cinquefoil, and sundews, extraordinary to behold with their trim reddish leaves, tall and pointed, spiked with jewelled hairs glistening in the sunlight, leaves which attracted small insects, trapped them, then slowly killed and digested them. Between clumps of various mosses there grew the butterwort, with its rosette of large, fleshy, greenish-yellow leaves on a long, sleek stalk; the small, beautiful, pink flowers of the cranberry; the brilliant orange-yellow flowers of the bog asphodel, a striking contrast to the green hues predominating.

Above, the sky was blue as the harebells, only one or two fluffy clouds to be seen. It was a perfect September day, one to uplift the spirits and exhilarate. Athena and Paul rode for some time admiring the scenery, then, reaching a pleasant copse earthed with dry, springy moss, they reined in their horses and dismounted.

Picking up his lute, which was never far from his hands, Paul began to sing.

'My lady fair, with moonlight hair,
And eyes like precious jewels,
I shall be sad, I shall despair,
If –'

'Paul!' Athena exclaimed. 'You are not to sing such personal songs about me, it is not right.'

'I did not mean to offend you, Athena,' he told her humbly. 'When I sing and compose verses they come straight from my heart. I cannot conceal my feelings.'

Athena looked away, embarrassed. This was the first time they had been alone together and she was having her doubts about the wisdom of it. He was so good-looking, so charming and appealing, seeming to possess all the best qualities of her former suitors, plus a quality of sincerity which was irresistible. Besides, he had so much to offer her, so much that was different from her experiences of her morose and taciturn husband. She had been forced into marriage with Hamish Mullally. With Paul it was very different. She had warmed to him of her own free will; if she were out here now riding with him, sitting in this pretty copse on emerald green moss enamelled with marsh buttercups, then it was of her own choosing, and that meant a great deal to her.

She looked at Paul. He had such a sensitive face. She could not see him employing any roughness towards her. She could imagine his wooing; it would be smooth and sweet, never jarring, never harsh.

She had no intention of being unfaithful; she had taken her marriage vows seriously. But she could not evade that feeling of coercion. To have been married to a man she barely knew, who was still a stranger to her, even more so now that she was in a strange land, was anathema to love, so she felt. Love must be nurtured, it could not be raped into existence. It was a quality which she needed, perhaps more than any other; she could not survive without it. But her husband had shown, by his every action, that he was not interested in letting love grow between them. The hours when he had cared for her while she was seasick seemed to be very far away now and quite intangible. If he had only shown, in even the smallest way, that there was some hope, how different she would have been feeling at this moment.

'Athena –' Paul had stopped strumming his lute and was staring intently at her, 'you inspire me to compose a score of sonnets, two score,' he said. 'How could anyone have moonlight for their hair and Egyptian turquoises for their eyes? It is just not possible, I do not believe it.'

'Paul, your compliments are very cheering, and I do appreciate them, but you must not forget that I am Lord Mullally's wife, that I belong to him.'

'But are you happy with him?' Paul leaned forward intently. 'I have seen the misery in your eyes, although you try to hide it. Is he cruel to you? Tell me that. Does he beat you? Oh, what I would do to him if I found out –'

'No, Paul, he certainly does not beat me. No, there is nothing like that. We had – an arranged marriage. I know that is quite normal and I am fortunate not to have been married to an old or ugly or repulsive man, for that might have been so.'

'He might as well be old and ugly and repulsive if he fails to love you. What manner of man could know you and not love you?' Paul's earnest, boyish face was closer to hers now, his fingertips brushing hers, his lute forgotten on the emerald moss between them. Slowly, his fingers slid along her skin until his hand palmed hers. She felt a wave of colour rush into her cheeks, a sweet, stormy feeling rise in her breast. Soon both her hands were caged in his.

When Paul kissed the palms of her hands she did not stop him. His lips were warm as velvet, smooth as satin. He held one wrist and kissed that, too, then kissed the other. Then she was lying back against the brilliant green moss, crushing scores of brilliant yellow buttercups, as Paul took her lips, trapping them with his own. The kiss was gentle and languorous, and Athena forgot everything except Paul's touch.

The kiss became two, and then three, Paul's finger tracing its way down her white throat, across the top of her breasts, so that she sparkled with desire.

It was the thud of a horse's hooves against the turf which disturbed them. They sprang apart guiltily, Athena turning her head to see none other than her husband dismounting from a great black horse. Never had she seen Hamish's face so blackly enraged. He stood glaring at them, riding crop in hand and, with a dreadful feeling of foreboding, she knew that he was going to thrash Paul.

Athena stumbled to her feet, ashen-faced, while Paul backed away, stuttering and stammering apologies, his golden hair ruffled, his face white except for two spots of colour in his cheeks.

'No, Hamish, please –' Athena gasped as Hamish continued to glower, his right hand half raised, holding the crop. He took one step, two steps, towards them, his anger seeming to make him tower over them.

'Oh no, Hamish! Please – no! I will do anything –' Athena cried again, as Paul turned and began to stumble away from them.

Hamish did not speak. He stepped towards her, grasping her wrist in one iron hand. She struggled to free herself, but it was quite impossible.

'Get on your horse, mistress, we are returning to the house,' he hissed between clenched teeth.

'You – you will not hurt Paul? Please, promise me that you will not hurt him, it was not his fault.'

'Get on your horse!' Hamish half-pulled, half-dragged her towards her mount and tossed her into the saddle. She fought back her tears; he was not going to see her cry.

Hamish took the reins of her horse and mounted his black stallion. Then he was leading her back to the Hall like a naughty child, her cheeks pink with fear and mortification. He had not touched Paul so far, but what would he do to him later? She felt so helpless – it was all her fault; she should never have let Paul kiss her, nor take her to that lonely place.

Thankfully, no one saw them enter the Hall as Hamish dragged her along by the wrist, up the stairs and to their room, where he flung her unceremoniously on the bed. He locked the door behind him and turned to face her, his face livid, his eyes burning with fury.

'*I* am your husband, mistress, and do not forget it,' he said, through clenched teeth. 'I will not have you behaving like a harlot with every man you meet. This is not the Court of France, and I will not support such behaviour from you here or there.'

'I meant no harm,' Athena whispered, her voice faint. 'Paul – I – he has done nothing.'

'But what *would* he have done, had I not arrived on the scene? Tell me that. It was quite plain to me what would have taken place next, and I remind you again – you are my wife, *mine*.' He thrust his face into hers, grasping her forearms until the flesh scorched. 'Take off your clothes,' he ordered. 'Now! Do as I say! It seems to me that I must show you all over again that I am your husband, that you belong to me, that you are my property to do with as I wish.' He began to throw off his own clothes.

Trembling, Athena began to fumble at the laces of her gown. She was slow and nervous; he grew impatient. She was very much aware of his bronzed and naked body sitting on the bed beside her as she struggled. Finally, she was in her shift and she lay looking at him, not daring to allow any expression to show on her face.

'Your shift, also, mistress,' he said sternly. 'I want to see you naked.'

With sinking heart, Athena did as she was ordered, until she lay there before him as he desired: quite naked. He leaned over her, and clamped his mouth on hers. It was a ruthless kiss, leaving her jaw aching, her desires unaroused.

She was terrified. How could she respond when fear was the only emotion throbbing within her?

He climbed on top of her quickly, thrusting himself almost angrily between her legs. She could feel the fury and the tension within him transmitting itself to her. His weight was crushing her and she felt suffocated, tears trickling out of the corners of her eyes as she prayed for it to end. He crashed against her body brutally, again and again, until she was on fire with pain. He did not seem to care that she was not roused nor likely to be. He cared for nothing except his own selfish pleasure. On and on he went, arching in and out of her body, with each movement bringing himself hard against her so that she was reminded of his violent strength, his power and authority over her.

She felt as if there were a stone in her breast, constricting her breathing. She wanted to scream, but dared not for the thought that it would bring Aunt Kathleen running, and that would be too shameful to face. Aunt Kathleen must never know of this. Her cheeks went white, then red, then white again; she clenched and unclenched her fists, tensing her body against the pain, the brutality. She was on fire with the agony. Would it never end?

Finally, to her exquisite relief, he finished, rolled away, his back to her. She heard his gasping breathing as she curled up into a protective ball and pulled the coverlets up to her ears. She felt numb and broken. She could not have felt worse if he had whipped her. Shame palpated within her; she felt degraded. She saw her life stretching before her, composed of these terrifying onslaughts upon her body, and she knew the deepest despair. How could she stand it? She would go mad: it would crack her spirit and her mind. Was this how he treated his mistresses, his lights of love? If so, why had they flocked round him so eagerly? Her mouth curled wryly. Perhaps it was only with his wife that he felt obligated to behave like this, showing her who was master. Why, oh why could he not have been like

Paul: gentle, sweet, sensitive and romantic? she thought longingly.

They had planned to stay at Mullally Hall for some months, but the next morning a messenger arrived, a man who wore the salamander and the *fleur-de-lys* upon his livery: he had come directly from King Francis to consult with Lord Mullally. The consultation took less than an hour, and then Hamish announced grimly that he was going to Paris, for his foster-brother had need of him.

Athena was stunned by the news. She had just begun to settle in, she said, and now they were to leave. But Hamish told her that she was to remain in Ireland; that the business he had with the King concerned only him. He would, he said, return to collect her when his business was completed.

So she was to be deserted; he was going back to France without her! No doubt he would be exultant at the thought of seeing his mistresses again: indeed, that was probably the reason he was returning, for what possible business could be so urgent as to summon him back to the King? He had far more urgent matters to deal with here in Muldara, on his estates. She would have Aunt Kathleen, of course, and the warm and friendly Irish people who had made her feel so much at home, but would that be sufficient salve for her wounded pride? Surely the Mullally relatives would whisper behind their hands at the new bride being deserted so abruptly and so soon after the wedding?

Hamish rode away within the hour, his leave-takings curt; it was obvious that his mind was on other matters. Athena watched him disappearing into the distance with mixed emotions in her heart. There would be no more of the savage love-making to endure, but there would also be a gap in her life. She had not realized it until having to part with him.

Kathleen's soothing arms were there to console her, but Paul had ridden away some hours before, immediately following the débâcle in the copse. All his companions and servants had gone with him. Mullally Hall was a cold echoing place without them; how would she survive the days until Hamish came back?

But days, then weeks, and finally months were to pass, all of autumn and much of the winter, before Hamish returned to Muldara.

He was pale and exhausted when he arrived at the hall late one January afternoon, and Athena feared that he was ill, but there was nothing lacking in the strength of the orders he gave to the servants and to her: on the morrow they would both leave for Paris, he told her.

That evening, as Athena packed for the journey, she prayed that the Channel would be smooth this time. The weather was bad and she dreaded another stormy crossing. Kathleen muttered beneath her breath as she fussed around, helping Athena, and both the women knew that they would miss one another dearly. They kissed and hugged warmly on saying goodbye the next morning, and Kathleen made them promise to return soon.

Athena would have liked to have said goodbye properly to all the cousins and other relatives, but that was not going to be possible. Heavy-hearted, she took her seat beside her silent, saturnine husband and their carriage bowled away from Mullally Hall towards the coast.

She looked out of the carriage window most of the time, eager for her last sight of Muldara's beauty. How lush and verdant it was, even in winter, much as she imagined the Garden of Eden to be. An unspoiled paradise – but it had been spoiled for her.

Hamish did not say one word to her during the journey to the coast, nor she to him. They embarked on board the ship in the same silence. The sea looked calm and satiny, for which Athena thanked God, but they had hardly been out at sea for more than two hours when the storm began.

Immediately Athena was assailed by the conviction that the ship was going to sink. It was like a powerful premonition, pushing all other thoughts from her mind. She lay helpless in her bunk, white and terrified, while her stomach churned and the boat's rocking increased, up, down, up, down. She gripped the sides of her bunk, trying to control her nausea as the storm increased in velocity and the ship's timbers creaked and groaned as if in despair. The experience was to be even worse than during the voyage to Ireland, and, within a short time, Athena began to be very sick indeed.

It was as if there had never been any quarrel between them, Hamish taking one look at her greenish face, then caring for her tenderly. He placed cool cloths on her forehead, stroked her brow, and fetched fresh water for her to drink. He held the bowl when she vomited, and helped her to lie down again afterwards. He spoke soothingly, saying that the voyage would soon be over, that the storm was not as bad as she thought, that they were in no danger, that the ship was certainly not going to sink.

'We are all going to be drowned,' she moaned, feeling quite convinced of it, for now the ship was juddering as if unable to hold out against the barrage of lashing rain and raging wind.

'No, we are not going to drown,' Hamish said firmly. 'There is no danger of it. Captain McFahy is an excellent man and most experienced; he has been doing the Channel crossing for years and there is no weather he cannot handle.'

'This must be the worst storm he has ever known,' Athena groaned.

'I have known worse,' Hamish said, almost sternly, as if putting her to shame for her imaginings.

The nausea was almost enough to make her forget Paul and Aunt Kathleen. She did not know what had happened between Paul and her husband, she only knew that very shortly after Hamish had found them together in the glade

Paul had ridden off. She had not been able to say goodbye to him, which had sorely distressed her. She looked up at Hamish's features, composed as they now were in such a solicitous expression. Where was the grim and stony-faced husband of a few hours ago? Vanished as if he had never been. Was it to be like this always, she thought in despair? I have to be ill or about to drown before he can be kind to me. She did not realize how ill she looked with her deathly white pallor, the smudges beneath her eyes, the greenish tinge round her mouth and cheeks.

The storm soon blew over, and the ship did not sink. They reached Paris eventually, on a day of blustering snow. This time, Athena did not go to her old apartment in the Louvre but to Hamish's suite of rooms, where his servants awaited him. He undressed, taking off his dusty travelling clothes, washing, and dressing in green and gold brocade. He seemed not to notice his wife sitting on the bed in silence.

Soon he was ready for the audience with his foster-brother, the King – or so he said, his tones curt. He had attired himself with such care that Athena was positive he was going to meet one of his mistresses, and she felt extraordinarily gloomy. When he had left, she ordered the servants to begin unpacking. A few moments later the Comte tapped at the door and came in, beaming, to embrace her.

'My fair daughter, how I have missed you!' he exclaimed. 'And how was the honeymoon?'

'As well as can be expected, Father,' Athena said wryly.

'What did you think of Muldara?'

'Beautiful: I loved it and the people I met there, especially Aunt Kathleen, Hamish's aunt. They are all so warm and sincere and uncomplicated, so easy to make friends with. Father –' Athena paused. 'Did you – have you seen Hamish here at Court recently?'

'Here? Was he not in Ireland with you?'

'No. He left Ireland last September, and I did not see

him for over three months. He said that he had urgent business in Paris . . .' She flushed. 'And now he says he has gone for an audience with the King.'

'You sound doubtful. I can assure you that that is where he has gone, straight to the King. They have some business to discuss, I believe.'

'More likely it is women.' Athena's mouth twisted. 'They are two of a kind.'

'You sound disillusioned, *mon trésor*. Is he not a good husband?'

'I do not wish to be disloyal, Father.' She changed the subject, speaking of the rigours of the sea voyage, telling him how ill she had been, and how well Hamish had cared for her. 'He would make an excellent physician,' she told the Comte.

'So he is a good husband then?' the Comte pressed her anxiously. 'You are happy in your marriage?'

'Father, it is too early to say. Ask me later, another time.'

And with that the Comte had to be content. They were sitting talking, sipping wine and eating honeyed cakes when Hamish returned. He looked from one to the other of them unsmilingly.

'I must leave Paris for a short time, Athena,' he said, his voice terse. 'I have business to attend to, vitally important business.'

'You are leaving? But we have only just got here, Hamish!'

'I know. This is unavoidable, however.'

'But where are you going?'

'I cannot say, nor should you ask. It is enough for you to know that I shall be back eventually.' Abruptly, he turned on his heel and was gone.

'He has gone to one of his mistresses, I know it,' Athena whispered to herself immediately the door had closed behind Hamish. 'That is why he rushed us back to Paris. He was missing his mistresses, and now he is here he cannot wait to get back to them!' She twisted her hands together in despair. She had no defence against her husband's disturbing behaviour. Everything he did upset her in some way.

The Comte took her hand in his, squeezing it. 'Men can love their wives and still take mistresses,' he said.

'It is plain he does not love me, Father,' she said miserably.

'Teething troubles, *mon trésor*, just teething troubles. They will sort themselves out. Every newly married couple has teething troubles.'

Despite all the Comte's efforts, however, Athena remained inconsolable. She could not shake off a feeling of impending disaster. How badly things had gone in Muldara – but how much worse they would be now that Hamish was back at Court with all its temptations and promiscuity. Their marriage had barely begun, and yet it seemed destined to be destroyed. If only they could have stayed together in Muldara, allowing its lush and verdant peace to work a miracle on them. For that was what they needed now – a miracle.

PART II

QUEST FOR THE IMPERIAL CROWN

CHAPTER TEN

The audience with King Francis had gone well. The recent visits which Hamish had undertaken as Francis's secret ambassador to Germany had proved fruitful. This time there was a great deal at stake: the Holy Roman Empire. News had just reached the French Court that the Emperor Maximilian was dead, and King Francis wanted the Crown as he had never wanted anything before. His mother was convinced that he would win it. But many more secret negotiations would be necessary, and Francis could think of no one more suited to carry them through than Lord Mullally, whose brilliantly shrewd mind, diplomacy and fidelity had already served him so well.

There were, however, other contenders for the Imperial Crown, who had already proclaimed their intentions – King Henry the Eighth of England for one, and King Charles of Spain, the grandson of Maximilian. Luis of Hungary had also laid claim to the Crown, but no one took him seriously. Francis knew that there would be a fierce battle between himself, Henry and Charles; they would all pursue their aim with every means at their disposal. Bribes, gold, promises of land, annuities and property would be used to coax the German Electors into supporting one claimant above the others, for it was the Electors' task to select the new Emperor.

'I want you to visit the Archbishops of Mainz, Trier, and Cologne, and the Count Palatine,' Francis had told Hamish. 'These are the key Electors. We must have their support, no matter what it costs. I have the greatest faith in your powers of persuasion, Hamish. I do not envisage your failing in this task. You must promise these men anything – anything at all that they desire – if they agree to elect me as the next Emperor. I shall provide you with a good horse, a squire and a valet, and all you need for the journey. You will also take with you some small chests of gold, which are to be divided out amongst the men you visit. And let them know that there is more where that came from.'

'Undoubtedly they will have been approached by Charles's ambassadors, and by those of Henry the Eighth,' Hamish put in.

'And you must outdo all their promises,' the King said. 'However much gold has been offered them before, you must increase it – double it if necessary, or even treble it.'

Hamish had been further instructed on his embassy, and then he had gone to his suite of rooms to inform Athena that he was going away. His loyalty to the King was unquestionable, but he knew that his departure could not have come at a worse time. What would she do in his absence? He thought of all the courtiers who would be more than willing to occupy her time. There was the King, too, although it was rare for him to take up with a mistress once he had discarded her. There was a strange, bitter feeling in his heart as he rode away from the Louvre. He could not remember having experienced it before. Usually, when he set out on the King's business, he felt exhilarated, full of elation and anticipation, but this time he was leaving his young bride behind him for the second time . . . It seemed to make a great deal of difference, and yet, had he not been forced into the marriage with her, and surely he resented her for it? Had he not found her flirting outrageously with Lord Marningham? She had made it obvious that she set no store by her marriage vows. He should have known it. He remembered what the Comte had told him: she had been but a common urchin before he had rescued her from the London streets. Bad blood would out, there was no denying that. But he must remind himself that he had not married her with any thought of loving her, nor of she loving him; he had done it to please his foster-brother, and the satisfaction of doing that would have to be enough.

He rode straight from Paris towards Rheims, bypassing that city, and on through Luxembourg to Trier, stopping occasionally to rest and water the horses, but taking only the minimal time about this procedure, for Hamish knew that others would also be setting out to visit the Electors with the same objective in mind.

Richard Greifenklau, Archbishop of Trier, had every intention of allowing himself to be bribed. Archbishop he might be, and one of the seven Electors in whose hands the fate of Europe lay, but the thought of being generously bribed with gold was temporarily overruling all other considerations. Privately, he believed that the election of Charles, King of Spain, would be disastrous, and he told Hamish so.

'If I might be allowed to speak frankly, Lord Mullally, then I will say that I believe a German Prince should be elected as the next Emperor. Perhaps the Duke of Bavaria, the Elector of Saxony or the Margrave of Brandenburg. The Elector of Saxony is quite the godliest amongst us; he is wise, shrewd and pious – qualities which I feel are essential in a future Holy Roman Emperor. Do you not agree?' The Archbishop leaned forward quizzically, while Hamish thought of his sybaritic, lecherous and self-indulgent foster-brother.

'I am inclined to agree, my Lord Archbishop. However, I believe the Elector of Saxony is most reluctant, for, as you say, he is shrewd, and he does not wish to have the immense responsibility of such a position thrust upon him.'

'Another German princeling, then . . .?'

'My master, the King of France, is more than willing to reward those who support him in his claim,' Hamish said. He gestured to one of his valets, who came forward with a small chest which Hamish took into his hands, pushing open the lid. He held the chest forward so that the Archbishop could see inside it. It was filled with gold coins.

The Archbishop gulped audibly, his plump fingers with their ragged nails twitching, seeming to have difficulty preventing themselves from thrusting into the casket.

'There's a great deal more where that came from, many thousands more, in fact,' Hamish said coolly. 'This would be but only a small down-payment to demonstrate that King Francis is serious in his quest . . . Do you *still* feel that a German Prince would be the most suitable for the next Emperor?'

The Archbishop swallowed again. He seemed to be having difficulty finding his voice. His eyes gleamed; he bit on his lip, showing black, decayed teeth.

'How much more is there where that came from?' he said at length.

'Many thousands more, My Lord Archbishop. Enough to make you rich, a man to be reckoned with; enough to make Trier great.'

'Power is good.' The Archbishop seemed to be speaking almost to himself. His fingers reached out and caressed the pile of gold coins lovingly. As Hamish did not stop him, he lifted up a handful of the coins and held them tightly in his damp palm. He could feel the heat from them flowing right through his body, and after the heat came a surge of excitement. Riches! He was going to have wealth, tremendous wealth, thousands of gold coins in his coffers. He would be the richest Archbishop amongst the Electors, he would have untold authority. And all he had to do was promise to vote for King Francis at the Imperial Election in June. For him, the oak-panelled room receded. He did not smell the scent of the pine cones burning on the fire in the great hearth, nor the odour of roast capon being prepared in his kitchen. His head was filled with gold, an unending stream of it, and so easily procured. All he had to do was agree to vote for the King of France. It seemed so simple. He suppressed a chuckle, thanking God for having brought this splendid opportunity to him. If he had known when he had awoken that morning that this was to be the day of the greatest good fortune ever offered him, he would not have been feeling so morose when Lord Mullally had been ushered into his presence. He should have had more faith: but then only he knew how lacking in faith he was. Now it seemed that prayers he had not even known he had prayed were answered, and he began to understand the value of his position as one of the seven Electors. He decided that he would take full advantage of it.

Hamish left the presence of Richard Greifenklau in high spirits, riding out into the town square, his valets behind him. The Archbishop had fed them well, so they had no need to stop and eat, and Hamish gave hardly a glance to the Imperial town of Trier with its great sandstone Porta Nigra, the amphitheatre and the ruins of the Emperor's baths; he paid no heed to the Roman bridge over the Moselle as they rode across it, nor to the houses and other buildings built of local red sandstone. His mind was occupied with thoughts on how best to accomplish his next mission, in Mainz.

A cold wind was blowing in their faces as they headed in the direction of Mainz, across the desolate country of the Hunsruck, a rugged highland region broken up by some pasture land, where animals grazed in summer, and forests. There was very little sign of cultivation.

That night they slept in the open, curled up on the rough unyielding earth, wrapped in their blankets and cloaks and huddled together for extra warmth.

The next morning they were coming out of the Hunsruck, riding between overhanging crevices of rock, when Hamish's instinct told him that there was danger ahead. Instantly, he halted his horse, his attendants doing likewise. As they paused, a rock skittered down the slope of one side of the crevice, loosened by a careless foot high above them.

'Ambush!' Hamish hissed.

Immediately they turned their horses back the way they had come, only to see four riders blocking their way. Turning again, they saw four more facing them.

The brigands were ragged and unsavoury-looking, their dark faces heavy and scowling. They held swords in their hands, and began to advance steadily towards Hamish and his attendants.

'Swords at the ready!' cried Hamish to his men, and they all reached for their weapons.

The next moments were chaos. Men's roars filled the air, and the squeals of terrified horses. It was a narrow crevice and there was little room to manoeuvre, but Hamish fought like a madman, wielding his sword with strength and courage, taking on three of the brigands at once, slashing with his sword to left and right, parrying their thrusts, forcibly beating back their encroachment. It soon became obvious to the swarthy-faced brigands that they had taken on more than they could cope with. They were small-time bandits accustomed to rapid conquests, to frightened travellers falling to their knees and begging not to be harmed, delivering up all their money and treasures with barely a fight. Now here they were, faced with a giant of a man with fierce black eyes and night-black hair, a man with the strength of three and perfectly capable of taking on a trio of bandits at one and the same time. Shortly, only two of them were still alive, and they, terrified, were heading for the hills on their panicking horses.

Hamish sheathed his sword and turned round to see how his companions had fared. One had received a gash in the upper arm, which Hamish proceeded to bandage; the other had a scratch on his forehead and a V-shaped wound on the back of his hand, but that was all.

'Well done, men,' Hamish said, proud of them. 'They'll

not ambush anyone again.' He looked round at the six dead bodies lying crookedly about them.

They rested for a time, leaning against the rock face, and then remounted and set off towards Mainz, Hamish forcibly clearing his mind for the business ahead. In Mainz he was to see the Archbishop Albert, brother of Joachim of Brandenburg, another of the Electors, who because of his notorious greediness had been given the sobriquet of 'the Father of All Avarice'. Hamish wondered how the Archbishop would compare to his brother. Would he also be avaricious: open to corruption and bribery? King Francis had said that the vote of the Archbishop of Mainz would certainly carry with it that of the vacillating Archbishop of Cologne, and he might also have some influence on his brother, Joachim – although at the moment it seemed that, after Hamish's recent visit to him, Joachim was fully in favour of Francis being the next Emperor. Hamish had the authority to offer the Archbishop one hundred and twenty thousand gold florins and the perpetual Legateship of Germany if Francis became the Emperor.

Albert of Brandenburg was young, ambitious, and up to his collar in debt. He had been made a cardinal the previous year. He was already Archbishop of Magdeburg, and administrator of the See of Halbestradt. Desiring to hold the Archbishopric of Mainz, which carried with it the right to elect the Holy Roman Emperor, he had set about acquiring it. For this he had needed twenty-one thousand ducats for the pallium alone and ten thousand ducats for the papal dispensation which would enable him to be Archbishop of more than one See. He had borrowed money from the German banking house of Fugger, then found himself faced with the problem of repaying the loan. The solution was the massive sale of Indulgences – all the faithful being told that their purchase of Indulgences would go towards the building of the new St Peter's in Rome, and particularly the shrine which would house the relics of the Blessed Apostle, St Peter. An Indulgence promised four privileges: a plenary remission of all sins, the choice of a confessor by the purchaser of the Indulgence, participation in the saintly virtues, and the freeing of souls languishing in Purgatory.

The sale of Indulgences was now a widespread and thriving business, part of the money going to the building of St Peter's, part to paying off the Archbishop's debt to the Fuggers. Seen as a brilliant scheme of absolute genius by its promoters, it was vilified by Martin Luther, who for some years had been preaching throughout Germany that the practice of selling Indulgences went against all the teachings of the Gospel.

All that mattered to Hamish as he asked for an audience with Albert of Brandenburg was that the dual Archbishop was impossibly in debt, a greedy man who was even more worldly than the Archbishop of Trier. What would he say to the one hundred and twenty thousand gold florins and the Legateship of Germany soon to be offered him? Any moment now Hamish would know.

It seemed strange to see such a young man already a dual Archbishop and Elector. The youthful face was worldly and yet goodnatured, for Albert of Brandenburg was very much a humanist, despite his corruptibility.

Without hesitation, Hamish launched into his speech. When he had finished, Albert of Brandenburg looked at him boldly, tapping his slender fingers on the surface of his oaken desk.

'A hundred and twenty thousand gold florins, a Legateship? That is very tempting.' He smiled at the thought: it was an open, almost boyish smile, revealing perfect teeth. 'Will you take wine?' The Archbishop gestured to a servant, who fetched them goblets of fine Moselle wine and a platter of almond and honey cakes.

'You are visiting others?' the Archbishop went on. 'All the Electors? Can King Francis's money stretch that far, and is he offering one hundred and twenty thousand gold florins to each of us?' His lip curled slightly.

'Importance takes precedence,' Hamish smiled nonchalantly, his relaxed manner belying the tension of the moment.

'So in that case I am extremely important. I see . . .' The Archbishop smiled again, taking a sip of the wine and helping himself to a cake.

'I would not deny that, My Lord Archbishop.'

'You would be foolish to do so.' Another cake followed the first, and a second goblet of wine for both the men. 'What makes you think I might be open to bribery? I might well be insulted by your approaching me with gold, for the inference is that I am corrupt.'

Hamish shrugged. 'I would not ask you to do anything which goes against your religion, My Lord Archbishop. I wish merely to bring to your notice the fact that King Francis is extremely eager to become the next Emperor. He pledges that, as Emperor, he will carry out his duties religiously and with every benevolence. He promises to lead a crusade against the Infidel within three years of becoming Emperor . . .

'He knows that he has rivals?'

'Yes indeed, My Lord Archbishop. Charles, King of Spain, Henry of England, Luis of Hungary.'

'Luis of Hungary is hardly a serious contender, I think; nor is Henry of England: although one does wonder there. But Charles of Spain, grandson of the late Emperor, great-grandson of the previous Emperor – his claim would appear to be premier to that of Francis of France.'

'He is but a callow youth, My Lord Archbishop, only nineteen years of age. He would lack sagacity, assiduity, and other vital qualities. The Empire needs a man of breadth and wisdom, tolerance and justness; a man who is fearless in battle, as King Francis proved himself to be at Marignano.'

'You are right, My Lord, but you speak of King Francis

as if he were a great, ancient and wise man when, in fact, he is only in his mid-twenties himself.'

'That is so, but he has had great experience of ruling –'

'Of ruling only a small Kingdom.'

'What experience has Charles of Austria had? His aunt Margaret, the Archduchess, has ruled for him since he was a small child: she has made every decision for him and guided him.'

'The same might be said of King Francis, who looks to his mother for guidance and advice – and also, so I have heard, to his mistresses.' The Archbishop's mouth curved into a sly smile. 'One does not envisage the Holy Roman Emperor being governed by mistresses . . .'

Hamish suppressed his irritation and returned the smile. 'One has only to look back in history to see Charlemagne with his harem –'

'But Charlemagne never allowed his women to govern him, my lord.'

'I have never known King Francis to be overruled by any woman, My Lord Archbishop. He might listen to their advice, but he would never take it if it did not agree with his judgement.'

'Then one must only conclude that his judgement frequently concurs with that of his mistresses,' retorted the Archbishop tartly.

King's ambassador and Archbishop sat staring at one another thoughtfully, sipping at their wine, each taking the measure of the other. Hamish had known that Albert of Brandenburg would be a trickier proposition by comparison to Trier, but he had not really expected arguments of this kind. Knowing that the Archbishop was deeply in debt, he had expected the talk of one hundred and twenty thousand gold florins to outweigh all other considerations. However, knowing what he did of human nature, he found it very difficult to believe that the Archbishop would unequivocally refuse so much money, money which carried with it the Legateship of Germany. But as the conversation progressed, it became clear that the Archbishop was deliberately holding out in the hope of gaining even more gold. The first day's audience ended in a stalemate, Hamish and his men being offered accommodation overnight. Next morning Hamish was shown into the Archbishop's presence for the second time, and the bargaining began.

The Archbishop seemed an expert at haggling and Hamish wondered how he had acquired these skills, for they seemed remarkably out of place in a man of God. The latter declared that, if more gold were not forthcoming, he would want more than just the Legateship of Germany.

'If King Francis can find me another post befitting my station, and if he is willing to offer me that as well as the Legateship, I will reconsider,' the Archbishop said blandly, as if he did not care about the outcome of this audience. And with that Hamish had to be content, for he did not have the authority to offer more at this juncture.

He rode away from Mainz with a deep feeling of dissatisfaction, as if he had failed his Royal master. He could not understand why the Archbishop had been so reluctant to display his true thoughts on the matter. He had been evasive, not declaring for any of the proposed Kings, not even hinting which way his favours lay. Hamish was unused to failure, even partial failure, and it rankled. He was glowering and angry as he rode along, and beset with an even greater feeling of urgency than before. He believed it quite possible that someone had got to Albert of Brandenburg before him and offered him more gold and an even more important position than that of the Legateship of Germany. Hamish suspected that that person was none other than Charles of Austria.

Ahead lay a longer journey than that between Trier and Mainz, for Hamish was now aiming for Cologne and its Archbishop, Hermann von der Wied. Messages had been carried to Hamish already saying that the Archbishop of

Cologne had declared for Henry Tudor, then that he had declared for Luis of Hungary, then that he had declared for Charles of Austria. Such a vacillating temperament should prove beneficial to Hamish's embassy, or so he thought, for Hermann von der Wied could surely be bribed if the money were right.

Cologne itself had over thirty thousand inhabitants, and ever since the twelfth century when its Cathedral had been built it had attracted merchants and traders who had settled within the precincts. In the year 1000 the Holy Roman Empire had comprised fifteen towns. Now it comprised three thousand, of which Cologne was vitally important. The Cathedral, with its great twin Gothic spires, dominated the river front and was surrounded by the streets and buildings of the Altstadt, the Old Town. Down-river were the ancient Roman settlements of the Lower Rhine valley, for Cologne had been originally a Roman fortress town, Colonia Agrippina, on the left bank of the Rhine. Now it was the main trading artery of Western Europe, an importation route into Germany for cloth and textiles and many other items.

In the presence of such illustrious architecture, Hamish had not expected to see anything sordid, thus he was startled to be suddenly accosted by a tall, heavily-painted strumpet with hair so harshly bleached that it stuck out around her rotund face like a thicket of straw. She had appeared from a dark alleyway, running up to Hamish's horse and gripping his stirrup, then his leg.

'Handsome sir, would thou come with me? I have much to give: no one is more generous with her body than Arta Liebling . . .' The woman's husky, sensual voice trailed away as she gazed up into Hamish's steely eyes.

He tried to disengage his leg from her hands, but she gripped all the harder, so he leaned down to remove her fingers with his own.

'Handsome lord, do not refuse me,' she whispered throatily, thrusting her breasts against his hands, and letting her cloak open so that he saw the naked, pendulous flesh beneath, the rouged nipples erect.

'I have no time to dally,' Hamish said sternly, finally freeing his leg of the harlot's hold, and spurring on his horse in haste. What a frivolous welcome for his solemn mission, he mused, as he continued on his way leaving the woman standing behind him, scarlet with fury at her rejection.

Hermann von der Wied would be a very different proposition from the other Archbishop Electors, for he owed his position of power to the late Emperor Maximilian, and it seemed reasonable that he would now give his support to the grandson of Maximilian, Charles. Much would hinge on Hamish's making him change his mind, but could such a man be bribed even if, as he had vowed, Francis was prepared to spend three million in gold to buy the Imperial Throne?

The room in which the Archbishop greeted Hamish in his Palace blazed with heat from a massive fire banked high in the great hearth. He sat in an impressive carved armchair lined with furs. He had sable-lined boots upon his feet, mittens on his hands, and a cape of marten draped round his voluminous shoulders.

The Archbishop came straight to the point.

'I fear that you are wasting your time, my son. I owe my position, my See, to the late Emperor Maximilian and to him I have sworn to remain loyal.'

'But he is dead, Your Grace,' Hamish began.

'But has he not a fine grandson, Charles, King of Spain and Archduke of Austria.'

'A mere boy of nineteen, Your Grace; an unproven boy. Already he is King of Spain, Sicily, Jerusalem, the Balearic Islands, the Canary Islands, and the Indies. He is Archduke of Austria, Duke of Burgundy and Flanders, Luxembourg, Athens and the Tyrol. He is Count Palatine of Burgundy and Roussillon. He is Landgrave of Alsace and Count of Swabia. Would you have him, at nineteen, add to that long list the title of Holy Roman Emperor? No Christian ruler since Charlemagne has held such immense power.'

'And that power would, of course, threaten your French master . . .' The Archbishop gave a small, conspiratorial smile, pressing the tips of his fingers together and hunching down into his marten cape. 'Do you not find it chilly in here? The February weather is so treacherous, do you not find?' He reached out a jewelled hand and rang an engraved silver bell beside him. Instantly two pages came running, and within seconds were banking up the fire to an even greater height, so that Hamish began to squirm inside his clothes and wish that he were elsewhere. 'Will you have some Rhenish wine with me? Our local wines are superb, and I vow that you will find them a pleasant change from French.'

Hamish nodded and the pages returned, one carrying a silver-gilt platter holding goblets encrusted with emeralds and rubies and a flask of gold studded with diamonds, the other bearing a tray laden with marchpane sweetmeats, sugared comfits, honey and almond pastries, nut and sugar cakes.

All Hamish could think of was his thirst in the heat of the room, so he declined the sweet food and took more of the Rhenish wine, which was indeed fragrant and refreshing. Strong, perhaps, but then there was nothing wrong with his ability to hold wine.

When the pages had gone, the Archbishop leaned back in his fur-covered chair, sipping from one of the jewelled goblets, lightly caressing the gems with his fingertips as if their texture brought him comfort. He helped himself generously to the food, sweetmeats and comfits, cakes and pastries disappearing at a startling rate.

'I have found that good food heats the body, you know,' he explained to Hamish, his mouth crammed, crumbs falling from his lips and down the front of his robe. 'The world is a cold place, and it will be even colder for he who sits on the stone throne of Charlemagne.'

'Then would you rather not see a French King on that throne, Your Grace?'

'What qualities does this French King possess that would endear him to the people of the Empire?'

'He is a staunch Catholic, Your Grace.'

'But a lecher.'

'It is true that he enjoys women's company . . .'

'To extreme, to extreme. His chronicled mistresses are many, only God knows how many unchronicled mistresses he has.'

'But he is married, and he has a fine healthy family. Surely the stability of family life is essential in one who must rule over so many thousands of people? And the Archduke Charles is not married – indeed, Your Grace, he has been betrothed in the past to innumerable Princesses and not one of them has become his bride. What if he remains celibate? What if he abjures marriage and never has a family, no heirs to govern his countries? Imagine the strife, the discord, civil war . . .'

'So you would have him a priest, would you, My Lord? But I do not see him as a priest, only as a careful man, for he knows how important it is for him to select exactly the right Princess, one who will be eminently suitable to be an Empress.'

'Then you have decided already, Your Grace: you will vote for Charles of Austria –?'

The Archbishop reached for a cake decorated with sugared cherries, crusted with spiced nuts, and munched on it slowly, pensively.

'Now, I did not say that, did I, My Lord? Who knows what God's plan is until He formulates it? I am merely His helpless servant; I must obey His will. When I pray to Him for guidance it might well be that He instructs me to vote for King Francis.' The Archbishop's eyes twinkled. 'He might be so pleased by certain gifts made to me for the charity of our city, for its poor and needy, that He tells me to support the French King. As I have said, I am merely His servant, here to carry out His wishes.'

'King Francis also cares for the poor and the needy, My Lord Archbishop: for the poor and needy of Cologne as well as those of France. He wishes to send you a generous gift, largesse for your paupers.' Hamish picked up the small carved chest which was on the table beside him and flicked open its lid. 'I have here a small advance on the one hundred and twenty thousand gold florins which King Francis is willing to hand over to you to use for your charitable purposes or whatever other objectives you have in mind. He also wishes you to know that, should he be elected Holy Roman Emperor, you will receive the perpetual Legateship of Germany.'

The extreme heat of the room seemed to be having some effect on Herman von der Wied, for his cheeks glowed and a tiny trickle of sweat eased its way down his face. Reaching out his mittened hands to take the casket, he gazed down for some time, silently, at the gold florins nesting there. Finally, his voice rasping, he said:

'The perpetual Legateship of Germany, ha! And one hundred and twenty thousand gold florins – for my paupers, of course, you understand.' He flicked his eyes up at Hamish, who said that, of course, he did understand that the money would go to charity. He managed to hide his exultation, for he was quite sure now that the Archbishop would vote for King Francis.

CHAPTER ELEVEN

It seemed to Athena that there was a conspiracy of silence wherever she went in the Louvre. When she made cautious enquiries about Hamish's whereabouts, everyone said very much the same thing: they had not seen him for some time, they did not know where he was, nor what he was doing. Athena had convinced herself that this was because everyone was rallying around her husband, helping to hide the affair he was having with some courtesan; they wanted to protect her from hurt, and so they would not reveal where he was. But the invariably negative replies only infuriated her more, and growing daily more enraged, she determined that she would find out the truth. Finally she sought an audience with the King himself.

Francis was now deeply involved with the Comtesse Beaumont, who was expecting his child. Like his other paramours, the Comtesse was swarthy, sultry-skinned, dark-haired, heavily built. Pregnancy did not seem to tire her as it did Queen Claude, and she continued to appear at every Court function to dance far into the night with the King.

Athena was reminded of her entanglement with the King as she took the proffered seat before him and began to tell him of her fears. When she had finished speaking, the King gave his lazy, sensual smile.

'It is not unknown for a wife to be ignorant of the whereabouts of her husband,' he said, fingering an emerald on his sleeve.

'But Your Majesty, no one in the Palace seems to know where my husband is, nobody. I have asked so many people and they all say the same: they do not know where he has gone or what he is doing.'

'Perhaps in all truth they do not know where he is.'

'If that is so, then he will have disappeared from the face of the earth, for surely there is someone, somewhere, who knows of his plans?'

The emerald on the King's sleeve seemed to be giving him trouble, for he pecked at it with his nails, pushing it to left, then to right, then polishing it with a fingertip.

'I can only think that if he went off without telling you where he was going, then that is what he wanted. Had you thought that his friends might feel they were betraying his confidence if they told you what they knew?'

Athena leapt at his words. 'Then they *do* know something?'

'I did not say that, I was only surmising.'

'But Your Majesty, you are his foster-brother; surely *you* know where he is? He had an audience with you and then he rode away and he has not been seen since. He would not tell me where he was going, nor has he sent me any note. He may be dead for all I know.' She fretted her hands together, feeling desolate and very much alone. The thought of Hamish lying dead somewhere, unaided, brought a spear of pain to her heart.

'I am sorry that I cannot help you, Madame.'

'So not even you know where he is, Your Majesty?'

'I am sorry that I cannot help you,' the King repeated, averting his head to show that the interview was over.

Heavy-hearted, Athena rose, made her obeisance and left the King's audience chamber. Weeks had passed since Hamish had ridden away from the Louvre, weeks of loneliness and supposition, wild imaginings and desperate fears. She saw him in the arms of his paramour. Always, in her mind's eye, they were naked, relishing one another's bodies, making violent love, their arms caging one another fiercely. And the paramour she always pictured as a shapely, sturdily built woman with a body made for child-bearing, not one who became ill because of a mere storm at sea. At night she lay awake, tormenting herself, tossing and turning in her bed. When she did manage to rest, she would have the same wild, jumbled dreams which had begun in Muldara: the dreams which haunted her and yet which could not be dissected, nor made into any sense.

Strangely, she found herself yearning for Hamish's presence, for his arms around her. Why that was she could not imagine, remembering as she did so clearly his onslaughts upon her body, the violence with which he had taken her. Frequently he featured in her dreams, and these dreams she did recall, waking with his face brilliantly clear in her mind, seeing the midnight-blue eyes, the jet-black hair, the powerful, autocratic lines of his face; and her cheeks would blaze, her body throb, as she remembered what he had been doing to her in her dream. Then she would remember the reasons for his absence, the secret paramour with whom he had probably spent that night, kissing and caressing *her* body, not thinking of his rejected bride.

If only they were back in Muldara, where at least for a time she had had her husband to herself . . .

The Comte did his best to console her, but as he frequently took his mood from hers, being miserable when she was miserable, and happy when she was happy, his comfort was of little aid. Nonetheless, she drew warmth and strength from his proximity. He had blossomed on the King's annuity, buying himself a new wardrobe of clothes, taking on new confidence with his gambling colleagues. To have one's daughter married to the King's foster-brother was a fillip indeed, and one which he intended to put to good use. And, since he had played Cupid to the King and Athena, it was rumoured that he was to be given the estate of Clermont on the outskirts of Fontainebleau Forest (the King making doubly sure that if the Comte should discover the truth about the relationship, he would feel so indebted to the King that he would not breathe one word of it).

And so the weeks passed, and Athena tried to fill her days by taking part in Court life. But she found it empty and unsatisfying without Hamish nearby. More fool you, she told herself, for he is off with some other woman, caring not one jot for you. And she believed that, for what else could take a man away from his bride? Did not the conspiracy of silence in the Palace prove that? If he had been on respectable business there would have been many to have told her so, including the King. March winds and rain lashed at the Palace, and April's capricious season began, and still Hamish did not come home to her. She began to feel that she would never see him again; that she had lost him; that in some indefinable way it was her own fault. Where could he be? Oh, if only she knew. She ached for him. Often the Comte would try to prise information from her: why did she look so pale, why did she seem so downhearted? But she found it difficult to tell him, especially when she was not sure herself. Could it really be true that she longed for a man who had shown her nothing but violence in the marriage bed, a man who detested her because he had been forced to marry her? Even if he were here in the Louvre, he would be dallying with his other mistresses; he would not want her – a virtual stranger foisted upon him to please the King. She thought longingly of Paul, Lord Marningham, wishing he were at Court to cheer her. She frequently chided herself for being the only person in the Palace who found the frenetic activities of the Court both facile and boring.

She began to think of herself almost as a widow; and there was a tinge of accompanying grief with this thought, the hours she had spent with Hamish seeming like a poignant, evasive dream. Then, after the moments of grieving, would come the long moments of anger as she thought of Hamish and what he was surely now doing. All right, so he had been forced into marrying her, so he did not love her, but did he have to show it in such a blatant way, deserting her so cruelly, leaving her alone and unprotected from jibes at Court? For there was no doubt about it, there were some taunting expressions on various courtiers' faces – especially female ones. Tortured as

Athena was, she saw every pretty face as belonging to one of Hamish's former mistresses, and she did not feel that she could trust anyone. What if she were to strike up a friendship with a girl, then discover that that girl had spent some time in Hamish's bed? The thought brought dismay in its wake.

So she grew more aloof, more insecure, with each passing day, having no friend but the Comte. She knew that Queen Claude was giving her pitying glances, but her pride balked at such reactions. The Queen had troubles enough of her own, with her sybarite husband; she had little enough sympathy to spare for others. And yet that was what she began to show towards Athena as the days stretched into weeks.

One day, she deliberately sought out Athena as they were walking on the terraces of the Louvre in the spring sunshine.

'Ma Dame, you look so pale, so *distrait*; will you share a few happy hours with me in the Royal nurseries playing with my children?'

'I would be delighted – and honoured, You Majesty,' Athena said, pink suffusing her cheeks.

'Then come with me and I will show them to you.'

The Royal nurseries were attractive rooms, light and airy, and filled with attentive nursemaids. Here, somehow, the Queen's pronounced limp and her objectionable sniffing did not seem so noticeable. She was obviously an excellent mother with a powerful maternal instinct, loving to be close to her children.

'My husband is a doting father, but his time is limited, unfortunately.' The Queen sniffed. 'Nonetheless, he manages to spend many hours here in the nurseries, even more so now our son, the Dauphin, is born.'

At that moment a nursemaid approached them with the little boy, who was now just over a year old. He was a handsome, angelic-faced child, his nature matching his features, so said Queen Claude, the nursemaids all agreeing warmly.

'The easiest of babes to raise,' the Queen smiled adoringly. 'When he was born I told the King that he was even more beautiful than himself, which was true. Alas, since we lost the poor Princess Louise last year we have become anxious parents.' Queen Claude had lost the baby she had been carrying the previous summer, but she was now expectant again and she expressed the hope that this would be another son. 'The Dauphin needs a brother,' she said.

The Princess Charlotte was a pretty and exquisitely dressed toddler. She hung on her mother's hands and cooed up at her engagingly.

'Charlotte is not so even-tempered but we love her all the same,' the Queen laughed, taking the little Princess on her knee and planting kisses on her cheeks. 'Do you not long for a child of your own, *Ma Dame*?'

Athena felt a spear of heat rise in her throat. Managing to find her voice, she said, 'Alas, Your Majesty, God has not seen fit to grant me a baby.'

'Sometimes such things take time,' the Queen consoled. 'No doubt, when your husband returns –'

'*When* he returns,' Athena said, her mouth twisting.

'You speak as if you do not expect to see him again. Have you heard news . . .?'

'News, Your Majesty? Why no, should I have done?'

The Queen looked away uncomfortably. 'I did not mean anything, *Ma Dame*, simply that you might have heard from your husband.'

'No, I have not, not one word. It is as if he is dead. I fear that our marriage was a sad mistake.'

At that moment the Princess Charlotte flung her quilted velvet ball across the nursery and it landed on the nose of the Dauphin, who looked as if he were about to burst into tears and then decided to chuckle instead.

'Poor nose, poor nose,' cooed the little Princess, gently

patting the Dauphin's face, at which he chuckled even louder.

For a moment the Queen's back straightened. 'Nothing that my husband, the King, does is a mistake, *Ma Dame*.'

'Oh, I did not mean to criticize His Majesty. Indeed not, Your Majesty, far from it. I know that he had our best interests at heart, but my husband's sudden disappearance, this long silence . . . What else am I to believe, what must I think?'

'Do you not have a proper faith in God and His Blessed Mother, *Ma Dame*? Do you pray to Them, do you ask for Their will to be done?'

'I say my prayers, Your Majesty.'

'But do you ask for *your* will to be done or *Their* will to be done? There is a world of difference. We do not always know what is best for us, but God and His Blessed Mother know.'

'But is it not true that God says a man and his wife must not be parted?'

The Queen looked flustered and colour rushed into her cheeks. 'But it is not a permanent division; your husband is going to return to you, you must know that.'

'You have some information perhaps, Your Majesty, which I do not?'

'It is not always wise to ask too many questions,' the Queen smiled, sniffing loudly. She turned to one of the nursemaids. 'The sun is dying and this room is growing cold. Build up the fires, close that door over there, draw the arras across to keep out the draughts. The Dauphin must not catch cold.'

Athena had the distinct impression that the subject had been changed very deliberately, and she decided not to persevere. But she was sure that the Queen knew something about Hamish's activities, and what reason would she have to conceal her knowledge from Athena except to protect her from hurt? That was surely it. The Queen knew that Hamish had a secret paramour; that he was with her even now, at this very moment, somewhere in France or possibly even out of the country, and she was evading Athena's enquiries to save her from being broken-hearted.

CHAPTER TWELVE

The Archbishop of Cologne was reknowned for his vacillations, but, even so, Hamish was sure that he had made such a powerful impression on the man that he would vote for Francis at the coming election. He had left the casket of gold florins 'for the poor of Cologne' and let the Archbishop know that the rest would follow immediately he got word to his Royal master.

Hamish had received word by a secret diplomatic messenger that Pope Leo the Tenth was actively against the accession of King Charles as Emperor. Now, Hamish was on his way to see Frederick, the Elector of Saxony, whom he had visited late the previous year while Athena was in Ireland. Knowing already that the Emperor Maximilian was ailing, and very much aware of the importance of Frederick's vote, Francis had despatched Hamish to visit Saxony, to sound out its Elector, a key figure in the negotiations and one whom everyone wished to cultivate.

And so, on his way to see the Elector Frederick, Hamish and his men rode into Leipfurt, a hubbub of voices greeting them. Reaching the main square they saw a massive crowd of people gathered to listen to a monk who was preaching. Having no wish to become involved in the crowd, Hamish reined in his horse, gesturing to his men to do the same. But he was curious. Why was there such a seething mass of humanity, and why were they now so raptly silent? Who was the monk? What did he have to say that was so important? Hamish looked at the man. With a blunt, square face and dark hair, a broad, heavy chin and a pugnacious nose, he looked more like a butcher than a monk. He was raising his balled fist and crying that people must put aside the sinful ways of the Roman Church and look again to God and God alone.

'Priests are not needed to intercede between man and God! There must be no one to come between them! God wishes to speak with *you*, not with your intercessors!'

Hamish turned to a man at his side, asking him who the monk was.

'Why, it is Martin Luther,' the man replied. 'Have you not heard of him? He is famous. Listen to what he says, for it is full of marvels.'

Hamish could vaguely recall having heard the name, something like two years before, in connection with some Theses which had been published criticizing the Catholic Church. There had been ninety-five of these Theses, challenging Papal Christendom, and they had been nailed to the door of the Schloss Kirche in Wittenberg on the Feast of All Saints in 1517. The Theses had propounded very much what this monk was now saying: that all Christians could go straight to God without needing a priest, without needing Indulgences.

Hamish was disturbed as much by the rapt attention of the massive crowd as by the rhetoric of the speaker, whose voice was mesmeric, commanding attention. He did not hesitate or bluster; he clearly knew exactly what he must say, and he was busy saying it. He sounded highly logical, convincing, erudite. Instinctively, Hamish felt that the man threatened all that his Royal master stood for – indeed, all that the Catholic world stood for. He wondered if the Electors knew what was going on in their land, and, if they did, whether they were attempting to silence this heretic. The man had such an air about him that even Hamish – staunch Catholic that he was – felt himself being drawn, persuaded, cajoled.

He looked at the faces of his two companions. They also were listening, watching intently. There was no shock, no horror on their faces; neither of them seemed to be aware that the man was preaching heresy. Indeed, they seemed to be absorbing his every word. Hamish knew that he could not fail to report what he had seen to his Royal master when he returned to the Louvre, but for the moment he wanted to get his companions away from the monk's dangerous preachings. Abruptly, he ordered them to ride on, and he led them out of the town. They did not stop until they were far away from Leipfurt and dusk was drawing in, and then they heard the strains of music, saw the camp fires, and realized that they were on the border of a large gypsy encampment.

Was it the tribe that Hamish knew, the one that he had stayed with before? Yes. So that meant that Zita Rosa would be amongst them. Thinking of her, he was suddenly conscious of how he had been punishing his body in the last weeks, denying his natural appetites while he pursued his Royal master's business. Zita Rosa – with her knee-length jet-black hair, peacock-green eyes and voluptuous body! He felt a stirring deep within him. She would be here, somewhere in this camp: the dancer who had captivated him on previous visits, who had danced for him and him alone in a swirl of crimson and emerald skirts, flinging herself at his feet at the end of the dance to show the entire encampment that she wished to be his. They had lain together beneath the stars or in her tent: it did not matter where as long as their bodies could fuse and become one.

'*Hamish!*' He heard the voice before they had ridden halfway through the encampment, and there she was, his Zita Rosa, as gloriously beautiful as he remembered, with her *café au lait* skin, brilliant eyes, luxuriant hair. She wore a gown of flame and lemon, and there were gold chains at her neck, tinkling bracelets at her wrists, and in her ears wide gold hoops. '*Hamish!*' she cried again, holding up her arms.

He dismounted and she ran to embrace him. She smelled of chamomile and cloves and her arms were like steel round his back, crushing him close to her. She dragged down his head to kiss him passionately again and again.

'My Hamish – oh, my Hamish,' she repeated. 'How I

have missed you, how I have dreamed of you! All these long months and you did not return – I thought that I would never see you again! I do not know how I have survived without you. Life has been black as the pit, lonely as Purgatory. But now you are here with me and I can be happy again. Come, come to my tent. Tell your men to settle themselves wherever they will, to treat the camp as their home. They will be fed and their horses given water. Come, come, my lover, come to my tent . . .'

The scent of cloves and herbs was stronger in the tent as Zita Rosa continued to kiss Hamish with all the pent-up desire of long drawn out months. They sank onto the pallet at the edge of the tent, Zita Rosa hastily unlacing her gown and freeing her breasts, taking Hamish's hands and placing his palms on her soft, heavy flesh.

'I am yours, oh, you know I am yours,' she whispered. 'Take me, take me now, I can wait no longer!' Her fingers fumbled at Hamish's breeches while he tore of his doublet and shirt. The lusts within him could not have been stronger had he been without a woman for ten years. He was swept away in the ecstasy of Zita Rosa's proximity, her velvet, scented flesh, the creamy breasts, narrow waist and broad, shapely hips.

Within seconds they were naked in one another's arms, Zita Rosa's body crushed beneath that of Hamish. She panted like an animal as he drove himself into her, clawing at his back like a cat and moaning his name.

He was a man, with a man's animal needs, and for weeks he had been stifling them. Nonetheless, he was aware that there was something different about this fusion: it was simply fornication, lust, the satiation of powerful, beast-like appetites. Once, he had thought he loved Zita Rosa; now he knew that he did not. She had a body which would drive a saint to ecstasy and which he found irresistible, but there was no tenderness, no caring, in what was happening. He could no more have stopped than ceased to breathe, but awareness was irradiating his mind before he had finished. He did not love Zita Rosa, his thoughts being filled with memories of Athena. She had come to him as if in a dream, filling his consciousness, eradicating any tenderness he might have felt for Zita Rosa. He closed his eyes, and his hands were fretted through moonlight-coloured hair and not black; the eyes which were gazing up at him were turquoise jewels, not peacock-green; the body he had entered was that of his wife, not a passionate and promiscuous gypsy girl. His wife, who had been a virgin until he had deflowered her . . .

Zita Rosa had sensed that something was wrong, but she did her best to respond as lustily as ever, to coax Hamish to the all-consuming heights of passion. But she knew. She could tell. His heart was not in it; his mind was elsewhere.

'Lover,' she whispered, and there was *tristesse* in her voice, 'My lover . . .?'

There was no answer. Hamish rolled on his back, one arm across his forehead, eyes closed. Silence reigned in the tent. Normally he would have curved his arm round her shoulders and pulled her close in the afterglow of love, but tonight he did not. His face was saturnine and she dared not speak again. She waited in vain for him to say something.

Hamish was beset with homesickness, with longing for his bride, and there was a sick, empty feeling in his heart. Was he, then, in love with a girl who loathed him, a girl who had been forced to marry him? How she would laugh if she knew what he was feeling now. Here beside him was the most sensual and beautiful gypsy girl he had ever known, a girl who had only to dance by the light of the camp-fires to inflame a man's lusts and yet he would have given anything for her to be Athena . . .

A tear trickled out of the corner of Zita Rosa's eye. She had lost him. The only man she had ever loved and she had lost him. She remembered the early days when she had dreamed of his joining her in the gypsy camp, staying with her forever; when she had dreamed of bearing his children, of living with him by the camp-fire, of roaming the countryside as his woman. Now she knew that he would never be hers: some other woman had claimed him, she could sense it. With her supernatural gypsy instincts, lying there beside Hamish, she could almost visualize the woman that he loved: a woman very different from her both physically and mentally. The letter A floated through her mind and then what she thought was a T, but no, it was an M – or was it? She could not be sure. There seemed to be some confusion about the woman's name: did the woman have a double identity? How very strange. She wanted to question Hamish, to find out more about this woman that he loved, but he was lying beside her so silently that she guessed he must have fallen asleep after the long hard hours he had spent in the saddle. How unlike him to fall asleep after only one bout of loving. She could remember nights when they had never slept. Gently she rested her head against his shoulder, curving her arm across his stomach, revelling in the feel of his naked flesh against hers. She must make the most of this, relish every second, for instinctively she knew that this would be the last time he would ever come to her. Many tears had trickled out of the corners of her eyes before she, too, fell asleep.

It was an unlikely place for an ambush but, nonetheless, the men galloped towards Hamish and his attendants as if pursued by devils.

'*Ambush!*' cried Hamish, remembering the last time they had been attacked. Instantly his men were ready, swords in hands. The ambushers did not look like brigands: they were clean and neatly dressed in plain clothes, and, as Hamish began to fence with the nearest assailant, his sword point ripped at the man's doublet, tearing open the sombre material to reveal beneath it the emblem of the double-headed Habsburg eagle. So, his embassy had been discovered and King Charles's men had been sent to despatch him and his attendants . . . The fighting was fierce and violent, swords slicing through the air, horses neighing and rearing on their hind legs in panic, raising clouds of dust to choke the men, to blind them. There were six assailants, and again Hamish fought untiringly, putting paid to three of the men himself while his companions finished off the other three. When the bodies lay on the ground, they tore open each doublet to see the double-headed Habsburg eagle embroidered on every tabard.

'Fine work for one who would have himself a future Holy Roman Emperor,' Hamish commented bitterly. 'To set murderers upon us, to slaughter us as we go about our business. And a very serious business it must be, if Kings are ready to kill for it.'

'We have finished them all off, My Lord, so no messenger will get back to the Habsburg,' one of his aides said.

'But what if there are others? King Charles is a scrupulous man, even if he is but nineteen years of age. He is already accustomed to fighting strenuously for what he wants: he has battled with the Duke of Guelders for years to keep Flanders free from his encroachment. We must trust that these are not the first of many, and that others who are also in the race have not sent their assassins after us.'

'You think that Henry of England . . .'

'I would put nothing past that man. He has his father's avarice, and the size of this prize is incalculable. Who knows what Henry is getting up to at this moment, and King Charles?'

Hamish and his aides rode on toward Wittenberg and the palace of Frederick the Third – 'the Wise' – Duke-Elector of Saxony, who, unknown to Hamish, was Luther's protector and champion, whilst also having been put forward as a possible future Holy Roman Emperor himself.

Frederick, however, had refused to co-operate, being above bribery.

Frederick the Wise was a great builder. He had ruled since 1486, had founded a University, had rebuilt the Castle and Church of Wittenberg, the City Hall, the Augustinian Friary, and two Residents' Halls for students. He was an energetic and enlightened Prince, fired by the new Renaissance spirit, quite fearless in his dealings, pious, and a shrewd politician. By hereditary right he was the Imperial Vicar for the eastern half of the Empire, so he had authority over all the Princes of that eastern section and thus was revered. He was famous, too, for his massive collection of holy relics, situated in the new Castle church which had been designed for the permanent exhibition of this enormous collection. There was a constant stream of pilgrims visiting the holy relics who, for their pains, would be given spiritual privileges and Indulgences if they carried out specified acts of respect and contribution to the relevant relics and said prescribed prayers. Frederick managed to be a champion of Luther, who spoke so angrily against Indulgences, while himself dealing in them to a vast extent.

On entering the Duke-Elector's audience chamber, Hamish saw a man in his late fifties with a shrewd and ascetic face. He was on his knees praying at a prie-Dieu, and on a small dais in front of him was a relic of the True Cross in a gold case encrusted with rubies.

The interview which followed was to be the most difficult Hamish had yet encountered, for Frederick proved to be above bribery, above suggestion or persuasion. Many and generous had been the offers put to him by the Habsburg Charles and the Tudor Henry, and he had rejected them all, spending even more time at his prayers with his holy relics.

He listened carefully to everything Hamish said, especially to the offer King Francis had made that he would lead Christendom against the Infidel within three years of his being voted Holy Roman Emperor. That statement seemed to have some effect upon the Duke-Elector, for a thoughtful expression veiled his features. But Hamish soon realized that he was wasting his time attempting negotiations with the man they called 'the Wise'. He thought of the three Archbishops whose worldliness had disturbed him, and yet here was a Duke whose piety put those Archbishops to shame.

The Duke Elector then stunned Hamish by asking him if he knew that Pope Leo had suggested that he, Frederick, become a contender for the Holy Roman crown.

'I had no idea, Your Grace,' Hamish said. 'And will you stand?'

'I am unwilling to discuss my feelings on the matter,' the Duke-Elector said gently. 'Time will tell. No doubt you will hear eventually.'

'Your Grace, I would deem it a great favour if you would tell me now.' The thought of bribing one of the contenders himself would not only be foolhardy but a total waste of time.

'As I have said, My Lord, I am not willing to discuss the subject.' The Duke-Elector's gnarled fingers rested on the gold and ruby casket containing the relic of the True Cross. 'God has not yet shown me the way I must go, but I know that my prayers will be answered soon.' He crossed himself, his eyes closing as if he were praying silently.

Hamish was conscious of an aura about the Duke-Elector, a warmth and sincerity totally lacking in the three Archbishops he had previously visited. He believed it was quite possible that he was in the presence of a saint and he felt humbled.

Afterwards, when the audience was over, Hamish wandered absently out of the palace and into the town. Although he had not managed to sway the Duke-Elector, he felt reasonably assured of the three Archbishops and thus felt that he could now give some time to personal pursuits. Wittenberg took its name from the white sandhills rising nearby in the middle of a plain speared by the river

Elbe. On the northern bank stood the town, which consisted of a long, straggling, wide street running from end to end intersected by others, there being in the region of three or four hundred houses and some two thousand inhabitants. Hamish had heard that the people were said to be fond of religious plays in Passion Week. They were also fond of ale, for the town abounded in breweries. Although Hamish did not know it, Luther had come here to live as a monk and then as a professor, in a house near the Elstergate in the eastern section of the town. Here, he had studied the Bible and St Augustine, writing hundreds of comments and lectures, sermon upon sermon, a myriad letters. Here, shortly after his arrival in 1509, he had written: '*But now, at God's command or by His permission, I am here in Wittenberg. If you desire to know my condition I would say it is by God's favour very good.*'

Even had Hamish known all this, that the monk who was to endanger and transform Christendom had a secure home in the town, his thoughts would not have been upon Luther. He was finding himself filled with yearning to see Athena's face again, to hold her in his arms. It was a strange and unfamiliar sensation and he did not quite know how to deal with it, but he did know that he wanted to buy her gifts. He visited several shops, purchasing a jewelled hood in the German style and a pair of lavender silk sleeves fretted with silverwork and sewn with seed pearls. Then he saw some sumptuous sables which he knew she would love, for she found great pleasure in furs, so he bought the sables, too, and a necklace of plump pink pearls, which, in his mind's eye, he saw gracing her swanlike throat. When he had made his purchases he felt very pleased with himself. He came out of the last shop laden with his packages, walking past the Stadt Kirche without seeing its double tower surmounted by two smaller ones like pepper-pots. He made straight for the lodgings which he and his men had taken for the night and unburdened himself of his parcels. Suddenly he knew the reason for his restlessness. He had been away from his bride for many weeks now, and he was missing her.

He sat down at the supper table, one of his men placing bread and roast beef, capon pie and Wittenberg beer before him. He began to eat, his mind occupied with thoughts of Athena. So he had missed her – his sojourn with Zita Rosa showing him this as nothing else could – but what of Athena herself? Was she missing *him*? No, he thought. Why should he imagine that she had changed? How frequently she had shown her revulsion for him, her manner always cold. She had always flinched from his lovemaking, preferring Lord Marningham's tender wooing to his earthier approaches. He drank deeply of the beer, trying to visualize his return home. No, he could not see Athena running towards him, arms outstretched, to embrace him – far from it. Most probably she would have had a splendid time without him and would feel nothing but dread on his return. He glanced at the pile of gifts. Would those alter her feelings? No, of course not, he chided himself, for love could not be bought. When had he started to think so cynically? She did not love him. She did not want him. He was nothing but a burden foisted upon her by the King.

Suddenly he was no longer hungry. He pushed away the food, but finished the beer and asked for his goblet to be replenished, letting the strong brew nullify the anguish he was beginning to feel. But he knew that he could not remain in an alcoholic stupor for the rest of his life. He would have to come round, face the fact that he was married to a girl who abhorred him. But how he had missed her! And he could fight it no longer: the anguish was like a knife cutting into his heart. God help him, he loved his wife but she despised him. How, in the name of the Holy Virgin, was he going to eradicate himself from this wretched situation?

CHAPTER THIRTEEN

It was good to be back at the Louvre. Hamish went straight for a private audience with the King, where he relayed to Francis every word that he had spoken to the Electors and every word that they had spoken to him.

'I would say that we have them all except the Duke-Elector of Saxony, brother,' Hamish concluded with a grin.

'And I feel that I myself have won over the Elector of Brandenburg, for he seemed well pleased with being offered Royal status in diplomatic ceremonies and the office of Vicar of the Empire after I become Emperor.' Francis beamed. 'And, of course, the hand of the Princess Renée has been greeted with an excellent response. There is, too, the Princess Charlotte; even though she is only an infant, she would prove a precious pawn in the negotiations if that should be necessary. You have done well, brother, and I am pleased with you.' Francis clapped a hand round his foster-brother's shoulders. 'Now, take wine with me. I vow that you will be nauseated with Rhenish wines and longing for the sweet wines of France.'

They went on to talk of the Empire and what its achievement would mean to Francis, and then Hamish went straight to his wife's suite. His heart was pounding as he strode along the corridors of the Palace towards her apartments. In a few more moments he would see her again, his beautiful Athena with the moonlight-coloured hair and the turquoise jewels for eyes. His body throbbed with anticipation. Nonetheless, he knew a moment of misgiving as he opened the door and stepped inside.

Athena was sitting in the window embrasure, sipping fruit juice and eating *petyperneux* – honeyed pastry cakes – with her father. The Comte gaped as Hamish burst into the room, but it was not his face which the latter wished to gaze upon. Words of warm greeting were upon his lips, his arms were raised, held out to Athena – and then he saw her expression.

Seeing him, Athena felt a wave of faintness, a sick and dizzy sensation, the colour swooping from her face. Ashen, with wooden lips, she stared at him, the goblet crashing from her hand. She did not seem to notice the broken fragments on the table, nor the finger-shaped wine stains on her ivory silk gown. She stood up, her lips moving soundlessly, and then swayed as if about to fall. Instantly, the Comte was at her side, supporting her, his face turned angrily to Hamish.

'How dare you burst in here like this and upset my daughter?' he said coldly. 'Can you not see what a shock you gave her? Have you no feeling?'

Hamish found himself stammering apologies. He stepped towards his wife, meaning to speak to her, to tell her how he had missed her, that he was back now, that they would not be parted again. But she turned her face away, hiding her head in her father's shoulder, both their backs turning to him. He knew an instant of white-hot anger, then commonsense prevailed. He must put aside his dreams. In his silly romantic haze he had forgotten how she loathed him. How could he have been so witless as to imagine that she would respond to his loving warmth? Hope evaporated in that moment. He had come back and he had spoiled her happy and contented existence. How could he have forgotten that she despised him? He thought of the gifts he had brought: they were in the ante-chamber waiting for her to open them. He would send a servant in with them.

Athena sat surrounded by the gifts which she had just finished unwrapping. The sables were the most sumptuous she had ever seen; the pink pearls, the German-style hood and the exquisite sleeves would have delighted her in any other circumstances. But she was thinking of her husband's long absence, his sudden return, without one word intervening. Undoubtedly these were guilt-gifts for his secret *affaire* with another woman. He thought to buy her good nature with these presents. She felt cold and sickened, telling the servant who had brought the gifts to take them away.

'Take them back to your master, for I do not want them,' she said, her voice low.

'Away, My Lady? But –'

'I said *away*! Back to your master!' As Athena turned her head with a gesture of dismissal, the servant obeyed her instructions, a puzzled frown on his plump, heavy face.

When she was alone, she plunged her face into her hands and wept. If only he loved her, if only he had told her where he was going, sent letters to her, let her know whether he was alive or dead. Instead, he returned like a whirlwind, laden with gifts to silence her reproaches. He must be feeling very guilty indeed to have given her so many fine presents. She pictured Hamish as he had burst into her apartment an hour or so ago. She thought he looked thinner, but so he would if he had spent the past weeks in arduous lovemaking with his harlot. She swallowed, feeling sudden nausea, pressing a cold hand to her burning cheek. How she hated the woman who had kept him away all this time! If that woman were here now, she would seize a dagger and drive it into the woman's heart over and over and over again until she was dead! A fire of jealousy inflamed her whole body, setting her limbs trembling. It was too late to think of what might have been, to ponder upon the rupture of a love lost forever – a love which had never been given the smallest opportunity to grow and develop. Two lives wasted, his and hers, and she was powerless to do anything about it.

*

When his servant came back to him bearing the returned gifts, Hamish went cold with shock. So, she would reject everything – him, and even his gifts. He smashed his fist into his palm, suffused with an unbearable, aching longing. He spent the next hours in contemplative mood, racked with indecision, thinking first of Athena, then of his ex-mistresses about the Court, and then of Athena again. No doubt she would be delighted if he did not seek out her bed, but he was her husband and she was his wife, and he did have a longing for a son to inherit his estates. Indeed, it was more than a longing: it was absolute necessity, for, without a son to inherit them, his possessions would revert to the Crown and although he loved his brother dearly, he could not die happy knowing that his marriage had been without fruit. Yes, he must have a son.

That night he went to his wife's apartment, steeling himself against the acrimony in her eyes. Wryly, he thought of how he had longed for her when he had been in Zita Rosa's arms. Now, here he was with Athena and she was as cold as an ice-maiden, his very own Snow Queen.

The ensuing hours were the most unsatisfactory either of them had ever spent. All Hamish's attempts at tenderness were rebuffed coldly. Athena was tense, rigid in his arms, her mind thronging with thoughts of his secret mistress. All Hamish could think of were his decimated dreams: the dreams which had carried him back so urgently to the Louvre.

Finally Athena hissed, 'Get it over with and be gone!'

A harsh fury swept through him. They had made a bad match, it was a disaster, he would admit that, but did she have to be so merciless? Could she not have some pity for his feelings? He tried to kiss her, but she turned away her head. He kissed her cheek, her neck, her shoulders. She was as rigid as if paralysed. He cupped her breast, marvelling at the satiny smoothness of her flesh. She was like a woman carved out of ice: no response did she show. He almost despaired, but it was not his nature to retreat before the battle was done. Ah, Holy Virgin, why did it have to be a battle when it should be love and love alone? But nothing was going to make him admit it while she was so chilly with him.

His hand caressed her stomach, her hips, her thighs. His mouth twisted. To beget an heir without love: a bitter thought, but one which he must repress. There was nothing else for it.

She smelled of roses and gilly-flowers. How he would have loved to kiss her all over, from head to toe, gently, sweetly and slowly. But her eyes were screwed tightly shut, her face averted, almost as if she were in pain. His fingers traced an arc through the moonlight coloured hair between her thighs. It was soft as swansdown, and she gave a little jerk as he touched her there. Was it response? But no – her head was still averted, her hands clenched at her sides. Perhaps, if he continued, she would relax. His fingers slid between her legs. How warm she was there and, surprisingly, moist. He had hoped to rouse her, but suddenly she moved, pushing his hand away angrily.

'Did I not tell you to get it over with and go?' she choked.

Deeply disappointed, he caged her in his arms, lowering himself on top of her and driving into her body. She gave a cry, but it sounded more like anguish than enjoyment. He scythed in and out of her body urgently, wishing that he could speak to her, tell her how he felt about her, tell her that, even unresponsive, she was the most desirable woman he had ever made love to.

She wanted it over quickly, so that was how it would be. He felt the beginnings of his passion and let it freely flow, jetting fiercely into her body. After, he rolled away from her, and she turned her back on him, curling up into a tight little ball. He waited until he had regained his breath and then he slipped on his nightrobe and silently left the room.

Hearing the door close behind him, tears of acid pricked

behind Athena's lids. He was gone: it was over. Only by keeping the most supreme control over herself had she been able to bear it. When he had told her that he was only there to get himself a son she could have gouged out his eyes. So, his secret harlot for pleasure and herself for begetting sons, she thought. Well, he would get nothing else from her; certainly no visible sign of pleasure or delight in his lovemaking. She had fought hard to repress her every response, succeeding admirably. But it had not been easy: she had longed to curve her body against his, to return his kisses ardently, to murmur that she loved him, that she had missed him desperately, that she could not live without him. Now all her vain and empty hopes were dashed: he had got what he came for and he had gone.

Far into the night she wept, wondering if tonight she had, indeed, conceived a son and, if so, whether it would mean that her husband would not come to her bed again. She did not know how she would take such news. Would it be better to endure further such assaults as the one which had just gone before, agonizingly loveless as it had been, or never to share another night with him, to see him about the Court with his other women? She did not know if she could bear either.

The following weeks were no better, Hamish and Athena glaring at one another if they should happen to meet about the Palace, not one courteous word being exchanged between them. There was only one consolation: Athena did not see Hamish surrounded by a bevy of beautiful courtesans. Not at any time, not even when she caught him unawares, was he accompanied by any of his ex-mistresses. She thought of them as ex-mistresses, but how was she to know that they really were discarded? She thought again and again, most bitterly, of the words she had heard him exchange with his Irish cousin in the window embrasure at Mullally Hall, and, as the weeks progressed and she did not become pregnant, she began to think that Hamish's cousin had been right.

The night-time visits continued every few days, but Hamish never remained in her bed after making love to her; for all she knew, he went straight to one of his mistresses' beds, where he would be sure of a warm welcome. Matters did not ease between them: she was as cold and forbidding when he bedded her as she had been on his return to the Palace, and he was as brusque, mindful of her earlier comments to make haste.

And then, in June, the Electors gathered at Frankfurt, as was the custom, each of them casting his vote for the Holy Roman Emperor. Despite all Francis's and Hamish's efforts, the voting went in favour of King Charles. On 28 June 1519, the Habsburg King was unanimously voted Emperor of the Holy Roman Empire, as Charles the Fifth. Charles was in Barcelona when the news reached him a week later, and by then all Europe knew.

Hearing the news, Athena had no way of knowing her husband's part in the intrigue which had gone before. She heard that King Charles had been elected, as did everyone, and although Francis put on a good face to the world, in private he was bitterly disappointed. It was rumoured that it had cost King Charles eight hundred and fifty thousand gold florins to gain his Imperial Throne, but all King Francis said before he went hunting at Fontainebleau was:

'I am well pleased not to have the Empire's cares.'

Unfortunately, the night before the news of the new Emperor had reached Paris, Hamish had asked Athena if she were with child. Paling, she had shaken her head. Next day, seeing Hamish's dour face, dark and glowering, she attributed his ill-humour to the fact that she was not expecting the son he craved. How he must be loathing her: for not only had she been foisted upon him, but she had failed to conceive.

In fact, Hamish was bitterly down-hearted by the news that his master had failed to gain the Imperial Throne. He felt totally to blame, totally responsible. He had never failed his foster-brother before, and he could not bear failure. For the first time in his life, he found Louise of Savoy looking at him with accusation in her eyes. She seemed to blame him personally for her son's failure to become Emperor: as well she might, for had he not been entrusted with all the important secret negotiations which were to have ensured that Francis won the Throne? And he had been so sure of those three Archbishops . . . He did not know what to do with himself. The King seemed not to want his company any more, not even on the hunting expeditions which they had loved to go on together. Louise of Savoy treated him to her most contemptuous stares, and the King's sister, Marguerite, composed a pointed verse about friends who turned into traitors.

Not having witnessed this, for she kept as far away from her husband as possible, Athena attributed Hamish's ugly moods to her own failings. He still came to her bed, now more determinedly than ever, she thought.

By mid-July Athena knew that Hamish had got what he wanted. She was with child. She decided immediately that she would not give him the satisfaction of knowing; that she would conceal the knowledge from him. She felt sick, guilty, and trapped in turn, not knowing how to pacify her turbulent thoughts. If she did tell him, he would stop coming to her bed and she had long ago decided that his visits were infinitely preferable to his absences. For some weeks she managed to conceal the information, telling only the Comte, who was with her more than anyone and noticed that she was looking peaky. But soon she began to suffer from morning sickness, the dry powerful heat of summer making her feel even worse than might have been expected. It was true that they were now ensconced in the Château of Amboise, far cooler and healthier than Paris, but, all the same, Athena thought that she could not have felt more debilitated.

For some reason known only to himself, now Hamish remained to sleep in her bed after he had made love to her. He had started to do this as soon as they had come to Amboise. At first she had thought that the woman who was interesting him at the moment had been left behind at the Louvre and that was why he no longer slept elsewhere, but although she examined the ranks of ladies carefully whenever she had the opportunity, she could not find one of them missing. All the ones who had been at the Louvre were here now at Amboise.

Hamish would have had to find out sooner or later, of course. One morning she woke before he did, feeling very sick indeed. Rushing straight for the dressing-room, closing the door behind her, she reached for a bowl. When she had finished she turned to return to the bedroom, hoping that if she crept in silently he would not hear her.

The door to her dressing-room was open, Hamish leaning against its frame.

'You have not been making any sea journeys that I know of, mistress.'

She stared at him dumbly, her heart frozen. Now he would learn the truth; he would stop sharing her bed, he would return to his mistresses and all their time spent together would be over.

'No, my Lord,' she whispered, unable to meet his gaze. 'Perhaps it was that supper we had . . .'

'But I am not sick, and I ate exactly the same food as did you.'

She was acutely aware of his bronzed, muscular body where his robe parted. This might be the last time they were together in such intimate circumstances. She felt totally wretched, a wave of dizziness engulfed her. Instantly he was at her side, his arms supporting her.

'You are with child,' he said.

'Yes, it is true.' Bitterness rasped in her voice. 'I am carrying your child.'

'My son,' he breathed.

'It might be a daughter,' she snapped. 'There is more than one sex in the world, even if you would have it otherwise.' She could think of nothing but the long, lonely months ahead without his company.

He scooped her up in his arms as if she weighed nothing at all and carried her across to the bed, depositing her gently upon it, almost with reverence. He plumped up the pillows behind her head and pulled the coverlet up to her waist. She looked up into his midnight blue eyes, astonished to find that they were brimming with warmth. So that is how it is going to be, she thought: I am his brood mare so he can be kind to me now. The mother of his son deserves tenderness, and that was all she meant to him – She was the vessel which carried his heir.

'Can I get you anything?' he smiled.

'No,' she muttered sulkily, but the smile did not drop from his face. He was obviously intensely happy at the news and did not intend to let anything dismay him.

'Fruit juice, perhaps; a madeleine?'

'Yes, perhaps a madeleine . . .'

He summoned the valet and asked him to bring a platter of madeleines, and when they arrived he sat upon the bed beside Athena, holding the platter while she selected a cake and nibbled at it.

'You feel better now, my love?' he asked.

So she was 'his love' now. 'Yes, I feel better,' she said irritably, not meeting his eyes.

He stroked a fingertip across her hand. 'If you should wish anything, anything at all, you have only to tell me, and it will be yours.'

'So, I am worthy of gifts now that I am bearing your child?'

'If you remember, I brought you gifts before but you rejected them all.'

'Those! They were but guilt-gifts!'

'Guilt-gifts? I do not understand . . .'

'No, you would not. Or rather, you pretend you do not. I *know*.'

'What is it you know that I do not?'

'If you do not know then I am not going to tell you.' Her courage had failed her: she had not dared to broach the subject of his secret mistress.

'If you persist in talking in this mysterious way I can see that we shall get nowhere,' he said, still smiling benignly.

'But have we not always gone in just that direction – nowhere?'

'You are dissatisfied with our relationship. Well, I cannot blame you. You were forced upon me, but –'

'And *you* were forced upon me!' she stormed. 'I have no say in the matter, no say whatsoever. I was less than a pawn, manipulated as if in a chess game. And who was the winner of the game? Not I, no certainly not I.' Tears glimmered in her eyes.

Immediately he took her hands in his. 'Do not weep, my love. I would not have you upset, not now.'

'No, certainly not *now*! It might upset your child – it might endanger your son, and that would never do, would it?'

He sighed. 'I had hoped that we might become friends, Athena.'

'Yes, it would be more fitting if the mother of your son were also your friend, would it not? But I fear that cannot be, not under the circumstances.'

He looked at her with puzzlement in his eyes, but knowing what she did how could she trust him? 'Athena, my love, if I had one wish in the entire world it would be that you were my friend.'

She almost softened then, but remembered in time his long absences, the manner in which he left her without explanation, his dark moods, the way he had forced himself upon her repeatedly to get himself the son he craved. How could she forget such intolerable things? If he thought that he could get away with such bad behaviour, would he not increase it? He would trample all over her if she let him; but she had no intention of being ground beneath his heel . . .

August passed, and Hamish's behaviour continued as considerate as ever. He was gentle, thoughtful, patient. He told her that he had consulted the King's physicians on her behalf and that he had been told it would be better for them to abstain from sexual union until his son was born.

The blood pounded in Athena's head. Yes, she had been right all along: all he had wanted was a reason to forsake intimacy with her. How blatant he was about it, not even attempting to conceal his eagerness to reject her body.

'Your *son*! Always it is your son!' she raged. 'Why do you speak only of a boy, never of a girl? I would not mind a daughter.' Her mouth twisted. How she longed to beg him not to desert her. The words were trembling on her tongue and she had to fight them back. She would never plead with him, humble herself to such an extent.

He was eager to pacify her, obviously thinking of the child lying in her womb. 'A son or a daughter, then,' he said. 'Whichever it is, that is what the physicians said.'

She was consumed by a desire to beat her hands against his broad, solid chest. Did he not feel one twinge of regret that they must lie apart? Was there no feeling in him? A thought entered her head: if she had a son would he be as moody and as cold-hearted as Hamish? Two of them like that – how could she bear it?

By way of rebellion, she stared him straight between the eyes and said: 'I have the strongest feeling that I carry a girl child. From the beginning I have felt that.'

She exulted at the look of disappointment which appeared on his face, and then she felt ashamed of herself.

She had wanted to wound him and she had wounded herself as well.

'If God wills our child to be a daughter, then so be it,' he said, but the words seemed forced from his throat.

'Would you not like a fair daughter, a pretty girl to show off at Court? You have a way with females,' she said pointedly.

'Daughters cannot inherit,' he said grimly.

'You speak of the Salic Law of the Franks. In England there is no such nonsensical law.'

'You seem to know a lot about England, my love.'

She put her hand to her lips. How had she known that there was no Salic Law in England? But, of course, the convent where she was raised; they would have spoken of it.

'You forget that I was brought up in an English convent,' she retorted haughtily.

'Nuns do not usually involve themselves with the laws of the land.'

'Well, they must have done, must they not, or else how would I have known?'

He shrugged, feeling dejected. If she truly felt that she was going to bear a daughter he knew that he would be deeply disappointed. But he would continue to care for her. How could he stop now, even though she had become a tartar since discovering that she was with child? He believed that she must be feeling bitterly unhappy, first being forced into marriage and now being forced into bearing a child for a man she did not love. He wanted to make amends to her, but he did not know how to go about it. She was so prickly, so unapproachable, these days. He would bring her gifts, peace offerings, but she seemed unmoved by them, sometimes giving them a scathing reception.

'I suppose, after what the physicians said, that you will no longer continue to sleep with me?' She said the words as coolly as she could manage, her back straight, her head high.

'Sleeping beside you will not harm the child. They have nothing against that.'

'How very generous of them. So you will stay by me at night?'

'Yes. Then I can take care of you if necessary.'

'I am not an invalid, you know.'

'All the same, I think it will be for the best.'

He cannot bear to be parted from his son even before he is born, she thought. If only I had the same attraction for him.

Even the baking August heat did not stop him from sleeping beside her each night. She grew to look forward to bedtime, when she would retire and he would join her soon after. He would ask her how she felt and if she wanted anything. Sometimes he would bring her a drink or some fruit, for she had a great appetite for apples. Then they would settle down for the night in almost companionable silence.

Amboise was beautiful in the late summer. The King had spent much of his childhood there. The gardens were ornate and expansive and Athena took to walking in them regularly, sometimes with the Comte, sometimes alone. It was on one of these excursions, as she walked alone through the rose arbours towards the woodland copse, that she saw Hamish sitting on a rustic seat with a beautiful young girl whom Athena had never seen before. She stopped, transfixed, feeling as if she had been struck in the stomach. Stepping back into the shadows of some tall rose bushes, she watched the two, while her heart pounded painfully in her breast.

The girl was about her own age, with glossy, jet-black hair coiled round her head and looped with seed pearls. Her gown was brilliant scarlet silk, her sleeves puffed and slashed to reveal gold silk linings netted with silver. Her face was glowingly pretty, her black brows fine and arched, her nose slightly retroussé, her mouth curved in a wide smile. Hamish was sitting very close to her on the rustic seat, his arm flung casually round her shoulders. He seemed intent on her every word, leaning forward and listening carefully.

Athena gripped one of the rose-bush supports, leaning heavily upon it, as she saw her husband take one of the girl's hands and squeeze it warmly. The girl continued to listen raptly. How could he betray her, oh how could he, and when she was expecting his child as well? Out here, where any eye could see, making a fool of her before the whole Court! It did not matter that the copse was some way from the rest of the gardens and that no one had seen the couple except herself, she felt humiliated all the same. She wanted to be far, far away from this spot, wishing she had never seen them together. Oh God, why had she walked in this part of the garden? She rested a hand on her stomach, thinking of the child lying within. Surely it would be experiencing the same waves of shock, which would surely be bad for it? She must get away, she must try to forget what she had seen.

Turning on her heel, she retraced her steps. But after the first bleakness, tears were coming, fast and fierce, and she made her way as quickly as possible to her bed-chamber where she locked the door behind her, flung herself on the bed, and sobbed.

Everything had seemed so much better between them. Athena knew that she had been waspish, but he had seemed so tolerant of her moods, and anyway expectant mothers were not known for their placidity. But it seemed that her acid tongue had driven him into another woman's arms, and surely this girl was his secret lover, for she had never seen her about the Court before, either in Paris or here. Such a striking girl, so proudly sure of herself. She lay there sobbing for some time, torturing herself with thoughts of Hamish making love to the raven-haired beauty. No doubt, now that he could not use her body he was seeking out his mistress with even greater energies. A spasm of jealous fury burnt through her body leaving her trembling. He was hers, *hers*! He had no right to pursue other women. She wept until she was exhausted, until there were no more tears, then she slept.

When she woke it was dark and Hamish's place in the bed was empty. The memory of what she had seen returned to sicken her, and she pressed the back of her hand to her mouth to repress her cries. It was well after midnight and he had not come to her bed. So, he was with the girl in the scarlet dress. No doubt at this very moment they were entwined, naked in one another's arms. She sat up, dragging Hamish's pillow towards her, pummelling it with her fists, wishing it were him. How could he behave like this, how could he do this to her? Had she not given him everything he wanted? She continued to torture herself with thoughts of her husband's infidelity, her anguish burgeoning. She lay there for long hour after long hour, thinking of him, sometimes with fury, at other times with a desperate love. She knew that everything she had ever dreaded had come to pass. She had known their marriage was doomed from the start. He was accustomed to promiscuity: how did she expect him to change just because of a simple ceremony in the Chapel of the Louvre?

The hours passed and still he did not come. Did he think that she was blind, that she would not know what he was doing? Oh, she knew, and the knowing of it was torture. Finally, wretched and bone-weary, she fell into a fitful slumber.

Next morning, she woke to find Hamish sleeping innocently beside her. What time he had arrived she could not say, but there was no doubt in her mind as to where he had spent most of the night.

Shock had been supplanted by numbness, and Athena lay in bed looking and feeling very ill. When Hamish awoke and saw how pallid she was, with dark smudges beneath her eyes, he hovered round her attentively, bringing her breakfast himself and sitting on the bed to help her eat. But she had little appetite. Then, just as he was carrying away the tray, she knew that she was going to be very sick.

'The bowl, the bowl,' she cried. He rushed into the dressing-room and fetched what she required, sitting beside her as she vomited, holding her head and comforting her with gentle words. She seemed to have spent half her life being sick while he comforted her. It was an ironic thought. She lay back amongst the pillows, her face as white as they were.

Hamish took her hands and patted them.

'*Ma pauvre chère*, how you suffer. But I want you to know that I shall not neglect you while you are pregnant.'

But what of afterwards, she thought bitterly. Why, have you not started to neglect me already? She wanted to scream in his face: 'Where were you last night? Who was that harlot I saw you with by the rose arbours?' but she dreaded the answer. If he responded frankly, admitting that the girl in the scarlet gown was his paramour, she would want to die. Life would be an eternal grave without her husband's love.

She could not fault Hamish's behaviour during the next few weeks. She stayed in bed for some days feeling weak and frequently nauseous. The King's own physician visited her, but he could not tell her anything that she did not know already: that she was carrying her baby badly, that the pregnancy was going to be a difficult one. She was told to rest, to lie down as much as possible, not to walk, and certainly not to ride. He advised a distillation of mint to soothe her stomach, sweet chervil and sorrel to stimulate her appetite, and motherwort to cheer her spirits and settle her womb.

The physician's presence was distasteful to Athena. Aged and decrepit, all his teeth had rotted, and his nails were thick with dirt. Yet he had attended Queen Claude through her pregnancies and so Athena thought that she must have trust in him. However, she balked at the instructions to remain inactive. She understood that she must give up riding, but to be deprived of her walks in the gardens was unbearable. She drank the herbal brews diligently, as instructed, but within a few weeks the enforced inactivity began to grate on her nerves. She lay on her *chaise longue* thinking of the scent of roses and gillyflowers, the feel of the September sun upon her skin. She felt that the room was closing in around her. She sent her maid away, saying that she was going to sleep, but then she got up, slowly, carefully, feeling dizzy but determined to get out in the fresh air. She put on a loose-fitting turquoise silk gown, leaving the stomacher unlaced. She felt like a fugitive as she walked along the Palace corridors and out onto the terraces, where she inhaled the fresh, invigorating air deeply. She had done little but lie around for weeks now, and her legs felt like paper, as if they might crumple. She held tightly to the filigree rails as she made her way down the first steps of the terraces. She walked across the chamomile lawns, inhaling their sweet scent with delight. How beautiful it was out here, like Paradise. She would sit by the Singing Fountains and allow the sunshine to restore her.

Something flickered out of the corner of her eye, a flash of brilliant scarlet. Her heart gave a massive lurch and pounded into life, the heat racing into her cheeks. At the same moment she lost her footing and fell down the rest of the stone steps with a sickening thud, the sky shaking above her.

She lay there, all the breath driven from her body by the impact, gazing up at the wildly revolving sun, then she felt the pain beginning deep in her stomach. A contraction! At once she panicked, waves of ice-cold shock sweeping up and down her body. Her baby: she was going to lose her baby! She fought back paralysing terror, calling out for help over and over, but no one heard, no one was passing. she tried to manoeuvre herself into a more comfortable position but fresh pain shot through her, as if someone had plunged a knife into her back low down between her hips. Tears burst from her eyes and she sobbed with the pain. She dared not move again. Perhaps if she lay very still she could save her baby.

It was more than three quarters of an hour later before a group of courtiers walked by and heard her cries.

'My husband – fetch my husband,' she begged. 'Lord Mullally – oh please . . .'

She wept afresh when she saw Hamish, who scooped her up into his arms and carried her into the Palace, placing her very gently on her bed. The physician arrived and immediately began to rail at Athena for having gone out when he had warned her to stay in and rest.

Hamish glared at him and instructed him to be silent. Immediately the man clamped his lips together, his face showing outraged pride.

'Your son – I am losing your son,' Athena whimpered and Hamish, his face stricken, cradled her in his arms.

'Can you not do something?' he said to the physician.

The man shrugged his shoulders, saying that one could not halt Nature, but of course, if Her Ladyship would submit to having clysters and leeches applied . . .

'My wife is already weak enough without being bled,' Hamish growled.

'Then I can do nothing,' the man almost snarled, turning on his heel.

Hamish at once sent a page for the Queen's midwife. She was a bustling, efficient person who was proud to have been at the births of all King Francis's children, and she immediately took control of the situation, shooing Hamish out of the chamber. With skilled hands she examined Athena, keeping to herself her serious misgivings. Shapely hips but what small, narrow bones: it was a blessing that the child was premature, for she doubted if he would have been born at all if he had been full-term. She had attended others of similar build and they had always lost their infants.

What followed was a vortex of pain for Athena. She sobbed and wailed and clung to the midwife, who soothed her gently. Even though labour had begun and Athena was not too far advanced into her pregnancy, it was a protracted miscarriage. When finally the tiny, perfectly formed body gushed into the world in a pool of blood, it could be seen clearly to be a boy. Tears flowed freely down her cheeks. A boy. Hamish would have had the son he wanted if only she had obeyed the physician's instructions.

Bearing up the tiny form, the midwife placed it on a sheet of linen to one side, and then she bathed Athena and helped her to put on a clean gown before Hamish came in to see her. The midwife beckoned to him and took him to one side to show him the little corpse. He looked at it and tears filled his eyes. His son. So white and dead and cold. His wife! He sat down on the bed beside Athena, reaching out his arms to enfold her. But she could not see the expression on his face for the tears in her own eyes. Misery was sweeping through her, and she turned away from Hamish's arms. When he attempted to move closer, she flung up her arms to push him away.

Deeply hurt, he let his arms fall to his sides, and then the midwife gestured to him to go outside for a moment, which he did. In the corridor, she begged him to be patient with his wife, explaining about the depressions which followed childbirth, especially when the child was born dead, and how some very sensitive women suffered agonies of grief. She would come round in time, the woman told Hamish, and the best solution would be another baby as soon as that could be managed. However, she warned, he must consider his wife's slender bones and how much he loved her.

'Yes, I love her desperately,' he said. 'What about her bones – ?'

'If you want an heir, all well and good,' the woman said, 'but if you love your wife then you must accept the fact that she could die having your baby. Had your son not been miscarried today, his size might well have killed his mother.' She explained that Athena's hips were among the narrowest she had ever seen. 'She is not made for child-bearing,' she concluded.

Hamish turned away, leaning against the wall, his head on his arms. The midwife waited while he fought for self-control. Finally he turned to her, his eyes hollow.

'Can you tell me no more? Is there no possibility she could survive a child's birth? If she should die . . .' He hid his face in his arm again.

'There is nothing more I can say, My Lord. Your wife or your son; perhaps neither: the choice is yours.' The woman gave him a glance of sympathy before she returned to her patient.

Alone, Hamish faced the awful truth. He longed for a son, but he loved his wife, however much she loathed him. If he made her pregnant she could die. How could he bring himself to make love to her knowing that the result might be her death? Had she not suffered more than enough already? God help him, he would never willingly cause her death. So, he must put aside forever his longing for a son.

Hamish did his utmost to cheer and comfort his wife after their loss, but she was tearful, weak and resentful at his presence. Nonetheless, he cared for her solicitously, bringing her gifts and little surprises. The Comte, too, was a constant visitor, and his gifts she welcomed, although she was contemptuous of Hamish's offerings, as she had ever been. But now, as her body adjusted to its loss, her emotional condition was, for a time, out of her control. Every time she saw Hamish she thought of her dead son, then she thought of the young girl in the scarlet gown and her stomach would churn.

But Nature, which can wound, can also heal, and gradually her mood began to improve, although she felt that she would never get over the loss of her son. She began to get up for longer periods and Hamish would accompany her in walks through the gardens. There was no doubt that he wanted her strong again, she thought – so that she could give him a living son next time!

One day, as they were walking by the Singing Fountains, Hamish told her that he had bought a château for them in the Forest of Fontainebleau, not far from Paris, and that as soon as she was strong enough for the journey they would move there. He believed that the rigours of Court life would be too much for her at the moment.

She stared at him. So he had bought them a home away from Court like other husbands did who wished to get rid of their wives! No doubt as soon as they were settled there he would vanish, leaving her alone. No doubt he would return immediately to Court to take up his life of lechery. She thought of her father and his kindly and innocent love for her. Compared to the Comte she saw her husband as a man of sly duplicity, a man who lusted after his secret paramour. She imagined what life in Fontainebleau Forest would be like: for a time sweet, until he got her pregnant again, and then he would desert her for the gay, laughing creature who wore bold gowns and, no doubt, had passions to match.

'You are not pleased with the idea?' Hamish could not understand the stiff look on her face.

'Will my father be able to visit me there?'

'But of course, as often as he likes.'

'What is the name of the château?' she asked, trying to show interest.

'The Château Blanche – the White House. It is a former Royal hunting lodge, used by the Capet Kings of France. It needs quite a good deal doing to it, but you will, of course, have a free hand. I want you to feel that it is your home, Athena, my love.' He took her hands in his. 'You do not look too happy. Are you thinking that you will miss the Court?'

She thought of the sexual licence at Court, of the immorality, the drunkenness, the frenetic tempo of life.

'No, I shall not miss the Court,' she told him.

'Then you are thinking that you will miss your father? But, as I have said, he can visit as frequently as he pleases. He must treat our home as his.'

So *you* can feel less guilty, she thought. She managed a pale smile and said, 'That will be good.' But she knew that her father would be torn, for he revelled in Court life.

'Then you will be happy?' he pressed.

How could she promise such an elusive emotion, feeling as she did? She did not reply.

CHAPTER FOURTEEN

The Château Blanche was an appealing fourteenth-century mansion built three years before his death by Philippe le Bel, who had used it regularly for his hunting sorties. It had a pleasing redstone façade, now faded to a dull pink, and a squat circular turret at each corner. The outside appeared in excellent condition, but the inside told a different story. Many years of neglect had caused crumbling and cracked plaster, dry-rot in the floorboards, ugly patches of damp in the salon, though Athena could see that it would be a most beautiful room when it had been redecorated and the damp stains cured.

A mixture of emotions filled her as she walked round the house with Hamish. She had vowed that she would hate the place, that she would be surly and hostile when discussing it. But that vow was now forgotten, for her heart had gone out to this old hunting lodge, so sadly neglected, and before they had explored more than half the rooms she was making plans for repairs and new colour schemes. So what if she was being brought here in order that Hamish could go off with his paramour? She was not going to sit around with a sour face, looking as dejected as the lodge: she would spend her energies on transforming her new home.

Hamish was watching her intently. It was important to him that she took a liking to the Château Blanche. He had seen that she was bored with the constant but meaningless round of Court activities and that she needed something to divert her attentions, something on which she could deploy her intelligence. He understood exactly how she felt: had he not managed to escape it during the frequent trips abroad, he could not have borne the facile Court existence. (He thought of some of the more recent jests devised to alleviate the tedium. The Comte Dunois had let a sow and her piglets loose in the corridors of the Louvre. On another occasion, dogs had been set on a wild boar to see which survived the encounter; all the dogs had been badly gored and had later died in agony, the boar being pronounced the victor. Already another bout was being planned to see if the dogs would be the vanquishers next time. Hamish knew that Athena had been nauseated by the latter event in particular, and that she had wept for the butchered dogs.) Wary of her favours being sought only because she was the King's ex-mistress, Athena had made few friends in the Palace. Hamish had seen that it was a state of affairs which could not be allowed to continue. There was her health to consider, too. Paris was not the most salubrious of places, whereas Fontainebleau Forest was idyllic. He hoped to see roses in her cheeks very soon. His only fear was that she would be lonely when he went off again on the King's secret business, which he must shortly do. He was desperately eager to win back the King's friendship, for Francis and the Royal Family continued to be cool with him after the débâcle of the quest for the Imperial Crown. But it was his private agony which disturbed him most of all. He knew that if he remained with Athena he would be tempted to make love to her, and he could not forget the midwife's warning.

How could he say to his wife, 'Your hips are narrow: a child could kill you'? He phrased and rephrased the words in his head, but they always came out sounding callous and threatening. He could never bring himself to speak them. Besides, how could he destroy her hopes of having children of her own? He could see that she still grieved for their lost son – how would she feel if told that she must have no more, be they sons or daughters? If he was away on the King's business Athena would be safe from the danger of childbirth.

As he walked with her from room to room in the Château Blanche, his heart ached with love and desire for her, though his face showed none of this. They sat on a carved, corner bench, its design one of fleur-de-lis, gilly-flowers, roses and nettle leaves, and discussed how the main salon could be put to rights. All the time they were speaking Hamish was consumed with the urge to devour Athena's lips with kisses. He imagined himself taking her into his arms and thrusting his tongue between her teeth to explore her mouth. Slowly he would push down the bodice of her rose-pink gown to free her breasts, now more voluptuous since her pregnancy. While cradling the velvet mounds he would assault them with kisses, nipping at them tenderly to rouse her. She would gasp and move against him, her fingers probing inside his doublet, searching for his naked flesh. Then she would sigh that she loved him, that she needed him. Such acute happiness would soar in him at those words, at the feel of her hands on his body, that he would be instantly ready for sexual union. She would lie back invitingly, pulling up her skirts round her waist so that he could see her opaline skin glimmering with its silky heart of moonlight-coloured hair. Perhaps he would bend down to kiss that heart, to explore its crevices with his tongue. Perhaps by that time he would be too impatient and he would want to enter her forcefully, driving deep into her body. She would convulse and moan his name as if stirred to her very depths and that would rouse him even more, so that he continued to spear her over and over again. He would palm her milky buttocks, inflamed by the feel of them, so soft and round and velvet, then he would pull her hard against him so that they seemed forged into one being, one entity. She would twist her head from side to side, a cry on her lips, her hands clawing at his back while he curved to her body and tore into her more and more violently as his climax approached.

'Hamish! You are not listening to me! Hamish, I asked you if we should enhance this sunny room any further by using yellow or whether we should mute the brightness a little, perhaps with a softer pastel shade?' Athena looked at her husband quizzically. He seemed very far away. Were his thoughts at Court with his paramour? Anger twisted deep within her like a live thing. She thought of all the lonely nights she had spent since losing her son, nights when Hamish had not come to her bed and she had known he was with his harlot. Then there had been the two strange occasions when he had come into her bed-chamber suddenly, with a fierce expression on his face. Each time he had begun to make love to her with his usual ardour and she had begun to respond, despite herself. Then, having roused her, and when she was lying with legs parted waiting for him to take her, he had abruptly torn her arms from round his neck and hastened from the room, leaving her bemused, upset and bitterly disappointed. She could not imagine why he had behaved in such an odd fashion, unless he was feeling disloyal to his paramour by bedding her and could not bring himself to finish what he had begun. Yes, that must be it, she had decided, for what other solution could there possibly be? Angrily she had felt that her husband had made a fool of her, awakening her desires then leaving her unfulfilled. It was behaviour of the most cavalier kind, and she wished she could promise herself never to let him arouse her again.

Hamish was staring at her, his eyes narrowed so that their colour looked densely black, giving his face a cold, hard appearance. She repeated her question.

'I will leave everything to you to decide, Athena. This is your home and you must do with it as you wish.' He reached out and took her hand, pressing her fingers gently. How false a gesture, she thought; he seeks to placate me after his guilty thoughts. He knew every palliative trick and used them freely, but she was not deceived. Of course he would let her have a free hand with the Château Blanche, to allow himself two free hands for his harlot!

Athena discovered a deep delight in supervising the repairs

and redecoration to the Château Blanche. It was true that sometimes the noise of sawing and hammering, the shouts of the workmen, made her long for peace, but as she saw the hunting lodge gradually restored to its former glory, she realized what a satisfying task was hers. It was the first time she had had sole control of such a project, and now she wondered how she had managed before without such work. They had been here now for five weeks and on the morrow Hamish was going back to Paris. All he had said was that the King had summoned him. In truth, she had not expected him to stay for so long as five weeks, but he had, and she guessed that the tortured look she sometimes surprised upon his face was due to his long separation from his mistress.

The servants Hamish had found for the hunting lodge were good, sound people, their steward a man who could be trusted implicitly. Athena had no misgivings about being left alone with them. It was the thought of separation from her husband which unsettled her. How long he would be gone she did not know, but she knew that she would miss him desperately, even more, if that were possible, than he was missing his paramour. Five weeks at the château and he had kept well away from her bed, although there had been several occasions when she had seen a certain light in his eye and had thought that he was going to make approaches to her. But then that shuttered look had come over his face, as if he were barricading himself from her, and she had become crestfallen. She often thought of becoming pregnant again, but as things were that seemed an impossible dream. She knew that a baby would be a comfort to her. She knew, too, that Hamish wanted a son. Why, then, did he not come to her bed? There could be only one reason: he found her proximity repulsive and longed for his secret mistress.

That night, the night before Hamish left for Court, they dined together in the small dining hall, which was now decorated in blue and white, and looked at one another across the candlelit table. Strange how the tapers' light distorted one's vision, Athena thought; she could almost imagine there was fond, tender love in Hamish's eyes, his mouth curving sweetly.

'You are sure that you will not feel lonely here?' he said.

'My father will be here before the autumn is out.'

'So you are anticipating that I shall be absent a long time?'

'And will you not? When the *King* calls do you not always give him all of your time, all of your energies?' She stressed the word meaningfully.

'I have a certain duty to my foster-brother, it is true, but I shall try to be back as soon as possible –' he paused, then added, 'my love,' the words hanging crisply in the air between them.

'I would not have you hurry if it displeases you and His Majesty,' she commented sarcastically.

'Nonetheless, I shall be back here as soon as I am able.'

She wanted to shriek out: Enough of this pretence! I know why you are going away: not to see the King but to see your whore!

Instead, she looked down at her platter of capon in wine and orange sauce and felt revolted by the sight. She had never felt less like eating. He was going, and with no sign of regret whatsoever. She would be left here in the forest, thinking of her lost husband, her lost son, and yearning for them both. Pressing a hand to her lips, she pushed away her dinner.

'You are not ill, my love?'

'No, I am not ill. Do not fear that I shall try to keep you here by such means.'

'Indeed, I had not imagined that you would.' He sounded surprised.

The charade of their last dinner together continued as servants brought in pink and white blancmange, quince jelly and syllabub – sweetened cream flavoured with wine and beaten to a stiff froth.

When we have eaten this he will go to his room and I will go to mine, Athena thought dolefully. Then tomorrow he will be gone and I shall be alone. The tapers seemed to dim. She felt as if she were looking at Hamish from far away. Although they had barely touched during these past few weeks, how satisfying she had found them and how much she wanted them to continue. Nothing, of course, could make him stay; she knew that. And how forlorn it made her feel.

For the rest of the meal she tried not to meet his eyes for fear that he would see the desolation in them. When the servants had cleared the board, she and Hamish sat by the fireside in what could have passed for companionable silence. Athena tried to think ahead, to feel optimistic. In a few days a servant would arrive from the Château Deverelle bringing Carol to her. She had missed her dog, and knew that he would love his new home. Shortly the Comte would arrive for his first visit: that, too, should be pleasurable. And she had the rest of the renovations to oversee. So she would not be lost for activity. But somehow, even the sum of these did not cheer her. She knew what she truly wanted – an impossible dream – Hamish to love her, to stay with her here at the Château Blanche, where they would bring up their children together.

Feeling tears pricking behind her lids, she said that she would retire now.

'I shall be making an early start in the morning,' Hamish said, getting to his feet, 'so shall we say goodbye now?'

'Yes.' A twist of pain nearly took away her voice.

'Look after yourself, Athena. You will not feel lonely when your father and Carol arrive. Give the Comte my regards, for he will probably leave Court before I get there. Our steward is a good man and you can trust him with your problems: confide in him as much as you wish about the renovations, or any problems you may have with the Château. He will see that the workmen do as they are bid.' Hamish took each of her hands in turn, kissing them. His face looked aquiline with tension. He is impatient to be away, she thought. Her hands tingled where he had kissed them, her mouth aching for the touch of his; but he did not take her in his arms.

She had brushed out her long, golden hair and was sitting in bed in a fragile lace nightrobe, when the door to her chamber opened and Hamish stood there. There was an angry, almost hostile, and very determined expression on his face.

He has decided to get me with child before he leaves, even though he loathes me, she thought. She remembered what Madame le Brun had said: that only she, Athena, could be the mother of Hamish's legitimate sons. However much he loved his harlot, *she* could only bear bastards.

She was reminded of their first nights together in Muldara as Hamish flung off his clothes and climbed into bed with her. The next moment he had torn open her nightrobe and was branding her breasts with kisses. She tried to see his face: it looked dark and implacable, and she thought that he was forcing himself to passion solely to get her pregnant. But at least he was near her, touching her! He lapped at her breasts, catching her nipples between his teeth and probing them with his tongue, so that spears of ecstasy darted through her body. She wanted to moan his name, to abandon herself in his arms, but how could she, knowing that he thought of her as nothing more than a brood mare, the vessel which would one day carry his son?

It took all her self-control to keep herself from flinging her arms round his neck and joyfully returning his kisses. But she had only to think of his selfishness to strengthen that control. If he had loved her he would be staying with her at the Château Blanche, not riding off glad to be returning to Court. Just as she had suspected, he had brought her to this isolated place so that he could hide her away, miles from civilization, while he carried on with his former bachelor existence. If he left her encumbered by pregnancy, all the better for his plans.

Nonetheless, her heart was throbbing as he dipped his head to crush stormy kisses in the valley between her breasts, then lower, across her soft, white stomach, and still lower, his tongue tangling in the silky moonlight hairs between her thighs, before delving deep within her, hot and searching. She was caught unawares, going rigid for some seconds before scorching heat rolled into her cheeks. Clenching her fists, she pressed her hands deep into the mattress to prevent herself from urging him on. Sensing her rigidity, and taking it for an intense dislike of what he was doing, he stopped. Immediately she wanted to cry out, to beg him to continue, for sparkling sensations were veering up and down her body, coruscating inside her so that she felt she could explode with the powerful sensation. She remained silent with an effort, clamping her lips on her pleas, the words of love which formed in her mind so radiantly that they seemed to fill the chamber.

She heard him groan as if he were undergoing torture, felt him palm her hips, her thighs, his fingers delicately caressing between her legs so that a sweet tingling began. She wanted to beg him to take her; she wanted to cry out that she could not wait any longer; she wanted to be his now, *now*, her longing rapidly reaching a point where she could control her words no longer. She was pulsating with her craving for him, wanting him buried deep within her so that the deluge of their passions would flood together.

She looked at him, eager to see the expression on his face, yearning to see love and tenderness in his indigo eyes. Then she wished she had not looked. His face was chillingly cold, his eyes black and dense with what must surely be revulsion, and to her dismay, he drew away from her, his features rigid and unyielding, his shoulders stiff. He stood up – how cold the bed was without him – and went to retrieve his clothes in quick, jerky movements. Then he was gone, without having said one word, leaving her engulfed by an acute desolation.

Coiling into a ball, her fists clenched against her teeth,

she began to weep, racking sobs which speared her heart. Not even now to get himself a son could he bring himself to make love to her. On the morrow he would leave, go back to his harlot, and she, not his wife, would enjoy the delight of his passions. Athena pounded her fists against the pillow over and over until her arms began to ache. She wished that the pillow was Hamish's secret mistress, that the blows had been rained against her dark head.

Even if she invited every friend she had to the Château Blanche as well as the Comte, as well as Carol, her favourite hound, she knew that no one could compensate her for Hamish's absence. She wanted him, she needed him: he was her food, her air, her life. Without him she would crumble away, shrivel and diminish, forgetting what it was like to smile and laugh and dance.

She cradled her aching arms round her waist and stared unseeingly into the darkening chamber while heavy, salty tears rolled out of the corners of her eyes.

CHAPTER FIFTEEN

October's russet hues filled the landscape, reds, golds and browns captivating the eye wherever one looked. It was a particularly colourful autumn and somewhere in the recesses of her mind Athena remembered another similar season, one which she had sought to capture with her artistic talents. Wrapped in sables, she sat in the gardens seeking to transfer the golds and browns and reds onto parchment. She worked long and hard, gaining a deep satisfaction from her efforts. She would give the picture to her father for his birthday in December. He would soon be arriving at the Château Blanche, but she did not envisage him staying over long, for she knew how he hankered after Court life.

There was an all-pervasive peace about the Château Blanche which had invaded Athena's mind and heart. If only Hamish had been there with her it would have been paradise. She thought of him constantly, dreaming of him every night, each morning bringing the cold shock of knowledge as she realized that he was not beside her as she had thought in her dreams. She would lie on her pillows trying to conjure up the image of him beside her, his face tanned against the white linen, his eyes indigo, his hair black silk falling in a sweep across his forehead in the boyish way she loved. There were always sweet words of love on his lips when she imagined him like this. It was particularly poignant to awake to reality, to acknowledge that he was not there with her in her bed, but far away in Paris at the Court of iniquity and temptation. It was no good being consumed by rage and impotence: she must learn to cope with her ungovernable emotions or she would make herself sick with longing for him and grief over his errant behaviour.

*

The Comte and Carol arrived within hours of one another, the Comte laden with gifts for Athena, and they greeted one another rapturously, Carol leaping and bouncing around their legs. If only Athena could forget her unrequited love for her husband, it would be just like the old days at the Château Deverelle again. Looking back, how tranquil and idyllic they seemed. Perhaps if she tried hard she would be able to reconstruct the same tranquillity again, for she had the right ingredients: her father and her favourite dog. And now she had her own home, which grew more beautiful with each passing day.

When they had settled in the main salon before the fire, sipping at goblets of mulled wine, Athena asked how the Queen was faring and if the Royal children were well.

'Blooming,' replied the Comte. 'Since the Queen produced her second son she has never been more beloved by the King. Now it seems that he cannot do enough for her. He no longer makes cutting remarks about her piety.'

'That is good to hear, Father. And is the Queen responding well? Is she very happy at this new state of affairs?'

'One would think her a young, newly-married bride again; she has never looked so pretty and she seems to be taking a new interest in herself and in her gowns and her jewels, which, of course, pleases the King no end for he sets great store by display and modishness.'

'I remember that all too well,' said Athena thoughtfully. 'It is good to be here at the Château Blanche and to be able to relax, to wear whatever clothes I choose each day. If I want to potter in the gardens in an old pair of pattens then I can, without feeling that a thousand critical eyes are turned upon me.'

'My dear, you look more comely in an old pair of wooden shoes than the most stylish courtesan in jewelled slippers.'

'You are prejudiced, Father,' Athena grinned.

'It is an excellent way to be,' the Comte grinned back.

'Now, be honest with me, *mon trésor*, you are not lonely out here in the forest by yourself?'

'Loneliness is a state of mind,' she replied evasively.

'That's as may be, but is it a state of mind which you experience?'

'In truth, Father, I find this a very peaceful, restful place. Here I am cradled by the forest, by the scents and sounds, the scurry of little wild animals, the silver of birdsong; the seasons are so alive in a forest.'

'But do you not miss the colour of Court life, the excitement, the activities and entertainments?'

'I know you find this hard to understand, but no, I do not miss them. I have taken up painting again –' Athena paused, puzzlement showing in her face. She had said that she had taken up painting *again* but, as far as she knew, this was the first time she had shown any interest in such a pastime.

Hastily, his cheeks somewhat pink, the Comte interjected. 'Yes, you have painted before, *mon trésor*. The nuns told me that you were very interested in it when you were at the convent.'

'Ah, that explains it.' Athena's face cleared. For a few moments she had remembered another beautiful building, attractive gardens, herself sitting in their midst with paint and parchment. There had been a feeling of homeliness, of belonging, about that place, and now she felt a twist of homesickness which was silly, of course, for she belonged here, in the Château Blanche.

That night she had a particularly terrifying dream. A tall, powerful man, whom she knew was somebody very important, was raging and storming at her, crying that she had deserted his little daughter and left her to her fate. She woke with a leap of fright, finding herself drenched with sweat. Could the dream have been connected in some way with her lost baby? Somehow she did not think so. Who could the tall, angry man have been? She did not know. She lay in bed watching the pewter and charcoal of night give way to dawn's peachy light which confidently invaded her bed-chamber. Whatever her bad dreams, whatever her state of mind, morning always followed the night. She wished she could greet it more joyfully, but what was there to welcome about a day which did not contain her husband? She would have given anything to have been able to turn round into his arms, to feel his hands hard on her shoulders and waist. Then the truth hit her: how could the Château Blanche ever be her home unless Hamish were in it?

She called a name softly and Carol came bounding across the room from his pallet by the door, leaping up onto her bed, where he lay across her knees staring up at her with his solemn, devoted eyes. If only husbands were as devoted as hounds, she thought ruefully.

Winter had suddenly arrived, banishing the glorious autumn tints and replacing them with dull browns and greys. November brought storms and cold winds, and Athena and the Comte spent long hours huddled by the fire wrapped in fur rugs. Even Carol seemed reluctant to go into the frosty, biting air. There seemed little else to do but keep warm and try to cheer themselves by preparing for Yuletide. Again, no word had arrived from Hamish and Athena wondered where he had gone. Would he be cavorting at Court, taking full advantage of the absence of his father-in-law?

The Comte's birthday came and went. Athena showered him with gifts, many of them made with her own hands, including a shirt made of fine *toile de Paris* with full sleeves and a drawstring neck, as was fashionable, and a black velvet *toque* which she had trimmed herself with gold lace and pearls, but it was her paintings which seemed to delight him the most.

'When I am back at Court I shall hang these in my apartment, *mon trésor*, and be constantly reminded of you,' he said, kissing her warmly on each cheek.

Athena's heart plummeted. She knew that the Comte was growing restive, that he longed to be back at the Louvre. The Yuletide festivities and the Twelve Days of Christmas would be so elaborately and joyously celebrated that he would not want to miss such a time. And yet he was going to, because he did not want to leave his daughter alone, as her husband did.

Athena had steeled herself to celebrate Christmas without Hamish, telling herself constantly over and over that she would not miss him, that she would not feel lonely without him. Deliberately she tortured herself with thoughts of him with his paramour so that she would feel anger instead of misery, for anger seemed an altogether more bearable emotion. So none could have been more surprised than she when, just as the priest was finishing celebrating Midnight Mass on Christmas Eve, who should ride up to the Château Blanche but her husband. He had two men with him, a squire and a valet, whom Athena had never seen before. Hearing the commotion in the inner courtyard, she knelt to make the sign of the cross before the altar, then slipped out of the tiny chapel to see what was happening.

Hamish stood in the grand salon, travel-stained and looking weary, but filling the room with his vibrant masculinity. Although the salon was large it seemed like a doll's room with him standing in it.

He made no move towards her and she fought back the desire to rush into his arms. How she longed to bury her head against his shoulder, feel his powerful embrace encircling her, be safe in the cocoon of his arms. But he was staring at her so strangely, his face inscrutable. She dared not remove her guard while he looked like that.

Finally he said, 'I have come home for Christmas. Am I too late for Midnight Mass?'

'The priest has just finished celebrating it.' Athena had been stifling yawns as the Mass came to an end: now weariness was the farthest thing from her mind. Her husband stood there, taciturn it was true, but her husband, nonetheless. She could not imagine why he had left the Court festivities to come to her. Perhaps he had had a quarrel with his paramour? He did look strained and unhappy. Maybe that was it: a lovers' tiff and he had come to her, Athena, as second best. Her anger would have flamed but she took pity on him, looking as he did, sending servants for wine, meat and cheese for their master. Then the fire in the great hearth was built up with logs and pine-cones which filled the room with a heady, invigorating scent. They sat by the fire together while Hamish devoured the food as if he had not eaten for weeks.

Sipping at his wine, he said, 'I have gifts for you. My men will bring them in when they have supped. It has been a long, cold journey which few would choose to make at this time of year. There is a heaviness in the air; it might mean snow.'

'We are prepared for it. There are mountains of logs cut and the cooks have been working for weeks to prepare the Yuletide food.' Was he trying to make her feel guilty by stressing that he had travelled all this way in the cold for her sake?

He glanced round the room. 'You have decorated the salon prettily.'

'The servants cut evergreen branches for me and hung them about the walls after I had tied them with scarlet ribbons and baubles.'

'The baubles are very fine. I have not seen them before; where did you get them, mistress?'

'I made them myself.'

'So you have been busy indeed. Ah, that food was good; we have an excellent cook.'

'Surely not better than the Palace cooks?' Athena said pointedly.

'Food tastes like broth from Paradise when one is ravenous.' He smiled. It was the first time he had relaxed his stern expression.

'Did you not have viands on the journey?'

'We passed so many starving beggars on the way that we had nothing left for ourselves.' He shrugged, as if apologetically.

'It is true that the beggars at our door have increased since the cold weather came. We feed them daily. The cooks make a special soup.'

'You give them bread with it, also, of course?'

They were strangers, discussing trivia, in no way behaving like a husband and wife. Was this how it was to be, then, during his visit? A pall of gloom descended upon her. She felt stiff and awkward, as if he were indeed a stranger and someone she feared. She wondered what would happen in their bedroom: would he fall upon her as he had fallen upon the food, like a starving beast? Soon she would know.

At that moment Hamish's two attendants appeared, laden with packages. No wonder he had needed two men to accompany him, when he had brought so many gifts. There was even something for the Comte, and a jewelled collar for Carol. Oh, in truth, her husband was feeling guilty and ashamed of his behaviour.

When the packages were unwrapped, Athena was surrounded by gifts which would have delighted a queen: bolts of material, gold satin, turquoise lace as fine as gossamer, lemon silk embroidered with silver stars, rich rose-pink velvet. Stroking the rose-pink velvet, a memory stirred at the back of Athena's mind: something about a visit to Court in a gown of this colour with a pink jewel to match, a jewel on a chain round her neck. She pulled at the memory, trying to formulate it more clearly, but just as swiftly as it had come it was gone. She looked up to see Hamish staring at her strangely. Then he picked up a miniver cloak which he had brought her and placed it round her shoulders. Was it her imagination, or did his hands linger longer than was necessary against her skin?

'I am overwhelmed,' she said, which was quite true. Why had he brought her all these presents? In their eighteen months of marriage they had spent more time apart than together, all of that by his design.

'I want you to be happy with these things I have brought you, mistress. I want to see you in gowns made from these bolts of cloth. I want you to wear the miniver cloak to keep out the cold – and, look, here are fur slippers to match. I want . . .' he paused, their eyes locking.

'What do you want, my Lord?' Athena whispered.

'Sleep; I need sleep.' He yawned and stretched. 'I am bone weary.'

She was filled with trepidation as she disrobed for bed, anticipating his harsh lovemaking, the satiation of his animal passions in her arms. Sex could be nothing but brutal without love.

Hamish tore off his travelling clothes and plunged into the bed, pulling the covers up around his ears, turning his back to her, and instantly his breathing showed that he had fallen into a deep sleep. She lay beside him, unwilling to admit that she was bitterly disappointed. He had ridden all this way to see her – or so he claimed – and yet he had greeted her coolly; now he slept without even having kissed her, everything he did confirming her worst fears.

The night was cold and she wanted to curl against his body, relishing its warmth, but she dared not for fear that he would reject her. She pulled the coverlets and the fur overblanket closely round herself and stared into the darkness. All those gifts he had brought her, beautiful things, but she would have relinquished them all gladly to have received in their place one kiss genuinely meant. She pondered once more over what could have have brought him back so unexpectedly. She supposed that there must have been some terrible quarrel between him and his mistress, and that the latter had told him to leave – although any woman who did that to Hamish would have to be truly witless. Who, having once possessed him, would wish to part with him? Athena thought, watching the curve of his shoulder in the darkness, listening to his even breathing. She thought of all the lovers in the world parted by circumstance, by tragedy: men and women who would give their all to be together. Yet here she was, lying in bed with her very own husband, and he did not want her. How ironic it was.

All problems seem to mushroom in the night and lying there through the black hours she felt very much alone. There seemed to be no answer to the furore in her mind, nothing but the thudding of her heart in the stillness.

'Oh Hamish, Hamish, why do you not love me?' she whispered. Her husband stirred, half turning in his sleep, and she held her breath, imagining that he had heard her. But no, he still slept deeply. Then a thought struck her: he had come unexpectedly and she had no gift for him. What could she give him for Yuletide? A hound would have been a good idea, but Carol's pups were yet to be born, their mother a friendly black bitch. She thought achingly of the child she might have given him had things been different, but he had given her no opportunity to replace their son. Then she remembered the trunk which had arrived a few weeks ago, filled with articles which she had ordered from a Paris merchant. There were some valuable books which she had ordered to while away the winter months: one was an illuminated volume of the Princess Marguerite's love poems and stories; another contained the verse tales of the Round Table by Chrétien de Troyes, another the poetry of Thibault the Fourth, Count of Champagne. She decided that she would give them all to Hamish, including the book of Thibault's love songs and poetry, for its cover was illuminated in black, white, gold and purple – the colours of King Francis.

Half the night had passed before she finally slept, dropping into a deep, heavy slumber. When she woke the room was filled with a pale pewter light, and Hamish's warm body was pressing against hers: but he did not know it for he still slept. She looked at his face, at its powerful sculpted lines, the full, sensual mouth, the thick black lashes lying on the strong cheeks. She had never seen blacker hair than his on any man's head. The Comte had said that the King had grown a beard of late, but Hamish was still clean-shaven and she hoped that he would remain so. She did not want him to change in any way.

Suddenly his indigo eyes were open, staring at her. She almost flinched away from him.

'My wife –' he murmured softly. His muscular arm curved round her waist, crushing her to him. Next moment their mouths were clamped together and the force of Hamish's embrace was driving the breath from Athena's body.

'My wife, my wife,' he said over and over again, between kisses. Then he tore her lace nightrobe from her shoulders and heated her neck and breasts with his lips. Flames of excitement soared within Athena, so hot and sharp that they seemed to pierce her very skin. Her nipples tingled deliciously; Hamish's left arm curved over hers, caging her to the bed, and she felt a sweet delirium of passion. He was going to make love to her at last . . . Anything, she would forgive him anything, even his infidelities, his disappearances, his neglect.

His hard, brown hand was slipping between her legs, encircling her womanhood and then tenderly invading it. Heat rushed into her cheeks and she gave a little gasp of pleasure. She could feel him hard and insistent against her thigh, his breath was rasping against her cheek. She was willing him to take her, to thrust himself inside her. The waiting was unendurable: he must do it now, *now*. She believed that he was going to, for he had climbed on top of her and she was spreading her legs to allow him room for entry. Then, to her dismay, she heard him groan out loud.

'*No!*' he cried, and then he thrust himself away from her as if she were burning him.

'Hamish,' she gasped, 'what is wrong?'

'I should never have come. I should have stayed away.' He groaned again.

'Tell me what is wrong, Hamish, I beg of you! Why should you have stayed away? What has upset you?' she pleaded. For answer he flung her a tortured look which struck her to the heart. The expectant heat had left her body and she felt chilled. Of course he could not tell her what was wrong. How could he say, 'I am missing my mistress. It is her arms I long for and not yours' – ?

Hamish stood up, his naked body golden in the pewter light.

'Where are you going?' Athena choked back on a sob.

'Out riding,' he said tersely, flinging on his clothes and slamming out of the room.

After he had gone Athena lay there feeling numb. Christmas morning and it was bleak and cheerless. But it had started out so well: what had made him change his mind about making love to her? Why did he have such complicated and puzzling moods? She wept for some moments, then the sounds of the household awaking intruded upon her consciousness. It was Christmas Day. She was mistress of the Château Blanche and she must make it a good day, a satisfying, happy day for everyone in the household – especially her father. She rose determinedly, shivering in the chill air, hearing the clatter of horse's hooves on the cobbles of the courtyard as her husband rode away. Was she really so repulsive that she drove him out into the cold dawn when he could have been tucked up in bed with her?

Deliberately she chose a gay dress, one of rich crimson velvet trimmed with swansdown. Solange, her lady-in-waiting, dressed her hair, decorating it with crimson love-knots and seed pearls. Athena surveyed herself in her silver-gilt hand mirror. How unseasonal she felt, how gloomy and bleak, but she would put on a brave show if it was the last thing she did. She had no intention of letting her husband know that his truculent moods could upset her.

*

The Comte was waiting in the grand salon. He wore breeches and doublet of brilliant emerald satin studded with amethysts. His hose were mustard yellow, his shoes green and gold, and on his head was a purple silk *toque* studded with golden brooches and jewelled pins. His face lit up when he saw Athena and he hurried to kiss her warmly on each cheek and wish her *Joyeux Noel.*

'Is His Lordship in a good mood?' he whispered in her ear.

She grimaced. 'He has gone riding, Father.'

'He preferred that to a warm bed? How very odd. Is the man loose-witted?' The Comte raised his eyebrows, his brown eyes twinkling. 'After his inclement ride last night I would have thought he would have sought to ease his body today. Do we break our fast before he returns, or shall we wait for him?'

'I have no idea when he will be back. Perhaps we should eat now. I do not think that he will expect us to wait for him.'

And so they sat down together at the board, with Carol placing himself strategically between them to collect stray morsels of food. After they had eaten they retired to the fireside in the grand salon, where Athena began to wrap up the books she planned to give to Hamish.

'Father, did you see the presents Hamish brought me last night?' Athena showed the Comte the miniver cloak, the bolts of material.

'Hmm, this is the best taffeta from Genoa,' the Comte said, fingering one of the bolts of cloth. 'It must have cost your husband a small fortune. He is certainly generous with his gifts.'

Athena shrugged, her face expressionless. 'I do not know how to take his gifts. He brings me all these things and yet he is so distant, so cool. He upsets me so much with his moods that I sometimes wish he would stay away from me . . .'

A footfall sounded in the doorway, Athena flinging up

her head, her cheeks bright pink. It was Hamish. Had he heard what she had said? She waited for some angry retort, but when none came she began to relax a little.

'Will you break your fast, husband, and then we shall open our Yuletide presents.'

Hamish nodded but said nothing. When he returned from the dining hall he took a seat by the hearth with the Comte and Athena and they began to unwrap their gifts.

The Comte was delighted with the black velvet doublet and fine lawn shirt and the other smaller gifts that Athena had given him, and he kissed her warmly by way of gratitude. She was equally delighted with his present to her: sleeves of *toile d'or*, a material of great delicacy, the weft being of gold thread and the warp of silk. The Comte had also given her a diamond ring engraven with her initials. They were so enthusiastic over one another's tokens that it was some time before they noticed the silence from Hamish. He had opened the verses of Thibault, the songwriter, and was reading them to himself.

'Could I forget her gentle grace,
Her glance, her beauty's sum,
Her voice from memory efface?
I'd end my martyrdom.

Her image from my heart I cannot tear;
To hope is vain;
I would despair,
But such a strain
Gives strength the pain
Of servitude to bear.

Then how forget her gentle grace,
Her glance, her beauty's sum,
Her voice from memory efface?
I love my martyrdom.'

He was reading with a sinking heart, for the verses seemed to fit his very feelings. It was a 'martyrdom' for him to love Athena knowing what he did, that she could die having his child, and he could not forget her 'beauty's sum', nor could he 'efface' her voice from his memory. There she sat, only a few feet away from him, bright and beautiful in a crimson gown, with loveknots in her hair, and he should be the happiest man alive. But instead he felt nothing but the blackest dejection. Her life was in his hands; he could let down his guard and take her as he longed to do, spending long sweet hours making love to her. But there was a natural conclusion to that act, and if she died in childbirth he would have murdered her as surely as if he had struck her through the heart with a dagger.

Wherever he travelled, however much he was occupied by the King's business, he could not repress his longing for her. When he should have been thinking of the King's confidential matters, he was thinking instead of his wife and aching to be back with her at the Château Blanche. How many times had he said to himself, 'Yes, I will go back. I will make love to her: she is my wife and I need sons. She will not die, she will be safe.' And then would come the second thoughts: he would hear again the midwife's warning, remember Athena's suffering when she had lost their son. If he claimed his conjugal rights she would inevitably become pregnant, and then she would die in childbed. And so he had kept away, until the previous night when his yearnings had got the better of him. How he had longed to spend Christmas with her in a warm cocoon of love, her kisses for wine, her body for food. Now here he sat beside her, knowing that he could not do it. But if he stayed with her any longer, if he had to share a bed with her again, how would he control himself? Last night he had been exhausted, but tonight he would be refreshed . . . Holy Saints, but how he longed to be spared this terrible burden.

'You like the books, Hamish?' His wife's voice broke through his thoughts. He looked up at her, seeing her fragile beauty, the wide turquoise eyes, so young, so innocent.

'I like them,' he said gruffly, 'particularly the verses by Thibault.'

'I am so glad. I was not sure that they would meet with your approval.' Athena clasped her hands together.

'But they do. Thank you, my love.'

He had called her his love: if only he meant it. But on his lips it was only a hollow phrase, a palliative . . .

'You have been travelling widely, Hamish?' put in the Comte, at which Hamish started almost guiltily.

'Why, what makes you say that?'

'Athena has shown me all your gifts: the Genoese taffeta and velvet, the silks from Italy and so on. I merely thought that you had gathered them on your travels.'

'I purchased them from merchants,' Hamish said casually, 'in the usual fashion.'

'But of course,' the Comte smiled, but he was sure his son-in-law was hiding something. The man had reacted very strangely to his innocent question. He was pleased that Athena seemed able to cope with Lord Mullally's moods so skilfully. His changeability never seemed to deter her. Whether he blew hot or cold she carried on as before. Which, of course, relieved him of a great deal of guilt, for he could not have borne to see her heart-broken and misused. What was Lord Mullally up to? No doubt his wild Irish blood had something to do with his odd behaviour, for if he were French he would surely behave with a great deal more gentility. A Frenchman, even when he took a mistress, knew how to pacify his wife. Was it that his son-in-law was finding it more difficult than he had expected to cope with both mistress and wife? If so, perhaps he would come to his senses and realize which was the most valuable. The Comte knew that if he were married to a woman like Athena he would be as likely to commit adultery as to jump naked into the Seine in full view of the Court. But young men were foolish; they had fires within them which burnt uncontrollably, sometimes scorching everyone around them, particularly those closest. If only he dared take his son-in-law aside and have a quiet little talk with him, but, if the truth be known, he did not have the courage. He contented himself with the thought that things might have been much worse. Lord Mullally might have been a wife-beater, for although common law called on a husband to treat his wife mercifully, civil law said that he could beat her violently with whips and sticks or thrash her with a cudgel. And many husbands did just that. He did not think that he could stand to see his beloved Athena physically ill-treated. But, on the other hand, it was against God's laws to interfere between man and wife. The Duc de Marne had whipped his wife so savagely that she had died, and the wife of the Comte de Malle had been a simpleton since being beaten about the head with a cudgel by her husband. Lord Mullally might be a difficult and complicated man, but at least he did not resort to brutality.

Watching her husband's face, Athena shivered despite the heat of the blazing fire. He was reading Thibault's love verses, the book open upon his knee, but he looked morose and unhappy. She guessed that he was thinking of his secret love and wishing that he was with her on this Christmas Day. Most probably, he was bitterly regretting his hasty departure from the Louvre now that the anger of the lovers' tiff was spent. She felt helpless, knowing that she was not the object of his love, knowing that she could not make him happy however hard she tried.

The day would have been extremely quiet had not a band of travelling gypsies called at the Château. They looked pinched with cold and their clothes were ragged, but they soon cheered up after being ushered in and fed coney pies and ale. Having rested after their meal, the gypsy band was more than eager to entertain the occupants of the Château.

Athena, Hamish, the Comte, and all the Château servants, gathered in the grand salon to watch the entertainment. Four of the gypsy men began to sing and play their lutes, which were decorated with coloured ribbons, now somewhat creased and grubby. After a few bars of the music one of the women threw off her cloak to reveal a dazzling scarlet dress embroidered with black roses. The bodice was low and revealed much of her ample bosom, and she danced with her feet and ankles bare. When she rotated, her skirt flared out, revealing naked calves and thighs. She flung back her thick, knee-length hair, arching her arms in the air and strumming her fingers and thumbs together to make a clicking noise. How proudly she danced, revived by the food and the ale and the warm salon. Round and round she whirled like a full-blown peony, her face deadly serious, eyebrows drawn together as if in disdain. Finally she sank to the ground, panting for breath, at Hamish's feet, looking up at him coquettishly as if awaiting his command.

While everyone loudly applauded the girl, Athena stared curiously at the tableau comprising her husband and the gypsy dancer. There seemed to be some unspoken message passing between them. Was he letting the gypsy know that he would bed her later, when everyone else in the Château slept? Athena felt an iciness descend upon her. Would her husband bring his whoring right into her home? Surely not. And yet . . . Athena watched Hamish dip into the leather pouch at his waist and draw out some coins which he threw to the girl. Joyously she scrabbled for them, lifting them up to her lips and kissing them, then blowing kisses to him.

For a few moments, as the girl had begun to dance, Hamish had thought that it was Zita Rosa, for they were very much alike. Then he had seen that this girl was taller, slimmer and not nearly half so beautiful. He remembered Zita Rosa as if she were a dream, a misty ghost in his past. But nonetheless, he felt a poignancy as he was reminded of those days when nothing had troubled him unduly, when he had bedded women wherever and whenever he chose, with not a thought for the consequences.

A young gypsy boy was singing now, his voice high and sweet, his song one of desperately tragic unrequited love which brought tears to Athena's eyes. The song told of a lady who believed her husband had died while away on the Crusades. Unable to live without him, she had fed poison to her three small children and then plunged a dagger into her breast. Only hours later her husband had returned from the wars to find his family all dead.

'*Love gone, love gone for all time. Love gone, love gone forever*,' finished the boy, before bowing low to loud applause.

'Sing us a Christmas song now,' someone called out, and at once the boy launched into verses which celebrated the birth of the baby Jesus. After, the gypsy girl danced again, this time accompanied by one of the gypsy men. Together they executed a bold and colourful flamenco.

Then the gypsies rested while there was a game of The King Who Does Not Lie. In this, the King and Queen were chosen by lot, and crowned with straw, after which he or she asked questions of each player, being required in return to answer a question from everyone taking part, the whole object being that no one must tell anything but the bald truth. Tiring of this, a game of Saint Cosme was announced. One player was chosen to represent the Saint, and he sat making strange gestures and grimaces while the rest of the players had to bring him offerings, which they must present to him with a perfectly straight face. Anyone so much as smiling at the Saint's antics had to pay a forfeit and become Saint Cosme himself.

Athena watched her servants good-humouredly, enjoying their antics, until it was time to dine. Hippocras, a wine spiced with ginger and cinnamon, sweetened with sugar and coloured with heliotrope, was served during the Christmas dinner, as were Malmsey, Romeyne and Muscadel, made from the muscat grape, with beer and ale for the servants and gypsies. To eat there were plump capons, venison, heron from the King's own heronries in Fontainebleau, six different varieties of fish, some baked in pieces with a batter of flour, pepper, ginger, salt and cinnamon, or with a vinegar or gravy sauce. And *Lèche Lombarde*: cooked pork pounded in a mortar with raw eggs, then boiled in a bladder with raisins, currants, chopped dates, peppers and cloves, after which it was cut into slices – *lèche* meaning slice – and served with a sauce of red wine, raisins, milk of almonds, all flavoured with ginger and cinnamon. There was a spicy mustard sauce for the beef and salted mutton; garlic, pepper and vinegar sauce for the goose; ginger sauce for the fawn.

Flambeaux were lit as the day darkened and course after course was carried in. Athena had been trying to avoid her husband's eye, for he was scowling and she did not want to arouse his displeasure, so it was with a sense of shock that she looked up to see how much wine he had drunk. A flask of Malmsey, a flask of Muscadel, and now he was starting on a second flask of Malmsey. She had never seen him drink to excess before and she did not know how to react to it. She thought better of making some comment and tried to carry on as if she had not noticed but, nonetheless, the meal was spoilt for her. The sweet courses were borne in: almond and cinnamon custards criss-crossed with sticks of sugar candy, flans, tarts and macaroons, jellies flavoured and coloured with rose-water, verjuice, preserved orange and lemon, and, of course, the great plum pudding served with hot custard sauce. Finally, Parmesan and Florentine cheeses, Marsolin and Brie.

By now everyone was in high good mood: everyone save Lord Mullally, who was scowling more than ever and taking little notice of the proceedings. Athena looked at him with dismay as he suddenly rose from the board and hastened out of the dining hall. Athena heard him calling the squire to saddle up a horse, and then the great doors were clanging shut behind him. He was in no fit state to ride, she knew that, but what could she do? She thought of running after him and trying to persuade him to stay indoors, for it was dark now and rain was beating against the windows, but he was beyond reason.

'He is driven by demons unknown to us,' the Comte said to her, his eyes full of commiseration. 'There is little you can do but provide solace when he needs it.' He was remembering the days of his own mental torture, before Athena's love and devotion had healed the schism in his mind.

'That time has not yet come,' Athena replied bitterly. 'If only I could give him comfort – but he resists all my attempts. He is determined to struggle on alone with his problems.'

The tables were being cleared and the gypsies were tuning their instruments in readiness for the evening's festivities. When the gypsy dancer had whirled and gyrated round the floor until she was exhausted, Athena's own minstrels struck up the tune to a lively *courante*, a swift dance with running and gliding steps and the occasional small jump. Soon, the entire household was cavorting to the music in great merriment. Next followed an energetic *gigue*, an English dance which took the breath away: then came a bawdy Spanish *sarabande*, the provocative movements of which made Athena blush. The *passepied*, a light and pleasant dance from Brittany, was more acceptable, as was the merry *branle* from Poitou.

Deciding that a dance might well cheer her fractured nerves, Athena ordered her musicians to play a stately Provençal *carole*. Originally this dance had been performed only in May, but travelling minstrels had spread it throughout the country. The dancers stood in a ring, some of them singing, turning from right to left in marching steps, beating one foot against the other as they moved.

Even the Comte joined in, although he confessed himself soon tired. To please him, Athena ordered a *pavanne*, the dance named after the peacock. It was a Spanish dance at more or less a walking pace, with simple steps in a slow rhythm which could be executed by even the most aged participant.

Night drew in and there was no sign of Hamish's return. For some time Athena had been repressing a feeling of anxiety. The lashing rain had not abated, but had grown indeed into a mighty storm. Inside the Château all was warm and cosy; outside, it would be diabolical for an unprotected rider.

Tired but happy, the Château occupants prepared for bed, dousing the tapers and flambeaux while suppressing contented yawns.

Kissing the Comte goodnight, Athena said, 'He has not yet returned. I am worried that something has happened to him.'

'He is a skilled horseman, *mon trésor*. He can outride anyone at Court in any weather. I remember once there was a contest between some courtiers to see who could reach the outskirts of Paris first. It was mid-winter then and your husband was an easy winner.'

'He has never struck me as being the energetic type.'

'He may surprise you one day.'

'He has surprised me more than once already, Father,' Athena said wryly. 'Tell me, what do you think made him leave Court to come here so unexpectedly?'

'He is not the only one who has forfeited a Courtly Christmas to be with you, *mon trésor*,' the Comte twinkled.

'You think he came here to see me? I do not.' Athena arched her brows. 'He came here as if he were fleeing from something – or someone.' But she had said enough. What if she asked her father directly if he knew of Hamish's paramour – what her name was and if all the Court knew of their affair? The Comte would be obliged to tell the truth and then Athena would know the worst, her fears verified. No, she could not bear that.

'Perhaps he is still out of favour with the King and they have quarrelled,' said the Comte, anxious to calm her fears.

'He is out of favour with Francis? I had no idea.'

'Something happened between them – do not ask me what, but for some months now relations between them have been strained. I fear your fine husband has found out what it is like to be on the wrong side of Louise of Savoy. All summer and autumn she was saving her most venomous glances for him.'

'Whatever can Hamish have done?' She was utterly mystified.

'Perhaps some dispute over a –' The Comte stopped, blushing.

'What were you going to say, Father? A dispute over a mistress? Possibly you are right.' Athena's mouth twisted. 'But now I think I had better go to bed. Would you like a spiced posset brought to your room?'

'That would be very pleasant, *mon trésor*.'

Having instructed a servant to take a spiced posset to the Comte's room, Athena retired to her own. A fire blazed in the hearth but, nonetheless, the room felt chilly. Her fears for Hamish were increasing: what if his horse had stumbled in the darkness? The forest floors could be treacherous at night. What if the storm had brought down a tree across his path or, worse still, what if Hamish had been struck by lightning? All manner of similar fears flitted through her head as she hastily undressed and climbed into bed, where she curled up tightly, shivering.

It was after one when Hamish finally returned, climbing on top of the bedcovers fully clothed and falling instantly asleep. Athena had pretended to be asleep when he came into the room, and as his breathing became more even, she reached out a hand to touch his doublet and breeches. They were soaked. He had drunk himself into a stupor and not noticed the rain, but he would catch a fever sleeping in his drenched clothes. She tried her hardest to rouse him, tugging at his arm, calling his name, but all her efforts were fruitless: he was in the deep coma-like sleep of the heavy drinker. She decided that she must try to undress him herself, difficult though it would be. Undoing the jewelled buttons on his doublet was easy, but easing it from his broad, muscular shoulders was another matter altogether. How heavy his arms seemed! She was breathing heavily before she had managed to remove the doublet and the soaked shirt beneath it. Once she had eased his breeches over his hips it was not too difficult to slide them down his legs and then to remove his hose. Panting, she pushed him to one side while she bunched up the sheets and coverlets. Then she rolled him back and placed the covers and one of the fur rugs on top of him. It had been an exhausting business for her, coming on top of all the energetic dancing of the evening, and although she had not expected it, she soon fell asleep.

Next morning she was awoken by his groans. Hamish, his hand on his head, was struggling to sit up.

Athena watched him, waiting to see what he would say, what his mood would be. For a moment his eyes were glazed, and then his expression was suddenly one of alarm.

'What – what happened last night?' he asked. 'Did I – did we – ?'

'You need have no fear that anything took place between us, my Lord,' Athena said coolly. 'You returned in your cups and got into bed with your drenched clothes on. I merely removed them while you slept.'

Relief transfixed his face. She had no idea that he was horrified at the thought that he had made love to her while he was insensible from drink.

'I am sorry if I put you to any inconvenience, mistress,' he said, but his features looked grim and not apologetic.

It had been a fortunate escape. He was luckier than he deserved. He could so easily have let down his iron guard last night and would now be spending the first of many, many days of dread and anxiety. What sort of Christmas gift would it have been to have got her with child: a cruel present indeed.

Hamish rose and dressed hastily, as if hurrying somewhere, Athena thought, as she lay on the bed watching him: her handsome, virile husband who seemed horrified at the thought of any sexual conjuntion between them. She thought back to the days when he had spent every night with her at the Château of Amboise, when their relationship had seemed to be improving. But that had been before she had miscarried of their son in that stupid, fateful accident. After that, Hamish had changed – and not for the better. She watched silently as he finished dressing and slammed out of the bedchamber.

Breakfast was a silent, uncomfortable meal, even the Comte unwilling to speak because of his son-in-law's black, glowering face. They ate roast beef, crumbly fresh white bread and honey, with mulled wine to warm them, Carol sitting at Athena's feet waiting for morsels of meat to be passed to him surreptitiously.

'That dog should not be allowed to beg at table,' Hamish suddenly growled. 'He should be properly trained.'

'He is but a pet,' Athena exclaimed. 'He is not meant to be as disciplined as a hunting hound. Besides, he is soon to be a father; did you not know? So he merits special treatment now.' Immediately she had spoken she wished that she had remained silent, for her words hung in the air like a taunt, as if she had said: My hound can be a father but you cannot.

She darted a glance at her husband's face to find it frozen, his fist crushing the piece of bread which he had been about to eat.

'You seem altogether over fond of fathers, mistress,' Hamish muttered, a furious jealousy beginning in his breast. She doted upon the Comte and upon her pet dog but he, her husband, received only icy rebuttals. He should never have come; she was far happier here without him and every moment that he spent with her was fraught with danger. It would be better if he went now and did not return. She would soon forget him.

Sadly, Athena watched her husband and his valets ride away. Why had he come? He had not said one tender word to her during the entire visit, but had behaved like a man demented. Now he was returning to his *belle amie* – he should never have left her if it tortured him so.

Surprisingly, he had kissed her goodbye. She had not been expecting it, but he had scooped her into his arms, crushing his lips to hers with such passion that she thought she would faint from it. For long moments she had been supported only by his caging arms, wishing that the kiss would last for eternity. How strong he was, her husband, and yet his lips could be like molten satin. She would live on that kiss during the long, lonely weeks ahead until she saw him again – if she did. She had the strangest sensation that he might never come back to her. Tears beaded her eyelashes. Her husband, her heart, her soul, riding away into the distance – lost to her, gone back to his paramour. Athena tried to pretend that she did not care, that he and his harlot were welcome to one another, but she would have needed a heart of steel for her pretence to work. A tear trickled out of the corner of her eye and she clamped her lips on the words she longed to call out, to bring him back.

Would she ever see him again? Would she ever enjoy his kisses again, or be crushed in his arms? As his broad-shouldered figure disappeared into the distance, she turned to walk into the Château, determined not to weep out loud, determined not to care. But once in the privacy of her bedchamber her rigid control shattered like a piece of glass and she flung herself on the bed and sobbed.

PART III

LOVE'S BATTLEFIELD

CHAPTER SIXTEEN

The winter of 1523–24 was one of the severest in living memory. All around the Château Blanche lay a wonderland of white, beautiful, sparkling, but treacherous. Inside the Château, as Athena sat by a roaring fire, sometimes with the Comte, sometimes alone save for Carol and two of his offspring sprawling by her feet, she would often think back over the past three years.

When she was in high mood she would make jests about the Château Blanche being a convent and she its Mother Superior for living such a nun-like existence, but at other times she was eaten by desolation and longing for Hamish. She had seen little of him, his visits being infrequent and brief. Why he came she did not know, for he only glowered and growled, drinking heavily and riding until he was exhausted. Her husband was a man possessed by demons but there seemed little she could do about it. She lived only for his visits, even if he spent them in surly moods. At least he was near her, no matter how terse and bad-tempered, she consoled herself. She had become almost resigned to the fact that he did not seek her bed, sleeping in the adjoining bedchamber, always making sure that the intercepting door was firmly closed and locked. She found even the brief accidental touch of their fingers a heady brew, and if he should forget his surliness and drop a light kiss upon her forehead or her cheek she was thrilled beyond measure.

She had adjusted to the life of a country lady. After overseeing the renovations to the main part of the Château she had turned her attentions to the low stone stables, which had been falling into disrepair, and now they were bright and new. The worm-eaten panelling in the grand salon had been replaced by gleaming new oak; and the ancient neglected dovecote had been cleaned, repaired and furnished with doves, whose velvety, tremulous calls filled the air on summer days. The Château saw her supervising a constant round of activity. There was soap and lard to make, flax to prepare, thread to spin and wool to card and spin, clothes to sew and to mend, hassocks and bed-curtains and coverlets to embroider and to fringe, timber to be felled to keep the fires going. Autumn, when bees yielded their wax stores, was the time for candle-making, some two hundred candles being made a day in candle moulds; for the servants, rush lights were made, bark being stripped from rushes and dipped in melted tallow. A mountain of bread was baked daily in the brick oven, then, when it was cooled, it was stored in the oak cupboard hanging on the wall in the kitchens.

Athena had become quite adept at mixing medicines, salves and unguents using recipes given her by the Comte. When anyone in the Château had an ailment of any kind they could come to her for a remedy rather than go to the wisewoman who lived deep in the forest in her ramshackle little hut. Athena had also begun to embroider a crimson and gold cloth for the altar in the small chapel in the Château. When she had finished that, she intended to embroider the Mullally emblem on pillowcases, bedcurtains and hassock covers. She had already sketched out the design, showing the two-headed falcon and the salamander on an azure ground. She clearly remembered the time she had spent sketching the design, for a strange thing had happened: intent upon drawing the two-headed falcon, she had found her quill outlining a smaller bird which seemed to resemble an owl, with a single rose held in its beak. Puzzled, she had stared at the owl while some long-forgotten memory stirred in her mind. The owl and the rose . . . She knew they meant something very pertinent to her but she could not think what. The owl and the rose: over and over she said that phrase to herself, trying to delve into the depths of her innermost memory and failing.

She had tossed away the parchment and begun her sketch again, this time completing it without interruption.

In the summer the gardens were a delight with the throaty, burbling coo of the doves, and there was always at least one graceful slender heron watching for fish at the lake's edge since Athena had had the waters re-stocked. Now it contained eels, carp, trout, tench, perch, sturgeon, minnows, pike, bream and others, for there were three fish days each week, Tuesday, Friday and Saturday, together with all the fast days and, of course, all the long days of Lent.

Athena herself tended her herb garden, where she grew sage, comfrey, borage, thyme, rosemary, dill, parsley, and many more which featured predominantly in her herbal remedies. Even wild flowers had their uses and were cultivated, old nettles being spun into nettle linen, groundsel used to cure gout, daisies and celandines to treat ulcers, heal sore eyes and aching teeth, foxgloves for dropsy. It was vital to stay busy during every waking hour in an attempt to evade the lonely longings for Hamish. If she sat thinking too long she became morose, for memories all too often reminded her of the colourlessness of her present existence.

Hamish had visited three or four times each year, and always laden with gifts. On his last visit, in readiness for winter, he had brought her a collet, a round cape without armholes, of stout Moroccan leather to keep out the rain when she went walking or riding, and, along with it, two beautiful pairs of Spanish leather shoes tooled with gold, four lengths of exquisite satin from Bruges in Flanders, three pairs of taffeta hose and three pairs of velvet, and a hatbox of scented Russia leather. There had been a handsome wolfskin cloak for the Comte and even a token for Solange for her devoted duty to her mistress: a set of silk buttons and shoulder knots, which she immediately attached to her best dress and wore proudly.

However, no amount of gifts could alleviate the tensions

of the visits, for Hamish never came to her bed and only kissed her on leaving to return to Paris, or wherever the King happened to be at that moment. One particular visit had gone even more badly than the others. Noticing that her husband's shirtsleeve was torn, Athena decided to mend it and to check on his other shirts to see if any of those needed sewing. She would do it without telling him, hoping to surprise him, hoping for once to banish the scowl from his face and to see a smile. In her search for shirts, she looked in his dressing-case of Russia leather and there saw something which shook her to the core: a crushed red rose, a lace kerchief wrapped round it. Her legs like crumpled paper, she had sunk onto the bed, staring at the rose and the kerchief with tears biting behind her lids. How unlike Hamish it was to preserve a sentimental token, and how much he must love his paramour to do so. (Athena did not recognize the kerchief as one of the Comte's which she had borrowed many months previously and forgotten to return, the rose being one which she herself had picked while in Paris.) In a frenzy of jealousy she ripped her nails through the fragile lace and tore it into a dozen shreds, following suit with the rose. The shirt that she had been mending had also ended up in tatters. She would not mend his shirts ever again – in future she would leave that to his paramour!

When that visit had come to an end, Athena had turned her face away from her husband's goodbye kiss, wounding him deeply, though she had not guessed it. When he had found the torn remnants in his room he had imagined that they were a direct message from his wife: do not waste your time in loving me, for I do not love you, and he had felt sick with grief. It was plain that his appearances only injured her, disturbing her tranquil life at the Château Blanche. If he left her alone he would not be happy but at least he would know that *she* was. She had her doting father who stayed with her regularly, and her many pets, the cats and dogs and birds which flocked to her gardens.

How many times he had ridden to the Château Blanche determined that this time he would bed his wife, but each time, on seeing her, he had been torn in two – by his love for her, and by the renewal of the knowledge that his lovemaking could kill her. He was a man, with a man's fierce appetites, and he loved his wife and would die for her, but he would not see her die for him.

Athena had no notion of all this as she sat cosily by the fire with her hounds at her feet. Soon she would be joined by the Comte for a game of cards, perhaps *mal-content* or *renette*, and then they would eat honey and almond tartlets and drink mulled wine before retiring to bed. How restful and satisfying her life would have been but for the gnawing emptiness she felt, the void which hungered to be filled with Hamish's love.

The camaraderie of the Field of the Cloth of Gold had long been forgotten. At that historic meeting, Francis the First and Henry the Eighth had appeared like peacocks outvying each other in splendour and panoply. They had danced and feasted and visited one another's tents and exchanged priceless gifts. Their Queens, Katherine and Claude, had gone to Mass together. For a time it had seemed that the bonhomie of the Field of the Cloth of Gold would survive all dilemmas, all pressures, but now King Francis and his foster-brother, Lord Mullally, together with the Constable of France and other generals, were discussing the heinous treaty made between King Francis's arch-enemy, the Emperor Charles, the Duc de Bourbon and Henry the Eighth. It was a treaty drawn up in the utmost secrecy but discovered by Lord Mullally's network of spies. The treaty gave Burgundy to the Emperor Charles, while Henry the Eighth was to take Paris and the north–west provinces, and Bourbon was to have Provence, Champagne, Poitou and the domains he already possessed.

'It is a treaty which delivers up France's entrails,' King

Francis stormed. 'We have no alternative but to plan for battle. That cur Bourbon deserves to die. Have four thousand men despatched immediately to arrest him! He must not be allowed to escape.'

His generals hastened to comply.

'How dare he scheme against me, the King! And I have not forgotten how he insulted Madame Louise.'

'The man is an imbecile,' offered the Constable, 'turning down the hand of the Queen Mother in marriage! He must be moon-fevered. First he refuses to marry Madame Louise and then he wages war upon Your Majesty.'

'The man sees himself as your rival instead of your servant,' said Hamish, 'and as such he is an appalling danger to France.'

There had been trouble for some time with Bourbon. A Prince of the Blood, he ruled many Duchies and was Count and Lord of many more. For years, from his magnificent château in the Bourbonnais, he had governed central France, rivalling the King in splendour and riches. But Bourbon had a touch of madness about him. Since being replaced as Milan's Governor in 1517, he had believed the King's new favourite, Bonnivet, had stolen his laurels, and it was now obvious that Bourbon must have been seething with thoughts of revenge for some months, his complaints exacerbated by the death of his wife, Suzanne de Beaujeu in 1521. Suzanne was the niece of Charles the Eighth. All her children had died before her, and although she had left a Will naming Bourbon as her heir, Suzanne's possessions were to revert back to the Crown, the chief claimant for these now being Madame Louise. All, perhaps, could have been settled amicably, for Madame Louise was more than a little in love with Bourbon, even though she was fourteen years older than he. However, on being told of the Queen Mother's wishes, Bourbon had foolishly replied, 'Is it worthy of our friendship to bring me such an offer from such a woman? You are counselling me, to whom the best woman in the entire Kingdom of France belonged, to marry the worst woman in the world. I will not do it, not even for all Christendom.'

On hearing his words, Madame Louise had been infuriated beyond measure. 'The matter will not rest at that – by the Creator of our souls, those words will cost him dear!' she had blazed. She had then told King Francis that she would disown him and consider him a coward if he did not avenge her, whereupon King Francis granted his mother Suzanne de Beaujeu's lands, leaving Bourbon impoverished, no longer able to live in the bankrupting splendour to which he was accustomed.

And now Lord Mullally had discovered the consequences: Bourbon's treaty with the Emperor Charles and Henry the Eighth, his eagerness to divide up France and vanquish Francis. But Lord Mullally had discovered even more than was known by the Emperor and Henry the Eighth, for, when the time came, Bourbon intended to take Paris and proclaim himself King of France.

Despite everything, and believing that an ally was always preferable to an enemy, the King had despatched Lord Mullally to treat with Bourbon, begging the Duc to take part in the French Campaign in Italy. But the Duc had refused to give a definite answer. Finally, the King had sent four thousand of his men to the Bourbonnais to arrest its Duc, but he had taken flight. Bourbon was immediately proclaimed a traitor to the Crown.

There was another lusting after the French Crown – Henry the Eighth himself, who had decided to revive the ancient English claim to the French throne: a claim which had arisen when Edward the Second had married the daughter of the King of France. Twelve thousand English troops under the command of Henry's brother-in-law, the Duke of Suffolk, had landed at Calais and marched towards Paris. Within a month they had been only forty miles away from the capital. Suffolk, anticipating being joined by Imperial allies and discontented Frenchmen, had heard instead of Bourbon's terrified flight from Francis.

Winter set in. Frozen and deluged with rain, the English army had trailed to the safety of Flanders in preparation to return to England.

Spring was now approaching and a French plan of campaign must be mapped out, for even though the English had retreated, the Imperial forces were gathering in Northern Italy with Bourbon at their head.

'Bonnivet will hold them back,' the King now said, slapping his fist into his palm. 'Who could best him in battle? None that I know of.'

'Bourbon has reason to fight like the devil, Sire,' Hamish put in. 'He knows that if he fails he will be dishonoured, with years of imprisonment in front of him.'

'Even such fear cannot make a brave man out of a coward,' the King sneered.

'Nonetheless, Sire, I do not think we should celebrate until after the victory.'

'You are being unduly pessimistic, My Lord.' The King sounded angry. He could not bear to contemplate defeat. 'You will command the four thousand soldiers who are going to Bonnivet's aid at Sesia for the blockade of Milan, and keep me fully informed at all times of the battle's progress.'

'Yes, Your Majesty.' Hamish bowed his head, joyous at being given a full command, for he had not expected it.

'Ride safely, brother, and God go with you. I shall await news of the battle with impatience.' The King smiled.

'Thank you, Sire. God be with you, also,' Hamish replied, as the two men exchanged a warm embrace.

The French army rode out on a day of wintry sun and scouring wind, Lord Mullally at their head, behind him riding knights on horseback, and behind them, the men-at-arms. They marched south, going close by Fontainebleau, with Hamish seeing, in his mind's eye, his wife tucked up warm and safe in her château with her father and her pets. Then down through Orleans and through the Bourbonnais to Lyons, Vienne, Grenoble, and down to Embrun, where they spent the night before beginning the long and arduous trek through the Alps into Italy. It was to take them nearly five days, climbing through the pass of Mont Genevre and heading straight for Sesia, where Bonnivet was encamped with his men.

On arrival they were exhausted but they had made good time, their speed and their sheepskins preventing them from getting frostbite on the way.

Hamish went straight to Bonnivet's headquarters, where he and the Gascon greeted one another warmly, Hamish handing Bonnivet letters from the King. The Grand Admiral of France took the letters, tearing them open and reading them immediately, afterwards apologizing to Hamish, saying that it seemed like a lifetime since the last missive from Paris. Hamish was amused; he liked the swaggering, sometimes vain, sometimes foolhardy, man whose friendship with Francis was almost as close as that between Hamish and the King.

Admiral Bonnivet was a strongly built man who wore the fashionable beard, moustache and bobbed hair, his face broad, with Gallic cheekbones, high and fleshless. His mouth was a lipless gash, his nose large, strong and clean-cut, his eyes large and pale with short, almost invisible, lashes, his brows high-set and sparse. At the moment he looked haggard and there were bruised pits beneath his eyes, gouges beneath his cheekbones.

Having read the letters from King Francis, Bonnivet looked up, his eyes bleak.

'So you have brought only four thousand men? We could have done with double, treble, that. I have just received word that the Imperial forces have been reinforced by ten thousand men with Bourbon at their head.'

'Bourbon – that traitor!'

'Traitor, indeed. I would cheerfully gouge out his eyes myself,' Bonnivet sighed. 'The weather has been appalling.

We are desperate for food and fodder for the horses. There has been only one good thing about this winter: it drove back the English. I hear they got within forty miles of Paris. How did the King take it?'

'With fury – and courage.'

'What I would have expected. Camped here, frostbitten, desperate for supplies, I thought of little else but that – and the Unholy Trinity, the Emperor, Henry of England, and Bourbon. When I think of all those years Bourbon flaunted himself like a second King of France and Francis has behaved so amiably towards him throughout it all, never suspecting that Bourbon would turn out to be a viper, to bite the hand that has fed it so generously. Ah, that is venomous indeed.'

'There is a time when even the most poisonous snake is vulnerable,' Hamish told him. 'Their poison has to be repeatedly manufactured and it is used up when they have just killed their prey. After that, they have none until it is manufactured again.'

'You think that Bourbon will be vulnerable when he is backed by ten thousand *landsknechts*, lance-knights? And those are just the reinforcements! We would have had twelve thousand English on our backs as well had it not been for this severe weather.'

'I have never heard you so pessimistic, my friend.'

'Blame it on the cold – my very bones are iced. This is not a beard I sport but hoar frost.'

'Be sure that your ordeal is not going unnoticed at Court.'

'It is the waiting – the waiting, that is the worst of it.' Bonnivet wrinkled his forehead, causing it to furrow deeply, almost shrouding his deep, pale eyes.

On 30 April 1524 the Imperial forces, led by Bourbon, attacked Bonnivet and Lord Mullally at Sesia, the French being greatly outnumbered. The fighting was fierce and bloody, and Bonnivet was badly wounded. Hamish fought like a lion, seemingly indefatigable, slaughtering opponent after opponent. But the heart soon went out of the French army, especially when it was shouted from mouth to mouth amongst them that the Chevalier Bayard had been mortally wounded by a Spanish *arquebusier*. Bayard, fearless and pious, was one of the bravest men in France with a hero's reputation. He had been with the King at Marignano and it had been he who had knighted the Dauphin at his christening.

Seeing that Bonnivet was wounded, Hamish had dealt with his attacker and fought off five more Imperialists to save the Admiral's life. He stood bravely protecting Bonnivet for long, exhausting moments until the retreat was sounded and the French began to summon their strength and their wits for flight over the Alps. The ashen-faced Bonnivet, groaning with pain and bleeding heavily, was borne along on a hastily constructed litter.

Although spring's flowery fingers had touched Italy it had not reached into the Alps, where the French were to spend the next five days in arduous toil. Hamish saw them safely to Lyons and then he sped on ahead to take word to the King, for it was felt that the news of the crushing defeat would sound better from his lips.

The Court was at the Tournelles Palace in Paris, and Hamish strode through its rambling corridors wishing that he was the carrier of any other news but this. Reaching the King's inner audience chamber, he paced up and down like a restless tiger waiting for Francis to appear. He was aching and bruised from his long hours in the saddle, and desperately thirsty, but he would not attend to himself until the King was fully informed of the events at Sesia.

Hamish felt it would have been hypocritical to force a cheerful expression, and misleading for the King, so as he bowed low before Francis he allowed his feelings to show upon his face.

'It did not go well?' demanded the King.

'We were decimated, Sire. The Chevalier Bayard is dead, shot by a Spanish *arquebusier*. Admiral Bonnivet is seriously wounded. The army is even now in retreat. I left them at Lyons to lave their wounds and tend their sick.'

'*Jesu*!' The King sank into a chair, his head in his hands. After a few moments of silence, he said: 'God has seen fit to punish me, to punish France . . .'

'We shall fight back, Sire. We shall gather our forces and retaliate. There is no question of it.'

Francis lifted a strained and anguished face to his foster-brother. 'The Queen is ill, sick unto death – had you heard?'

'Holy Virgin, no!' Hamish gasped, crossing himself, the King doing likewise.

'The physicians say she will not last out the year. Such a good and saintly woman, Hamish, and she has given me so many beautiful children. I am distraught, stunned, and now you bring me this news of Sesia.'

'Sire, we shall lead an army again to victory over the Imperialists. You speak of your beautiful children: France must be made safe for them. We cannot rest while it is parcelled up by the Unholy Trinity. The Queen, God keep her, will recover all the quicker if she knows the Kingdom is safe for her family.'

'If only she *would* recover. I realize now how much I love her – but it is too late. The physicians hold no hope.' A noise suspiciously like a sob broke from the King's lips. Hamish had never seen his foster-brother so emotional, not even when they had been growing up together.

'Physicians can be wrong. Remember the Comte de Lailly; he was given six months to live and he is still with us ten years later, as fit as any man. And Madame de Bruse – did not much the same happen to her?'

'Ah, Hamish –' the King groaned, 'it is no use. She has had illness after illness since Marguerite was born last year. Hamish, I do not want her to die, I do not think I can stand it. How can I go on being King, pretending all is well, when she is no longer beside me? Let the Emperor and Henry Tudor and Bourbon have France – I no longer care, I no longer care . . .' Tears rolled out of the King's chestnut-coloured eyes and down his cheeks.

One can feel particularly impotent when faced with another's intense grief. Hamish tried from the depths of his saddle-weary and exhausted body to summon up some means of encouraging the King, but it was impossible.

Hamish resolved that no one would dissect France and share it out amongst themselves, not while he had anything to do with it. Whatever the King's mood, he would not stand by and see the Kingdom divided. He thought of the poor Queen, and of all the children she had borne one after the other. Even though small and with her bad limp and the constant snuffle, she had seemed so hardy, so invulnerable. He thought of her sweet tongue, her tireless devotion to the King and to her children. He could not envisage France without her. Daughter of its previous King, Louis the Twelfth, she had seemed part of the very framework of the Kingdom, but the lesson was clear: women were endangered by childbirth. The Church might teach that women were made for childbearing but it was as dangerous as the battlefield and as unpredictable. He had never anticipated Queen Claude's early death, nor, he believed, had the King. He wondered if the King would have abstained from lovemaking with his wife if he had known that her frequent pregnancies would precipitate her death. His mouth twisted as he waited for the worst of the King's grief to pass. Queen Claude was dying but *his* wife was safe, even if she was lost to him in her forest Château.

Hamish longed to rest. He had not slept in a soft bed for weeks. He had ridden across France like a demon possessed to bring word to the King. His throat felt bruised with thirst. But his heart was moved for the King, for he saw himself in the King's place, mourning Athena's death; he could understand.

Finally, the King said, 'Brother, forgive me. You are

travel-stained and you must be ravenous. Eat and rest and then we shall talk again.'

The Palace was a cowed and spiritless place after news of Sesia was circulated. That, plus the Queen's serious illness, seemed more of a burden than France could bear.

Knowing that he would soon be going on campaign with the King against Bourbon and the Imperial forces, Hamish decided to make a brief visit to the Château Blanche. While it was a place of secret torment for him, it was also the most peaceful place he knew. When he was far away on the battlefield, either blistering with the heat or so cold that he was frozen, he saw a comforting picture of Athena in her home. No trace of the world's discord, its wars and avarice, its hatred and brutality, invaded the Château Blanche's precincts. A convent would have envied its serenity, and at its heart was the beautiful beguiling Athena, ruling in her forest domain like the Faerie Queen in the Greenwood. Many times when he had been saddle-weary, aching and dispirited from the labours of battle, his eyes gritty from the sight of blood, shattered bones and dismembered bodies, it had been only the thought of Athena which kept him going. He lived to see her again. Yet, as time passed and his love for her grew ever stronger, he forced himself all the harder not to return to the Château Blanche. Whatever definition wise men gave to love, he could only say what it meant to him: to put her life before his own, her happiness and her future likewise. He was brand new to selflessness, finding it a disconcerting companion. He knew that love was no figment of man's imagination: even Francis the sybarite, the lecher, had succumbed to it, but too late to save his Queen.

As Hamish rode south to Fontainebleau he did not notice the prettiness of May all about him, the throaty, trilling birdsong of nest builders, the bouncing lambs in the fields. There was a blindness about him and yet he saw so much: his wife, every silvery flaxen hair on her head shimmering and sparkling like purest silver in the sunlight, the delicate laughter lines around her mouth, the plump and shapely lips just begging to be kissed, the neatly sculpted nose with its delicately arched nostrils, the clean, curving cheekbones and, above them, like twin jewels, the Egyptian turquoise eyes, of a colour surely never seen in any mortal being before.

Great billows of birds flew up, startled, as he approached the Château gates. May blossom was thick and creamy on every tree in sight. The Château glowed deep rose-pink in the sunlight and not for the first time he wondered why it had its name, the White Château, when its stone was pink.

She was sitting beneath a cloud of May blossom, an embroidery frame standing in front of her and three hounds at her feet. Languorously as a panther he dismounted, scrutinizing her face for every nuance of expression. He walked slowly towards her, as if he had all the time in the world.

The hounds saw him first, pricking up their ears, then she, seeing him, leapt to her feet, colour staining her cheeks.

'My Lord,' she gasped. 'I was not expecting you . . .'

He thought she looked dismayed, put out, at his appearance, and his heart sank. He wanted to see naked joy on her face when she saw him, wanted her to run to him, flinging herself into his arms. But want must not be his master.

Taking her hand he kissed it, apologizing for his sudden arrival. He had, he said, only a few hours to spare before going on campaign with the King.

'Campaign? You would go to war?' Her voice was husky. She was determined that he would not see her concern.

'Did your father not tell you about Bourbon joining forces with the Emperor?'

'Yes, I remember something of that, but surely Bonnivet –'

'Bonnivet was cruelly defeated at Sesia. Our army retreated, the Chevalier Bayard was killed.'

'Then the country is in terrible danger,' she gasped. 'And I never knew! We live such a quiet existence here at

Fontainebleau. Nothing seems to touch us – I had no idea.' She pressed her hand to her mouth, thinking of the Rabelaisian Bonnivet and the brave Bayard and all of the men who had died in battle while she had been here, embroidering, strolling in the gardens in the spring sunshine, making *pot-pourri*, and enjoying other trivial pastimes.

'How long ago did this happen? When did news arrive of it at Court?' she asked, thinking that everyone in France must have known of it but she.

'I brought the news to the King myself five days ago.'

'You – you were at Sesia?'

'Yes.'

'Fighting – in the army?' Her voice sounded constricted.

'What else would one do on the battlefield?' He arched a brow.

She was struggling against a bombardment of tangled emotions: terror that he might have died and she would not have known about it, fear that his life had been in danger when she had thought him safely enjoying his indolent, self-indulgent life at Court, confusion as she tried to correlate her picture of Hamish the languorous courtier with Hamish the valiant soldier. She examined his face. He looked strained, thinner than when she had last seen him. There were new lines of suffering round his eyes which stared at her in their inscrutable, mysterious indigo. She had no words for the force of her emotions, but she ached to fall into his arms, to rain kisses upon him, to shout out her thanks to God and His Blessed Mother for preserving him.

Food can be offered when other things cannot, and so she invited him into the salon and despatched a servant to bring refreshments. Hamish drank deeply of the wine which was from the much-praised vineyards of Graves, and then he cut a slice from the savoury pie and ate it with a piece of Brie.

Athena watched him eat, conscious that he might have

died at Sesia. She might never have seen him again. What would she have felt on hearing that he had died on the battlefield when she had thought him living aimlessly at Court? But why did she ask herself that question? She knew the answer, of course: she would have wanted to die, too. Her soldier husband. She tried to picture him in armour, wielding his sword, the clash of battle all around him, and pain switched through her breast. She saw him alone, dead or dying, forsaken, and she wanted to cry out. 'Never leave me again! Do not go back to all that danger. Stay here with me in loving peace!' The words echoed in her head, so loud that she almost believed he would be able to hear them.

When he had finished eating, it occurred to Hamish that Athena might not know of the Queen's illness.

'Did you know that Queen Claude is very sick, that the physicians say she is fatally ill?'

'She is going to die?'

'Alas, it would seem so, God save her.'

'I knew she was ill. She has not been well since the Princess Marguerite was born last year. She has been weakened by constant childbirth, poor woman. She was always so kind and understanding to me. She befriended me when I first went to Court, despite –' she paused. She and Hamish had never discussed her relationship with the King. It was not something which could be broached without embarrassment and difficulty. She had meant to say that Queen Claude had shown her friendship even though she, Athena, was publicly acclaimed as the King's mistress. Flushing, she ended, 'Despite my ignorance about Court matters and my father's previous disgrace.'

'He was never out of favour with the Queen, you know, only with the Queen Mother. He has always made much of the Royal children, and anyone who does that wins the Queen's heart.'

'Yes, they would. All those poor children to be motherless – Blessed Virgin protect them.'

'No doubt the King will marry again, as kings are wont to do.'

'How can you speak so callously, My Lord? You speak of him marrying again before his wife is even in her grave, and she whom the French call the "Universally Beloved".'

'I merely meant to comfort you with the thought that all the Royal children will, no doubt, have a new mother one day.'

'Some foreign princess, you mean: someone who will consider them her own children's rivals.'

'We must pray that the King makes a good choice. And do not forget that the Queen Mother and the Princess Marguerite will devote much of their time to the children.'

'It is so sad. She is only twenty-five and she has borne seven children without complaint. Methinks the King will miss her sorely, even if he does not realize it now.'

'I think he does realize it – he was quite heartbroken when he spoke to me. That, plus news of the defeat at Sesia, affected him badly.'

'Poor Francis, I do not envy him. A country to rule and seven motherless children to raise.' As she talked about the children a look of longing showed in Athena's face, although she did not know it. But Hamish saw and was stricken. Tomorrow, he would be returning to the Palace and soon after he would be setting out with the army. There was every possibility that he would be slain or, at the very least, badly injured. He had been lucky at Sesia, but luck was an unpredictable entity. If only he could go into battle having ensured that his line would continue, if only he could leave his wife with child, his estates secure . . . For a few moments he battled with his thoughts, and then he made a decision. Die without heirs? Not he! Tonight, especially as it might be the last thing he would ever do, he would make his wife pregnant.

CHAPTER SEVENTEEN

The forest was eerily silent, a place of enchantment and mystery. A full moon, swollen with silver light, hung suspended in the air as if by magic. The chilling cry of a hunting owl split through the darkness.

Inside the Château Blanche, Hamish was sitting on a bench in the grand salon kissing Athena's palms, kissing each of her fingers in turn, with such tenderness that tears nudged at her lids. This could be their final parting, she thought, as he took her in his arms. This could be the last time he held her, the last time he kissed her. Within days he might be dead on some ignominious battle-field, his body bloody and broken. She suppressed a sob, moulding herself against his hard chest and curving her arms round his back. Their goodbyes were sweet and poignant, heady and potent as wine. In the fearful days to come she wanted to remember this time, to revive it in her mind over and over, to give herself support for her ordeal. The touch of his flesh against hers caused a singing in her heart.

Gently, he took her by the hand and led her out of the salon and up the stairway to her bedchamber. There, he scooped her up in his arms and tenderly placed her on the bed. Then he proceeded to undress her slowly and sensuously while covering every inch of her face with small, sweet kisses. When she lay naked, he stood looking down at her body, glimmering like purest alabaster, her hair a milky cloud. When she was like this he could well imagine her the Queen of the Faeries, transported to his side from her faerie kingdom. If he looked about him carefully he might well see elves and pixies secretly observing their lovemaking. This is the last time she might ever enchant me, he thought, and there was a renewed poignancy deep within him as he stroked her body with exploratory hands, as if he could in some way memorize her form. He wanted to remember everything about her, every line and curve, every softness, every hair and every tiny filibert nail. He would take her image into battle with him, a silver and turquoise banner. He would need nothing else to hearten him. Then the thought of dying in battle became uppermost in his mind, in all its bleak and painful finality, excluding the fear he had nursed for what seemed like an age regarding Athena dying in childbirth.

'My sweet, sweet love,' he murmured, circling his tongue round her ear so that her body was invaded by a sweet sharpness, the warm wetness inflaming her. Then he nudged the line of her throat with his mouth, making little wet circles with his tongue after each kiss. 'Oh, my sweet love, my rose, my joy.'

He kissed the hollow at the base of her throat with particular tenderness wishing that he could be as small as an elfin sprite so that he could nestle there and never have to leave her again. He lowered his mouth to her succulent breasts, the colour of creamy onyx but warm and with a now wildly pounding heart beneath them. He rested his head on the insistent thud-thud, his mouth opening slightly so that he seemed to inhale her very heartbeat, absorbing her into himself. Then he caged each erect nipple gently between his teeth, feeling her sigh and rise beneath him.

'My soul, my life,' he whispered, aching to absorb every part of her into him.

Athena's delight was so overwhelming that she felt there was every chance she might not survive it. Who was this sensual and solicitous lover, so delicately nurturing her body as if she were some rare bloom which might die without his attention? Spirals of exquisite ecstasy were twisting through her. Her lips were burning: she wanted to feel his mouth on hers, on her breasts, her throat, her thighs. She quivered as his tongue thrust between the silver lacy hairs at the base of her stomach. Again and again he darted in amongst them, probing at her flesh, while shock after shock of passion scored through her. Then his tongue explored more intimately still, circumventing her womanhood, once, twice, until she reached an intolerable peak of ecstasy. Then he thrust his tongue deep within her so that she squirmed and cried out his name.

'I am here, my love,' he murmured.

She looked down at his jet-black head: such a stark contrast against her pale thighs. Never had she known such bliss, such torment. She had not known such an act as this existed. It was like nothing she had ever encountered before. She remembered Ireland and his brusque, violent lovemaking. Where now was the man who had raped her repeatedly? She could not believe that this was happening to her, that he really wanted her in this way. Could it be that he was imagining she was his paramour? Or was it that he wanted a son before he went into battle? She remembered what he had said months ago about an heir for his estates. But this was no time to feel bitter about such treatment of her, for war and possible death lay ahead of her husband, and this was a time to treasure, to hold to her breast and savour. Whatever had gone between them before she could forget and forgive, for if she had his child, his black-haired, blue-eyed son or daughter, she would have something to live for.

Now she was burning for him to take her, but still he lingered, wanting her to be fully roused, wanting this night to be unforgettable for them both. He kissed the sensitive insides of her thighs and then her knees and lower legs and down to her slender, shapely ankles and feet, pressing kisses on each instep and each toe. Then he retraced his way, kissing as he went, thrilling at the little cries which escaped her lips. He had been erect since he placed her on the bed and he was conscious of a hot, insistent throbbing, a feeling of intolerable pressure. His senses were demanding that he take her now, without further preamble. He saw himself lying dead and bloody on the battlefield, having died childless if he did not now impregnate her . . .

Moving on top of her, he felt her hands reach down to guide him to her womanhood. Then he was at its entrance, hard and pulsating, urgent for admittance.

'Now, now, I can wait no longer, my darling,' he heard her gasp and it was then that he saw, instead of himself lying dead on the battlefield, Athena's body as she struggled to bring forth the son which would kill her. A cry broke from his lips. It was of torment and not of passion. He was lanced by anguish and longing and despair, and such a conflict that he thought he would choke on it.

'Hamish, what is wrong?' she gasped, but he did not answer. Instead, he tore himself out of her arms with a groan of suffering and fled the room.

Athena lay in bed, shocked and trembling, the peaks of ecstasy diminishing. Her mouth was tight as she thought of his lovemaking and how he had sought to rouse her. But, in the end, even though he was going to war on the morrow, he had not been able to betray his secret paramour by making love to her, his wife. Tears sprang from her eyes, drenching her face and neck. She would give her life to be Hamish's love, which, though she did not know it, was just what he was not prepared to see her do.

Next morning they parted in constrained silence, he bending to kiss her goodbye, she woodenly responding. Then he rode off, accompanied by a handful of the Château's servants: men whom he had handpicked for battle. Harness jingled and glittered in the sunlight, horses neighed and frisked, exulting at the sun on their flanks. She watched them go, her eyes remaining on her husband's handsome, straight-backed figure. His standard bearer, a blond-haired boy of fourteen, carried his banner aloft, the emblem of his House, the two-headed falcon and the salamander, winging in the breeze.

She thought of all she might have done the previous night. She could have gone after him when he left her, begging him to make love to her, begging him to leave her with child. Regret tore through her, leaving her white and shaking. She wanted to scream his name out loud again and again until he was forced to return to her, to stay with her. She knew that such desires were both hopeless and cowardly. Solange stood at her side, her pale, pointed face full of concern for her mistress. When Athena swayed, she caught her arm and helped her to the rustic seat beneath the May blossom trees.

'I will never see him again, Solange. He is gone to his death,' Athena moaned, plunging her face in her hands. 'He will die on the battlefield and a messenger will bring me the news. I know it, oh, I know it!'

'He survived Sesia, Madame.'

'But he is not used to battle. He has lived so long at Court,' wailed Athena, who knew hardly anything of the truth. 'How will he fare with seasoned soldiers, men who slaughter for a living? There are three men who would kill the King and all his armies and divide up France between them: the Emperor, Henry of England and Bourbon.'

'But surely the English have retreated, Madame?'

'That is true: the severe winter drove them back. But the Emperor alone has armies enough to conquer France twice over. Flanders, Spain, Austria, Germany: there is no end to the Emperor's Kingdoms and Duchies, and all of them will provide men for the coming fight.'

'The French have more to lose, so will they not fight all the fiercer?'

'That may be so, but they will surely be outnumbered.' Tears trickled down Athena's cheeks. 'I can do nothing but wait and pray. We will say Novenas for their safe homecoming and for France's deliverance. Come into the chapel, Solange. Come and pray with me that they will be saved.'

Athena had asked her husband to keep her informed, and

he did as he had promised. She heard that Bourbon had crossed the Alps and captured Antibes, Toulon, Frejus, and many other places, and that now he was laying siege to Marseilles. Hamish said that they were preparing to march with forty thousand men to relieve Marseilles. It was August, and a blistering heat beat down on the army. Victualling them, and finding fresh drinking water was a nightmare and there was an outbreak of the sweating sickness amongst the camp followers; a tawdry, bedraggled lot at the best of times, but a necessary evil.

The Marseillais had behaved with incredible courage, holding their position against the invader when his great guns thrashed their walls. King Francis had sent them shiploads of provisions and fifteen hundred reinforcements, along with a letter speaking of his pride at their courage, telling them that he would never forget them and that he was on his way with further aid.

The King and Lord Mullally marched towards Marseilles in the blazing sunshine, barely pausing to rest. Reaching Avignon, their exhausted men could go no farther and they were forced to make camp. Immediately Bourbon heard of their proximity, of the forty thousand men on their way to attack him, he retreated in great panic.

'So we do not have to lift a finger.' The King forced a grin. He had barely smiled since the death of Queen Claude in July. The physicians had assured him that she would last until the autumn, and so he said goodbye to her quite confident that he would see her again after battle was over. But he had only been gone a few days when she had died. The thought of Bourbon and his treachery had made her wretchedly ill. She had wept over the thought of France being divided and her husband losing his Throne, and Francis was filled with a searing desire to get his revenge on Bourbon for all the suffering he had caused. The little Princess Charlotte, only eight years old, had also died, doubling Francis's grief. But he still had six children left whose futures must be made secure, and the only way he could do that was by defeating Bourbon and the Imperial troops. Now it seemed that the traitor Duke had, after all, been nothing more than a clay-footed coward, for he had fled at the mere breath of the approaching French army.

Hamish had been chastened by the Queen's death, visualizing Athena in her place. He thought of the King's words to his sister. Francis had told Marguerite that if he could buy the Queen's life with his own he would have done it with all his heart and that he had never thought the bonds of marriage ordained by God could be so hard to break, which exactly reflected Hamish's own thoughts.

While Bourbon ran, Francis and Hamish led their army over the Alps back to Italy and Milan, the coveted jewel. It had been Louis the Twelfth who had laid claim to Milan because of his Visconti grandmother, and it had been he who had first conquered it, then re-conquered it after it had been snatched from his grasp. After, it had been French for twelve whole years. But by 1514 France had had no footholds left in Italy. When Francis had come to the Throne he had added the title of Duke of Milan to his other titles and, as Spain was attacking Venice, he had made a promise that he would come to their aid. It had been a glorious dream, fuelled by Louis the Twelfth's Italian victories. The result had been the Battle of Marignano, at which Hamish had bravely fought beside his King and which brilliant victory had made Francis the hero of Christendom. The King and Hamish made their triumphant entry into Milan, the King in rich blue velvet embroidered with golden fleurs-de-lis and Hamish in darker blue velvet barred with silver. They had given thanks in the Cathedral and then they had celebrated. While they had been there news had arrived from Paris that Queen Claude had given birth to her first child, the Princess Louise. How long ago all that seemed. Now they must defend Milan against the Emperor Charles and his allies, and Queen Claude and the Princess Louise were dead.

In her richly furnished sitting-room in the Tournelles Palace, the Queen Mother, as Regent of France in the absence of her son, was busily composing a letter to him. Messengers had brought her news of the Imperial forces gathering in Italy intending to conquer Milan, this knowledge further increasing the sense of foreboding which had gripped her for some days. Marignano was nearly ten years in the past – and, in truth, she had no cause to think of Italy with dread, except for Sesia – but, nonetheless, whenever she thought of Francis marching towards Milan, she felt faint and slightly nauseous, prickly sweat breaking out on her forehead and palms. Her premonitions were famous: they had frequently proved to be true. Flinging back the trailing sleeve of her crimson samite nightrobe, she moved her pen furiously over the parchment, begging Francis not to make war in Italy. She felt better when the letter was completed, but in case it should go astray or not reach the King for some reason, she wrote a second, this time her entreaties virtually a command, and sent each by different messenger to make doubly sure of their arrival.

When the messengers had left, the Queen Mother paced up and down the room, gnawing at her fingers until they ached. Her son, her Caesar, was in dire peril: she knew it, she could feel it in all the sinews and cells of her body. As her blood raced through her veins it seemed to beat out a message: *Danger, danger!* If her son did battle in Italy she saw nothing but disaster, carnage and death.

It began well. Hearing that Pescara, one of the Emperor's commanders, was heading for Milan, Francis became determined to beat him to the city. Marching at an almost inhuman speed, Pescara reached Milan one day before

Francis. However, his men were in a sorry state and the city was being visited by the plague. Deciding that it would be foolhardy to remain, Pescara marched his men out of one of the city gates while King Francis marched his men in through another. What they saw was enough to turn the hearts of even the most hardened soldiers: a beautiful city assaulted by the Black Death. Everywhere they looked were doors with crosses painted on them to warn that within were sufferers from the plague. In the streets lay corpses of rats, cats and dogs who had died of it and, as they rode on, they saw human bodies, too: black-speckled, bloated, bubbling and seething with blow-flies. They saw twisted faces, arms and limbs; eyes wide and staring in horror and pain; mouths a distended O filled with dried blood and vomit. At one street corner they saw a man and a woman huddled together, fornicating in the very face of death. The man was heaving up and down, gasping and panting, his face flushed and swollen, its colour an unnatural dark red. Hamish turned his head away, but not before he had seen that the woman was already dead. The man on top of her did not seem to have noticed.

Finding Milan a death town, they did not long remain in it. The army needed somewhere quiet to recover from the enforced race across the Alps and so, for the next two weeks, they made camp and recovered their strength before turning their thoughts to Pavia. Pavia, situated south of Milan and Marignano, was on the River Ticino and it was being held by Antonio de Leyva. There was reason for optimism. While they were encamped a secret messenger had arrived from the Pope, Clement the Seventh. Hitherto, as was to be expected, the Holy Father had been anything but Francis's ally; indeed, he had been in league with the Emperor and Henry Tudor. Now, he wished to make a secret pact with the King of France, saying that he felt it might be possible to get Florence and Venice also to treat with him.

When the messenger had gone, King Francis turned to

his foster-brother with exultation in his chestnut-coloured eyes.

'God has answered our prayers! He knows that we are to win and He has sent the Holy Spirit to inform the Holy Father of this.' He lifted up his shoulders and his hands, palms uppermost, in a characteristic gesture. 'What did I tell you, Hamish? With the Holy Trinity on our side we can beat the Unholy Trinity!'

Hamish was mystified. Why should the Pope, whose See they were in, whose cities they were planning to conquer, declare himself for them? Could he, in truth, have received a Divine visitation that the French would win, and he wished to be allies with them so that he could get the best terms? But why should he turn against the Holy Roman Emperor himself: a man who was God's temporal representative on Earth just as the Pope was God's spiritual representative? As, between them, they ruled most of Christendom, it did not seem right that they should not be together in all things. Could it be a trick? But no, the Pope would not indulge in such low games. Having pondered upon this for a few moments, he smiled at the King, but somewhat tardily. He could not forget the stream of urgent letters which had kept arriving from the Queen Mother, each letter begging, pleading with Francis not to fight in Italy. Even more disturbing was the King's reaction to his mother's letters, for he who had always listened to her advice, even if he did not always take it, was totally ignoring her warnings.

'Well, now that we have the Holy Father on our side we must show our mettle. I shall send a force to conquer Naples.' The King slapped his knee, his face bright.

'What number?' Hamish's heart had sunk, for they could not spare any men from their ranks. Besides, it was winter again: the best time to lay siege to a city, for in the coldest months food was scarce even when all was well. Inside Pavia's walls there would be starvation and shortage, disease and terrible hardship.

'Six thousand men – no, fifteen thousand. Naples is worth it. The Duke of Albany will lead them.' Albany was a Scot: he was accustomed to hard winters and his men would follow him devotedly through any weather conditions.

'So many, Sire? Do not forget that there are five thousand *landsknechts* under de Leyva in Pavia, and that they have already resisted our first assault.'

'How could I forget?' The King frowned pettishly.

'And that our efforts to re-route the River Ticino proved fruitless.'

'I have not forgotten that either,' snapped the King.

'We might well be here for months and the winter will be an ordeal for *us*, as well as for the men in Pavia. To have our forces reduced now will only deplete morale.'

'Do you not think the news that the Holy Father is on our side will elevate it again?'

'Sire, the Pope is not a general: he does not command armies. He has only spiritual power.'

'But that is a power above angels. His influence is inestimable. Where he goes men follow like ducklings.'

'Antonio de Leyva is a brilliant general: some say that he is supreme.'

'They have been saying that of me ever since Marignano.' The King's mouth curved up at the corners, making his long nose appear to overshadow his lips. 'Besides, de Leyva has gout. They say he suffers torture with it. A general distracted by pain is only half a general.'

'But he and his men have a roof over their heads. Our soldiers are exposed to the elements, standing in the mud, feeling the beat of rain on their backs.'

'There is fever in Pavia.'

'There is fever in our ranks also.'

The King glared. 'I would let none but you argue with me, brother.'

'But has the argument dissuaded you from deploying so many men, Sire?'

'You expect me to listen to your advice *and* to take it?' the King roared. 'You ask too much of me, Lord Mullally.'

Days seemed to merge into one another, all of them bitingly cold, deeply demoralizing. Lying in their muddy entrenchments, men thought longingly of their homes. Sweet, benign France: its flowery summers, the trees ripe with blossom, the orchards crammed with fruit. They thought, too, of the girls they had left behind them: wives, sweethearts, sisters, mothers. And, while days seemed to drag, weeks took an age to pass. Few were without some ailment or fever, the ones who escaped disease succumbing to frostbite; some helpless, watching as their fingers turned into what looked like charred sausages. There was dysentery and strange fevers which, taking hold on a healthy man, squeezed the life from him before nightfall. Men spoke of comets and God's Will, magicians and wizards and portents of disaster. Starved of food, of exercise, of love, superstition ran rife amongst the soldiers. It was said that Madame Louise, the Queen Mother, had had a terrible premonition of death and disaster, that she had written daily, pleading with the King not to fight in Italy, but that he had disregarded all her entreaties. It was said that Antonio de Leyva, the commander of Pavia, was a great and dreadful wizard whose powers were limitless and that, while the French armies bivouacked outside the city's walls in the most appalling squalor, cold and discomfort, inside Pavia de Leyva and the citizens were living like kings for, by sorcery, the commander could re-stock his larders with sumptuous foods, his wardrobes with splendid clothes. Envy thrived and made the French discontented and truculent. Albany's victory would have cheered and elevated them, but word came that he was enjoying no better luck than they.

Meanwhile, in Germany, Bourbon was recruiting men: six thousand *landsknechts* and five hundred Flemings. He,

Pescara and Lannoy, the Emperor's other commander, planned to deliver Pavia as soon as they had gathered enough men.

Hearing of their approach, King Francis made camp in the Park of Mirabello, employing a hunting lodge there. It was an excellent situation, for he was protected at the front by a tributary of the Ticino on one side and the *castello* of Pavia on the opposite side. On the farther bank of the tributary the Imperial troops lay encamped. There was something like fifty yards of mud and waste between them.

It was February now and there was still no sign of spring. Hearing the rumours which were burgeoning amongst the men, King Francis made sure that word was passed amongst them that the inhabitants of Pavia had not eaten flesh nor drunk wine for over a month, and that buildings were being torn down to provide firewood, gold from churches and even de Leyva's own gold chain having been melted down to pay for his army of *landsknechts*. But it was useless. No army's morale had ever been at a lower ebb.

Towards the end of February, six thousand of Francis's mercenaries returned to their homeland. Then two thousand German mercenaries deserted. Consulting with his generals, Francis discovered that most of them thought he should retreat.

I have never known such an unhappy army, Sire,' said Marshal de la Palice. 'They are like men without souls, mere ghosts of themselves. They mope or quarrel and fight one another venomously. There is a badness in the air, Sire. I have never experienced anything like it before in all my years as a soldier. Sire – I beg of you to retreat. The Imperial army is fresh and well-fed. They have not been languishing in freezing ditches for months as our men have. If we go now no one will think any the worse of us for it. There will always be another time, another place, for a confrontation.'

Bonnivet, now recovered from the wounds he had

received at Sesia, spoke up hotly after la Palice: 'You speak like a dotard, la Palice: a dotard and a coward! And all those others who have spoken of retreat are cowards!' He glared from one to the other of them. 'We French are always victorious when we are led by kings. We never avoid fighting or skulk like knaves. We fight like heroes, proudly displaying our banners, especially when we have at our head a courageous King who can make even cowards fight. Sire, give battle!'

Both sides had an excellent argument, as the King realized, but four months bivouacked in Italy would have been wasted if they retreated now. Nonetheless, he wanted to hear more opinions.

'Lord Mullally, what say you?'

Hamish folded his arms, his face thoughtful. 'As our armies are about equal in number now, it seems to me that we have an equal chance of winning. That is, if all things were equal, but they are not. Our soldiers are half starved, miserable, and they yearn to return home.' As I do, he added silently. 'Demoralized troops have never fought well, they have not the heart. Lannoy and Pescara will have heard that our men are eight thousand less in number and they will be exultant. Their morale will be higher, higher than ours has been since last summer. Lannoy has been lurking across the river for three weeks, too scared to attack us. If it is a battle you want, Sire, I vow that we shall have it before long, unless we retreat this very night. The Imperialists will be down on us like sparrowhawks.'

Hamish was right. At dead of night the Imperialist army moved along the river banks until they came to a narrow section where they could cross. A violent storm was raging and rain battered down on them. At regular intervals bifurcated spears of eerie lightning split the sky. There was no moon and the Imperialists donned white shirts over their armour for easier recognition. No one apprehended them as they crossed the tributary and approached the Park of Mirabello. Unbelievably, they attacked the walls of Francis's headquarters three times with battering rams and any implements which came to hand and yet no one in the French camp appeared to hear them. Shortly, the enemy was occupying the Mirabello camp. But they did not have Francis as their prisoner, for he was roughing it with his men.

Next morning Francis and Hamish looked out and saw the Imperialists marching towards them. The March day was cold, it seemed like winter again, especially in their hearts. With his headquarters taken, the King had to re-form his men in great haste, which he did immediately. But de Leyva, as if acting with a sorceror's knowledge, attacked the French who were protecting a section to the far left of Pavia, thus preventing the latter from regrouping with the King.

'We can wait no longer,' Francis said to Hamish. 'Our men are flung all over; they have lost their ranks. If the enemy attack now we will be ripped to shreds.'

The first attack went well, the French guns detonating an entire Imperialist company. A charge, led by the King and Hamish, forced a number of Flemish horse to scatter, their commander being slain. The Imperialists wavered, it becoming obvious that they had been badly shaken by the French, who were now beating them back.

Turning to Hamish with a triumphant grin, the King said, 'Now I can really call myself Duke of Milan!' Hamish grinned back.

But the King had exulted too soon. He had commanded his infantry to charge while the way was open for them but they were tardy in obeying, and the Imperialists overcame them. Soon the German mercenaries, under their commander, were overcome by the Imperial *landsknechts*, who decimated them while Pescara was gathering his forces. Even so, the day might have been won had it not been for the Imperial *arquebusiers* firing mercilessly at the King's Swiss pikemen, whose sturdy defence gradually faltered.

The King galloped back to them shouting heartening commands, but the pikemen failed to respond. Seeing that it was useless, Francis gathered his men-at-arms around him, charging the enemy repeatedly, while *arquebusiers* shot at them from all sides. There was plenty of cover in the Park and it seemed that every tree, every bush, concealed an *arquebus*. The French were not used to being shot at in this way. They knew about lances and cannon and hand-to-hand combat, but being fired upon by these small, portable guns which could attack from all points was something which bemused them. Not a few dived into the River Ticino to avoid the gunfire and, in the horror of the moment, drowned, while others retreated, leaving the King and Hamish and their Court to battle on alone. Two great Marshals of France lay dead: la Palice and la Tremouille, both veterans of Charles the Eighth's army. Bonnivet, believing that the end had come for his King and for France, tore open his visor, crying: 'I cannot survive such disaster, such destruction, for anything in the world. I must die –' A sword thrust granted him his wish.

Francis and Hamish fought on valiantly while all around them men were dying; men who had been their companions and friends since they were infants, men who had fought beside them at the great victory of Marignano. There was no time for tears, however, only for fighting with rigid determination to stay alive, for any who fell were being slaughtered by the Imperialists rather than being taken prisoner.

The King's horse was shot from under him and he crashed to the ground in a swirl of silver surcoat. Immediately Hamish leapt from his mount and helped him to his feet, then they stood back to back, beating off assailants, the King wielding his massive great golden sword. Between them they killed a good number of Spanish officers, but then the King was wounded in the arm and over his eye. He fell to the ground.

At once Hamish stood over him, beating back the Spanish one after the other, wielding his sword like a god, as if possessed of limitless energy. But the enemy came in droves and he was alone. Eventually he was overcome and beaten down to the ground beside the King. Stepping forward, a Spanish officer plunged his sword into Hamish's side, the blade slicing through flesh and tissue and muscle, narrowly missing his heart. As Hamish lost consciousness the King was surrounded by the enemy who, unaware that he was the King, tore off his surcoat and armour and prepared to kill him.

A Frenchman rushed up and, thinking to save the King's life, begged him to surrender to Bourbon.

'I will never surrender to that traitor,' Francis hissed, his face twisted with pain. '*Never!*'

'Sire, Sire, to save your life: they will kill you else!'

'I will never surrender to a traitor!' the King repeated.

The Imperialist commander, Lannoy, appeared, pushing aside the crowd who surrounded the King. Lannoy kissed the King's hand, then fell to his knees to receive Francis's gold-hilted sword, while the air was filled with cries of 'Victory, victory! Victory for Spain!'

Eight thousand Frenchmen and their mercenaries were dead, while only seven hundred Imperialists lay slain. Weak and bleeding profusely, the King requested that he should not be taken into Pavia, at which Lannoy accompanied him to a nearby monastery to have his injuries tended. The exultant Bourbon was there, but the King totally ignored him. After his wounds were tended and bandaged he was taken to the fortress of Pizzighettone, where he immediately wrote to the Queen Mother.

> *'Madame, to let you know the extent of my misfortune, nothing remains to me but my honour and my life which is safe. And so that news of me may be of some small*

comfort to you, I have begged to be allowed to write this letter, which favour has been given to me freely. I beg of you not to lose heart but to employ your usual good sense, for I have confidence that in the end my God will not desert me. I commend unto you all my little children, who are also yours, and beg you to hasten the bearer of this on his road to and from Spain – he is on his way to the Emperor to enquire how he wishes me to be treated. And I recommend myself humbly to your kindness.

'Your very humble and obedient son, Francis.'

Then, to the Emperor Charles Francis wrote:

'I have no comfort in my plight other than in my esteem for your kindness. I pray you decide in your own heart whatever you may be pleased to do with me, certain that the good pleasure of such a Prince as you can only be joined with honour and magnanimity. If you would be pleased to have pity upon me then you would find a friend in place of a desperate man.'

The Emperor did not reply to the King's letter. On being told of the victory at Pavia, he immediately fell to his knees to pray.

In England, Henry the Eighth leapt from his bed, calling for wine to celebrate, telling the messenger who brought the news that he came like St Gabriel announcing the coming of Christ. But privately Henry was bitter. Had his army not been forced to retreat in the appalling winter of 1524 he would have been able to share in the spoils of this great victory.

In Paris, the Queen Mother as Regent of France summoned all those Lords and Princes who had stayed in France. She raised a skeleton army to guard the borders and brought back Albany and eleven thousand men from the disaster of Naples, and she ransomed many of those who had been taken prisoner at Pavia. She began negotiations with the Pope, with Venice, with England, but most especially with the Emperor Charles.

In Pizzighettone a messenger arrived from the Emperor, who demanded that Burgundy be returned to him along with the Dauphiné and Toulouse, and that Bourbon must have his possessions returned to him along with Provence, which he would rule as King. Not surprisingly, Francis rejected these suggestions, asking instead for the hand of the Princess Eleanor, sister of the Emperor.

Francis would not have left the battlefield so willingly had he known that Lord Mullally was not dead but only wounded. Surrounded by the wreckage of France's army, Hamish lay unconscious for much of that day, while those who could still walk were making up a rough field-hospital for the wounded. Then, scouring the battlefield, they searched for those who were still alive and could be helped. They would have left Hamish for dead had he not emitted a groan as they passed. He was drenched in blood and at first sight it appeared that he had been wounded in the heart; it was a miracle he was still alive. Lying him on a pallet of coarse straw in the field-hospital, two of the men looked down at him dispassionately, believing that he was nearer death than life; he had groaned agonizingly as they had transported him across the battlefield and blood gushed from his wound in a never-ending stream, while all around him the groans and shrieks of the dying and wounded filled the air.

He had lost consciousness again until he felt a gentle hand raising his head and the edge of a goblet pressed to his lips. Eagerly he gulped down the cold water whilst looking through a grey haze at the ascetic face of a cowled monk. There were monks everywhere now. They had come from a nearby abbey to tend the thousands of wounded. The monks would have stayed, providing what little aid they could, if they had not been ordered to withdraw by the Imperialist commanders who had no wish to see any French saved if their deaths could be hastened. The wounded were left where they lay, to freeze by night and to starve, to suffer desperate thirst. It was to be the last drink Hamish was to have for a long time. That night he lay looking up at the stars, shivering with cold, passing in and out of unconsciousness, trying to ignore the searing pain in his side. When he was awake he thought of the wife he would never see again, imagining her in his mind's eye in her little château with the Comte and her pets, and he thanked God that at least she was safe. But what would become of France now? The monks had told him that Francis was being tended in a nearby monastery but that the Emperor Charles meant to have France for himself. In his weakened state he wanted only to sob at such crushing news. How gloriously they had begun this battle, but if only they had listened to the Queen Mother's warnings.

Next morning a young French officer walked through the ranks of wounded, taking down names and details, for he had bought himself free and intended to return immediately to Paris. Hamish managed to gasp out his name, to tell the man to inform the Queen Mother that he was seriously wounded and in the field-hospital outside Pavia. Then, exhausted from fever and loss of blood, he sank into a coma.

CHAPTER EIGHTEEN

Athena had not received a letter from her husband for ten weeks and she was sleepless and nerve-wracked with worry. He had been writing regularly, as he had promised, keeping her informed of the siege of Pavia. She knew that it could not have been easy getting letters out of war-torn Italy but, nonetheless, Hamish had succeeded and she was grateful. She was in the grounds of the Château, by the lake, watching a heron flapping away in a flurry of wings, when the messenger arrived from the Queen Mother. The Comte had seen him first, for he was crossing the courtyard as the man rode in; noting the gravity of the man's expression he felt the cold pinch of shock. He was not so possessive that he did not wish his beloved Athena to have happiness with her husband, and he knew that she loved Hamish. If something had happened to Hamish . . .

The messenger dismounted, bowing courteously to the Comte. 'I have news for My Lady Mullally,' he said.

'I will fetch her, wait here.' His heart heavy, the Comte hurried off.

Athena was gazing deep into the waters of the lake, watching the sleek, silvered bodies of the finned creatures as they darted about. Some scurried to the bottom of the pool into the mud as her shadow fell across them. But others, braver, dared the upper reaches of the water. Hearing footfalls approaching, Athena turned, seeing the Comte hurrying towards her, his face rosy from exertion.

'There is news?' she gasped. 'News has arrived of Hamish?'

The Comte took her arm, his face grim. 'There is a messenger from the Queen Mother, my dear. I fear it is not good news. Be prepared, my daughter.' His voice cracked.

The earth trembled, she felt faint. She saw a multitude of silver fishes darting hither and thither across her vision. All the colour ebbed from her face. 'No, oh *no*!' she moaned, pressing her hand to her mouth.

'Come, *mon trésor*. Come and hear what the man has to say. He is waiting for us.'

Athena needed all the Comte's support as they made their way through the gardens to the courtyard. Immediately on seeing her, the messenger dropped to one knee, his plumed hat in one hand.

'My lady,' he said, *Madame la Régente* has received news of the Lord Mullally, your husband, and instructed me to bring that news to you. I have ridden here non-stop –'

'And the news is . . .?' Athena's voice was a whisper.

'His Lordship was seriously wounded while defending the King's life on the battlefield at Pavia. He fought fiercely and bravely when all about the King had fallen. He killed many of the Imperialist troops who would have slain His Majesty. He was –'

'Wounded – seriously? Then – then he is not dead?'

'His Lordship was well enough to send a message to *Madame La Régente* after the battle, but the messenger did say that he looked sick unto death.'

Again the earth trembled and tilted. Athena felt as if she were poised on the edge of a great precipice where violent winds scoured at her body. She was alone in the blackness of night, in a foreign land, without friends, wind and rain gouging at her flesh, rending at her clothes.

'Help My Lady to the bench,' the Comte gasped as Athena's full weight collapsed against him. He and the messenger carried Athena to the rustic bench and gently laid her upon it.

'Inside – her maid,' the Comte instructed the messenger who did as he was bid, returning a few moments later with Solange.

'Ah, *ma chère* Madame!' Solange cried, kneeling down beside her mistress and chafing her hands.

Despite all their efforts, it was some time before Athena recovered consciousness and when she did it was to the weight of a knowledge that was intolerable. Her darling Hamish mortally wounded, perhaps even now lying dead somewhere, lost and forgotten, on a foreign battlefield. If he had died unshriven, as so often happened in battle, his soul would even now be in Purgatory enduring appalling horrors. She shuddered and pressed her face into her hands as the tears flooded. So short a time they had had together and now God had parted them. For nearly a year now she had been awaiting his return, praying for him, offering up Novenas for his safe return. But all in vain, so it would seem.

Later, when she was a little recovered, she questioned the messenger closely, wanting to know all the details of the battle: how it had gone, who had been slain, how the King had fared. And, on hearing that the King was now the prisoner of the Emperor, she gasped out loud.

'What will become of France? The country will be cut up and shared out amongst the victors, Bourbon will be King!'

'Not while *Madame la Régente* lives,' the messenger said. 'She is negotiating even now with the Emperor and with the others involved. She has ransomed many of the officers who were taken prisoner by the Imperialists after the battle and she will do the same for the King. All that remains to be settled are the terms on which he will be released.'

'The Emperor will release him? Can we be so sure of that?'

'He is prepared to treat, Madame, but so far the terms he has asked for are scurrilous; the King has refused them all. But it is hoped that the King will make a match with the Emperor's widowed sister, Eleanor, and that peace will be made with a grand alliance.'

Athena had heard of Eleanor, the swarthy, splendour-loving widow of the King of Portugal, by whom she had conceived and borne one child, the Princess Maria. Since her widowhood she had lived in Malines with the Emperor's aunt, Marguerite of Austria. But Eleanor was the Emperor's favourite sister; they had always been extremely close. Would he allow her to marry a man who had been his bitterest enemy?

When the messenger had been refreshed and sent on his way, Athena fetched quill and parchment and began to write a list.

Grief has turned her brain, thought the Comte, watching her as she wrote down item after item. Seeing his eyes upon her questioningly, Athena said:

'I am making a list of all the things I shall want on the journey.'

'The journey? Where do you plan to go, *mon trésor*?'

'Why – to Pavia; where else, Father? Would you have me stay here, smelling roses, embroidering shirts and making *pot-pourri* while my husband is lying there sick unto death?'

The Comte felt a zig-zag of alarm course through him. His beloved Athena, the only being in the entire world whom he loved, and she was talking of going into war-torn Italy to look for her husband!

'*Mon trésor*, you cannot do it, it is not possible! You will die! Why, you will never get even halfway across the Alps. Have you no idea how strenuous the journey is, how long it will take you? Even in summer the Alps are freezing at night. Then there will be brigands and mercenaries, looting and raping,' he shuddered. 'Seeing a lady they will not think twice: you will be set upon, raped, murdered –' He stood up, his heart pounding loudly. 'You cannot go, I forbid it.'

'Father, I am going. You have no right to forbid me and you know it. If you think that I will be easy prey as a woman then I shall go dressed as a man, but nothing is going to deter me, *nothing*. I shall take two men with me and we shall go well equipped for the journey, never fear.'

'Oh, my daughter, my dearest, I beg of you –'

'Nothing that you can say will change my mind, Father. If I stay here, leaving Hamish to his fate, then I shall die, it is as simple as that.' Fierce determination shone in her face.

The Comte sank into his chair, a groan escaping his lips. He would be left with nothing in the world, nothing and no one. He was cursed, oh yes, he was cursed. God had turned His face against him . . .

'Yes, I shall wear men's clothes,' Athena went on, 'simple, plain clothes. Nothing that would look rich or attract attention. And I shall take one of the servants' cloaks, lined with sheepskin; that should keep me warm, even in the Alps.'

'Daughter, if you carry gold they will find out, they always know.'

Would you have me go penniless, travelling all that way into a strange country with no money to buy victuals and medicines for Hamish when I get there? I will take gold, Father, but I shall have it sewn up inside my cloak between the cloth and the sheepskin where no one will see it.'

The Comte groaned again, 'But the dangers, the risks –! It will not be safe: marauding bandits will view even the sheepskin cloak as a fine and rich article to steal.'

'Then I will go without it, and freeze in the Alps. Would you have me do that instead?' Athena's face was grim and set. She had made up her mind and she was not going to change it.

First she chose two of her sturdiest retainers, men who knew how to wield a sword and who were of unquestioning loyalty. While they were selecting suitable clothing for the journey and filling panniers with food and flasks of water for the journey and other requirements, Athena summoned one of the young manservants, a man of her own height and of very slight build. Explaining her intentions, she was soon wearing a pair of his breeches, doublet and hose. The clothes were ill-fitting; but they would do. It was strange to be wearing man's garb, and highly embarrassing to have her legs unconcealed by skirts, but she was not going to let modesty deter her. Shoes were the main problem, for even the smallest of the menservants seemed to have large feet. Finally, she found a woman servant who owned a pair of leather shoes in a masculine style which fitted Athena reasonably well.

Solange was busily sewing gold pieces into a cloak, and packing herbs and unguents, bandages and ointments into panniers, along with food and changes of clothing. Athena bound up her hair tightly and put on a round-brimmed hat with a plume. It was large and came down halfway over her ears, which satisfactorily disguised her feminine features.

When they were ready the Comte again begged her not to go.

'I *must* go, father,' she said simply. 'I feel that Hamish needs me. You have taught me a great deal about herbs and nursing the sick and now I see why that was. It is my duty to go to him, but I go because I love him. Wherever he is, he needs me.'

The Comte wanted to sob, 'But I need you too! I cannot live without you!' But he knew that such an utterance would be cowardly and selfish, so he forced himself to bid her Godspeed and a safe journey. Then he watched her and the two squires riding away from the Château and he felt as if his heart had died.

The older of the two squires, Pierre, had fought at Marignano ten years before as a foot soldier, having been wounded so badly that he would never be accepted into any army again, but it meant that he knew the quickest way into Italy. They rode directly south, resting overnight at wherever they happened to find themselves when it became dark. Pressing their horses on with cruel haste, Athena discovered what it was really like to be saddle-sore. She felt as if her hips and thighs were aflame and her back throbbed with a dull ache. She was so exhausted that it seemed she had barely closed her eyes at night before it was dawn, but she was determined that her own frailty was not going to delay them: time was of the essence. Hamish might even now be sinking into the final oblivion.

Passing through Sens, Lyons, Vienne, eventually they reached Grenoble, where they replenished their supplies for the last time before tackling the Alps. Merely looking at the snow-limned peaks made Athena shiver. Hitherto, the journey had been arduous because of its very length and the necessity to remain in the saddle during the daylight hours. But now there would be danger and difficulty in their passage. They had a choice between the passes of Mont Cenis or Mont Genevre, and decided on the latter. The horses were sturdy and sure-footed; nonetheless, Athena felt she was riding at the very edge of a precipice.

The May sky was cornflower blue when they set off and flowers and greenery were in abundance. Pierre told Athena that once they got over the pass they would be near Turin and from there it was a straightforward journey to Pavia, which lay to the south of Milan. It was necessary for Athena to keep in her mind's eye a picture of Hamish lying wounded and near death, otherwise she would have faltered and begged to turn back. By now her very bones ached: she felt as if she had been kicked and pummelled all over. Curling up beneath the sheepskin cloak at night, their camp fire glowing, she was conscious of a feeling of unearthliness, as if she no longer belonged to the world, a weird, disorientated feeling.

She always woke cramped and sore, but to come out from under the cloak into the chill morning air took courage. Pierre or Gaston would collect cans full of snow and heat them over the fire, adding herbs and spices. They would each dip a metal goblet into the steaming liquid, nursing it welcomingly between their palms as they sipped. Then they would slice up cold sausage and eat it with stale bread and hard cheese, while the horses munched on their oats, after which they would set off again on the now precipitous trail, leading their horses by their bridles for it was too steep to ride.

They seemed to have been in the Alps for months, with nothing but peaks in front of them, and the biting cold which cut into Athena's forehead like a blade. They had spent six nights in the Alps before they emerged in the Plain of Saluzzo where, exhausted, Athena slept the night round, the squires keeping watch in turn.

'Now that we are in Italy, My Lady, we must beware of mercenaries,' said Pierre. 'After battles they haunt the countryside looking for loot and for unaccompanied women.' Colour flooded his cheeks. 'They are called the Scavengers.'

'I have been warned about them, Pierre, but they will take me for a man, will they not? And we none of us look wealthy: certainly not after that ordeal through the mountains.' Athena gave a faint smile. She felt a century old and she was sure she looked it at the moment.

'We will take care of you, My Lady,' Gaston grinned. 'I have some skill with a sword.'

'And I,' Pierre added. 'I was at Marignano, remember.'

'I think avoidance will be our best tactic,' suggested Athena. 'I was told that even a sheepskin cloak would be looked upon as loot.'

Squaring their shoulders, the two men assured her they would defend her with their lives.

They had paused for refreshment in the shelter of some rocks when Gaston suddenly put a hand to his ear.

'Horses – coming this way!' he said, his broad face alert.

Instantly Pierre flung handfuls of soil over their fire, while Gaston led their horses into a sheltering niche in the rock. Keeping their hands on the horses' harnesses to stop them jingling, they pressed themselves against the rockface while the horsemen rode by on the other side. They heard guttural voices conversing in German and knew that the horsemen were Scavengers, Germany mercenaries. They heard, too, muffled screams as if from women who had been gagged or who had had cloaks flung over their heads. Each time there was a scream it was followed by the hearty slapping of a hand against bare flesh and more screams.

'Jesu, they are carrying off women,' Athena whispered, her face ashen.

'Stay silent, My Lady,' Pierre hissed. 'They are nearly past us now, God be praised. May the Holy Saints see that we escape unscathed.'

The thudding of hooves, the guttural German voices, and the screams of terror gradually died away as the horsemen put distance between themselves and Athena. She was rigid with terror, her skin icy and beaded with sweat, by the time Pierre and Gaston decided it was safe to come out of their hiding place.

Those poor women being carried off like that, never to see their families again! Athena crossed herself, feeling a great wave of pity for the Scavengers' victims. 'Where do you think they are taking them, Pierre?'

'Possibly they have a lair in the mountains, My Lady, somewhere where they can take their victims without hindrance or danger from other looting parties. It is always a time of chaos and horror after a great battle, and Italy has been the scene of many wars for decades now.'

'Let us put as great a distance as possible between the Scavengers and ourselves,' Athena said, shuddering, as they mounted their horses to continue the journey.

But worse was to come. They came upon a village still smoking after having been burnt and looted, its buildings charred and desecrated. Bodies lay everywhere in hideous testimony to what had happened. Women had been raped and then knifed: they lay on their backs, their skirts up round their necks, their legs wide. A young boy had been crucified against a stable door; he gave his last gasp as they approached. One cottage lay apparently untouched, its door wide open. Glancing inside was like seeing a vision of Hell, for on the heavy wooden table lay four women's heads, just the heads, no bodies, the eyes wide open in shock and unbelievable agony.

'Do not look, My Lady!' Pierre gasped, for the sight of the heads was grisly enough but he had seen something else. Four of the village men had been castrated at some point and their hacked off members thrust into the women's mouths. Pierre felt a ball of ice lying deep within the pit of his stomach. As vomit seared the back of his throat he gulped, swallowing over and over. What would his mistress think if he showed weakness now? He seized Athena's arm and led her away.

As quickly as they could, they turned their backs on the village and headed towards Pavia. There is a point where so much horror has been registered upon the mind that nothing is felt but numbness and that was how Athena felt now: stunned and reeling from the horrors she had just seen. It was a different matter to talk of the vicissitudes of war than to experience them so shockingly. At the first suspicion of what would be seen in the village, Athena's mind had clamped itself shut, knowing full well that white-hot hysteria would be the result of her pondering upon the outrages.

Hamish. Hamish. She repeated his name over and over in her mind, keeping his image as a beacon to lead her onwards. There was no turning back now: no, not for any reason. She seemed to hear his voice in her thoughts, to see his haggard face before her. His eyes were entreating, begging her to make haste and, with each passing mile, her conviction strengthened that he was still alive and in urgent need of her.

They nearly blundered into a Scavengers' camp. They had just passed a village where all seemed well, and the sight of a goatherd sitting peaceably with his herd of goats grazing around him had put them off their guard. They had stopped to take refreshment in the village, making it clear they would pay for everything they ate and drank. At first the villagers were hesitant, but when they relized that the trio were not about to loot or attack them their natural hospitality showed itself. By making various gestures, Pierre and Gaston made it clear that they were very thirsty and hungry, and soon they found themselves sitting on low, carved stools in a small garden in front of a wood and adobe cottage, being pressed to eat delicious crumbly goats' cheese and to drink fresh frothing goats' milk. Athena had never tasted the musky flavour of the milk before; wrinkling her nose, she decided that it was an acquired taste, but she was thirsty and weary of the sameness of the previous few days' repasts. A child had come up to them with a large loaf of coarse bread, and Gaston tore it up into sections for each of them. By now a circle of children stood watching them, faces agog. Athena had wished that she could speak to them, but she knew no Italian. They were healthy, sturdy children, with glowing, tanned skins, and their clothes were coarse and threadbare but clean. One boy had a streaming nose which he kept wiping with his sleeve. Athena had found herself loath to leave the peaceful, rustic village. It would have been nice to stay there for the night, but there were still some hours of daylight to go and they could not spare the time.

They had ridden on, refreshed and relaxed, certain that there could be no Scavengers in the area. They were skirting a sloping hill. Almost too late, Gaston, riding a little way ahead, saw the spiral of camp smoke twisting its way into the sky.

'Back, My Lady,' he hissed at once, his broad face filled with alarm. He had seen the camp ahead, spread out beneath them on a small plain, what looked like dozens of German mercenaries cramming their mouths with food and swigging wine. As Gaston urged them to retrace their steps as silently as possible, other things registered in his mind: poles set round the camp, one every few feet; and on the poles, lifeless heads with bulging eyes and grotesquely twisted mouths, the long hair on each head proclaiming its femininity.

A war against helpless women and children, Gaston thought, his mind reeling. But for him, their mistress's head might have joined those others. But what unspeakable things would have been done to her first . . .?

Avoiding the Scavengers' camp added three hours to their journey, and they slept the night in a small, wooded copse. The earth was dank and smelled of mushrooms. A hunting owl's cry stabbed through the darkness above them, followed by the unearthly scream of its victim. Cuddled down inside her sheepskin cloak, the rank smell of the copse filling her nostrils, Athena shuddered. Which was more brutal: nature or man? God and His Sweet Mother seemed far away from battered, bloody Italy, and she was sure that the men who had destroyed the village they had seen could not have consciences. Every night of their journey she had said her prayers diligently, entreating God and His Mother to preserve and protect Hamish wherever he was and to lead her to him safely. She prayed also that King Francis would be returned safely to his country without mishap; nothing was going to make her lose faith in God, whatever she saw, whatever happened to her. This was the testing time; it would either make or break her. Grimly, she determined that she would not be broken. She hungered to have Hamish lying beside her, his arms around her body. If she contemplated finding nothing but his corpse once they reached Pavia she knew that she would have no reason to go on.

The field-hospital was spread across a great area of pasture beside the Ticino river. Crosses filled one section where the dead had been hastily buried before disease spread throughout the camp. The moans and wails of the sick and dying were terrible to hear, and Athena was chilled to the heart as she rode along the perimeter of the camp looking for someone well enough to give her the information she wanted. Many of the men lying on rough straw pallets were corpses, for there were few now sufficiently strong enough to dig graves. Those who were recovered or partially recovered had long ago left for home. She stared hard at every pallet, aching to see Hamish and yet dreading that one of the bone-white, filthy and bloody bodies might be his. Her eyes rested carefully upon each face before she rode on to the next pallet. At last she found a man who was conscious and bright-eyed, despite a shattered arm bandaged with tattered linen that was black with dirt. She asked him about Pavia and he told her of the carnages of battle, of France's most chivalrous and best-loved knights slain, of the bloodthirsty Spanish Imperialists who would have wiped out the wounded too after the battle was over.

'Do you – do you know of Hamish, Lord Mullally, His Majesty's foster-brother?' she asked, her heart lurching, beating so noisily that she was sure the man would hear it.

The bright eyes looked at her with pity. 'Lord Mullally? He is dead. Only two days ago I saw the gravediggers carrying his body to the burial area.'

It was a moment of decimating agony for Athena, who pressed her knuckles to her mouth and sank to her knees. After all this she was too late. The injured man looked at her compassionately; her squires stood by, grim-faced and awkward. Time seemed to alter the whole world; the sky, the air, the clouds, had become a different place, strange and alien. Unconscious of the hard ground biting into her knees, unconscious of anything but the searing fact that her beloved Hamish was dead, Athena felt her life was over: she would lie down on one of the pallets and die.

Then a voice piped up from nearby. A French man-at-arms, with a deep gash over one eye and a throat wound which had made his voice high and thin like a woman's was calling out to them.

'You are wrong, Melville, wrong! I do not know who you saw going past, but it was not Mullally. Did you see his crest, the falcon with two heads and the salamander on an azure ground?'

'Yes,' replied Melville emphatically. Then he gasped. 'Why, no! A falcon, yes, but not two-headed. God forgive me, mayhap it was not Mullally whom I saw carried to yonder graveside.'

Athena leapt to her feet. 'Then where does he lie?' she asked, her voice hoarse.

The man with the throat wound pointed to that section of the pasture where the knights and nobles were being tended.

The next few minutes were wild and distorted as she hurried along each line of wounded, scanning grey, unshaven faces, some with hideous wounds, some paling with death, one after another of them, but none of them Hamish. Her fists were clenched, her nails scoring into her palms fetching blood, but she did not notice. *Hamish!* Where was he, where did he lie? Then she saw the beloved face and a moaning cry escaped her lips. *Her husband.* He was not dead, but nearly so.

Ashen and raging with fever, he lay on the same pallet where he had been placed by the monks weeks before. The pallet was filthy with earth and blood, some brown and caked, some fresh and scarlet. Flies were hovering and alighting on it and on his improperly bandaged wound in a sickening mass. Nights of rain had drenched the pallet and green mould had grown on it like some loathsome disease. For days now Hamish had barely eaten, having had nothing but slops cooked in an iron pot over a camp fire kept alight by some of the stronger wounded. It was fortunate that the river was close, for at least they had had water at hand, although its purity was dubious for dozens of men had drowned in it during the battle.

'Jesu, thank you!' Athena gasped as she sank to her knees beside her husband, her fingers tracing his pinched and shadowy features. How thin he was and there were deep pits beneath his eyes and hollows in his cheeks, his hair stark black against the deathly pallor of his skin. His eyes were closed, his heart thudding, sweat beading his brow. She realized that he was in the midst of a raging fever. With disgust, she looked at his suppurating chest wound: how he had survived with that she did not know.

After a few moments of exquisite delight at finding him still alive, even if in such a sad state, she reached into her horse's panniers for a sharp knife and cut away the stinking brown bandage. As she did so she had to compress her lips against sudden nausea. The wound was filled with foul pus. She clasped her hands together, momentarily deterred. Could he survive such a dreadful condition as this? Ordering Pierre and Gaston to boil water, she reached for lint, linen and bandages and began to clean the noisome wound.

Hamish did not stir as she worked, but she could feel his heart pounding with the force of the fever. How shockingly near his heart the wound was, barely a finger-width away. She remembered what her father had said about fevers: that, contrary to popular opinion, it was wiser to bring down the body heat rather than to increase it by swathing the body in heavy covers. But they were in the open air here – dare she do what she really wanted to do: remove his filthy, tattered clothes, thoroughly wash his body, and dress him again with one of the spare outfits they had brought with them? Might he not take a chill on top of the fever? She deliberated as she cleaned out the wound, bathing the festering area with fresh linen dipped in the boiled water, which Gaston brought her in a leathern bucket. Now that the wound was bathed it looked enormous, glowing white ribs showing at one point. It was a miracle that he had survived. If he could only best the fever . . .

'Gaston, Pierre –' she looked up at her two squires, who stood nearby awaiting her orders, 'there must be a town or a village nearby where you can buy a clean pallet and fresh blankets. And we want some sort of shelter to keep off the rain.' She gave the two men some coins and told them to make all haste with their errand. Looking closely at the wound to make sure that it was completely free of pus, Athena opened her medical box, taking out medicinal oils and herbal unguents which she had made herself with comfrey and other ingredients that would reduce inflammation. Choosing the relevant oils, she packed the wound with them. It gaped wide and she felt that he really needed stitching, but she did not have the instruments or the courage to do this. Besides, if it began to suppurate beneath the stitches, it would prove difficult to clean it out again.

She bit on her lower lip, wondering what was the best course to take. How thin and pallid he looked, and the sweat was rolling off him, drenching his clothes. First she washed his face, and combed his tangled, sweat-streaked hair. She dared not move him to remove his cumbersome leather doublet, so she cut at it with her sharp little knife. The leather was stiff from repeated exposure to rain, and Hamish began to moan while she was working. Each time he winced, she winced too, feeling the pain that he was feeling. Beneath the doublet his shirt was creased and discoloured with sweat and blood, and she quickly cut it off him. She remembered how tanned he had looked the last time she had seen him naked; now, his body was white and wasted. A sob caught in her throat at the sight of him. Then, keeping her emotions under a rigid control, she washed his chest and arms and as much of his back as she could reach without disturbing him too much. She slit one of the spare shirts down the back and draped it over his torso and arms, tucking it beneath him, and unfastened the points of his breeches and slid them down, along with his hose. It struck her, then, that he was wearing no armour: someone must have removed it at some point. She bathed the lower part of his body, patted it dry, and dressed him in clean clothes. She wished that Gaston and Pierre would hurry up, for it could not be healthy for Hamish to continue lying on the mouldy and filthy pallet.

She knew that loss of the body's fluids could be highly dangerous in a fever, but was it safe to try and get a semi-conscious man to drink? Perhaps the safest way would be to soak the clean linen in the freshly boiled water and hold it at the corner of his mouth so that the water would trickle down his throat in such small quantities that it would not choke him.

It was a slow, not entirely successful business, but Athena persevered, tenderly watching his throat move as he swallowed minute amounts of water. The sun was too hot to cover him with her sheepskin cloak, for she knew that would only increase the fever. She sat beside Hamish, drinking in his every feature: his coal-black lashes and strong brows, the greenish pallor around his sensual mouth, the hollows at each side of his nose and in his cheeks caused by loss of body fluid. Lying out in the open here, in the Italian spring, he should have been tanned like a chestnut and, indeed, his hands were, but his face was ghostly.

It was almost nightfall when Pierre and Gaston returned. They had found all they needed at a nearby monastery, where they had been generously treated by the Father Superior and the monks. Gaston had a clean pallet rolled up across his saddle. There were blankets, hassocks, cheese, a leg of mutton, two flasks of wine, and four loaves of light and crumbly white bread.

'The monks certainly live well here,' Athena commented, breaking open one of the loaves to sniff its fresh-baked aroma. 'And wine, too; that is excellent.'

'I have brought skins, My Lady, and poles to make a shelter. We shall have it erected before dark.' Pierre smiled down at his mistress encouragingly.

Athena added some of the wine to the water she had been feeding Hamish. She dearly wished that she could feed him the mutton and cheese and bread and that he was well enough to drink more of the wine. She spent the next hour easing the watered wine into his mouth while

Gaston and Pierre erected the shelter of skins. Was she imagining it, or was there some colour in Hamish's cheeks? She hoped that it was so. Her back was aching agonizingly from leaning over him for so long and she sank back onto her haunches with a sigh.

'Eat, My Lady,' said Pierre. 'We do not want another invalid.'

The mutton was pink and succulent in the middle and crispy brown round the edges, and the cheese was crumbly and fragrant. The wine tasted like herbs, quite unlike anything she had ever drunk before, and instinctively she knew that it would do Hamish good. She drank half a mugful then put the rest aside for him. She had heard of tonic wines made by monks and knew that they had very powerful restorative properties. This must be one of them, she decided, and she felt much refreshed after only a few sips.

A slight breeze was springing up as darkness fell, and so Athena placed one of the loosely-woven blankets over Hamish. He looked much better now that he was on the clean pallet, in clean clothes, and with some fluid in his stomach. Satisfied that she could do no more for now, she curled up beside him under her sheepskin cloak, the shelter of skins above them, while Gaston and Pierre slept outside with the horses.

She woke twice during the night, once when an owl gave a particularly piercing hoot and the second time when one of the horses whinnied. It was eerie lying there in the darkness of a moonless night, listening to the faint moans and sighs of the wounded who lay all around them. She could not help but think of the graveyard so close by and of all the many dead who were buried there. Would their spirits looking for release haunt the camp, as tortured as their bodies had been in life? She shuddered, reaching out for Hamish's hand with her own. How good it was to hold him, to lie beside him. She was deeply thankful that she had come; nothing in Christendom would ever separate them again.

The next four days were much the same. Athena kept Hamish clean and comfortable and she managed to get a surprising amount of watered wine down his throat. Gaston and Pierre, when they had done all that they could for their mistress, went amongst the other wounded and helped to tend them. Athena gave them gold to buy more of the restorative wine, bread, cheese and meat from the monastery to dispense amongst the other soldiers.

On the morning of the fifth day, as Athena was bending over her husband, smoothing back his hair, he opened his indigo eyes and looked directly into her face. Shock speared her breast; she was sure that her heart had stopped beating. The world became silent around them.

For some time he stared at her, then his lips moved but no sound came, for his throat was tight and raw.

He groaned, thinking that he was hallucinating. He could not take his eyes from her. What a brilliant vision it was, this mind-image of his wife bending over him, her face tender and sensitive with concern. He could see the dimples at the corners of her mouth, wisps of silky moonlight-coloured hair escaping from the strange mannish hat which she wore. And why was she wearing a man's doublet? Why should he conjure her so?

'Hamish. Hamish, my darling . . .' Athena took his hands, watching the astonishment spread across his face, followed instantly by delight as he realized that she was no conjured spirit, but really Athena, really there in front of him.

It was the turning point. He began to mend immediately, and when he had drunk two cups of the wine, gulping it down as if he had never drunk before, he lay partially supported on one of the hassocks, staring at Athena as if she would disappear if he closed his eyes. For much of that day he drank in his wife's image along with a generous amount of water and wine. He was still too weak to chew, but by nightfall he felt hungry and Athena placed small pellets of the fresh white bread in his mouth. It was so crumbly that it dissolved without any danger of choking him.

The next few days showed a marked improvement in his condition. His body being desperate for fluids, he drank constantly, Athena always ensuring that the water was boiled first, for Gaston and Pierre had told her of the bodies in the river. Colour had returned to Hamish's face and he had expressed a wish for meat but had little energy to chew it, so Athena chewed it for him, feeding him tiny slivers which he could digest. He said very little, for his head was spinning with weakness for much of the time. He just lay and stared constantly at his wife, feeling stronger with every moment that he looked at her. As he sat up for longer periods, seeing all the misery and suffering around him, he thanked God for having sent his wife to him. All this way she had come, down through France, across the Alps and into Italy, to search for him. He never ceased to marvel at her stamina, fortitude and courage, but as yet he did not ask himself why she had come: it was enough that she was there and he felt blessed by her presence. He had lost track of time, and when he was told how many weeks he had been lying sick and fevered in the field-hospital he found it hard to believe. He could dimly remember somebody taking his armour: whether it was being stolen or whether it was to help him he did not know. He could also remember someone feeding him gruel and bread sops and the monks, who, in the early days, had tended him and the other victims. The Imperialists had ordered the monks away, saying that if they returned they, the victors, would slaughter all the wounded and the monks along with them.

Hamish asked Athena what had become of the King. She told him that Francis was a prisoner in an Italian fortress awaiting the pleasure, or displeasure, of the Emperor, and that the Queen Mother was negotiating with the Emperor and everyone else involved to try and free the King.

'So, he is the Emperor's prisoner . . .' Hamish groaned, seeing his proud and splendid foster-brother languishing in a cell in a foreign land. Kings imprisoning Kings: what had the world come to? He grieved for Francis and for France.

'The Queen Mother seems to be coping superbly, Hamish,' Athena told him. 'She has organized the Council and is being advised by the best men in the Kingdom. She has ransomed as many as possible from the Emperor.'

'Did she not try to ransom me?'

'It was thought that you were dead, Hamish. The King saw you fall, he thought he saw you mortally wounded. He would not have left the battlefield had he known you were still alive. Someone must have seen that you were not dead and brought you here to the field-hospital.'

'The monks – they were scared away by the Imperialists, who said that they would murder us all if the monks stayed. It seems to be their policy to let us all die, and yet they have allowed some to be ransomed. I find that puzzling.'

'The Emperor needs every coin he can get after impoverishing himself to win the Imperial Crown,' suggested Athena.

'And yet many knights and lords were slain after the battle was over, so I was told. The flower of French chivalry. Had they been allowed to live they could have been ransomed for many small fortunes. The ways of the Spanish and the Germans are beyond me.'

'You are tiring yourself talking, My Lord; sleep now. Gaston will be here when you wake up.'

'And not you?' Alarm leapt into his eyes.

'I am going to the monastery. Now that you are well enough to be moved we will find a place for you there, where you will be more comfortable. There, I will be safe and perhaps I will be able to wear a gown again. My skin is irritated by the roughness of these men's clothes.'

'Have you brought gowns with you?'

'I – I brought two nightrobes.' Colour swam into her cheeks. 'I could not very well pack a gown, with all its petticoats and underskirts and hoops and padding. We would have had room for nothing else.'

His indigo eyes twinkled. 'I wonder what the monks will make of a lady in their midst, and one who has only men's clothes or nightwear? It will certainly brighten their lives – as it has brightened mine,' he added, making Athena blush all the more.

The monks were Franciscans, whose lives were supposed to be dedicated to the greatest poverty as well as sexual abstinence and obedience. It was true that they wore harsh brown robes and that their feet were bare, but as Athena was shown into the Father Superior's sanctum she could not help remembering all the good food, the blankets and the pallet which Gaston and Pierre had been given by these very Franciscans. The Father Superior's room looked bare at first glance, but his chair was padded and there was a hassock for his back. On a table at one side stood a wine flask and a goblet, and as Athena was ushered into a chair facing the Father Superior's desk a cupboard door swung open to reveal, hastily thrust inside, a tray laden with food. She suppressed a smile as she waited for the Father to speak. She had come here dressed as a man and at some point she would have to divulge her sex.

'How can I help you, my son?' The Father Superior smiled genially. As she had been told, his French was excellent. There was a strong smell of wine on his breath and a few cake crumbs nestled in a fold of his habit.

'Father, you were very kind; you sold us food and a

pallet and blankets. My squires came here to purchase them from you, remember, about a week ago?'

'So many have come to us for aid . . .' He shrugged.

'You have been very generous, Father, and I know it must be difficult for you being so near the battlefield yet unable to help.'

'It is the cross that we must bear, my son. We pray for the wounded.' His deep-set dark eyes looked sombre.

'Father, I do not know how to say this,' Athena paused. 'You see, I came to Pavia looking for my husband, Lord Mullally.'

'Your *husband*?' The monk's voice came out as a squeak.

'Yes, my husband. You see, Father, we decided that it would be safer for me to travel dressed as a man.'

'So you are – you are female?' He said it as if he had found out that she was a deadly snake.

'I'm afraid so, Father.'

'No woman has ever been in our monastery before. It – it is unthinkable, quite unthinkable, that you should be here.'

'Nonetheless, I am here. I have come to ask you if you could help us yet again. Oh, we can pay, of course.'

'We do not take money, young – mistress.'

'I realize that, Father, but you must collect alms for the poor? The gold can be used to support the poor –'

'Gold?' he interrupted, leaning forward.

'Yes, gold, Father.'

'And what is it that you want, my daughter?' He sat back again, folding his hands across his ample stomach.

'A room where my husband can recover in comfort, where he can be nursed back to his full strength.'

'I think that would be possible. We have many brothers here who are skilled in the use of herbs and medicines.'

'Oh, but I would wish to nurse my husband myself, Father.'

'Ah no, that would not be possible,' he said abruptly. 'To have a – a female in our precincts would be to court

Satan. It is against all our laws and the teachings of the Church.'

'Surely you have a room somewhere away from the main building? I do not mind how small it is, or how isolated, as long as it has a roof. My husband has been sleeping outside night and day for weeks now. He received a terrible wound, close to his heart, and he has been burning up with fever. If I had not come here to nurse him he would have died by now. I want to continue nursing him, but properly, away from the rain and the night mists . . .'

He shook his head. 'The brothers are skilled – highly skilled – with medicines and herbs. You could leave your husband with us knowing that he would be hale again very soon.'

'And where do you expect me to stay while he is being nursed, Father? Would you have me languishing in the open in the field-hospital, wondering how my husband is faring?'

'It would be an opportunity to carry out many charitable deeds, my daughter. I am sure that your qualities as a nurse would be more than welcome amongst the wounded.'

'I have travelled all the way from Fontainebleau, near Paris, so that I could find my husband and nurse him myself – and nothing is going to detract me from that purpose. *Nothing*.' She sat back, her lips set in a stubborn line.

'Then, alas, it will not be under my roof, my daughter.'

'Father, I know that you and the brothers were ordered off the battlefield, and I know how that must have distressed you, but we are now talking about a man's *life*. If my husband took a chill now, when he is still in such a weak and vulnerable condition, he would have no resistance. This is one life which you can save, Father. Do it any way you wish. There is no need for me to see or speak with the brothers. Food can be left for us outside the door and I will open it when whoever has brought it has gone, or my squires, Gaston and Pierre, can deal with such matters.'

'It is against all our teachings and beliefs to have women in the monastery,' he repeated sternly.

'Father, if the world went according to your teachings and beliefs there would have been no battle at Pavia, there would be no field-hospital filled with suffering and dying men. My husband would still be strong and healthy. The world is not an ideal place. I have seen terrible things since I came into Italy; I shall dream about them for the rest of my life. If the world was as you would have it, there would be no need for any particular beliefs or teachings, for everyone would be meek and mild and without sin.'

'You have a very convincing argument, my daughter.' He looked anything but convinced.

'What would have happened if King Francis had been imprisoned here, Father? Would you have forbidden him all female visitors, his sister, his mother?'

'No, but –'

'My husband was raised with the King. He is his foster-brother. There are few as close to King Francis as Lord Mullally.'

'You should have told me earlier.' His manner changed abruptly. 'Under the circumstances . . .' Smiling benignly, he went on to say that a room would be put at their disposal immediately and that they must occupy it for as long as they wished.

While Athena thanked him courteously her mind was raging. What manner of Franciscan was this, who had charity for kings and their intimates but not for the ordinary man and woman? She wanted to tell him what she thought of him but she could not afford the luxury.

Gaston and Pierre made up a comfortable litter from the skins with which they had built the shelter, placing their master's pallet on the litter and then gently lifting him onto it, the strongest of their three horses dragging it along. A cowled brother with downcast face and arms tucked in his sleeves led them through the cool corridors of the monastery, along the greystone cloisters, out through a small door, into a paved terrace and then through another door, which led to a separate huddle of buildings, somewhat more dilapidated than the main part. There were three rooms put at their disposal: one for Hamish, one for Gaston and Pierre and one for Athena at the very bottom of the corridor. She could not help but smile at this, although she hid her smiles from the brother.

Before the monk left, she told him that her squires were strong and experienced at many tasks and that they would be pleased to help the monks with their labours while they were resident at the monastery. The monk bowed his head, still keeping his eyes averted from Athena, as if the sight of her might corrupt him. When he had gone, Gaston and Pierre gently lifted their master from the litter, placing him on the narrow wooden bed in his room. Hamish had winced at every jolt during the journey and now he lay back, bone-white, on the coarsely woven brown pillow, his breath sounding raw.

'Gaston and Pierre, you will have the room at the end of the corridor. I will stay close to My Lord. I paid the Father Superior handsomely for this arrangement, so will you see that he keeps us well provided with food and some more of that marvellous wine? My Lord wi'l take refreshment now.'

'Yes, My Lady.' Gaston and Pierre left to do as they were bid.

Athena leaned over her husband, touching his forehead lightly with her fingers. 'Get your breath, My Lord. Food and wine are being brought to us.'

'You have done well, Athena,' he said, his voice momentarily faint. 'It is not the Royal Palace of the Louvre but it is a great improvement on the battlefield.'

Athena grinned. 'And the cuisine is superb. You will soon get your strength back here.'

'It will take more than good food to restore me, Athena.'

His tanned hand reached up to take her little one. 'To recover I need the fairest nurse in Christendom as well.' He squeezed her fingers meaningfully.

Athena felt the heat rushing into her cheeks. She looked away, unable to meet his midnight-blue eyes for they were filled with an emotion she had never thought to see in them: deep admiration. There was no doubt that he was feeling grateful to her for all she had done. He would have been a boor not to have done. She had thoroughly enjoyed nursing him; she had never felt so useful in her entire life. To be needed, to be indispensable: she asked nothing more. Of course, she knew that this was only a brief sojourn and that as soon as he was recovered and back in France he would probably return to his adored paramour, who would, no doubt, be desperate for news of him. She wondered if the Queen Mother had sent a note to her too, telling her that Hamish had been wounded at Pavia, for undoubtedly Louise of Savoy would know of his clandestine affair, as she knew of everything concerning her courtiers.

But for the bleak decor, it would have been idyllic at the monastery. Food was brought to them at regular intervals, with wine, fresh milk and spring water for them to drink. Hamish looked a little better each day, responsive to everything his wife did for him. Gaston and Pierre helped with tasks about the monastery, reporting that the brothers seemed grateful for the help. They also said that they had never seen any monks, let alone Franciscans, eating so well, drinking so heavily and talking so much.

'There seems little discipline, My Lady. They eat meat every day and do not keep the fast days, and most of the wine they make seems to go down their own throats in somewhat large quantities.'

'It might be that Luther is right,' Pierre said.

'Luther? What do you know of him?' Hamish interrupted.

'I know that he speaks of the corruption and decay in the Catholic Church, My Lord. I have heard that he talks of worldly monks and nuns who neglect their vows.'

'I heard him talk once, in Germany,' Hamish said, off his guard. 'He seemed to me a totally convincing speaker, a man whom one would feel compelled to believe.'

'When were you in Germany, My Lord?' Athena asked.

Realizing that he had spoken rashly, Hamish said, 'Some time ago. The King and I went on a hunting expedition.'

'On the Emperor's lands? Have you met Charles the Fifth, then?'

Hamish's mind filled with alarm. How could he turn the conversation? 'No, we did not meet him,' he said quickly. 'It was planned that we should, but one of his sisters was ill at the last minute and he could not make it.'

'It is said that he dotes on his sisters,' Athena mused.

'That is true. He worships them, and his brother, Fernando. They are a very close-knit family, despite the fact that Fernando was brought up in Spain and Charles in Flanders with three of his sisters.'

Athena was experiencing the strangest sensation: a feeling that was brought on by the thought of Charles's sisters. Three sisters. How familiar, almost intimate, that sounded, as if it referred to her. But she knew that she had no siblings; she was the Comte's only child. But, deep inside, she was experiencing a feeling of grief, of loss and, inexplicably, it seemed in some way connected with the Emperor's three sisters.

Hamish seemed tired, and he dozed a little while Athena sat on the bench beside his bed examining her feelings. Sisters, losing sisters. Could the Comte possibly have had another daughter and years ago the child had died and she had forgotten about it? She knew that her memory was imperfect since her accident, but her father and the physicians had said it was only to be expected; they had said that the fevered dreams and the headaches would grow less and less. And it was true that they had. She was very strong now: had she not travelled through France into Italy, as hardy as any man, believing herself to be fully recovered from the effects of the blow to her head? But now, here came all these swelling sensations pouring through her mind and body, and in some way they seemed to be connected with sisters. Why did the thought of Charles the Fifth's three sisters make her feel so disorientated, so uneasy, so sad? She wished she knew. In an attempt to pacify her thoughts she imagined her father waiting for her in Paris. She wished that she could get word to him that she was safe and that Hamish was alive, but it was impossible. She knew that he would be anxious, for she remembered how she had felt when Hamish had been away at war for a year: waking in the mornings with a feeling that something was amiss; not being able to settle to any tasks satisfactorily; dreading the sight of a messenger riding towards the Château. Looking back, she did not know how she had survived that long, lonely, aching year. She had lived it as if cursed by a faerie who had ordained that she would feel no contentment or happiness until Hamish returned to her. Now, here she was beside him . . .

Feeling his eyes upon her, she looked up. His mouth was sweetly curved in a smile; she had surprised a look of longing on his face. Was he thinking of his paramour, that young, radiant brunette waiting for him in France? No doubt he would return to her immediately they got back to their homeland, under some pretext of the Queen Mother needing him now that she was Regent. Yes, Hamish would stay in Paris, sending Athena back to the Château Blanche. She was certain of it. But until he was fully recovered he was hers, and she was going to make the most of it: all else would be folly.

'Athena, what are you thinking of?'

'Of France . . . and of you getting strong again.'

'I will, never fear. I cannot wait to have my health back.

When I think of the King locked away in a fortress I feel as if part of me is locked away with him.'

'You are very close to him, My Lord, it is only natural that you should feel that way.' Comfortingly, she took his hand, feeling his bones sharp against her fingers. He had lost a great deal of weight.

'I have failed my foster-brother –' he muttered.

Athena's eyes opened wide. 'How can you say that, my Lord? You all but lost your life defending him.'

'He is the Emperor's prisoner. If I had fought harder, longer, perhaps he would be free at this moment.'

'And perhaps you would be dead.' Athena's mouth twisted. 'You have only the strength of a man, not of an angel. If God had wished the King to be rescued then He would have sent a miracle to free him.'

'So you think it is God's Will that Francis should be kept under lock and key by the Emperor, that France should be without its King, that all those French lords and knights should have been so cruelly slaughtered by the Imperialists?'

'If it is not God's Will then whose will is it, My Lord? If men must go to war then they must be prepared to pay the price. If the battle had gone the other way, what would the French have done to the Imperialists?'

'If only the Emperor had been at Pavia, if only *we* had taken *him* prisomer. But he would not put his own life in danger. He is a weakling and a coward: there is none of the blood of his grandfather in him. But then, his father was but a courtier and a womanizer and his mother, Queen Juana, is insane. She has been shut away for years now, and Charles calls himself King of Spain when *she* is rightfully its ruler. His lust for lands and Crowns knows no equal. Oh, if only I were well enough . . .'

'Well enough for what, My Lord?'

'Well enough to go straight to the Emperor, to intercede for Francis. There must be some way of arranging a compromise, some way of having Francis freed.'

'And you think that you could do that?' Privately, Athena thought that he must be fevered again. What did he know of such matters? And anyway, he would not be well enough to be moved for weeks.

Hamish would say no more on the matter. He had already revealed more than he should. He set about making as speedy a recovery as possible, but, as the days passed and he grew accustomed to Athena's presence, her sweet smile and patient nursing, he began to realize that he was torn; half of him wanted to be well so that he could intercede for the King, the other half wanting to remain here as long as possible with Athena. He knew that had he been stronger he would not have allowed the conflict to get the better of him. Had he not succeeded in putting the King first for years now? But the tranquil haven that was the monastery was having a softening effect on him: the serenity, the fact that he was bedridden, all were playing their part. He felt his love for Athena being freed from the cage in which he had kept it. One by one, the bars were falling away; soon his love would be blazing on his face and in his breast. But what would she think of him? She was loyal and brave, she had travelled across two countries to find him when she had heard that he was wounded, but it did not give him the right to demand that she love him. He must be grateful for each sweet smile, for every gentle touch of her hand, for her skill with herbs and unguents, for the fact that she had come at all. He must ask for no more than that.

What was worrying him was the thought of his growing stronger but still being too weak to leave. There would be a natural result to their being alone together: he would start to desire her again. And here, in this haven, where they were flung together night and day, how would he be able to control himself? He would be the vilest of animals if he repaid her courage, her selflessness, by making her pregnant. But even now, when he could do little more than lie still to quiet the ringing in his head caused by loss of blood, he could feel the echoes of desire. Pointedly, they thrust their way into his mind, his emotions, and, when she thought he was dozing, he would lie there thinking of her soft, curving, white body, her breasts snuggling in his palms, her warm satin lips. Then passion would sear through him with an almost intolerable savagery. She never guessed, of course: his gentle, patient nurse.

Oh God, he did not want this time to end! He wanted to walk into eternity with Athena beside him. He saw the life to which he must return as a hollow, superficial and vainglorious existence. Love, in all its generosity, tenderness and contentment, that was what truly mattered to him now. The depths of his feeling stunned him. He felt somewhat akin to a visionary experiencing his first vision. It was as if another part of him had come into being. But to what purpose? He could not answer that question. If she had loved him and he was responding to that love, then he would have understood. But his feelings had developed unkindled by her loving him; they had simply sprung out of nowhere, taking him by surprise. He, who had always had his life so well organized, so perfectly under control. But he had vowed that he would not make her pregnant, and nothing would make him alter that vow.

They got on well together. The hours did not drag. Athena was able to expend some of her love in tender ministrations, while Hamish could gaze upon her face as he liked. They talked and laughed and made plans for themselves and for the Château Blanche, but all the time each considered this truce to be a temporary state of affairs – Athena believing that her husband would go straight back to his mistress when he was well, that he was only being dutifully grateful to her, while Hamish gradually began to reconstruct that iron control which was so vitally necessary to protect her from himself. Nonetheless, it was an idyllic time, blossoming as it had out of tragedy, chaos and bloodshed. When it became obvious that Hamish was strong enough to travel, they both hid their disappointment as they prepared for the journey to Paris. Both of them needed all their skill at pretence to conceal their true feelings. Athena had longed for Hamish to touch her, to kiss her and make love to her, but he had made no sign in that direction. He had been a very sick man and near death, and she had no intention of forcing him into behaving in any way which did not spring from his own needs. Desire was one of the first things to go when a man was seriously injured and the journey back was taxing for them both. At night-time they lay close to one another but not touching, Hamish wrapped in blankets, Athena in her sheepskin cloak. Both of them would lie there pretending sleep, Athena longing for Hamish to take her in his arms and Hamish only wishing that he could.

CHAPTER NINETEEN

The Comte rejoiced to have his daughter and his son-in-law returned to him alive, and the Queen Mother wept as she kissed Hamish, forgetting any acrimony there had been between them. The next few days were filled with subdued festivities to welcome back Hamish and his wife, subdued, naturally, because no one could forget that their King was a prisoner of the Holy Roman Emperor. Athena was quite prepared to remain at Court for some time – anything to stay with her husband – so when Hamish began to talk about her returning to the Château Blanche she was dismayed. She found that he had already arranged for her journey with the Comte, though nothing had been said to her before.

It was futile to be angry: the idyll was over. He wanted her out of the way so that he could court his paramour once more without the embarrassment of her presence. A sick grief engulfed her. It seemed that nothing she did for him could make him alter towards her. She remembered the happy, relaxed times they had spent together at the Italian monastery. He had been like a different man then, and she had thought he was beginning to love her. Now, her pride came to her rescue; indeed, she had little else to save her from foundering. She would go back to the Château Blanche with her father and no one would know the burden of misery and dejection which she was carrying; certainly not Hamish. She would put his callous ingratitude out of her mind and she vowed that she would not think of him in his mistress's arms. When Hamish kissed her goodbye she kept her face wooden, saying nothing. Then she rode off with the Comte, Pierre and Gaston in the blazing heat of summer, her heart a prickly ball in her breast.

*

Hamish was with the Queen Mother, who was telling him all that she knew about the King's whereabouts and what had happened to him recently. Louise of Savoy looked strained, as if she had not slept; she had lost weight and there was ill-concealed anguish in her eyes.

'My son has, of course, refused outright the heinous terms put to him by the Imperial Envoy when he was at Pizzighettone. Such terms would have divided France – destroyed it completely. And that scurrilous knave, Bourbon, would have been made King of Provence.' The Queen Mother's lip curled. 'The Emperor refused to give his sister Eleanor to my son as his bride which only shows his foolhardiness. The Habsburgs have long been famous for gaining by marriage what others gain by war, and yet now the Emperor has refused to make an alliance in this way.'

'The King has now left Pizzighettone, has he not, Madame?'

'In May he left Genoa, in June he landed at Barcelona. As soon as I knew he was at sea I sent out French ships to rescue him but, alas, the attempt was a complete failure. Francis was taken from Barcelona to Madrid, and that time was not so bad. He was allowed to dress as befits a King and he was given a worthy steed. It is said that he awed the Spaniards, that they were overcome with admiration for him. He was entertained and presented with gifts and feasted all along the route.'

'And when he reached Madrid, Madame –?'

'That was a different story. Straight into a tower of the Alcazar like a common felon. It is a small room, and there is a double iron grille over the only window. It is sparsely furnished; there is a drop of over one hundred feet from the window, even if one could get through the bars, and the tower is under constant guard by two companies of soldiers. On rare occasions they allow him to ride a mule, but only when he is strongly guarded. I fret constantly, knowing he needs exercise, activity. Louise clenched her hands, pressing her lips together and biting upon them. 'I think of him shut away in that tiny, airless room and I know that he is suffering. His letters are sad and spiritless. It is as if he has given up. Oh, how helpless I feel.' She paced about the room. 'I have written letter after letter, I have sent envoys, ambassadors, couriers, gold, ships. Nothing seems to work. When I heard that you had been wounded, that you were not dead, I knew that you had been given to me by God, that you had been saved for one purpose and one purpose only. Hamish, I want you to go to the Emperor. I want you to intercede for my son. But you must act quickly, for every day that passes drags him down further into despondency and lassitude. You will be France's saviour: only you can save him now.'

'Give me your instructions, Madame, and I shall ride immediately to the Emperor.'

PART IV

THE CONVENIENCE OF MARRIAGE

CHAPTER TWENTY

The Emperor was cold and vindictive. He was barely listening to a word that Hamish said. Looking at Charles's long, thin face with his huge, deformed jaw and the teeth which would not meet so he could not shut his mouth properly, Hamish felt a wave of revulsion. This man, bony, twenty-five years old, dressed in funereal black, with spindly legs and a misshapen jaw, was God's temporal representative on Earth, a man with boundless power. An autocrat, a despot . . . He showed no remorse, no pity for King Francis, but only an all-pervading iron chilliness.

'King Francis is becoming ill because of his imprisonment, Your Imperial Majesty. Every day that passes sees him more dispirited. His mother fears for his health. He has always been an active man: to be shut in one room –'

'And where would he have put me had the positions been reversed? I am sure that I would not have been given a palatial room at the Louvre. Battles between Kings must be decided by Kings and not by menials.' Charles's eyes were icy. 'I have no intention of answering any of the feeble, pleading letters which King Francis has sent me, nor do I have any intention of listening to such as yourself, My Lord. There is no reason why I should change my plans. I have given Francis the terms of his release and he has refused to accept them. If he wishes to be free, he has merely to agree to the Treaty.'

'A treaty which divides up his Kingdom and makes the traitor Bourbon King of Provence –? Such terms would kill His Majesty,' protested Hamish.

'If he wishes to die then that is his concern,' the Emperor sneered. 'But if he accepts the terms, then he will be freed from the Alcazar. It is as simple as that, My Lord.'

'Your Imperial Majesty, the Pope has let it be known

that he deplores King Francis's imprisonment in your lands. He is sympathetic to the King's plight.'

'I have not heard of this, My Lord.' The Emperor said it in such a way that Hamish felt he was being accused of lying. 'Do I have to remind you of the persecution which my Duchy of Burgundy has received from French Kings?'

'But not from King Francis, Your Imperial Majesty, only from French Kings who are now dead. If you wish to take revenge upon King Francis for what his forebears have done then I think that you have had it now.'

'So you think that I should free him, just like that, as if I am weak and easily swayed by argument? That is not my way, My Lord, nor has it ever been.'

Hamish fought for control over his anger. He tried another approach. 'I believe that King Francis suggested a marriage alliance between himself and your sister, the widowed Queen of Portugal. Have we not seen enough of war? Is it not more Christian to make peace now with a marriage?'

'I might have considered that if Francis had no children and I could one day see my sister's son wearing the French Crown, but he has sons, has he not, a large healthy family, all of whom would rule before any children of my sister's. Such an alliance would be repulsive to me, My Lord, and to my sister. She has been a Queen once and would accept no lesser role. As the second wife of King Francis she would live in the shadow of Queen Claude's children. Such an inferior position would be untenable to both my sister and myself.'

'Your Imperial Majesty, I can promise that Queen Eleanor would be treated with the utmost courtesy, love and devotion by my master. She would be First Lady of France; there would be no question of her children coming second to those of Queen Claude.'

'So Francis would make my sister's son his heir? You cannot expect me to believe that,' sneered Charles, 'nor would the French people accept it: it would be unconstitutional, a blight upon Queen Claude's name. There would be insurrection and uproar, my sister would be vilified. You are wasting your time, Lord Mullally. There is only one way King Francis can get out of the Alcazar, and that is by agreeing to my terms. You may tell the King what I have said; it may make a man of him.'

Hamish choked back his rage. Swallowing hard, he said, 'Is there any message of hope that I might carry to the King from Your Imperial Majesty?'

'Only that he may put his trust in God.'

'Then I shall be allowed to visit the King?'

'But of course.'

The audience was over.

Hamish left the Emperor's presence with a heavy heart. Charles's lack of feeling was unnatural, and yet he must have a normal man's emotions, for it was well known that he doted upon his blood kin. But at least he, Hamish, had received permission to visit King Francis in the Alcazar, and that was where he was riding now, as fast as his horse would take him.

Francis and Hamish wept at being together again, flinging their arms round one another rapturously. The effusive greeting over, Hamish glanced round the dull and depressing room where the King was imprisoned. It was shockingly grim and enough to quench the spirits of a jester. He must get him out of here as soon as possible, whatever the price paid.

During the journey to Madrid a plan had formed in Hamish's mind. He was going to urge the King to agree to the Emperor's terms, to agree to them all, as if he were cowed, then, once the King was freed, he would make it known publicly that he had been forced to agree to the terms under duress and that, as a result, they were not legal.

Hamish had thought it a satisfactory plan, but he had not considered Francis's response.

'If I did such a thing my honour would be in ruins,' the King exclaimed. 'To *lie* my way out of this situation – what would men say of me? Posterity would condemn me; I would never be trusted again, no man would ever believe my word. I appreciate the idea behind your plan, Hamish, but I cannot agree to it.'

Hamish swallowed a groan. 'Would you stay here a prisoner, brother, in this accursed place, when you could be free and back in your own Kingdom again?'

'It is true that I yearn to be in France once again, that I long to see my children. How are they? Tell me how they are, Hamish.'

'All well, and longing to see you again, as is your mother. Please, I beg of you, do as I say, Francis. It is a way out –'

'A poor way out, Hamish, and not to be entertained by an honourable man. No, I cannot do it, much as I might want to. You return to France?'

Hamish nodded glumly.

'Then you will take messages for the Queen Mother and for my children.'

'Of course.'

That night Hamish slept in a small room in the Alcazar, feeling its all-pervading gloom seeping into his bones. Next morning he headed back to Paris, rehearsing what he would say to the Queen Mother, imagining her dismay and grief when she knew that he had been unsuccessful, that one more effort had failed.

Louise wept brokenly, cupping her face in her hands. When she had recovered somewhat, she told Hamish that she thought his plan to free the King was a fine one and that she would pursue it if at all possible.

'The Princess Marguerite is to be allowed to visit my

son in the Alcazar. I will tell her of your idea and she will try to talk the King into changing his mind. If anyone can do it she can; he listens to her. Now, Hamish, tell me how my son looked. Was he well? Is he still confined to that dreadful room?'

'He looked pale, Madame, as is only to be expected, for he rarely sees the sun. The food is none too good: it is oily and flung together anyhow. I would not vouch for the cleanliness of the Alcazar's kitchens. I have letters for you and for the Royal children.'

Hamish passed them to the Queen Mother. 'The King lives for the letters he receives from you and the rest of the family – he told me to tell you that.'

A sob broke from Louise's lips. She pressed a hand to her mouth. 'His family has always meant more to him than anything. This is a vicious end for my son.'

'Let us not consider it an end, Madame. The Princess may well succeed in talking the King round. Let us pray that it will be so.'

'And may God in His goodness hear our prayers,' added the Queen Mother. 'Now, take a brief holiday with your beautiful wife, Hamish. You have earned it. I will keep you informed as to what is happening.'

CHAPTER TWENTY-ONE

Going home. Part of him was exultant, part apprehensive. To live with her would be sweet torture: he wanted it and yet he did not want it. He would continue to sleep separately from Athena, with the door between their rooms securely locked and bolted. He would not allow any physical contact between them, not even so much as a brush of the fingertips. When he was near her he would try to keep uppermost in his mind the picture of her suffering in labour, dying in childbirth.

She was waiting for him in a gown of moonlight-coloured silk embroidered with sky-blue loveknots and roses. She did not look a day older than sixteen. When he was away from her he almost forgot how protective he felt towards her. He knew that she had crossed the Alps to reach him, had nursed him through appalling conditions, and yet she looked as fragile and ethereal as an elfin creature from the forest. He kissed her lightly on the brow.

'Did your journey go well, my husband?' She was watching his face for some sign of his happiness to be back with her, but his indigo eyes were inscrutable, his face set in rigid lines. He has not changed, she thought, her heart sinking. I must go on taking care with every word I say to him.

They dined together on herb and capon pie and a selection of luscious summer fruits. Hamish washed down the food with copious amounts of wine, Athena watching him with dismay. Surely it was not going to start all over again, his heavy drinking, the black moods, the rages, the midnight gallops through the forest? She did not think she could bear it. She wanted them to be lovers, but they always seemed to be haters. She tried to keep the alarm from her face, behaving as if nothing was amiss, reconstructing in her mind the tranquil and easy-going days they had spent together while he was recovering from his wound. He had seemed a different man then, relaxed and goodnatured, with gratitude shining in his eyes.

'How goes it with the King?' she asked.

'Badly. He is shut away in the Alcazar like a common felon, in a small, dingy room; he has no exercise, no respite from the boredom and humiliation.'

'We have been saying Novenas for his safe return to France.'

'If prayers could release him then he would have been free by now.' Hamish's mouth twisted. 'He is hardly allowed out of his cell, and for an active man that is tantamount to torture. His mother fears for his health, as do I.'

'The Emperor is adamant about the terms for his release?'

'Quite immovable.'

'Are the terms completely unacceptable to the King?'

'Completely. If he accepted them he would be nothing more than a puppet, a laughing-stock, lower than a peasant and completely in the control of the Emperor, Bourbon and the King of England.'

'I would have thought the Emperor would have leapt at a marriage between his sister and the King. It seems such a sensible solution to the problem.'

'For the King, yes; but the Emperor believes that his agreement to a marriage alliance would be seen as weakness. After all, he is the victor: it is he who has captured and imprisoned King Francis, not the other way round. Why should he settle for a marriage alliance when he can have France added to the Holy Roman Empire?'

'Then he must be an exceedingly greedy and avaricious man. He already has enough dominions to suit six kings.'

'They say he will not be content until Habsburgs rule the world.'

'And will people just stand by and let him do this?'

Athena clenched her fists. 'What of the Pope? Can he not speak out for King Francis?'

'Since my foster-brother was put into the Alcazar the Pope's affiliation has changed. He has let it be known that he wants Francis to be released and returned to his Kingdom as soon as possible.'

'Surely the Emperor will listen to that?'

'The Emperor is a law unto himself. He fears no man, not even the Holy Father. Do not forget that he comes from a dynasty of Emperors, men who for decades have ruled Christendom. It is in his blood to be all powerful.'

Athena tried to imagine this merciless despot, the Emperor Charles the Fifth. 'He sounds a monster,' she said.

'At times he is. He is cold and emotionless as glass.'

'So nothing can be done?'

'All that can be done is being done, believe me. I would not be here otherwise.'

She took that to mean that he would not leave Paris if he thought urgent news was on its way regarding his foster-brother. She felt so helpless. She wanted to show her love, to reach out her hand and touch him lightly, smile into his eyes. He filled his goblet yet again, drinking deeply. When the meal was finished he said that he had business to attend to and that he would see her anon. Alone, she silently prayed for patience and tolerance, for understanding, but she felt as if she were blundering in the dark. He was an enigma, her husband, with his inscrutable, basilisk expression, his variable moods. She longed to find the secret way to his heart: there must surely be a path, if only she could find it? Meanwhile, she would go blundering on, ignorant and bemused, with heartache as her closest companion.

Athena and Hamish seemed to be living on a tightrope. In the ensuing days, Hamish returned to his former, scowling self, constantly finding some fresh task to do which kept him from Athena's side, and sleeping in his own room, on the other side of the locked door, while Athena tried to console herself with her pets. It was worse after the message came from Paris. The King's enforced inactivity had made him seriously ill and it was feared that he would lose his life. The Princess Marguerite was even now on her way to Spain to nurse him, and, wrote the Queen Mother, the Princess would be doing her best to persuade her brother to agree to the Emperor's terms so that he would be freed at once. '*In the way that you suggested, Hamish,*' wrote Louise of Savoy. What could that line mean? thought Athena. She puzzled over it, but did not dare to question her husband. Had he thought of some plan which would help the King? Not for the first time she longed for him to confide in her.

Summer advanced. The land grew parched. The dogs lay on the grass, panting with the heat, the only ones to brave the midday sun. Letters arrived from the Palace: the King was worse; he had lost the power of speech and hearing; he failed to recognize anyone, even his sister. Mass was celebrated in his cell: the priest was in readiness to give him the last rites.

On reading this, Hamish crushed the letter in his hand, banging his fist down over and over again on the table, an agonized groan escaping his lips. Athena could not restrain herself; she flew to him, standing behind him, placing her hands on his shoulders, her cheek against his. They wept together. He turned, burying his face against her breast and sobbing like a child, while she stroked his hair and spoke soothingly. After a few moments, they went hand in hand to the chapel and knelt to pray for a miracle.

The tension of the next few days was brittle as ice, but the bad news seemed to have brought them together. And then another letter arrived from the Queen Mother: they had been granted their miracle, the King had recovered, God be praised. The Emperor had been told that the King had died and he had rushed to Madrid, only to find Francis recuperating. With not a word of concern for his health, the Emperor had put his terms to Francis again, and again Francis had been adamant in his rejection of them. The Princess Marguerite had returned to Paris with authority from the King to make his oldest son, the Dauphin, King in his father's place, while Louise of Savoy would act as the boy's Regent. However, the King's ministers and advisers had refused outright to accept his abdication, for they believed he had acted under duress.

France had been stunned by the King's almost fatal illness. Even the Emperor had been shocked out of his usual phlegmatic calm; the King of France was no use to him dead. It was said that Erasmus himself had written to the Emperor to intercede for Francis's freedom.

'*The King, my son, would not be persuaded to agree to the terms in the manner which you suggest*,' wrote the Queen Mother. '*Never has he been so obdurate – why I do not know. I am in despair.*'

Having read the letter, Hamish knew what he must do: return to Madrid to try again to change the King's mind. His efforts might prove fruitless but at least he would have done his best.

Ordering his valets to pack, he told Athena that he was going to Paris to give what aid he could to the Queen Mother. As soon as he was out of sight of the Château Blanche, they turned their horses for the direction of Spain.

It was winter before Hamish returned, and with him he brought the news of the King's release. Athena would never know the part her husband had played in having the King freed: how he had lived in the Alcazar with his foster-brother, trying to cheer him and keeping an eye on his health and, when he felt the moment was right, putting forward his arguments regarding the King's future. He was gentle but cogent. He reminded the King of his vital importance to France. He spoke of the Queen Mother's despair, of the sadness of the Royal children. Then he said that if the French Parliament had decided that the King's renunciation of his Crown under duress was invalid, then so was any treaty he might make with the Emperor. At last Francis had been won round. For him to go back on his word was one thing, but for others to decide that his word had never been pledged – that was different. He told the Emperor that he would agree to all his demands. The result was the Treaty of Madrid, in which Francis promised to relinquish Burgundy, Flanders and Artois, eschew his claims to Naples and Milan, forget his quarrel with Bourbon, and allow his two elder sons to live in Spain as hostages. The Emperor then agreed to give his sister Eleanor as Francis's wife.

Francis was still in Spain, meeting the widowed Queen Eleanor and putting the finishing touches to the Treaty and to the betrothal. Hamish had ridden to Paris in great haste to inform the Queen Mother, and, from there, had come to Fontainebleau to his wife. He had not felt so joyful for years; he was inebriated with his success. He had brought gifts for Athena: Spanish leather riding boots tooled with gold, scented riding gloves to match, a beautiful, slender dagger of Toledo steel with a gold hilt encrusted with rubies, Spanish leather collars for Carol and his pups, with golden bells suspended from them.

Having accepted her husband's kiss of greeting and all the presents, Athena said, 'Is this not Spanish leather, My Lord?'

'Indeed it is. I bought these from Spanish merchants,' he said, quite truthfully.

'They visited the Louvre then, despite the strife between our countries?' Fortunately she did not wait for his reply, for she had found the gilded leather collars with their tinkling golden bells and was enchanted by them, immediately calling the dogs to her, removing their old collars and replacing them with the new. When Carol shook himself to the accompaniment of tinkling bells, a look of astonishment stole over his face, which made Athena laugh out loud.

The next hours were good. They dined together and laughed over the dogs' antics, and Athena tried on the Spanish boots and gloves and walked up and down for Hamish to admire her in them. His mood seemed so cheerful that she was sure he would come to her bed that night. He kissed her and told her to sleep well and then she lay in her bed waiting – forever waiting. But in vain. Even with so much to celebrate he was not going to make love to her. Tortured with longing, she cradled her face in her hands and wept.

Next morning, Athena woke late and looked out of her bedchamber window to view the day. What she saw made her suppress a cry of horror and disbelief. A young woman had just ridden up to the Château with her retinue of servants. She had distinctive, unforgettable features, which became visible to Athena as she flung back her furred riding hood to greet Hamish, who was striding towards her, arms outstretched. It was her husband's paramour, come here boldly and openly to visit him! Athena fell back, knuckles pressed to her mouth, trembling from brow to toe. The strumpet – how dare she? Athena crept back to the window to see them locked in a loving embrace, spears of longing coruscating through her. Oh, if only it were she down there in her husband's arms. What was she going to do now: go down the stairs and face them? Perhaps – perhaps the creature had come to take him away? Perhaps when she went downstairs they would greet her hand in hand to tell her that Hamish was leaving her? A legion of similar thoughts throbbed through her mind as Solange helped her dress. She wore a gown of china-blue velvet lined with miniver, with a circular shoulder cape of matching miniver to keep out the cold. She half expected Hamish to come to her while she was dressing, to be courteous enough to warn her in some way, but he did not. Shakily, she descended the stairs and followed the sound of voices and laughter into the salon. She paused in the doorway, staring at them, waves of dizziness engulfing her. They were sitting close together on a bench, drinking wine. The girl was clasping Hamish's hand lightly and looking at him with adoration. She was even younger than Athena had thought, her sophisticated mode of dress and hairstyle adding ten years to her age. How old would she be: fifteen, sixteen? And Hamish was looking at her dotingly . . .

The girl saw Athena first, leaping to her feet, her face alight.

'Oh, Madame, I've so longed to meet you!' the girl cried, hurrying towards Athena and taking her ice-cold hands in hers. 'Oh, Madame, Hamish and I –'

'Hamish and you –?' Athena managed to hiss through wooden lips, dreading what was coming next.

'Hamish and I were waiting for you to come down so that I could meet you. Oh, I am so happy, so happy! You have no idea, Madame. May I call you Athena? We are almost like sisters, after all.'

'Sisters?' echoed Athena, feeling stupid and slow-witted.

'Yes, sisters, for Hamish has been like a brother to me. He is so kind, so understanding. I do not know what I would have done without him. And now we can be together again.'

Athena listened, her thoughts moving clumsily, her heart thudding. She was trying to make sense of what the girl was saying.

'You and Hamish, together . . .?'

'No, no, Madame my *father* and I together again. Oh, but I have not explained, have I? How stupid of me. It has been a secret for so long that I still find it difficult to speak the truth. You see, Athena, dear sister, my father is the King. While Queen Claude was alive I was kept a secret, you see, so that she would not be hurt. She never knew of my existence, thanks to Hamish. He looked after me for the King and carried messages between us and saw that I had everything I needed. My mother died when I was born. She was very beautiful and the King loved her dearly – but he was not, of course, married to her. Oh, how I have longed to tell the world that I am the King's daughter and now it will be possible, thanks to dear Hamish who has worked the miracle and freed my father from the Alcazar!'

Athena was trying to assimilate what the girl was saying. This beautiful, exquisite child was King Francis's illegitimate daughter and *not* Hamish's mistress, after all? But what did she mean about Hamish freeing the King from the Alcazar? How could such a thing be possible? There were so many mysteries about her husband: she believed that she would never learn them all.

'Come and sit down, Athena,' Hamish patted the seat beside him, 'and we will tell you all about it.'

And so they did, and when they finished tears were sliding down Athena's cheeks as she gripped her husband's hand. The King's daughter, whose name was Bellonne de Veaux, watched them in delight. She knew how Hamish loved his wife, for he had spoken lovingly of her many times to Bellonne. How good it was to see them so happy together when so many married couples squabbled and avoided one another's company.

Bellonne stayed with them all that day, and when she had left with her retinue, Hamish took Athena on his knee before the fire and kissed her adoringly over and over again. He had lain awake all the previous night longing to go into her bedchamber and take her in his arms, but he had fought back the desire manfully. Now, after Bellonne's visit, she seemed so happy, so glowing, that he could not resist her. It was as if all the years of inner conflict and torture had never been. He lifted her up in his arms, heavy furred skirts and all, and carried her up the stairs to her bedchamber, where he carefully placed her on the bed. A fire was roaring in the grate. Solange, who had been sitting waiting to undress her mistress, took one look at their faces and hurriedly disappeared, a smile on her lips. They drank wine, taking sips and feeding the wine into one another's mouths. They laughed and kissed and caressed, their minds and bodies in unity. It was as if the long years of abstinence had never been for Hamish, and for Athena there was the belief that at last her husband loved her.

'Your throat was made for jewels,' he whispered huskily, kissing it. 'Your ears are the most tiny and perfect I have ever seen; your skin is like Genoese velvet.' They gave one another sweet-wine kisses and passionate hugs, so tight that their flesh seemed to merge. 'My love, my sweet love,' he murmured. 'How I have missed you, how I have longed for you! If you only knew how I feel about you, how I cherish you, everything about you . . .'

Athena listened in delighted amazement to this eulogy. Could this be her taciturn, moody husband speaking to her as if she were a goddess whom he worshipped? She could hardly believe it, but all the same it was heaven in her ears. But she found that she was holding herself tautly in case what had happened before was to happen again: that he should suddenly turn himself from her and fling out of the room. She prayed that it would not be so, that he would stay with her and continue this fervid lovemaking.

'Athena, my darling, if only you loved me, if only I could hope that you would come to love me.' He lapped at her breasts, his tongue undulating across her nipples. She could feel him hard as steel against her thigh.

'Oh, but I *do*, Hamish! Did you not guess? I love you, love you, *love you*! That is the truth, my husband. Why do you think I went to Sesia to look for you? Would I have done that if I had been indifferent to you?'

'But I have treated you abominably, my darling. I knew that I did not deserve your love and so I dared not hope for it. I still do not deserve it, nor ever shall.'

'Love happens, it does not make moral judgements, nor is it calculating. I have loved you for years and I have waited all this time for you to learn to love me. I thought –' she blushed hotly – 'I thought that you had a mistress, another woman whom you loved desperately, and that you saw me only as a burden round your neck. All those times you left me I thought you were going to *her*.'

'My God, I went to no one,' Hamish growled. 'I could love no one more than I love you – unless you had a twin,' he grinned. 'And you put up with me patiently all this time, thinking that I was being unfaithful to you? You are a saint, an angel.' He circled her face with kisses, then lowered his lips to hers tenderly while their fingers interlaced and gripped tightly.

Athena felt tears of joy pricking behind her lids. She wanted to ask why he had not bedded her for so long, why he had so often started to make love to her and then stormed away as if in a great rage. But marvellous and beautiful sensations were searing through her body, taking her breath away, and Hamish's mouth was crushing hers.

He entered her in one swift, silken movement, plunging deep into her body, and she curved up her hips to meet his thrust, clinging to him, pressing her nails into his back and sighing his name. She could think of nothing but him, nor did she want to. Ecstasy filled her mind and veins, her heart beat his name, so that he seemed truly a part of her.

When she thought it must surely end, he went on and on, plunging ever deeper and harder inside her, making her twist her head from side to side on the pillow. Then she felt a curious scintillating sensation begin, as if she had unexpectedly reached the top of a mountain and was seeing a brilliant, unbelievable view spread out before her, a view which took her breath away. Currents of fire lapped through her blood, sweeping to her head and to her feet, gathering delicious momentum. Then she was embraced by the heady joy of her first orgasm, Hamish joining her.

Afterwards they lay in one another's arms, Athena's head on Hamish's chest, while he gently stroked her hair. It had been an overwhelming experience for them both and they were breathless. When they had recovered, Hamish began to kiss her again and soon they were locked together for a second time, as sweetly as before. Throughout that night they became one again and again; then, exhausted, they slept, bathed in an aura of contentment.

Next morning, waking in his wife's arms, Hamish felt a cold shock of horror. What had he done: how could he have taken advantage of her? Had he been mad, crazed, the night before, drunk on love more powerfully than on any wine? Oh God, he would never forgive himself. How was he going to live through the next weeks? He could not bear to look upon her, this woman whom he loved, whom he had wronged so grievously. He leapt from the bed as if her touch burned him, making her wake with startled eyes.

'Hamish, my love,' she whispered, holding out her arms. But he flung her a tortured look filled with self-loathing. He stormed into his own bedchamber and she heard him crashing around in there. Trembling, she went after him, calling his name. Seeing that he was packing his belongings, despair twisted in her heart. Nothing had changed: it was as if the previous night had never been. He was going to leave her yet again, and she could tell from the expression on his face that it was hopeless for her to try and stop him. Sick and shaking, she went back to her room and plunged beneath the bedclothes to curl into a tiny, self-protective ball. She lay there while all her hopes and dreams evaporated one by one. He did not love her, it was all lies. He had behaved lovingly towards her to lower her defences because he wanted a legitimate son. He had tricked her . . . Too shocked, too stunned, for tears, she lay there listening to him pack, then heard him clattering down the stairs, calling for his squires. Then they were riding off into the distance and it was just as if the last night had never been.

Bellone de Veaux was having a marvellous time at Court.

She was truly her father's daughter, and she adored junketings and masques, feasting and dancing, balls and banquets, as much as Francis did. She enjoyed being the centre of attention too, after the long years of being raised in the country by her solid, loving, but so boring foster-parents. But all that was behind her now, and she was receiving the accolades due to her as the King's lovechild. The Court was *en fête* now that the Treaty of Madrid had been signed, freeing Francis, and he was expected back in Paris in a few weeks' time. Bellonne had been taken under the Queen Mother's wing and the Princess Marguerite had welcomed her as a sister. After visiting the Château Blanche she had returned to Court to attend the ball being given in her honour. She had relished every moment of the meeting with Hamish and his wife, thinking them admirably well-matched, and so no one was more surprised than she when the King's foster-brother returned to the Louvre the next day, his face as black as a storm.

Bellone had always known Hamish as a kindly, tolerant father-figure; she had never seen his thunderous moods. She did her best to cajole him out of them, to question him, to ask him what was wrong and why he had come back to Court so suddenly, but she met with a stony lack of response. Topaz eyes glittering, she determined to get to the bottom of this mystery. Athena had said that Hamish would be staying at the Château Blanche for some weeks. They had obviously been very happy together, and now here he was at Court, sulking and storming about as if something terrible had happened. She started to make discreet enquiries of those closest to Hamish at Court, trying to find out what had happened, but no one seemed to know. Hamish told her that she was too young to trouble her head about such matters, that children should take care to mind their own business. This had stung her into determination to meddle as much as she was able. She was not the Queen Mother's granddaughter for nothing. Finally, all her efforts having proved fruitless, she went direct to Louise of Savoy. There was nothing that her grandmother did not know.

Bellonne told the Queen Mother that she believed something had happened between Lord Mullally and his wife.

'He has been so kind to me over the years, Madame, bringing me letters and gifts from the King, seeing that I have everything I need, giving me pocket money – and now I want to do something to help him in return.'

'It is not the first time that Lord Mullally has stormed round the Court like a thunderbolt, my child. He has a volatile temperament.'

'But, Madame, only a few weeks ago I was at the Château Blanche with him and his wife and they seemed so happy – it was obvious that they were going to spend some time together. And then, within a day, he returned to Court, black-faced and biting everyone's head off.'

'It is no secret that Lord Mullally dotes on his wife, but it is quite possible that she is the only one who does not realize it.' Louise said shrewdly.

'And why is that? Why should he hide his love from her? Love is such a beautiful thing, but it does need nurturing.'

'You are young and still very romantic, my child, and it is right that you should be so at your age. Lord Mullally and his wife were forced into marrying one another by the King. It was not a love-match.'

'But you said –'

'I said it was *not* a love-match. I think that Lord Mullally only realized that he adored his wife after they had wed.'

'Then what is to stop them being happy together, Madame? I do not understand.'

'Lady Mullally was with child. She had an accident, a fall, and she lost the baby. It was obvious to the midwife that if the baby had been full-term his arrival would have endangered his mother, for she is not built for child-bearing. Now, in those circumstances, what would a man do if he truly loved his wife?'

Understanding suddenly dawned on Bellonne's beautiful, intelligent face. 'Why, he would be terrified of getting her with child again in case she died . . .'

'That is it, my child; that is at the heart of it. Why do you think he spends so much time away from his wife? If he stayed with her he would be tempted to get her with child. He is a very passionate man.'

'Then what is the solution – or is this problem insoluble?'

'Lord Mullally certainly thinks so.'

'And you, Madame?'

'I am no miracle-worker, child, nor would I elect to interfere between husband and wife. And neither must you.'

Bellonne sighed, thrusting her shoulders back. 'But does Lady Mullally know the circumstances? It seemed to me when I met her that she was innocent of them.'

'The midwife told only Lord Mullally and he thought it best to keep it from his wife. He did not think that she could face a lifetime knowing that she must remain childless, for she was deeply upset by the loss of her baby.'

'Then there *is* something I can do.' Bellonne rose and dropped a kiss on her grandmother's forehead.

'It would be wiser if you did not meddle, my child.'

'But you will not forbid me?'

'No, I will not forbid you, but take care, and be prepared for all eventualities.'

Flakes of snow, soft and white as flax, drifted against Bellonne's face as she neared the Château Blanche with her retinue. She was in a very determined and purposeful mood. When she was shown into Lady Mullally's presence, they greeted one another warmly, and, over mulled wine and honeyed cakes, they began to talk.

'My Lady – Athena,' started Bellonne, 'I owe a great deal to your husband. I am in his debt for all that he has done for me while I was growing up in the country. Now

I want to help him. He is at Court at the present time, in the blackest of moods. No one can do anything with him: he snaps and snarls and no one can comfort him. It distresses me to see him thus when he should be here with you, loving you as he obviously wants to do.'

Athena was astonished. What did this girl mean? 'My husband is far from being an equable man,' she began, but Bellonne interrupted.

'He loves you, Athena. The whole of Paris knows how he dotes on you; it is common knowledge at Court.'

'He – he loves me? If only that were true, my dear, but I fear that it is not.'

'But you are wrong! I do not wish to pry,' Bellonne said, meaning that she did, 'but did you and your husband have a disagreement? Can you think of any reason for him to have returned to Court so suddenly and be in such a foul mood?'

Athena sighed. 'It is not the first time this has happened, my dear Bellonne, and the solution is quite beyond me.'

Bellonne had no intention of telling Athena what the midwife had said. That would be altogether too cruel, and, in any case, would not be what Lord Mullally wished. But she could reassure Athena that her husband truly loved her.

'Well, I think it is a tragedy that the only husband and wife at Court who love each other do not seem to know it,' Bellonne declared. 'Life is too short to waste time. You two should be together.'

'I do not see how that can be so, Bellonne. I can hardly order my husband back to my side, and I do not think that he would come even if I asked him.'

'Why do you not try it? It will certainly give us some breathing space at Court,' she grinned impishly.

'It was very kind of you to come and talk to me like this,' Athena said, forcing a smile, 'and you have my thanks for it, for the kindness that you intend. If only I could believe that what you say if true.'

'But it *is*, it *is*! Why should I lie to you? Oh, Athena, I should so much like to see you two reunited. Soon I shall be reunited with my father because of Hamish and I want the same for him.'

'I do not see what I can do, Bellonne, I really do not. But I shall think about what you have said, my dear. Now, will you stay and dine with me and meet some of my pets?'

When Bellonne had gone, Athena walked round her home, thinking hard. The King's love-child had ridden all this way in winter to tell her that her husband loved her. Could there be something in it? She clasped her hands round her waist. Her woman's time had not come for two months now, and she believed that she was with child again. She had not known how to tell Hamish. She had imagined him revelling in Court life, surrounded by worshipping courtesans, and had supposed that he would be filled with resentment if she wrote to him to tell him that he was to be a father again, that he must leave the Palace and return to her side. But now she was beginning to think differently. Before she slept that night she composed a letter to Hamish, re-writing it half a dozen times before the wording seemed right. She had no wish to sound demanding or to make him feel pressured into returning. Using a light tone, she merely asked him to come for a few days' visit. If he wished, he could ignore the invitation. Then Athena climbed into bed, thinking of her baby and praying that it would be a son for Hamish.

Within hours her husband was at her side. Taking her in his arms, he thought that she had never looked more radiant or more desirable, but for some reason she kept her eyes lowered and welcomed him lightly. He had brought her gifts, as usual: two of the most gorgeous gowns she had ever possessed and a sapphire pendant, a gift from Louise of Savoy. The gowns were so inviting that she wanted to try them on immediately, and Hamish followed her to her bedchamber where he helped her unfasten her day gown, his fingers burning to caress her neck and his body rigidly controlled as she stepped out of the dress and appeared in her underskirts. Excitement had brought down her guard, and she was laughing and pink-cheeked as she donned the first gown of rose samite, asking Hamish to hook her up. But the gown would not fasten! She suppressed a gasp: she had forgotten about her expanding waistline.

Hamish was puzzled, for the gown was exactly his wife's size, made specially for her by her Paris dressmaker, who knew her shape perfectly.

He looked so hurt that his gift would not fit that Athena blurted out the truth, her face covered in blushes. She was not prepared for the look of anguish which crossed her husband's face. It was like a physical blow and upset her so much that she burst into tears, sobbing helplessly in his arms, expecting him to curse her. But he did not. Instead, he kissed her tenderly, holding her close and whispering that he loved and adored her. But his voice sounded choked, his eyes were bleak.

'I thought you loathed me, that you did not want me; and that was why I kept away, my beloved.'

'Loath you? Never, my husband. When you are away I miss you desperately, I long for you!'

Lifting her up in his arms, Hamish carried her to the bed and gently laid her on it, then, slowly and tenderly, he made love to her, determined that in the coming months he would make her the happiest woman in Christendom.

CHAPTER TWENTY-TWO

It was spring when the visitors arrive at the Château Blanche: two of Hamish's Irish cousins and a party of their friends from London – one of whom was none other than Marjorie, daughter of the Duke of Chester, who was expecting to meet the daughter of the Comte de Deverelle and who instead saw a woman who appeared to be the double of her long-lost sister.

But surely it could not be, Marjorie thought, as she gazed at the fair-haired woman. The Comte's daughter might be the double of Amrica, but was she not French by birth? Then Athena spoke, and the strangest thrill coursed down Marjorie's spine. That voice, the timbre exactly like her sister's . . .

'*Amrica*,' Marjorie whispered hoarsely, moving closer. 'Amrica – is it – can it really be you? But I do not understand – how did you come to be here?' Hesitantly she approached Athena as if terrified that she might vanish again.

'My wife's name is Athena,' Hamish smiled at Marjorie, who ignored him.

'But this is – yes, it truly *is* my sister Amrica! We all thought she was lost, dead. Oh, sweet sister, how did you come to be in France? Do you not remember me? I am Marjorie, your *sister*!' Tears poured out of Marjorie's eyes as she gripped Athena's hands.

Then it all came out, Marjorie explaining how she and her family had gone to London on their way to Court, and how her sister Amrica had inexplicably vanished.

'We were all inconsolable. Our mother wept for days, weeks. A black depression settled on us all. Our father scoured London, all England, in search of you, Amrica, but there was no trace. It was as if you had never been, dear sister. There was talk of murder, or sorcery. Oh it was terrible, terrible!' Marjorie shuddered at the memory, and began to weep again.

'But I do not understand,' Athena whispered. 'The Comte de Deverelle is my father. I was brought up in a convent in England. My mother died long ago. How can you be my sister?'

'But I am, I *am*!' Marjorie cried. 'And you are *not* the daughter of the Comte de Deverelle, you are the daughter of the Duke and Duchess of Chester. Without a doubt – oh, without a doubt, you are! Tell me, do you have three tiny moles on your left shoulder-blade? Because my sister Amrica does?'

Athena's cheeks flushed crimson, her head spinning, her legs giving way beneath her. Hamish caught her in his arms. He knew that his wife had a trio of moles on her left shoulder-blade, for he had kissed them frequently. Could it be true that his wife, whom he had thought a street urchin, was really the daughter of one of England's premier Dukes, a cousin of King Henry the Eighth himself? It seemed too unbelievable to contemplate.

When Athena was sitting on a *chaise longue* with Hamish beside her, holding her hand, Marjorie continued the story.

'But I cannot remember,' Athena kept saying. 'Oh, I *wish* that I could remember! There is just a darkness when I try to think back.'

'I shall make sure that you will remember soon, sweet sister,' Marjorie said softly.

That night, Athena lay in Hamish's arms while he stroked her hair.

'Do you really think that it is possible that I am this girl, this Amrica, the Duke of Chester's daughter?' she asked him. 'It all seems so strange, so puzzling. Marjorie was adamant – and yet how can I doubt that the Comte is my true father? No father has ever been more devoted and loving than he.'

Hamish, who knew full well that there was some mystery surrounding Athena's origins, continued to stroke her hair tenderly. He was looking into the future with mixed feelings. What if she really were the Lady Amrica, daughter of an English Duke and Duchess, and what if her memory returned? She might well decide that she wanted to go back to her real family in England, believing that she had been married under false pretences, for if she were Chester's child then the Comte would have no call upon her, no jurisdiction over her at all, and certainly not the right to have arranged her marriage. Hamish had met the Duke when he was King Henry's ambassador to the French Court. He was a shrewd and intelligent man, tall and broad-shouldered, with gilt hair and startling blue-green eyes. Now that Hamish thought about it he could see a resemblance between Athena and the Duke. His arms tightened around his wife.

'My love, you have not answered me,' Athena said.

'If you are this Amrica, then you will make your true family very happy indeed. They had thought you dead.'

'What will you think of having a Duke's daughter for a wife, Hamish?'

'Your origins have never mattered to me, my darling. It is you I love.'

'Oh, how I wish I knew the answer to it all!'

'We shall know a little more tomorrow when the Comte arrives. My messenger will have reached him by now.'

'Oh, my poor father – if he *is* my father. Oh, but he must be, Hamish. How could he have lied to me all these years?'

'We shall know tomorrow, beloved.' Hamish stroked her hair thoughtfully, a great weight crushing his heart.

The Comte de Deverelle looked a lonely, broken, old man as he knelt before Athena, begging her forgiveness with tears streaming down his wrinkled face. Athena kissed him and told him how much she loved him and how good he had been to her and that she would never forget it, then she begged him to tell her all he knew about her past. And so the story came out of how the Comte had found her unconscious upon the cobbles in London and how he had been stunned by her likeness to his dead daughter, how he believed that the real Athena had been sent back to him by a miracle.

'I owe my life to you,' Athena whispered.

'God forgive me for what I have done!' the Comte wailed.

'It seems to me that if you had not rescued Athena – Amrica . . . she would not be here now safe and alive,' Hamish put in.

Marjorie, after a moment's hesitation, agreed. She thought the Comte de Deverelle had been a wicked old man, but, on the other hand, he *had* saved her sister's life and cared for her lovingly in the ensuing years.

'You will *always* be welcome at the Château Blanche,' Athena assured the Comte. 'Come as often as you please, just as before; nothing has changed. And you will, of course, be our baby's godfather.'

'Thank you, thank you, *mon trésor*,' the Comte sobbed, flourishing a lace kerchief and blowing his nose loudly.

The Irish cousins, who had been standing in the background, watching and wondering what was going on, looked at one another with raised brows. What a story they would be able to take back to Muldara: wait until Aunt Kathleen heard all about this!

During the following days Marjorie did her utmost to help her sister to remember her past. She told her childhood tales, anecdotes, anything she could think of to jolt her memory. A messenger had been sent to Cheshire, informing the Duke and Duchess that their lost daughter had been discovered and was awaiting them at the Château Blanche – that she could not travel to England to meet them for she was with child.

The Duke and Duchess did not arrive alone: they

brought Violette, Arabella, and Paul, Lord Marningham, too. Violette had never married, and Arabella, newly-widowed, was the mother of two young children who had been left with her mother-in-law for the moment. Paul was now married and his young bride had come with him to France. She was small, sweet and golden-haired. Her name was Alice and Athena took to her immediately.

There was a very tearful and emotional reunion, the family clustering together, talking until late and rising early to be together again. There was also dismay and embarrassment when Athena and Paul recognized one another as brother and sister and thought back to the stolen kiss which they had exchanged in Ireland. But after the first awkwardness they were able to laugh about it, though they kept it to themselves.

The Duchess, red-eyed, clung to her long-lost daughter, trying, as Marjorie had, to make her remember, but making little headway. After a few days of such intense excitement and stimulation, Athena found herself very tired and Hamish insisted that she remain in her bed, where he cared for her tenderly, allowing only her mother to visit her on the understanding that the Duchess would not upset her daughter. The Duchess could not take her eyes from her child and she frequently wept, silent tears trickling down her face. She seemed both overjoyed and subdued, as if she were in the face of an unbelievable miracle, for that was what it seemed like to Athena's family.

When the Duke had learned how the Comte had passed off Athena as his own daughter, he had been purple with rage, slamming his balled fists together, making his wife wince.

'The rogue! The knave! The soundrel! I shall have him flogged and flung into prison!' His eyes bulged.

'Now, now, my dear,' gentled his wife. 'He is a French citizen and you have no jurisdiction over him.'

'I shall speak to King Francis! I shall see that this

blackguard is punished as he deserves – forcing my daughter into marriage with an *Irishman*!' The Duke's lip curled.

'He is half English, my dear, and he *is* the French King's foster-brother. He and Amrica do not seem unhappy together, now do they?'

'It is for *me* to arrange her marriage, not some foreigner.'

'My dear, what do you think would have happened to our daughter if the Comte de Deverelle had not found her that night? She had been set upon, her clothes torn from her by thieves, the Rosetta Jewel taken . . . She had received such a bad blow to her head that she still has not regained her memory all these years later. What do you think would have been the result if she had recovered consciousness alone? How long do you think she would have survived in those appalling back streets? She would have been attacked in – in other ways. And with her memory gone she would never have found us again.' The Duchess shuddered, imagining all the terrors her daughter would have faced had the Comte not rescued her.

The Duke snorted, flinging back his head. 'He had no right to call her his daughter, to give her another woman's name, to deceive the King of France!'

'Suddenly you care for the feelings of the French King, My Lord?' The Duchess raised her brows. 'The Comte nursed our daughter for weeks; she was near death but he saved her life. The least we can do is forgive him. Think on it, husband. Lord Mullally is not angry at the deception.'

'And why should he be? An *Irishman* finding that he is married to the daughter of one of the premier Dukes of England! The man has every reason to celebrate. When I think of my fair daughter in an *Irishman*'s bed . . .'

'The Duchess suppressed her impatience. 'It is plain that they love one another, my dear – and did we not always say that we wanted love matches for our children, to ensure that they would be as happy as we have been together?'

'That is so, but –'

'Then we must give thanks to God and His Blessed Mother. It seems to me that the Virgin has been smiling on our child, that She has been caring for her all these years when we could not.' Tears had sparkled in the Duchess's eyes.

'Is the Duke – my father – still angry with the Comte?' Athena asked her mother, a day or two later.

'A little, my darling.'

'But the Comte has been so good to me. He nursed me for weeks after I was attacked. Many times I would have been so lonely here at the Château Blanche without his visits. And I think at times he truly believed that I was his real daughter. In his home there is a portrait of the real Athena when she was a child. No one could tell us apart, Mother. I imagine that if she had not died, she would have looked exactly like me when she grew up. You have so much now, Mother – Father, your children, and you have found me again; but the Comte has nothing.'

'I know, I know.' The Duchess patted her daughter's hand. 'I have done my best to talk your father round, and I think I am winning.' She smiled. 'Now, did I ever tell you about what happened when you were seven years old –?' The Duchess launched into yet another reminiscence intended to try and jolt her daughter's memory.

One week later they were waving goodbye to Violette, who had to return to England to be with her children. She and Athena kissed one another warmly and promised to meet again soon.

'I look forward to seeing my nephew and niece. It is strange to think that I am an aunt,' Athena smiled.

'You must come and see the children as soon as you have had your baby and you are recovered.'

'I shall look forward to that very much.'

A few days after Violette had left, Athena started to have

her vivid and disjointed dreams again, and this time she found that she could remember something of what she had dreamed when she woke, only the odd thing here or there like mysterious pieces of a gigantic jigsaw, but they made her yearn to put the pieces into place, to remember all of her past.

The Duchess became very excited when Athena mentioned her dreams to her.

'Oh, your memory is returning! I knew it would if we all tried hard enough.'

'But it is such a slow business, Mother – so frustrating.'

'If only you were not with child, my darling, you could come back to Cheshire with us and see your home. That would surely make you remember. But as soon as your baby is born you must return with us to England. That is where you belong, after all.'

Hamish, joining the family group at that moment, felt trepidation at her words. The Duchess was a commanding woman; he suspected that she was accustomed to getting what she wanted. And the bluff Duke, for all his heartiness and bonhomie, was a man who would brook no interference with his plans. Athena – he still thought of her as Athena – was his wife and about to become the mother of his child, but, after all they had gone through, he could see that the Duke and Duchess had an excellent claim upon her. He greatly feared that, if her memory returned, he would be excluded from her life. How could he blame her if she wanted to go to Cheshire to see the home where she had grown up, or if she wanted to stay there . . .? He was filled with foreboding.

The Duke, Hamish knew, looked down on him as being an Irish adventurer, who would never have risen to such heights as marriage to a daughter of a premier Duke of England if that daughter had known who she really was. In the following weeks, watching his wife so happily content with her new-found family, he reached the nadir of depression and gloom. He was the only one who knew how dangerous it was for her to give birth, but whatever happened he felt that he was going to lose her and he could blame no one but himself. After all, what had he ever given her except grief and loneliness, and now her very life was in danger because of him. These days Athena seemed to talk of little else but returning to Marningham Hall and Hamish could not refuse her this wish, especially as it might heal her mind. But the birth of their child must come first . . .

News reached the Château Blanche that King Francis was exceedingly happy with the Emperor's sister, Eleanor, and that theirs was a love-match. Eleanor was dark-haired and stately; in fact, Francis's favourite type of woman. So Hamish was happy on that score, at least. Then his wife went into labour and everything else was pushed from his mind.

Athena alternately burned and froze with pain as hour after hour passed and she fought to produce her child. It was unbelievable torture and her screams rang throughout the Château.

Hearing them, Hamish groaned in agony, leapt onto a horse and galloped away into the forest to escape the sound of her cries. But they seemed to follow him wherever he went, resounding in his ears, spearing at his heart. He was a foul and callous murderer. He would to go Hell – he wanted to go to Hell – for what he had done to his beautiful wife. He wanted to be put on the rack, his body stretched and broken until he died, as she was dying. It was useless trying to seek solace in the forest, and he returned to the Château, grim and white-lipped. The Duchess was weeping and the Duke was pacing up and down the salon, a dazed expression on his face.

'My wife –?'

'The child is not yet here,' the Duchess whispered through her tears. 'The midwife has arrived, and the

King's physician. They are tending her now.' The Duchess's voice quavered and cracked. 'Come, My Lord, we must go into the chapel and pray.' She tugged at her husband's hand. It was plain that she had no wish to say more than was necessary to Lord Mullally.

Hamish smashed his bunched fist against the doorjamb, oblivious of his grazed and bloody skin. He reached into his belt for his dagger, balancing it on his palm, looking at the sharp steely blade and imagining it sinking into his heart. A fresh scream rang out from his wife's bedchamber and he sank onto a bench, his head in his hands. She had been in labour now two days and a night. He got up, walking along corridors and in and out of rooms like a zombie. The servants huddled anxiously in the kitchens, and Carol lay outside his mistress's door, whimpering and refusing to eat.

That night Athena's daughter arrived. She was small but healthy. Athena was very weak and deeply shocked from loss of blood, but she had survived.

The baby was baptized immediately. Her name was Alysa, after the Duchess of Chester who, along with Louise of Savoy, was her godmother, the Comte being her godfather.

Hamish could not believe that his wife was still alive. He came to her bedside as if fearing to find her dead, and, when he saw her bloodless face, he could not hide his tears. Athena was too weak to speak, and she drifted off into exhausted slumber.

Hamish was at the door when he remembered that he was now a father. Tip-toeing back, he looked into the cradle at his wife's bedside. He saw a minute, wrinkled, rosy face surmounted by a sprig of moonlight-coloured hair. A smile curved his lips. He had a daughter – and his wife was alive.

CHAPTER TWENTY-THREE

Athena smiled happily from her bed at all the visitors who came to see Alysa. First to call was Bellonne, who brought the new baby a silver-gilt christening casket; then came the Comte, humble and contrite, tears in his eyes as he stared down at Alysa who might well have been his first grandchild. He brought the baby a rope of perfectly matched pink pearls and blushed with pleasure when her finger curled round his and gripped hard. The Queen Mother sent a silver filigree bracelet for the baby, set with one cabochon emerald, and there were gifts from other courtiers, friends of Hamish.

Athena was easily tired by visitors and surprise gifts and she slept a great deal: as did the baby, who was sweet-tempered and rarely cried. Solange's sister, Marie, was the baby's new nursemaid.

'I suppose I had better start thinking about a governess,' Athena said to her mother some weeks later.

'A *Frenchwoman*?' the Duchess wrinkled her nose. 'Will that be necessary, my darling? As you are returning to England you will be able to select an English lady of good breeding.'

'She will have to speak French, of course,' Athena said.

'Why, my dear? If you are to remain in England . . .' The Duchess smiled persuasively, steely determination behind her sweetness.

'It is unthinkable that I remain in England, Mother. My place is here with Hamish.'

The Duchess managed to conceal her revulsion at this idea, for she knew that she must tread carefully. She intended to take her daughter to Cheshire and there, if not before, make her see that her present match with a mere

Lord of dubious origins and nationality was hardly befitting her status as daughter of the King of England's cousin.

The Duchess smiled winningly. 'Do you realize, my dear, that if you had not been lost to us all these years you would by now have been married to someone eminently suitable? For example, the eldest son of the Duke of Portlingly, or the Duke of Barton's heir. Anthony is such a charming boy; you will meet him when we are back at Marningham Hall – and all the other ladies and gentlemen with whom you should be mixing.' The Duchess glowed at the image she was creating and, in her enthusiasm, forgot the need for caution. 'Marriages which have been proved to be against the bride's wishes can easily be annulled, my dear. When the circumstances are known, that this wretched Deverelle fellow was pretending to be your father and that he coerced you into marrying a totally unsuitable man, there should be no difficulty in having you legally freed of the union.'

'Mother,' Athena spoke firmly, though she felt far from sturdy, 'I cannot allow such talk. I am married to Hamish: we love one another and I have borne his child. I will not hear talk of an annulment. The mere thought upsets me deeply.'

The Duchess leaned forward, patting her daughter's hand. 'That is only because you have not thought seriously about it, my sweet. When you are stronger and when we have discussed it at length you will begin to see that I am right.'

'Mother . . .' Athena began, but she was too weary to argue, gripped by one of the sudden attacks of sleep which had beset her since Alysa's birth. Seeing her eyes close and her body relax, the Duchess tip-toed out of her daughter's room, a knowing smile on her lips.

Hamish was at the bottom of the staircase when the Duchess came out of Athena's room. His arms were filled with roses which he had been about to take into his wife's chamber. He had overheard the conversation between mother and daughter, a fine sweat breaking out on his brow, a throbbing ache beginning deep in the pit of his stomach. He was going to lose her. He knew it. He had known it from the moment Marjorie had cried out her sister's name and embraced her. All these years he had merely had her on loan for the time when her family reclaimed her, and that time had now come. She would go back to England, she would see the life from which she had sprung and eventually she would agree to have her marriage with the half-Irish upstart annulled. The English aristocracy had a low opinion of the Irish at the best of times. But the thought uppermost in his mind was that he did not deserve Athena's love. For years he had forced her to endure a loveless existence; she had not wanted to marry him, she had had no choice.

Hamish went to the stables, saddled one of the horses and rode out into the forest. He did not halt his horse until he was deep in amongst the trees and undergrowth, where branches and leaves knitted overhead, excluding the sun. Dismounting, he sank down onto a rotting tree stump to think, to mourn. This time he must give his wife the freedom of choice which had been denied her before – otherwise he would have no peace in his soul.

The sunless glade was damp and chilly; no animals cavorted here, there was no birdsong to sweeten the air, only crawling earth creatures, squirming and repugnant. But it was an inner chill that caused him to shiver. When Athena left him, he knew he would never feel warm again; there would always be this desolate, penetrating cold, the icy palm cradling his heart.

Suddenly a frightened bird skittered through the undergrowth, its repetitive single-noted screech sounding to his ears like 'Lost . . . Lost . . . Lost'.

The old woman's hut was deep in the forest, in an eerie, sunless dell where animal noises sounded strange and distorted and the trees were packed so closely together that there seemed to be no sky above. Hamish stood for a moment or two, surveying the ramshackle shed, which was all that it appeared to be. Surely it was too small to house anyone –? And then he heard a croaking voice, and saw an old crone hobbling towards him, her skirt looped up and filled with pine cones, a cat bounding at her heels. Closer the cat came to Hamish, as if inspecting him, and he saw that it was grey and moth-eaten, but its eyes were bright and beady and filled with intelligence.

'Mistress Diable?'

'That is my name. What do you want? Who told you to come here? I never get men visiting me, only women. 'Tis women who have to suffer because of men, that is why they come to me.' The old woman paused to cough wheezily, and wiped her mouth. She seemed amused at something, and cast a knowing glance at her cat. Hamish could have sworn that the cat's expression matched her own.

'My wife . . .' He paused. He did not find it easy to speak of this, the problem which he had nursed so silently for years. 'My wife must not . . . That is, I do not want . . . She might die if she had a child.' A fine sweat broke out on his brow.

'Want to bed her but not to kill her, eh?' cackled the crone. 'Well, ye have come to the right one. Do ye wish for a potion, or pills, or do ye want to know about the safe times for bedding?'

'There are – *safe* times?' Hamish was startled. He had never heard of this – what could the old woman mean? When he had come here, he had not stopped to think, to consider his actions. He had heard of Mistress Diable from the servants who spoke of her with a mixture of revulsion and awe. She had saved the life of Christianne, a girl who had nearly died giving birth to her son and who was told to have no more children. Christianne had drunk one of Mistress Diable's potions monthly, ever since, and sure enough she had not conceived again. This news had sent Hamish straight to the old hag's home.

'But of course,' she snorted. 'The moon rules womankind, and the moon gives, but it also holds back. Come inside, and I will tell ye more.'

Hamish had to bend double to get into the shack, where he sat awkwardly on a tiny stool, being scrutinized by the cat. It was dark and smelly in the shack, and he imagined fleas and lice moving about in the filth. He longed to be outside, but not until he had what he had come for. Mistress Diable wanted to know when his wife had had her last woman's time, then she scuttled to a corner and poured over a chart. Again, she seemed secretly amused.

Finally she looked up at him. 'Between the fourth and the twelfth of the month, your wife will be safe from pregnancy.'

'You are sure of this? It sounds . . . too simple somehow.'

'Ask Christianne, Helene, Marguerite, to name but three who are no longer burdened with children because they visited old Mistress Diable. That is my proof.'

'I cannot argue with that. Thank you, mistress.' Hamish handed over some coins in payment, and retreated from the stinking hovel.

Before he put the hag's advice into practice, he checked the names she had mentioned. He knew about Christianne, but not about Helene and Marguerite who also lived at the Château Blanche. Sure enough, they had both visited Mistress Diable and been given similar advice, and they had not become pregnant again. Overjoyed, he thought longingly of making love to Athena before she left for England. Just one more time together, before he lost her. He had hardened himself to be brave, to give her her freedom. He was determined that he would not try to influence her by emotional pleas or entreaties. This time, she must make her own choice. She had suffered enough, she must suffer no longer.

*

It was the most rapturous coming together they had ever shared. Hamish relished every moment, memorizing it for eternity. But he had to steel himself against those words which ached to be spoken. He wanted to plead with her to stay with him; not to go. He wanted to pour out his desperate need for her, his love and longing. But, if he did, he would be influencing her unfairly. She had lost many years of family life; now, she must make up for them. He had no right to interfere, even though remaining aloof nearly broke his heart.

In view of their recently improved relationship, Athena had expected anything but silence from her husband. But silence was what she got, and it affected her deeply. He would let her go after all, just like that, without a word, a plea. How could she have forgotten what a complicated and baffling man she had married? One moment, she thought she knew him; the next, he was a stranger. He had made love to her passionately, tenderly, yet he had said nothing about her departure, nothing about wanting her to return, and soon. This was their last night together before she left for England, and he was staying silent, as so many times before. He need only have said that he needed her, that he could not bear her to go, and joyfully she would have stayed. But the night wore on, and it was time to sleep, linked together in one another's arms; still he said nothing. She believed that she knew the reason. All along, he had been a reluctant husband, marrying her only to please his foster-brother. Now he had seen the opportunity to rid himself of her, once and for all, and he was taking it. It was a bitter thought, but she must accept it as the truth. What other choice did she have? However, she knew one thing for certain: if he wrote to her while she was in England, saying that he needed her, that he wanted her back, she would fly on wings to his side. But the words must come from *him*.

*

Athena was spellbound by Marningham Hall, memories beginning to ficker into her mind almost as soon as she saw it. At first they were disjointed and unclear, but as the days passed and she explored the Hall over and over again, visiting her childhood haunts – the hollow in the meadow by the River Dee where she and her sisters had played, the water gardens where she had had a swing, the mossy glade where she had been thrown from her pony when she was seven years old – gradually the healing process began.

She visited her old Irish nurse, Hannah McCorbe, now bedridden with the rheum. Hannah lived in a little house in the grounds of the Hall, well cared for by the Duke's other servants. Her reunion with her long-lost charge was joyous but tearful; she wept with unquenchable happiness.

'I've prayed for your return, that I have, *macushla*, and always, deep in the pit of me heart, I knew you'd come back one day.'

'Hannah,' Athena gently kissed the old nurse's cheeks, tasting the salt of her tears, 'you must forgive me if I seem somewhat dull-witted, if I do not appear to remember everything at once.'

'They've told me what happened to ye, *macushla*, that ye've married a fine Irishman, and me heart is blessed to hear it, that it is.' The old woman beckoned to Athena to come closer. Then, speaking in a sibilant whisper, she said, 'But do not let the Duchess know what I have said, will ye, for she thinks the Irish are fine servants but not suitable husbands for her daughters. 'Tis raging inside she is with the scandal of it all. Old Hannah knows.'

'I love my husband, Hannah,' Athena said, 'very much. And I want nothing to separate us.'

'That is the right spirit *macushla*. If he is the one for ye then ye make sure ye keep him. Now, tell me of your daughter. Will ye bring her to see me next time? I have heard she is just like you were as a child. When I see her 'twill bring it all back to me as if it were yesterday.'

'Of course I will, Hannah.' Athena put a box into the

old nurse's hands. It contained marchpane sugared sweetmeats which the old woman loved, displaying an almost toothless jaw as evidence of her weakness.

Old Hannah had called her '*macushla*', which was a loving endearment, but since returning to England the Duke and Duchess had insisted that Athena was called Amrica at all times, even though she found it difficult at first to respond to that name. When letters came to her from Hamish, which they did and frequently, they were addressed to the Lady Athena Mullally, a fact which made the Duchess frown pettishly.

'That is all in the past now, my dove, that silly name which is not you at all. You must forget it; you must remember now that you are Amrica, our daughter. That, after all, is the name by which you were baptized. In my view, to call yourself anything else is blasphemous.'

'Yes, Mother,' Athena – Amrica replied with a sigh.

Hamish wrote that the King was deeply grieved at being parted from his sons, who were the hostages of the Emperor to ensure that King Francis kept his part in the Treaty of Madrid. The Royal Family all sent their love, Hamish said, and hoped that she and her daughter were well. Athena – Amrica always wrote by return, telling Hamish everything that happened at Marningham Hall, describing the Hall to him, and how it felt to be back in Cheshire. She always signed her letters lovingly and sometimes she would draw a heart and a rose entwined at the bottom of the page.

What Hamish noticed in particular about his wife's letters was that she never mentioned returning to France, and his desolation increased with each day. But he had vowed not to try to change her mind by unfair methods: she must choose her own happiness. He had tampered with her life too much by far and now she must find her feet and her lost memory, enjoy her family again, and then . . . He did not like to contemplate the outcome of her going to England. She was tasting freedom for the first time in her life: who could blame her if she snatched at it to the exclusion of all else? He kept his letters restrained, giving his wife only the most cursory news of France's politics. What he did not tell her was that he was on the King's business yet again, for Charles was delaying the arrival of his sister Eleanor in Paris and Bourbon was still loose and gathering men to sack Rome itself. He was even now preparing for the journey to Rome.

The Holy City was a bloody battlefield. Saintly relics had been stolen or destroyed, nuns abused and raped. The Pope was cringing in terror, there was looting and carnage in every direction, screams and moans filling the air and hordes of mercenaries sacking and pillaging wherever they rode. In all his years as a soldier and envoy Hamish had never seen such horrors as he saw in Rome. To ride through its narrow, sun-baked streets and to come upon a murdered nun, her habit twisted up round her neck, a dagger through her heart, her legs wide apart after being brutally raped, her nose broken and bloody, smashed across her face, to see castrated monks hanging from trees, to hear that monks had been forced to rape nuns at swordpoint after a dozen mercenaries had done the very same: all these things were like the shadow of Satan across the land, that shadow growing ever larger and darker with each passing day. The Devil was triumphing, aided and abetted by man.

Everywhere that he went, dressed in his dowdy merchant's disguise, Hamish heard the same talk from everyone's throat. These mercenaries who shouted for the Pope's death, for the Catholic Church's downfall, were all Lutherans, followers of the monk he had heard preaching in Germany some years before. This was the outcome of Martin Luther's stirring, rousing eulogies. These men who professed to be his followers wanted blood and more blood, destruction and death. They talked animatedly of their leader, the Duc de Bourbon.

Wandering round the Holy City, which was slowly being destroyed and burnt, Hamish saw horses tethered in St Peter's itself, saw men and women fornicating beside their tethered horses. Everywhere he looked there was horror upon fresh horror, but, despite all his efforts, his enquiries, both openly and in secret, he could not discover the hide-out of Bourbon. That was, until one day when he met the Florentine goldsmith and metal-worker, Benvenuto Cellini. Cellini, a dashing young man of twenty-six, had written to King Francis in secret, letting it be known that he wished to deliver Rome from those whom he considered as pagan as the Infidel. The Florentine, who would one day be King Francis's goldsmith and jeweller, met Hamish in secret in the Street of the Angels.

'This Bourbon is in league with the Devil,' Cellini growled, punching his fist into his palm. 'I saw him once, years ago, when he had the face of a mournful angel, but now he rides the streets dressed like a warlord in furs and plumes and jewelled brooches.'

'Then you have seen him? That is more than I have since I came to Rome, Master Benvenuto.'

'*Si*, I have seen him. The *landsknechts* – the German mercenaries – who are all Lutherans, are besotted by him. They will do anything he asks.' Cellini punched his palm again. 'My heart is black and heavy with the pain of seeing the desecration of the Holy City. Bourbon and his men came here in May, shouting for blood, and there has been no let-up since then. There has been nothing like this since the Goths came to plunder us. His Holiness shudders in the Castle of Sant'Angelo. They say the Holy Virgin weeps, that tears pour from Her statues wherever they stand in the city – not that many of them have been left in one piece. Bourbon has everyone on his side. It is not right that such an evil man as he –'

'Not everyone, Master Benvenuto. The English are no longer in league with the Emperor.'

'Henry Tudor never got over missing out on the plundering after Pavia.'

'It is not that, Master Benvenuto. As you know, Henry Tudor is married to the Emperor's niece, Katherine of Aragon.'

'And –?'

'And Henry Tudor now wants to marry his mistress, Anne Boleyn. Henry's Cardinal Wolsey has asked to meet King Francis with a view to a treaty with him. It is hoped that there will be peace between England and France and that this will enable King Francis to get back his sons.'

'Those poor *bambinos* shut away in Spain; it is a crime that the Emperor keeps them there. It seems to me that it is his ambition to have everyone locked up: King Francis, his heirs, the Pope himself. My Lord, as an artist my overriding ambition is to preserve the Holy City. That is why I wrote to your King asking if I might meet with one of his envoys, that is why we are sitting here together discussing the situation.'

Hamish nodded. 'If we only knew where Bourbon has hidden himself.'

'I shall find out, My Lord, have no fear of that. I have my spies – my apprentices are faithful and loyal, to Rome and to me. We shall find out where Bourbon is, but, more important; we shall find out what his plans are. And when we do we shall intercept them. I have good weapons in readiness: an arquebus each. We shall ambush the devil and fire upon him together.'

'Master Benvenuto, if you would rather take the glory for yourself alone . . .'

'Indeed no, My Lord. It is fitting that an envoy of the French King who has suffered so much at Bourbon and the Emperor's hands should be involved in that devil's death. Now, we shall dine together and you will sleep in my house – no one suspects a mere artist of being an anarchist.' Cellini grinned, his boyish face lighting up.

The waiting seemed interminable, but finally their patience was rewarded. Giorgio, one of Cellini's apprentices, returned to the Master's workroom filthy and dishevelled, his cloak torn, his side badly bruised.

'I overheard some of Bourbon's men discussing the sacking of Sant'Angelo,' Giorgio said, coughing on the choking dust which had settled in his throat. 'They became suspicious of me sitting nearby them and only by pretending to be in my cups did I divert their attentions. They made a fine joke of me.' Giorgio winced as Cellini examined his bruised side. 'They picked me up and flung me out bodily into the street, right into a mound of dung. A group of horsemen came riding by and cantered over me; that is how I got these bruises.' He winced again. 'But it was worth it: I heard all their plans. Today they intend to sack Sant'Angelo – everything.'

'Here, drink this wine,' Hamish offered the boy a goblet, 'and then tell us all you know.'

Hamish and Cellini waited in readiness, each armed with an arquebus. When Bourbon came into view, riding at the head of his wild band of mercenaries, they fired together. The Duc fell dead. A few seconds later one of the German mercenaries fired at them, wounding Hamish in the thigh when he stepped in front of Cellini to protect him.

It was an agonizing journey back to France, on a rough litter carried by Cellini's servants, but exultation that Bourbon was dead, and that he had had a part in it, supported Hamish along the miles. The mercenaries, panicking at their commander's death, had fled without troubling to see if the two men were dead or alive. Hamish had fallen on top of Cellini, blood spurting everywhere, which might well have saved their lives for, had the mercenaries investigated further, they would have seen that both men were still breathing. Cellini had been kindness itself. He and his apprentices had borne Hamish back to his workroom, where they had nursed him with every kindness. But as time had passed, and Hamish had felt that he was not going to get any better and knew that he certainly would not be walking for some months, if at all, he was consumed by a yearning to be back at the Château Blanche, where he could die in peace, if that were God's Will. And so he was taken back and, when they reached the Château Blanche after weeks of the slow, painful, jolting journey, he rewarded the Italian apprentices generously and sent them back to Cellini with his gratitude.

Hamish lay in his bed, in great pain. He had lost much blood and he believed that his wound was infected. The journey had done him no good whatsoever, and he realized now that he had been a fool to risk it. One of his servants had gone to the King to inform him that Lord Mullally was back in France and that he was seriously wounded, and Hamish had no doubt that the King would send his own physicians to tend him. When they came, their faces lengthened at the sight of the raw and desiccated limb which oozed pus, bone protruding through flesh. Hamish asked for the truth and they gave it to him. He was probably going to lose the leg. But, even if they managed to save it, he would never walk again, for the bone was shattered and quite beyond repair.

They did all they could for him, cleaning and binding the leg, but what they really wanted to do was to amputate it and they were fretful with him because he would not allow it. He wanted to give the limb a fair chance of healing, he said. Only if that chance failed would he allow them to remove the leg. That night he lay in bed, staring stonily into the darkness, trying to think of that time after Pavia when his darling wife had nursed him so lovingly. To think of that time only illuminated his loss and his grief. He wanted her, oh, how he wanted her. But look at him now: smashed and bloody, a suppurating mess. He would never walk again, they said. He was going to lose his leg. For some time he wallowed in despair, racked by anguish. Then he tried to imagine his bedchamber door opening and his wife standing there, a sweet smile on her face, her arms filled with herbs and unguents which would cure his leg in no time at all. It was a dream, of course; a foolish, witless dream, and he had no right to think it, no right at all to evade the truth. He had got what he wanted: Bourbon was dead. If he had had to pay a price for it, then that was unfortunate.

Had he been a woman he would have wept, sobbing far into the night. But he was a man, and tears are denied the lion. It was nearly dawn, when, having reached the stage of thinking he would never sleep again, he remembered the Comte de Deverelle and his skill with herbs and unguents: that skill which the Comte had taught Athena. In the morning he would send for the man, and possibly his ministrations would help. Hamish tried for a time to feel optimistic, but he knew that he was living on stolen dreams: dreams which were not his by right. His leg was a shattered, pulpy mass, a fiery length of agony. It would take a miracle to save it, and what he should be doing was spending his time adjusting to its loss. Nonetheless, he would send for the Comte.

The Comte kept his face inscrutable as he examined Hamish's damaged leg. He did not think that he had ever seen such an appalling wound. It scarcely resembled a leg anymore; it was merely bones and speared flesh, pulpy and crimson.

'Well, can you do anything for it?' Hamish said hoarsely.

'Do you want the truth?'

'Of course.'

'The physicians advise amputation. That would certainly save the poison from spreading through the rest of your body.'

'And is that what you advise?'

'It depends on what you want out of life, my friend. Do you want to live a full life or just a half life – the existence of an invalid, totally dependent on others?'

'Then I have a choice? The physicians seemed to think there was no choice, that I must lose the leg.'

'Physicians, being trained to cut out what is diseased, would naturally advise such a course. I will go away now and I will ponder upon the condition of your leg. I will think on the herbs and the other remedies which will best suit your wound. And I would ask you to keep in mind the thought that you have already recovered, and well, from a wound which would have killed any other man.' The Comte leaned forward with a smile. 'If you have done it once, then you can do it again. I will be back soon.'

When he had gone, Hamish lay thoughtfully upon his bed. Yes, he had recovered from a near-fatal wound once before, but then he had been tended by the woman he loved. There was no one now to love him, to kiss his brow, to give him a purpose for living. A year had passed since he had last seen Athena and her letters never spoke of her return to the Château Blanche. Of late they had grown scarcer. He believed he knew what that meant: she had chosen to remain in England. He would never see her again, nor their daughter. He had known it all along, of course. Why should she choose him when she could heave her brilliant heritage?

The Comte worked skilfully and patiently upon Hamish's wound. He removed the bandages which the physicians had placed around it, wrinkling his nose at the messy and unsuitable ointments which they had packed into the leg. With dexterity and patience, he cleansed the wound and applied his own healing herbal unguents. Then he fed Hamish a potent sleeping brew, made from the poppy, and left him tucked up for the night.

This procedure was carried out many more times in the following days. When the badness had been eradicated and the suppuration controlled, the Comte slowly and carefully fitted together the broken bones and lashed the leg between rigid splints. As the weeks passed, knowing that he had done all he could for the leg but that it would take time to heal properly, he began to realize that a profound change had taken place in his patient. The indigo eyes no longer held any brightness, alertness, or interest in life; they were dark, lacklustre. Hamish rarely spoke, he never smiled, he only picked at his food and sent it away barely touched; he tasted his wine and grew weary of it after two or three sips. He lay on his bed for many hours staring blankly at the wall. Remembering the active, indefatigable, tiger-like man that he had been, the Comte grew fearful. He would have given anything to see Hamish in one of his towering rages. Even a glowering mood would have been preferable to the dispassionate lethargy which now possessed him. To try and cheer Hamish, he spoke of the day when Athena would return, and he was shocked by the ashen pallor which swept across Hamish's face, the steely set of his mouth.

'She is not coming back,' he stated.

'*Not* coming back? But I do not see how you can say that. She is your wife, and husband and wife belong together. Of *course* she will return, she has only gone to England to visit her family.'

'You met the Duchess; she is a very powerful woman. Do you really think Athena will return to me when she can stay in England in the bosom of a family which dotes on her?'

'But . . . but she loves *you*, my Lord. You are perfectly matched. You were so happy . . .' The Comte's lips trembled.

'Yes – before her sister Marjorie came on the scene. Why should my wife be happy with dross when she can have gold?'

'Oh, but I am sure you are wrong!' The Comte nibbled at his lips in a paroxysm of alarm. He saw the long years stretching ahead with Athena in England and himself in France, and then he looked at the pallid, lifeless man lying on the bed. A life sentence for them both, only he did not think Hamish would survive it: for him it would be a death sentence.

After Hamish had fallen asleep, the Comte paced up and down in the salon, nibbling on his lips and clenching and unclenching his fingers. The breath of tragedy was in the air. He was stricken by inner conflict. He had a patient on his hands: one who needed his ministrations. But then he realized that however much he ministered to Hamish's leg wound, he could never reach his heart, his soul. Only Athena could do that, and she was in England. There was only one solution: she must be brought back to France as soon as possible. Then he contemplated the method. He could write to her, but letters went astray and, in truth, he longed to see her again, and the little Alysa, who would be two years old now. Once he had made up his mind, he set about putting his plan into action. Pierre had helped him nurse Hamish, and it was Pierre whom he now instructed in the care and nurturing of the leg wound. Then he made up a large supply of his herbal unguents and the poppy-based sleeping brew, without which the patient lay awake, fretting, all night. Then he told Hamish that urgent business had called him back to Paris.

'You know that I would not go if I did not have to,' the Comte said, trying to still the quaver in his voice, for he was sure that the eagle wits would divine what he was about. 'Pierre will look after you. I have instructed him fully in the care of your wound.'

'You have been very good to me. I thank you,' Hamish said. 'Remember me to the King and the Queen Mother.'

The Comte's reunion with Athena was ecstatic, but he did

not miss the Duchess's lip curling in distaste, nor the disapproving glance she flung him.

'Oh, it is so good to see you again!' Athena cried. 'You should have warned me you were coming.'

'I acted on the spur of the moment, *mon trésor*. I have something to tell you.' The Comte lowered his voice. 'Might we speak alone?'

'But of course. Shall we walk in the gardens? Mother, we will not be long.' Athena flung a placating smile at the Duchess.

'Athena, my visit was for a purpose. In truth, I am dreadfully worried,' the Comte began. 'I expect news of the sack of Rome reached you here?' Athena nodded. 'Hamish took part in it. He and Benvenuto Cellini were responsible for the death of the Duc de Bourbon.'

'So Hamish got what he wanted? Oh, I am so glad.' Athena clasped her hands together. 'So he is in a better mood these days?'

'Far from it, *mon trésor*.' The Comte took Athena's hands. 'A German mercenary fired at Hamish and Cellini immediately after they had murdered Bourbon. Hamish shielded Cellini from the crossfire and he was wounded, very badly wounded, I am afraid.'

A cry broke from Athena's lips. She clung to the Comte's arms, feeling the world buckling and spinning around her. 'He is dead! That is what you have come to tell me! He is dead! Oh, Blessed Virgin, why did I not go back to France before? Why oh why did I leave it this long? He is dead and I shall never see him again! Oh, God forgive me,' she wept.

'No, no, he is not dead. But without you he is as good as dead. The surgeons want to amputate his leg. They say that he will never walk again, and I fear that is quite possible. But there is something else, something far more serious. He does not *want* to walk again, he does not *want* to live. He has no reason to go on now that you have decided to live in England. He thinks that you no longer love him, that you will never return, so he wants to die. And the way that he is going about it, he will soon achieve that end.'

Athena gasped, her hand to her mouth. 'But – but . . . how can that be? His letters were so cool and detached. never, by any word or deed, did he give me reason to believe he wanted or needed me with him. I have waited, oh how I have waited for him to ask me to return, but he never has. You say that . . . he will lose his leg?' She shuddered, her face in her hands.

'I think – I hope – that I have saved it. He heals well, despite his *ennui*, but it is the sickness of his spirit which troubles me most. You know what a strange and puzzling man he can be. He finds it hard to talk of his needs, his feelings. But I know that he loves you, worships you, and that he has always needed you, whatever else he might have led you to believe. And he has never needed you as much as he does at this moment. Trust me, for I am right.'

'Where is he?' Athena's voice was a whisper.

'At the Château Blanche.'

'I am going to him straight-away. You will come with me?'

The Comte nodded, hope and joy in his eyes.

The Duchess's pleas and tears were terrible to see, and they cut her daughter to the quick. The Duke raged and stormed at the Comte, putting all the blame on him, saying that he had come to steal their daughter again.

'It is not so! Please do not say that, Father,' Athena begged. 'My husband is dangerously ill. He was in Rome, he was shot by an *arquebusier* and received a terrible wound. It is feared that he will lose his leg. I must go to him, Mother, Father. Do you not see? My place is with him. He is my husband and I love him.'

The Duchess flung her hands up in the air and stormed away down the length of the Great Hall, then returned, to begin her assault anew. But her daughter would not be moved. Hamish was in great need of her. The Comte would not have come all this way if it had not been so, and she must go to her husband.

'You can visit me in France any time. *Please* do so. Please feel free to come whenever you wish. And I will, of course, come back to see you. It is not the end, far from it. We shall be together again.'

The Comte shrank into the background, feeling shaken by the displays of emotion. If ever he had thought the English cold-natured he had altered his opinion now. Finally, when the Duke and Duchess had seen that their daughter would not change her mind, they reluctantly accepted her decision and the packing for the journey began.

History had repeated itself. Hamish woke from a drug-induced sleep to see his wife standing by his bed, her eyes shining with tears. He could not believe what he saw. It was a dream, of course: he was still asleep. A grimace of pain twisted across his face. He wanted to hold out his arms to the dream figure, but he knew that it would be pointless, for she was not there.

Athena looked down at her grey-faced, haggard husband. His eyes were dull; there were dark hollows beneath his eyes and beneath his cheekbones. Her heart felt too big for her breast: it seemed to be bursting out through her bones like a hundred tiny knives. She could see Death in her husband's face and she could not bear it.

Forcibly controlling her voice, she said: 'Now, what is all this nonsense about my husband being unable to walk? I am sure that I have been given the wrong facts, *chéri*, for it cannot be so. My husband is a brave, strong man, not a sickly invalid.' She leaned forward, lightly resting her hands on his shoulders, and he inhaled her scent, saw that it was really her, that she was really there.

'You do not want me now,' he whispered hoarsely. 'Go

away, make a new life for yourself. When I am dead, marry an English Duke and make your mother happy.'

Athena felt her heart shred into a thousand pieces. By way of reply, she called in her daughter, the little girl toddling up to Hamish's bed.

'This is your papa, Alysa. Remember all that I have told you about him?'

'Yes, Mama.' The little girl dimpled, then said, 'Hewwo, Papa,' and took Hamish's big hand in her tiny ones. 'We come home now, Papa,' Alysa went on. 'When will you be well 'nough to teach me and my bruvver to ride?'

Dazed by the exquisite beauty of the little girl with the turquoise eyes and rioting, moonlight-coloured curls, Hamish did not at first absorb what she had said. Then, slowly, realization dawned.

'Your *brother*?' he rasped, a choking feeling in his throat.

Athena smiled down at Hamish, then stepped out of the room for a moment, returning with a bundle in her arms. She sat on the bed beside her husband and lower the bundle so that he could look at it more closely. She pressed down the swaddling robes with one finger to reveal a round, rosy face with two indigo-blue eyes which stared at him unblinkingly.

'Your son . . .' she said, with a quaver in her voice. 'I have called him Hamish after you.'

'My son – my *son*? But why did you not tell me? All these months – *why* did you not tell me?'

'I did not want to force you into returning to me. I wanted you to find out, for yourself whether or not you could live without me.'

'I needed no persuasion, no coercion. I have known that for many years now,' Hamish whispered. 'It was *you* who had the doubts.'

'*Never*,' she said firmly. 'I adore you, I worship you. This last year has been the longest of my life.'

'Papa . . .' Hamish felt a tug at his sleeve. 'Papa, you

are going to teach me and my bruvver to ride?' Alysa piped.

'I am ill, little one. I do not think –'

'But Mama is going to mend you,' Alysa cried. 'That is why we come home. And I am going to help her,' she said proudly, beaming into her father's face.

Entreatingly, Hamish looked up at his wife. 'Go now, before it is too late. Marry an English Duke. Make your life with your family. You will regret it all the rest of your life if you stay here with me. I am a cripple.'

'That does not say much for the Comte's medicinal skills, nor for mine either,' Athena said, smiling tremulously. Then, placing the baby gently down on the bed, she began to smooth the sheets and plump up Hamish's pillows. Seeing her face, he became silent. It would have been easy to believe that he had already died and was in Heaven and that she was a beautiful angel.

When she had tidied the bed to her satisfaction, she turned to him with a glowing smile.

'If you want to get rid of me so much, my darling, there is only one way to do it. You will have to get well and walk again, will you not, and then you can throw me out bodily. For nothing else will move me: I am here to stay, where I belong, with my husband.'

The throaty coo of doves and the clap of herons' wings announced the arrival of a rider on a magnificent russet stallion. Pulling the animal to a halt, the rider sat watching the little group in the distance. Across the chamomile lawns, he could see a radiantly beautiful woman in a gown of china-blue samite, her lustrous pale hair coiled in a silken net. The woman was smiling broadly and holding out her hands to a small boy of about two years of age. Laughing joyously, the boy toddled towards his mother, catching at her fingers and gripping them tightly.

Nearby sat a sweet-faced little girl with a book on her

lap. The girl was very like the woman in colouring and expression, revealing their kinship. She wore a gown of terracotta silk trimmed with blue velvet ribbons, and her face too glowed with happiness.

It was an inspiring, reassuring scene and one which filled the rider's heart with gladness. He could not wait to join the group, to be a part of them. Dismounting, Hamish walked across the sweet-scented grass towards his wife and children. There was only the slightest trace of a limp as he moved.

Hearing him approach, his wife and children turned their faces in his direction, their expressions warmly welcoming. Within seconds, his son was climbing into his arms, his daughter holding onto his wrist, his wife resting her cheek lovingly against his. Such days were made for the gods.